RED + BLUE
A.B. GAYLE

Dreamspinner Press

Published by
Dreamspinner Press
382 NE 191st Street #88329
Miami, FL 33179-3899, USA
http://www.dreamspinnerpress.com/

Red Blue

Cover Art by Anne Cain   annecain.art@gmail.com
Cover Design by Mara McKennen

ISBN: 978-1-61372-520-7

Printed in the United States of America
First Edition
May 2012

eBook edition available
eBook ISBN: 978-1-61372-521-4

This book couldn't have been written without the contributions of several fellow authors, who encouraged and helped me along the way.

More specifically to Josh Lanyon for giving me initial direction, Charles Edward for pointing out my "Aussieisms," to Don Schecter for ensuring my guys are guys and encouraging me to continue whenever I felt like quitting, and to the incomparable Kate, who at times saw my characters and their story better than I did and made me do rewrite after rewrite until I did them justice. Then it was the turn of Vivian and Heather, whose enthusiasm gave me the courage to submit the finished product.

Finally, *Red+Blue* is dedicated to the canoe, because it allows us to leave behind the comfortable and familiar, and visit places like the Quetico, where long hours of paddling, and longer portages, both crush you and make you strong. (Thanks to Cindy for sharing the experience and letting me use her wisdom.)

PART
ONE

RED

INTRODUCING RED

SOME men can wear red, some can't. Being a redhead, I avoid it like the plague. The color suits my buddy, Jason. With his tanned olive skin and dark hair—thanks to his Spanish mom—when *he* wears red, you start looking for the charging bull. His ass looks great in tight black matador pants too. Pity he seldom finds an excuse to wear them. Mind you, in his dark pinstripes, he can double as a *GQ* model any day. He has that mandatory slim-hipped sexiness and the pout to match.

I, on the other hand, always look exactly like what I am—a country bumpkin. As for tans, I gave up trying after overdosing on UV as a kid, hoping my freckles would join up. All I got for my trouble was sunstroke, a face as red as a lobster, and a walloping from my dad.

Jason hails from Long Island but never talks about his folks much, always more interested in tales of my family. When we first met, he kept bugging me to do some Minn-speak. "Say, 'Ya, sure, ya betcha', Ben."

I told him to suck my cock for supper instead. *Geez*, one of the reasons I came to San Francisco in the first place was to get away from Minnesota. Why would I want to advertise where I came from once I got here? Yessiree, Bob. My older brothers might be happy staying there, but I wanted out. That's why I jumped at the offer of a summer internship when a rep for Sydney Sutherland Family Insurance came scouting around college back in February. My talent for number crunching gave me the chance to follow my dreams to Gay Central.

I met Jason in a bar in the Castro not long after I arrived. There I was, talking to my friend, Mick—well, I'd known him for ten minutes and he was still speaking to me, so that made him a friend in my book—anyway, Mick had asked me to ride on a tandem with him in the upcoming Pride Parade when this good-looking dude in a silky red shirt and black leather pants elbowed him aside and pulled me onto the dance floor. He acted like he knew me, but it wasn't until I was fucking

1

him into the mattress two hours later that I finally figured out he was one of the firm's top-gun salesmen.

You see, my traineeship role as an actuary keeps me apart from the snake-oil peddlers and their expense accounts. I assumed they were all conservative breeders with a wife and 2.5 kids, struggling to stay afloat with too much gearing on their five-bedroom McMansions and Porsches. It was real good to find I wasn't the only gay guy working for the firm.

I hadn't recognized Jason, but my hair makes me stand out in a crowd. Being six-two in bare feet also helps. Jason claims he's six foot, but hey, that's only if he's wearing his high-heeled Cubans.

We don't broadcast our relationship at work, although he always pinches my ass on the way to his weekly meeting with Adrian Sydney Sutherland, the head honcho of the western division. For some reason, my daily visit to the water cooler coincides with the time Jason walks past. No, wait, I remember—we planned it that way. Heh. Lucky no one has ever caught on. I think the boss saw him grope me a couple of times. The clichéd narrowed lips and hard eyes when he glanced our way indicated that something upset him, but maybe it was just acid reflux.

CHAPTER
┼┼┼
ONE

Red
December '08

THE rain had stopped, but a cold December wind whistled down the street between the tall buildings. I stamped my boots on the ground and shoved my hands as best I could into the pockets of my jeans. When choosing what to wear that Sunday morning, the last thing I expected was to be standing outside the office, waiting for my boss to arrive.

Two men in suits approached. Same walk. Similar build. Both about five-ten. Scratch that, waiting for the boss and his father to arrive.

Adrian Sutherland, the younger of the two men gave me a quick nod, and his greeting of, "Hi, Ben," echoed strangely in the empty foyer as we walked inside. On weekdays, there were always people coming and going. Not that there had been as many lately. A number of the offices were now vacant because of the financial crisis. Inside, my two companions spoke briefly to the out-of-hours security guard. The big, black dude had been eyeing me through the glass. Probably wondering what I was doing there. I was too.

"Thanks for coming in on your day off." The boss's quick smile transformed his face. Lately, the girls in the office had been arguing about whether his glum looks were due to the state of the economy or because he was still single after breaking up with his long-time girlfriend.

"No problem," I assured him. "My team was losing anyway."

As we waited for the elevator, the boss turned to his father. "Dad, this is Ben Dutoit, the trainee actuary I mentioned."

3

Strictly speaking, as Adrian Senior was the major shareholder in the company, he should be "the boss", but he spent most of his time in the East Coast office. I shook the older man's hand. The death grip matched his glare.

I straightened my purple throwback jersey as best I could. "Sorry about the gear," I pointed to my casual clothing. "I was at the Royal, watching the NFL when you called. You did say to come as soon as possible."

"Who are the Vikings playing today?"

"The Falcons." I swallowed nervously. When Adrian Senior asked his question, there hadn't been any trace of friendliness in his face. Now he was checking me out like one of those dogs who spend half an hour sizing you up before they decide whether they'll bite you or not.

"The Giants will walk all over you next week." The older man turned and stared at the floor indicator. *No wonder he didn't like me.* As soon as the elevator doors closed, I brought up the subject that had been worrying me ever since receiving the boss's unexpected phone call. "I couldn't hear properly because of the noise, but did you say Carl had a heart attack?" Carl Hausfeldt, the firm's chief actuary, while also technically my boss, had been more like a mentor to me.

"Yes, on Friday at the industry luncheon. We've just come from the hospital."

"Is he alright?"

"He is now, but it was touch and go there for a while."

Ever since the financial meltdown, Carl had been putting in stacks of overtime. I'd tried to help him, but there was only so much I could do. "Is he well enough to receive visitors?"

His father grew restless as Adrian gave me details about which hospital Carl had been admitted to and the visiting hours. "I'll be in your office," he barked and stalked off.

His son stared after him, tugged at his collar, then turned and smiled at me. Pure magic. I read a survey once where people rated photos of eyes in order of sexiness. Pale ones without any rims scored the highest. The boss's were a perfect example: the barest whisper of gray around a jet black pupil. Real come-to-bed eyes.

4

"Carl said you were helping him with the statement of actuarial opinion." Adrian handed over a sheet of paper. "Here's a list of instructions. When you're finished, my father will take everything back to the appointed actuary in the East Coast office. Carl says you know the password."

The handwritten note was brief and to the point, ending with a thanks for coming in on the weekend. My worry eased. Even from his hospital bed, Carl was on top of his game. "Okay, shouldn't be a problem." Adrian Junior gave another of those mouth-watering smiles before going to join his father.

I fired up Carl's computer and typed in "Chester"—the name of Adrian Senior's dog. Carl once commented that he chose the password as the animal reminded him of his master. If it barked as loudly as the man talked, no wonder he made the connection. Usually, with the normal background clatter, I wouldn't be able to hear a thing, but because the office was quiet, and the two men were arguing, every word of their discussion came through crystal clear.

"I thought from what you said that he was already qualified." The older man's voice still reflected his earlier irritation.

"Ben's done two of his exams, and if he passes the rest on schedule, he should be an associate by the time Carl wants to retire. That way we'll have less disruption." His son's more measured tones were easy to pick.

"Might happen earlier than he planned."

"The doctor said Carl should make a full recovery."

I sincerely hoped so. I liked working with Carl, and he'd already taught me a lot about the business.

"We should be downsizing, not employing new...."

The younger man's voice broke in over the top, "Ben joined the firm before Lehman Brothers went under."

"It doesn't matter. Now we need to shed staff to remain competitive, and you know my rule, last in—first out."

"If it comes to that, the new receptionist, Millie Carruthers, joined after Ben. At any rate, Carl's had no complaints about his performance, quite the opposite."

Their words faded to a blur as the impact of what they were saying took hold. The insurance industry hadn't been hit as hard as some, but because of all our high-risk policies, Fitch recently downgraded the company's rating from A- to BBB+. From the sounds of things, my future with the company was on the line. *Damn.* I enjoyed working here. Most of the people I came into contact with were really friendly, and Carl and I made a great team.

I downloaded all the data onto a memory stick and collected the supporting documentation as instructed. Luckily, most of the work had already been done, in readiness for the end-of-year deadline. I knocked on the door and handed over the material. The boss thanked me, but this time his smile was strained.

As the security guard—whose name, I discovered, was Tyrone— let me out of the building, my thoughts returned to the cause of the problem. According to Carl, the global financial crisis was brought on by politicians who lobbied for interest rates to be set too low, making it easy for everyone with a pulse to buy whatever they liked, assuming the boom would go on forever.

They forgot that taking risks has consequences.

THE firm's Christmas party was held the following weekend.

"Want a drink, sweetie?"

For a second, I thought I'd strayed into one of the Castro bars by mistake, but the husky, cigarette-coated voice belonged to our underwriting manager, Mrs. Christie. I took the tray laden with glasses of wine, bottles of beer, and cans of pop out of her hands.

She poked me in the ribs. "Not all of them."

"Ouch. That hurt." Mrs. C. was old enough to be my grandma and barely reached five foot. She couldn't harm a fly, let alone a big lump like me. She tried to take the tray back, but I lifted it out of her reach. "Nah, it's heavy. I'll do the honors. You go flirt with Mr. Simmons— he's got the hots for you."

Mrs. C. flicked me with her dishtowel. Years of mucking around with my brothers in the kitchen helped me dodge instinctively. I grinned and swiveled my hips to avoid the sting.

"Off you go then," she said and disappeared back into the kitchen.

After off-loading all except one of each drink, I headed over to the corner of the room where a floor-to-ceiling window overlooked the parking lot. Millie was talking non-stop, waving her hands around. It must have been a pretty good story. Pity Jason wasn't listening; his attention was fixed on something outside. Knowing him, he was making sure nobody touched his Corvette.

Call that a car? If I can't crawl underneath to scrape off the rust, forget it. Give me my Ford Ranger pickup any day, even if Andy did clock up a hundred thousand miles before off-loading it to his little bro.

As I approached, Jason ran his tongue over his top lip: his "gimme some action" signal. I ignored him and bowed to Millie. "Would you care for a drink, ma'am?"

Millie giggled and selected the pop. "Thank you."

Jason snorted and removed the wine. "You'd make a great Playboy bunny, Red."

"Stop calling me Red." I gave him the finger and propped the empty tray against the window.

"Red?" Millie's mouth dropped open.

After a quick mutter to Jason to behave, I turned to Millie. "My brother, Chris, calls me that whenever he wants to annoy me." I spared her the details about how Jason also screamed it when we fucked. Sometimes I wondered if he imagined we were in a bondage scene, and *Red* was his safe word. He had it back to front though, as his next words were usually: "Don't stop."

I drank my Heineken and scanned my fellow employees. Most of them were standing around, conversing politely; probably finding they had little in common outside work—assuming they *had* a life outside work.

"How long have you been with SSFI?" Millie's big brown eyes stared at me as she took another sip.

"Since July."

"Ben's a master of timing," Jason drawled from his position in front of the window.

"Timing?" Millie's eyebrows rose.

Judging by Jason's smirk, he was also referring to the fact we usually managed to come at the same time. "More luck than timing. After my summer internship ended, they invited me to stay on, but Lehman Brothers went under a few days later. Now it's hard to find good jobs."

"Do you think ours are at risk?" Millie whispered, glancing around the room.

Yes, yours and *mine, honey*, but I didn't have the heart to tell her.

Jason handed me the empty tray. "Time for a refill, Red."

I murmured my apologies to Millie and accompanied Jason back to the kitchen. At the doorway, he grabbed my wrist. "Careful, Red, I'll get jealous." Before I could utter a response, he placed his other hand around my neck, pulled me down to his level, and stuck his tongue into my open mouth.

The tray fell from my nerveless fingers as my whole body began to react. A voice inside my head clamored, "What the fuck's he doing?" We'd never outed our relationship to our workmates before. I broke away, stepped back, and eyed him warily. My heart was racing faster than a Minnesota wildfire.

Jason smiled, shrugged, and lifted his hands palm upwards. "Sorry, Ben, I couldn't resist. You look so cute when you blush."

As soon as my breathing returned to normal, I glanced around and noticed two more people had arrived—Adrian Sutherland and a petite blonde who clung to his arm as if she needed his strength to stay upright. Hey, maybe she needed his support because of her fuck-me trotters. Wouldn't you know it? Red. They matched her skintight backless dress. I checked out the rest of his date. Her skinny arms showed she'd never lifted anything heavier than a Gucci bag in her entire life. Was this chick Adrian's new girlfriend?

I glanced at the boss, and our gazes locked. *Damn*. He must have seen the kiss. Those come-to-bed eyes now resembled the business end of a double-barreled shotgun. He opened his mouth to speak. To avoid the imminent blast, I snatched up the tray and escaped to the protection of Mrs. Christie in the kitchen. Helping her clean glasses and collecting another round of drinks—mimosas this time—put me back into familiar territory. Mind you, I wasn't sure whether it was the boss's stare or Jason's kiss that threw me out in the first place.

When I left the kitchen, I noticed that the noise level had ratcheted up a notch since the arrival of the boss and his date. It was almost as if the man's presence added a degree of expectation to the air. Who would he talk to? What would he say? You see, Adrian Sutherland isn't one of those employers who buries himself in his office all day; on the contrary, he always stops to say hi and check up on how you're doing.

Double damn. He didn't have a drink. I took a deep breath and walked toward him and his date. I had to admit, they made an attractive couple. The flecks of gray in Adrian's hair gave him that George Clooney brand of middle-aged hotness. The suit, the haircut, the chiseled jaw, and the bimbo hanging off his arm all screamed "straight" though. Too bad. He looked like he needed a good fuck.

A warm smile spread across his face as I approached. *Phew.* At least he wasn't still mad at me for lip-locking with Jason.

"Thanks, Ben," he said when I reached him. The blonde selected one of the mimosas; he took a bottle of Heineken. "Laurel, this is our actuarial trainee, Ben Dutoit."

I couldn't shake her hand, as I was carrying the tray, so I said, "Pleased to meet you," and smiled, or at least tried to. It wasn't just the boss's smile that affected me. The smooth whiskey-tones of his voice also made my stomach do a backflip.

"Pleased to meet you, Ben, thanks for the drink." Laurel raised the glass to her lips. Her voice sounded sweet, but pale blue eyes raked me from tip to toe, assessing. Forget butter, even ice cream wouldn't melt in her mouth. I shivered.

"Are you cold, darling?" Jason's hand snuck around my waist.

Laurel's eyes flickered for a moment, then she turned and stroked the boss's shirtsleeve. "Adrian…." He looked down at her and smiled.

"Come on, Ben." Jason pulled me away, and I offloaded the rest of my drinks in super-quick time. Something about that female really set my nerves on edge.

From that night on, everyone at work knew I was gay, but no one seemed to care.

CHAPTER
┿┿┿
TWO

Red
January '09

MILLIE'S excited face greeted me at reception when I returned after a quick trip home to attend my brother Chris's wedding. It had been real good spending Christmas with the folks, but you could have cut the tension in the air with a knife: the bride was five months pregnant, Chris didn't look happy, and everyone bitched about the economy. To make matters worse, the Vikings lost to the Eagles in the first round of the play-offs.

"Hi, gorgeous." I gave Millie a hug. "New haircut? Sweet."

Millie blushed and giggled, straightening her skirt. "Hurry up, there's a start-of-year briefing in a few minutes. Mr. Sutherland's been looking for you."

"Sorry I'm late. Freakin' ice grounded the plane in Minneapolis." I peeled off my jacket, stashed it in my cube with the overnight bag, and followed her down the unusually quiet corridor. "Where is everyone?"

"In the conference room. Jason's saved us a couple of seats."

Jason pursed his lips in an air kiss and ostentatiously adjusted his cuffs when I sat next to him. Another new pinstripe by the looks of it. I felt like something the cat dragged in. Catnapping on the plane does that to you. Planes, trains—you name it, once they start moving I'm in la-la land.

"How was Minnesota, Red?" Jason sprawled out so our thighs touched.

I settled back in my chair and pressed my leg against his. "Colder than a witch's tit."

He smirked and adjusted his red tie. "And the rednecks?"

"They're pissed off at me." Geez, the man knew how to get under my skin. He'd probably worn that one on purpose.

"Why?"

"They're convinced I spend all my time clubbing instead of studying."

Jason snorted. "Well, you do, don't you?"

I shrugged. I laughed off their criticism at the time but the comment had stung. Because of lack of money, my four brothers ended up finding apprenticeships or starting work immediately after school. Winning a scholarship made college possible for me; however, as I stayed with my grandmother, who lived near the university, the only midnight oil I burnt was with my books, not the lube variety—at least not with anyone other than my own hand. So I'd been making up for lost time ever since.

"They also accused me of sounding like someone in *Queer Eye for the Straight Guy.*"

Jason turned and gave me a quick head-to-toe scan. "Which one?"

"They never watched it. They just think all gays are bitchy."

He laughed.

"Shush." Millie gave Jason a disapproving glare.

The familiar figure of Adrian Sutherland Junior stepped up to the podium and spoke into a hand-held microphone. "Now we've started a new year, I hope you all made a resolution to work harder and make SSF Insurance heaps of money." Everyone dutifully laughed. "There's no denying we have a hard slog ahead. The newspapers are full of dire predictions. I want to reassure you that our existence is not threatened by the collapse of the big institutions. In the past, we came under criticism for not being more aggressive in our investment practices. Time has proven the investment strategy developed by our recently retired chief actuary, Carl Hausfeldt, correct. According to the latest reports, we're weathering the financial crisis better than most of our competitors."

Huh? When I visited Carl in hospital before leaving for the holiday, he told me he'd be back on deck in no time at all. Hopefully that didn't mean he'd taken a turn for the worse.

The boss beckoned someone in the front row to come forward. "For those who didn't meet her at the Christmas party, it gives me great pleasure to introduce you to Laurel Marchison, the new head of our actuarial department."

Shit. The blonde chick. Gone was the sex-bomb outfit. Today she was dressed in a tight-fitting pale gray suit, her hair perfectly coiled into a neat bun.

The boss smiled as she approached and held out his hand. "Laurel is a fellow of the CAS. She earned her bachelor degree in actuarial science at Boston University and has a master's in business administration from Harvard. She'll be responsible for all actuarial functions in the policies handled by our West Coast division."

A wave of imminent dread came over me as the new head of my section took the proffered microphone. "Thank you, Adrian. In case some of you don't actually know what an actuary does…." She smiled and pointedly looked around the room, making sure we were all listening. "Apart from giving financial advice on current reserves, we calculate the appropriate pricing of our insurance policies and carry out modeling to determine what money will be needed to meet claims in various future scenarios."

Jason muttered softly, "Condescending bitch. Most of the staff have been here for more than five years. If they don't know what an actuary does by now, Lord help us."

Her lecture continued. "While our reserves may not be at risk, the new administration in Washington is proposing radical changes to the health industry. If these get through the House and Senate, our profession will be under threat. I will be reviewing all our policies to ensure the company remains viable."

The hairs prickled at the back of my neck. SSFI's involvement in high-risk policies had been one of the main reasons I joined the firm. *What were they planning?*

"Thank you, Laurel."

The boss accepted the microphone back and waited until she regained her seat. Mutters could be heard all around the room as he removed his glasses and polished them. Gradually the noise died down. He nodded in acknowledgement and resumed speaking. Immediately, I noticed the difference. With Adrian, you didn't get the feeling you were back at school, he sounded more like the coach before a game. He took the "family" concept literally. "The other day, Carl and I discussed a few measures we could introduce to help you. For a start, he feels that his lack of fitness probably contributed to his heart problems...."

Jason snorted and muttered under his breath. "Not to mention the fact he was an overweight, borderline diabetic with young kids from a second wife half his age."

Millie shushed him again.

"The training room on the second floor has been converted to a gymnasium. I encourage you all to use it whenever you wish. Guidelines will be displayed, and I trust you to treat both the equipment and your bodies with respect."

"*Woo-hoo*." My cheer was echoed loudly by a couple of guys in the back of the room.

The rest of Adrian's speech covered the usual topics. As the employees filed out, the boss approached me. "Ben, would you mind waiting in my office? I need to speak to you about something. I'll be there shortly."

"Okay, Mr. Sutherland." The ice in my stomach froze solid. *Here comes the axe.*

THANKS to the fact I had a few changes of clothes in my overnight bag, as soon as everyone left for home, I headed for the new gym.

Thump. The suspended punching bag shook under the force of my gloved right hand.

Whump. My left collected it on the backswing.

Thump. Each blow helped release the tension that had been building all day.

13

Whump. The new head of my section was already there when I entered the boss's office straight after the meeting. Shortly afterward, Adrian arrived.

Thump. As soon as he sat down, I apologized for being late. You'd have thought I had some control over the weather the way Laurel sniffed at my excuse and said JFK airport had also been affected, but *they* managed to arrive in time. From then on, she hijacked the interview.

Whump. First, she wanted to know what stage I had reached in my "attempt" to become an associate. She had my application folder in her hands, so she knew I passed Probability and Financial Mathematics before the internship began. I squirmed as I confessed I hadn't done any exams since.

Thump. Before she could say anything, the boss interrupted, calmly pointing out that I'd been promised days off for study when my internship switched to full-time employment, but due to Carl's increased workload because of the financial crisis, I hadn't been able to take any.

Whump. I could tell that she still thought I was a slacker.

Thump. Stupid bitch. It would have been in my best interests to complete my course as soon as possible because the firm offered bonuses for each exam I passed.

Whump. Not to be deterred, she sweetly informed us she completed all hers, first try.

Thump. I barely kept my temper in check as I explained I hadn't failed any so far and was preparing for Modeling in Life Contingencies in May.

Silence descended for a moment, as if we'd reached the end of the first round and the corner men were sponging the combatants down in readiness for a resumption of hostilities.

Thump. She came out all guns blazing, smiling sweetly and suggesting I should switch to a larger firm that could offer more varied experiences.

Whump. I saw red then. Sugar, if I wanted to join one of the big insurance companies, I would have applied to them in the first place. I tried to explain, but of course I didn't call her "sugar."

Thump. Then she hinted that there wouldn't be enough work for me.

Whump. The quick uppercut jab to the chin. After the talk I overheard between Adrian and his father, as soon as I heard of Carl's retirement, I knew my job was at risk.

Thump. I watched her out of the corner of my eye when Adrian promised there would be a place with SSFI as long as I wanted it. Laurel's whole body stiffened at the news. My heart started beating again. Knockout punch by the boss, shortly after the start of the second round. Seemed like he had won the battle. For the time being, at least.

"I thought I heard noises."

I turned to see who'd spoken, and staggered when the speed bag clipped me on the temple. A firm clasp on my arm steadied me, and the other hand stopped the weight from nailing me on the rebound. All the hairs on the back of my neck stood on end as I stared into two steel-gray eyes.

The boss quickly released his grip, allowing me to take a step back. I dragged my gaze away from his face and took a deep breath. With a spotless white towel draped casually around his neck and dressed in black gym shorts and a blue mesh-side tank, he looked like a regular at an upmarket health club. In contrast, I'd stripped off my T-shirt earlier because there was no one around, and my favorite old gray drawstring pants clung to my sweat-drenched skin.

Hastily, I toweled down and surreptitiously checked out my employer as he inspected the two punching bags: the speed bag I'd been using and the larger one. Now that he wasn't covered by pinstripe suits or business shirts, I could see he'd been in much better shape when he was younger. The muscles in his arms definitely didn't belong to a ninety-pound weakling. His only flaw was that he suffered from corporate "disease"—a definite paunch and thickening waistline. Reluctantly, I dragged my eyes upward and told myself to quit eyeing the boss off like a piece of meat.

"How come you're still here?" There was an edge to his voice that I couldn't identify. *Surprise or pissed off by my presence?* Hard to tell. So far, at work, I had rarely seen him being anything but smoothly professional. His face rarely betrayed his feelings, making him a difficult man to read until he unleashed one of his spectacular smiles.

"It was too crowded earlier." Peeling off my boxing gloves, I added, "Tyrone said to call him when I finished, so he could lock up and let me out of the building." I glanced up to find him staring at me as if I was speaking Swahili. "Tyrone—the security man," I explained.

"*I* know who Tyrone is; I'm just astonished that you do."

I shrugged. Once the big black dude realized who I was, we often compared notes on the performance of our respective teams. Another sports nut.

Mesmerized like a rabbit, I stared into those gorgeous gray eyes again, until he blinked and asked quietly, "What do you think of the setup?"

"Great." I grimaced as my reply came out higher pitched than usual. Damn, my voice hadn't cracked like that since I turned fifteen. The boss didn't respond, and I sensed he wanted more detail. I swallowed and struggled to find something intelligent to add. The man probably thought he'd employed a complete idiot. "The bikes and treadmill were going flat-out all lunchtime. So were the lat and quad machines."

Adrian placed his towel on one of the stationary bikes and walked around the room, checking the different pieces of equipment. Now he wasn't staring at me, my brain slipped back into gear. "Pity there's only one rowing machine, though." I missed canoeing on the lakes. The rowing action was better than nothing.

"Not enough room for any more, I'm afraid," he said and stepped onto the treadmill. "I'm sorry I didn't get a chance to talk to you before the meeting this morning. I wanted to tell you about Carl's retirement before making the announcement to everyone."

He was apologizing to me? "No problem. Is he okay?"

"Yes, he just wants to spend more time with the family." The expression on my boss's face didn't alter, but the tone of his voice suggested that he regretted Carl's decision as much as I did.

Suddenly I had this weird urge to say or do something to make him feel better, and bring that smile back to his face. All I could come up with was: "Thanks for giving us the opportunity to work out." The lines of his face softened a fraction. *Success.* I shrugged into my old cotton T. The boss didn't need to be exposed to my pasty white skin. So uncool.

"You don't have to go on my account." He turned back to the machine and pressed a few buttons until he was moving at a slow jog.

"No, it's fine." I stood there for a while, watching his running style. The boss might not be fit, but he moved well, fluidly. "Anyway, I've finished boxing for today." *Duh, what an inane comment! Of course you have stupid, he saw you take off your gloves, remember?*

"Fair enough." He turned, and this time he unleashed one of those devastating smiles at me again. "It sounded like you needed to work off some energy."

"Yeah." I blushed and grabbed my gear. "See you tomorrow, Mr. Sutherland."

He gave me a tight smile and turned away to concentrate on what he was doing.

In the safety of the corridor, I leaned back against the closed door and wiped my forehead. *Energy?* More like aggression. Not that I would ever actually hit her, but I *had* been thinking about his girlfriend.

CHAPTER
+++
THREE

Red
February '09

BY THE time February came around, I still hadn't done much preparation for the next exam. Panic set in. So much for my New Year's resolution. At least I had managed to track down a used copy of the latest edition of the course manual on the Actuarial Discussion forum.

The layout of my apartment didn't help my enthusiasm for spending time studying. Not that there was much of it: a tiny kitchenette, small table, a couple of chairs, bed, desk, closet. I needed to switch things around, but I couldn't manage on my own. The brass bars on the old-fashioned bed gave me an idea. I called Jason. "Hey, how about trying out those leather handcuffs I bought you for Christmas? Let's see if we can make those jingle bells ring."

"Sounds good." I could picture his smile when he heard my offer. "When?"

"Can you come now?"

Jason laughed. "Why don't I wait until I get there so we can come together."

I chuckled.

"But you will need to pick me up."

Lately, Jason had decided that parking his 'vette in Haight-Ashbury was too risky. Okay, the locals might be covered in tats and piercings, and always reek of grass, but given Jason's fondness for the stuff, I thought he'd feel right at home. Heh, heh. "Okay."

As usual, he waited for me on the sidewalk outside his house in Pacific Heights. Apparently the guy he lived with didn't appreciate him bringing tricks home. I'd never been inside, but it sure looked pretty grand from the street. No doubt *The Car* was tucked safely out of sight in the underground garage.

Over the last few weeks, we'd only seen each other a few times outside work. Jason's like that; blowing hot and cold like a faulty air conditioner. Today, he was hot. His black leather pants were so tight, for a moment there, I wondered if I'd have to get out and lift him into the Ranger. I wound down the window on his side and yelled, "Hey, did you damage anything getting those on?"

"Hey, yourself." Jason planted his hands on his hips and frowned at me. "Where the fuck did you get that shirt?"

I had to check to see which one I had on. "Goodwill."

He stared at me to see if I was joking. When he saw I wasn't, he shook his head and finally managed to lift his leg high enough to clamber in.

I glanced at him before driving off. "What's wrong with it?"

"Honey," he said with a smirk. "It's just as well we're going back to your place. I wouldn't be seen dead anywhere in the Castro with you dressed like that."

I flipped him the bird. "Not everyone can afford designer gear. It fits, it's clean. What more do you want?"

He rolled his eyes and shook his head in despair. "You wouldn't be bad-looking if you only had a decent haircut and didn't wear geeky shirts with stupid slogans on them—*Don't mistake me for somebody who gives a shit*. Puleease!"

"No wonder my family thinks I sound like someone out of *Queer Eye*, I've been hanging around you too long."

It was his turn to flip me the bird.

For once, a parking spot magically appeared outside the recently renovated two-story Victorian that I had found on the Internet before leaving Minnesota. The best part of the deal was my landlady, Mrs. Sanchez. As soon as I put my key in the lock, she rushed out of her apartment and handed me a large jar of cookies. From day one, she somehow knew I was gay and kept telling me to find a "nice boy" and settle down. Maybe she thought if she provided food, Jason might fall in love with me… or her.

They chatted loudly in Spanish for a while. Jason kept calling her "Tía Teresa", and I don't know what else he said, but soon she was giggling and patting her chest as if she had trouble breathing. I pulled him through the doorway before he broke her heart.

Immediately he was inside, Jason started stripping off his clothes. "Whoa, slow down," I said and pointed to the bed. "I need a hand with this, first."

"Why?"

"You'll see."

I lifted the heavy end and Jason staggered after me, doing his best, but he didn't have the muscles for the job. Hopefully, Mrs. Sanchez wouldn't notice the scuff marks on the linoleum. As soon as the bed was in place, Jason sprang on top and reclined on his side, watching me as I continued to rearrange the furniture. "Care to explain what you're doing?"

I placed the study desk under the window and sat in the chair, checking the view. *Great.* The tiny shared garden with its citrus trees, flowers, and lawn served as my daily reminder that the world didn't just consist of concrete and skyscrapers. Much better than rose-patterned wallpaper. "Fixing the room." I opened my briefcase and dragged out my latest purchase.

"Why?"

I threw the ASM manual at him. Jason let out a grunt as the heavy binder hit him in the stomach. "Because if I want to pass my MLC exam in May, I have to study."

"What the hell for? That's months away."

"I should have started months ago. There's a heap of problems and sample exams to work through."

Jason leafed through the pages and stared at me as if I had suddenly sprouted another head. "You *like* spending your weekends with all these weird formulas and things?"

I raised an eyebrow at him. "What did you think I was, just a pretty face?"

He laughed and dropped the book on the mattress. "I thought only nerds knew stuff like this." He toed off his loafers and started undoing his fly.

"Never judge a book by its cover." I rescued the course notes and placed them on the desk. "I may look like a lumberjack, but...." I sat on the chair and adopted the classic thinker pose. "Within this rough exterior resides a brain as big as Einstein's."

I caught the pillow he threw at me and proceeded to smother him with it as he giggled and writhed on the bed. After a brief tussle—which I won, as usual—I pinned his hands on either side of his head and smiled down at him. His cock pressed insistently into my stomach. Seemed the rougher I was, the more he liked it.

"Don't stop, Red," he said as I took my hands away.

"Just getting the handcuffs."

"Oh, yeah." He licked his lips. Dark brown eyes glinted from under half-closed lids.

The cuffs certainly turned him on. He was moaning before I even fucked him. In the end, I wasn't too sure which was louder: the bells or Jason. Noisy bastard. Just as well Mrs. Sanchez was nearly deaf.

Afterward, he wanted me to share a joint. I refused. I hadn't indulged in the stuff since my best buddy at college turned schizo from hydroponic weed. As we lay side by side on the bed, we talked about work. I complained to him about Laurel, and he listened sympathetically.

"You know she spent Christmas with Adrian at his father's place on Long Island?"

An image of the boss and the bitch he was dating flashed through my brain. "No, I hadn't heard that." *Damn. Sounded like things were serious. Too bad.*

A COUPLE of weeks later, I was busy updating our accounting software to the latest version—something Laurel hated doing—when I felt a presence at my side. Glancing up, my stomach dropped at the serious expression in my boss's eyes. "Ben, I need to speak to you."

Whoops. That didn't sound too good. I glanced at my co-workers, but only received shrugs in reply to my silent question.

"What's this?" he said as soon as I sat down, pinning me to my chair with those steel gray eyes of his.

Ever since the start of the month, he'd been visiting the East Coast office, and the place hadn't felt the same. I was real glad he was back, but I wished he wouldn't keep staring at me like that. Before taking the paper from him, I rubbed the sweat off my palms. "It's an NBA office pool sheet, Mr. Sutherland."

"Did you do this?"

I nodded.

"Laurel brought it to my attention."

I bit back a snort of disgust. In the boss's absence, Laurel had been a real bitch.

"She's concerned about this on two fronts." Adrian picked up the page and stared at it for a while. "Firstly, the gambling aspect, and secondly, that you're doing this on work time."

"I am not!" My anger spilled out. "I do everything on my own time, either at lunch or on Sunday nights." The first accusation didn't warrant a comment. Lots of companies did this sort of thing; as long as everyone kept quiet, no one worried.

Adrian removed his glasses and wiped them a few times. "Don't you think it might have been a good idea to run this by me first?"

"You weren't here." I squirmed in my seat as he didn't make a comment, just raised his eyebrows and continued to stare at me. Once again, I wanted nothing more than to stop him looking so serious, so sad. "I'm sorry, Mr. Sutherland. I'll return everyone's money tomorrow."

He sighed and waved the sheet of paper in the air. "You're missing the point, Ben. If you'd told me what you were doing, at least I would have known what Laurel was talking about when I arrived. Instead, I didn't know what to say."

"But everyone else thinks it's a great idea. Look at how many joined in."

Adrian replaced the pool sheet on the desk and picked up the progressive tally sheet that I'd drawn up. He scanned the page for a few seconds. "Hmn. So far June Christie is winning. Helps that she's a Laker's fan."

"For sure." I nodded, the tight knot in my stomach easing as his face lost its previous tension. Trust the boss to be aware of things like that. "But you have to pick the results of all the games, so it's all about knowing the stats. Plus there's a certain amount of luck involved."

"Isn't it a bit late to start now? The season's half over."

I shrugged. "Doesn't matter. Everyone's starting at the same time."

He stared at me for a second, and then started writing something. I sat up straighter and tried to see what he was doing. No luck. "I'm sorry, Mr. Sutherland, but while you were away, the office was real quiet. I thought it would be a good idea to give people something to talk about instead of just moaning about how much the value of their house has fallen, or what their shares were worth now." With my brain addled by all the coursework, it also stopped me going mental, but I wasn't going to tell him that.

He nodded, a wry smile twisting his lips. "I guess you're right. If I hadn't had to cover for my cousin when his wife was ill, there wouldn't have been a problem. You *would* have run it by me first, wouldn't you, Ben."

Not a question, an order. "Yes, Mr. Sutherland, I would have told you... um... asked you first." I scuffed my foot on the carpet, wondering why I felt so uncomfortable in his presence now.

"Good, but remember that while I'm away, Laurel is in charge."

Was that a note of sympathy in his voice? I glanced up, but the boss's face was an impassive mask. "Yes, Mr. Sutherland."

"I think I can convince her that you did it for the good of the company."

"But I...."

Adrian continued as if I hadn't opened my mouth. "...and encourage her to participate and show solidarity with the staff, suggesting she use her superior skills in probability and statistics to make her selections. If she wins, and she's worried about the legality,

I'll suggest that she can always donate the money to charity." I blinked in surprise at the twinkle in my boss's eye. Adrian Sutherland didn't look nearly as old and stodgy when he grinned like that. Almost as good as the slow, sexy version.

"Next time you have a brilliant idea, though, come and share it with me first, hey?"

The boss went back to scribbling on the paper. I headed for the door.

"Wait." He rose from his chair, handed me all the offending sheets, reached into his back pocket, extracted a few bills from his wallet, and handed them over. "I think that should be enough. I've missed a couple of weeks, but it's never too late, is it?"

I glanced at the top sheet. He'd filled in his picks for the next round. "No, it's never too late, Mr. Sutherland." I felt like pumping my fist in the air in a victory salute when I closed the door. *Go, Adrian.* Another win to the boss. Everyone smiled when I pinned the tally sheet back on the notice board and slotted the pool sheets into their folder.

CHAPTER
+++
FOUR

Red
March '09

THE rest of February and most of March flew by in a blur as I concentrated on preparing for my next actuarial exam. Dull. Dull. Dull. On the night of the twenty-fifth, the familiar strains of *"Don't Call me Red"* interrupted me while I was brushing my teeth and getting ready for bed. *Jason.* I'd given up trying to stop him using that stupid nickname so, as my own private protest, I changed the ringtone for his calls to the first few bars of one of Ry Cooder's songs.

"Happy birthday to you—"

Jason already sounded drunk. I interrupted him before he could make a total idiot of himself. He didn't need to waste time auditioning for *American Idol.* "Hey, thanks for remembering!"

"Where are you?" he demanded.

"Just about to hit the sack."

"It's your fucking birthday, Ben. Why aren't you out celebrating?"

"I was gonna wait until the weekend."

"Bullshit. It's not the same if it's not on the actual day. Just a few drinks. Come on."

I glanced at my watch. Ten o'clock. Maybe I could fit in a couple. "Okay, but remember I have to work tomorrow."

He gave me instructions where to meet, and the last thing he said was, "Wear something decent."

As luck would have it, Mom and my brothers had sent money for my birthday, so at lunchtime, in return for a promise to take her to see

Fast and Furious, Millie and I had gone shopping. An hour later, I was the proud possessor of my first pair of black leather pants and an Affliction tee.

Jason licked his lips and gave me an approving kiss when I finally located him in one of the Castro bars. "Nice."

After tossing back a few Coronas and bopping to the house DJs, he dragged me off the dance floor. "This place sucks. Let's go somewhere else."

I shook my head in regret and glanced at my watch. "It's late, and I'm out of cash."

"Think of it as my present, Ben."

The cold night air cleared my head as we hit the street and headed for his Corvette. "Where are we going?"

"Somewhere special. A private setup belonging to a friend of mine. None of those stupid *no sex on the premises* rules. You'll love it, Ben," he promised, flashing that sly, under-the-lashes grin he did so well.

"Okay." I struggled with my conscience for at least a second, heh.

Smoke-laden air greeted us at what looked like a dingy warehouse. *Yuk.* Who needs fog machines when you have cigarettes and weed. Upstairs, a couple of drag queens on a small stage exchanged campy one-liners, much to the amusement of the tanned, blow-dried crowd nearby. The barstools were all taken up by the leather and denim set. *Yeah. Gay central. Just the sort of place I came to San Francisco to find.* Jason led me to a crowded dance floor in the next room.

"I'm thirsty," I complained after we danced for a bit. The pink and green pulsing strobes mesmerized me, melding me into the mass of moving men. Many had removed their T-shirts, showing off their tans. I kept my ultra-pale skin hidden.

"Wait here," Jason said and scooted off. As soon as he left, guys started cruising me. I'd never had so much attention before. My leather-covered ass soon grew warm from all the pinches and pats. I sighed. *Where* was *Jason*?

He finally returned with some sort of fruit juice. "My hero," I said and scarfed the drink down, blinking as the alcohol hit me. "Hey. Are you trying to get me drunk?"

His wicked grin said, *"Who me? Never."* "It's a fine line, Red. I want you to relax and have a good time, but I still want you to be able to get it up."

"So thoughtful, " I replied and smothered a small hiccup. "I knew I liked you for a reason." We danced for another hour, Jason fetching me drinks every time I got thirsty.

At midnight, a slow number came on. Jason faced away from me, molding his back against my front. I clasped my arms around his waist and drew him in against my hard-on. No wonder people raved about leather. The silky lining against my legs felt *real* good. Each ripple of muscle in Jason's butt as his hips moved up and down with the music sent a shiver up my spine. I rested my chin on his head. "You shaid…." I tried to stop myself slurring the words after my fifth Everclear and grapefruit juice. "You were taking me shum… hic… where ssh… pecial."

Jason giggled. "Yeah, it's out the back." He grabbed my arm and pulled me after him. I only staggered a little bit.

"In here?" I paused at the entrance of the room all the guys had been disappearing into. Inside, a dark mass of bodies surged like the many-headed hydra.

Jason gave my arm another tug. "No. There's a better place down the corridor." He handed the burly man guarding the second doorway some money, but I couldn't see how much. Knowing Jason, it was plenty. Leading me into the dimly lit room, he turned with a shit-eating grin. "Happy birthday, Ben!"

Great! This one wasn't nearly as crowded. The recessed red lights shining up against the black walls added a touch of the devil to the atmosphere. Two guys were already fucking on one of the low, black leather cushioned benches, and a couple more stood by quietly watching. One had his cock out, frantically stroking its hard length. The other guy just held up his hand in a gesture halfway between a "hi" and a "don't interrupt".

Wow, somewhere to sit. "Thanks, Jason! This is cool." Staggering over to one of the other benches, I giggled. Definitely better than curling up in bed alone. "Did ya bring me a birthday cake too, with candles and everyfink?" The room swayed alarmingly. Just as well it was pretty dark.

Jason laughed. For once he was the sober one. He positioned himself in front of me and flicked the hair out of his eyes as he unzipped his crotch, proving he'd gone commando. "Nope. I haven't got any candles, but there's something here you can blow on, if you like." That set me off again. I couldn't stop giggling.

"The shaleshman... hic." I pointed at his rapidly thickening cock. "Sorry, the *salesman* shaid you should alwaysh wear underwear with leather."

Jason pushed my head back slightly so he could see my face. "Why?"

"Sh... shtains." I unzipped my fly. "Shee?" I said proudly and gestured to the wet spot on my red jockstrap.

"Well, at least you're not a morose drunk." Jason smiled and sank to his knees.

My grin turned into moans as he pushed the material aside and sucked hard. "Hey, go buy your own drink!"

He laughed and patted my honker.

I don't remember much after that. I know I fucked Jason at least twice, so I must have been able to get it up despite the alcohol he kept pouring down my throat. I'd never felt so horny. Afterward, I even wondered whether he had slipped me something. All I know is that I still felt under the weather when I rolled out of bed and just made it to work on time.

I shouldn't have.

As chance would have it, I ended up sharing the elevator with the boss. Luckily there was no one else there. Adrian took one long look at me, and this time those gun-metal eyes signaled a real blast.

"How dare you turn up to work in that state?"

Ow. His father wasn't the only one with a voice that could penetrate steel. I checked my reflection in the polished metal lining of the elevator and gasped. In my mad scramble to get to work, my shirt was buttoned up all wrong, the bottom of my tie protruded two inches below the top part, and my hair stuck up at all angles without the benefit of gel. I looked like an extra in *Dumb and Dumber 2*. "Sorry, Mr. Sutherland." With shaking fingers, I frantically rebuttoned my shirt.

After a brief flash of anger, his face settled into a stony mask. "Go home and report to me first thing tomorrow." The elevator drew slowly to a stop at our floor. "And make sure this time you're sober and not showing the effects of illicit substances." Excuses died in my throat as I silently watched the doors close softly behind him.

His last comment really shook me. Back home in my apartment, the bloodshot eyes staring back at me from the mirror suggested I *had* been smoking dope last night. In actual fact, it must have been secondhand, compliments of Jason. I spent the rest of the day curled up on my bed, unsure whether the pain in my stomach was from the aftereffects of the night before or dread of the day to come. Memories of actual events remained pretty vague. The urge to rip Jason a new one came and went. Each time I reached for my cell to find out if he *had* slipped something into my drink, I recalled that I hadn't been a totally unwilling participant. In the future, I would just have to be more wary of what he gave me.

That night, my dreams varied between visions of me returning to Minnesota, tail between my legs, and Adrian Sutherland whipping me on my way with that unforgettable expression of disgust on his face.

By the time I knocked on his door next morning, my heart had taken up permanent residence in an ash-dry mouth. It would have been better if Laurel had caught me; she already hated my guts. I rubbed sweaty palms on my pants at the sound of the quietly uttered invitation to enter.

Adrian sat at his desk, looking immaculate as ever—the crisp white business shirt and striped tie giving him an air of professionalism I could only dream about.

"Sit," he commanded, not bothering to look up from some papers in a folder.

Damn. My file again. Did the thing live on his desk lately? The suspense made my knees shake. "Are you going to fire me?"

His response sent my heart skydiving into my stomach. Anger, I sort of expected, but the boss's cold fury from yesterday had been replaced by bitter disappointment. I would have almost preferred the former. "Not this time," he said with a weary sigh.

The room spun as his softly spoken words registered. I breathed a sigh of relief and sank into the chair. "Thank you." I couldn't meet his gaze though, and stared at the familiar blue-gray pattern on the carpet.

"You've been a good employee, and I gather it was your birthday on Wednesday."

The sudden note of empathy made me risk a glance at my employer's face. Disappointment still lingered in that clear-eyed gaze, but the lines of his jaw had lost their rigidity. "Yes." I took a deep breath to settle my nerves. "It's still no excuse for turning up to work in that state, though."

He raised his eyebrows and inclined his head a fraction. "No, it's not."

Another deep breath. "I won't do it again," I promised.

"You better not." He shut the folder and sighed. "I understand that San Francisco can hold a lot of temptations for a guy your age."

I read the subtext he omitted—a *gay* guy your age—and blushed.

"But there's more to life here than drinking and dancing."

He rose to his feet and walked over to gaze out the window. Heavy drops of rain splattered against the glass. I wondered where this was headed. From the rigidity of his shoulders, nowhere good. After what felt like hours but was probably only a couple of minutes, my boss returned and stood behind his chair, folding his arms along the top of the backrest. When he spoke, he sounded more like Carl—mentoring me, not scolding. "Your profession requires integrity and responsibility, Ben, not just skill with numbers."

I stared at the dribbling raindrops and bit my lip as the image blurred. His voice, normally low, sank even deeper, mirroring the way I felt inside. "If you want to stay working for this firm, I need you to prove to me that you're committed to your career. Training to be an actuary is one of the hardest courses there is." He paused for a moment, waiting for an acknowledgement.

I swallowed and met his gaze. Or tried to. The knowledge that I had been the cause of his sad expression somehow made the day seem even more dismal. "Yes, Mr. Sutherland." This sympathetic understanding was much harder to cope with than the blistering Laurel would have given me.

"You have to hold down a full-time job, plus it requires a lot of self-motivated study. I believe the exams aren't easy."

I nodded. He wasn't telling me anything I didn't already know.

"I'm well aware that sitting at a desk all the time can be tough for a young man. You need something more active to balance your life."

His words gradually sank into my befuddled brain. "Like what?"

"I don't know." He waved his hands around. "There are lots of worthwhile things you could get involved in: Big Brother or Boys and Girls Club, for example. Maybe do some volunteer work for one of the charities we sponsor."

I returned his serious gaze, trying to work out what he was getting at. "Are you saying that because I turned up to work hungover, I should do community service? Like as an alternative to jail?"

The corner of the boss's mouth twisted up in a wry grin. "I suppose that's one way to look at it."

I thought about his suggestion. It wasn't that those things didn't interest me. Back home I had coached basketball at the local YMCA in Duluth and later in Minneapolis. "I'm not sure I would have the time," I said hesitantly. "Taking on something like that is a big commitment and, if anything, I should be doing more study. My next exam is in May."

"Well, you need something to burn off that excess energy. Do you play any sports?"

"Football and ice hockey in college." I flushed. "It's often too wet to go for a run."

He glanced at the rain outside and gave me a rueful smile. "Why don't you use the gym then? That's what it's for."

"The girls use it at lunchtime, most of them go home straight after work because they have families to look after."

"Well, you can use it after work."

"But you're usually using it then."

"So...." He drew up to his full height and raised his eyebrows in surprise. "That shouldn't stop you."

"I didn't think you'd want me there." I muttered the words at the floor, pushing my foot along the carpet.

"Speak up." Irritation clouded his voice.

I raised my head. "I said, I didn't think you would want me to be there too." I'd felt like a total idiot the last time I'd shared the gym with him.

"Why not?" Adrian bounced his fist on the backrest. "Actually, that's the answer. If I'm going to use the weights, I really should have someone to spot me." He smiled and rubbed his hands together. "There you go. We can meet up on a regular basis. Consider it as a form of community service: helping an out-of-condition executive get fit again."

I swallowed. "Yes, Mr. Sutherland. Thank you."

After that, we worked out for at least an hour Monday to Thursday. Before long, I began to look forward to our sessions. Seeing I was meant to be his personal trainer, I set some drills for us to follow: push-ups, sit-ups that kind of thing. At first we didn't talk much, mainly because I didn't know what to say and normal conversation seemed to dry up in my throat. The best I could manage was to recommend different remedies whenever his muscles were feeling the strain.

Some nights, he'd just sit on the bike and vent about the economy and what the government was or wasn't doing about the financial crisis. That meant I had to keep up with my online reading, so at least I'd sound intelligent. Not that he expected me to say much. I think he was just happy to have someone to talk to. A couple of times he asked how my studies were going. Much better, in fact. Every time I felt like slacking off, I remembered the disappointment in his eyes and made sure I finished the course content first.

He told me to call him Adrian, but I felt uncomfortable doing that, so I just called him "Boss". Whenever I talked to him in the office, though, especially if there were other people around, I still referred to him as Mr. Sutherland.

CHAPTER
+++
FIVE

Red

April '09

AT THE start of April, the boss had to visit the East Coast office for a few days—a board meeting this time. While he was away, I worked out on the aerobic machines, listening to the sort of music that used to waft out of Chris's room twenty-four seven. *"It's only just a little place that we called home sweet home. One old house trailer, two rusty Cadillacs, and five thousand country music songs."*

A hand landed on my shoulder. "Shit." I jumped a country mile. The boss was laughing at me. I tried to hide the big fat grin I felt inside at seeing him again. "Hey, I know my singing's pretty crappy, but I didn't think it was that bad!"

The corners of his eyes crinkled up, and the reflection off the walls turned his gray irises almost blue. A soft smile brought my attention to his lips. I'd never really noticed them before. The top one had a real curve to it, not thin like some men. I wondered what it would be like to nibble on. He said something, and I gave myself a mental kick when I realized I was salivating over my employer, not some random bar hookup. I turned off the music and removed my earpiece. "Come again?" My unfortunate choice of words sank in, and I felt my face grow red. "I'm... sorry... I didn't hear what you said."

As he stared back at me for a heart-stopping moment, the crinkle at the edges of Adrian's eyes grew even deeper. Then, with a sigh, he bit his lip, gave a quick shake of his head, and mounted the neighboring bike. "You can take the boy out of the country, but you can't take the country out of the boy."

"Hey! Ry Cooder's more bluesy than country," I spluttered in defense of my idol.

"Was that Ry?"

"Yeah. His latest CD."

"Can I have a listen?"

I wiped off the earpiece and handed it over. After a while Adrian handed it back. "Sounds good. I must get that one to add to my collection."

"You like Ry Cooder?"

"Yeah. I used to listen to him back in college."

"Wasn't his early stuff released back in the 1970s?"

He nodded and looked at me enquiringly.

I did some rapid calculations in my head. That would make Adrian around fifty. He had a lot of gray in his hair, but he wasn't that old, surely.

The man must be a mind reader; his eyes narrowed, and he replied testily, "I listen to Mozart also. That doesn't make me two hundred years old." His feet pushed the pedals faster than their usual steady speed.

Whoops. My face always betrayed what I was thinking. After a while, to break the uncomfortable silence, I blurted out, "My brother plays slide guitar. He thinks Ry Cooder is God."

"Well, he is. Isn't he?"

I returned his quick grin, glad to have made him happy again. "What other sort of music do you like, boss?" It was real good to discover we had something in common.

"Everything, really."

"Like what?"

He shrugged his shoulders. "Well, I'm not a fan of rap or country, but I do like U2, Queen, and lots of music from the eighties. But I also listen to other things." He stopped pedaling and ticked them off on his fingers. "The romantic composers: Beethoven, Brahms, and Vivaldi.

Then there's jazz, Afro-Cuban, gospel, opera. But mostly I listen to the blues: people like Tom Waits and B.B. King."

"But no country music?"

"No, even though I like Ry. Strange, isn't it?" He stayed silent for a while. "Have you heard any of the recordings he did with Cuban musicians?"

I shook my head.

"I'll bring in a CD for you next week." The boss started pedaling again, at a normal pace this time. I turned my iPod back on and moved to the rowing machine. At one stage, I glanced up and caught him staring at me. I had the feeling he still hadn't forgiven me for thinking he was old. I was proven right a few minutes later when I checked to see if he wanted to do some bench presses. His mouth twisted in a grimace, then into a half-hearted grin. "Are you suggesting that I'm also a weakling?" The rueful twinkle in his eyes stopped me from taking his words too seriously.

ONE person whose words I shouldn't have taken seriously was Laurel. While she made a lot of noise at the start about how I should be getting experience in all the different departments, as soon as the end of year report came due, she handed me a stack of her jobs on top of my other work. But the day she made Millie cry, she really got on my shit list.

Tickets for some big charity dinner were supposed to be delivered, and she kept hassling Millie, asking her whether they'd arrived. Millie tried to remain cheerful, but each time Laurel approached, I noticed her smile dim more. Eventually, Laurel found them on Adrian's desk. They'd been addressed to him, so Millie automatically delivered them with the rest of his mail. There are only so many times you can be called a clueless incompetent idiot before the waterworks start.

Adrian came out of his office and saw me comforting a sobbing Millie. "Why don't you take her down to Starbucks?" This time the smile didn't reach his eyes.

I plied Millie with coffee and cake until she gradually calmed down. "She does it all the time. No matter what I do, she finds some fault, and she remembers...."

I snorted in sympathy. "For sure, there's nothing wrong with the bitch's memory. She's one of those people who store up every little mistake and then tell you in great detail whenever she gets the chance. The banshee from hell, eh?"

Millie giggled at Laurel's new nickname, then her face grew more serious again. "And to think she might marry Mr. Sutherland." Rumors had been flying around the office for ages, but no announcement had been made yet. Millie sniffed and ate another piece of cake. All the girls loved the boss; there was something about him. It wasn't just his looks. If things were going ass-up, all I had to do was hear him speak, and the tension in my stomach melted away. Shit, if he'd been gay, I'd be first in line.

Millie gave me a sad grin as I wiped some cream off the side of her nose. "You probably don't read the society pages, but they're always getting their photos taken at the ballet or the opera. I think the photographers like them because they look so good together." She flipped through some magazines lying on a shelf near the door. "Look, here's the latest."

I saw her point. Laurel's black metallic dress caught the light, accentuating her big boobs. Her bottle-blonde hair was swept up at the back to show off her dangling diamond earrings. Adrian looked real good in a tux with a pale blue bow tie, but I much preferred the way he looked when he worked out in the gym with me.

AFTER that, life settled into a routine of sorts: work, gym, study, work, gym, study. Somehow the boss still had the impression I went out clubbing on weeknights as well as the weekend. He kept dropping gentle hints not to neglect my studies. He couldn't have been farther from the truth if he tried. My JO hand was starting to develop RSI.

Most days, when he wasn't out of town visiting clients, Jason stopped by to share some subs at lunchtime, perching himself on the edge of my desk, flirting shamelessly. Occasionally, we got together for some mutual "stress relief", but he kept trying to drag me to places that were downright scary. Leather bars and BDSM clubs. While I didn't mind a bit of bondage, bullwhips and water-sports were definitely not my scene.

A couple of times, I hit the Castro with Mick, the guy I went to the Pride Parade with. He was currently between boyfriends and, being in his final year at med school, he understood if we only met up on Friday or Saturday night. He even asked me to move into the spare room of his condo-loft in SoMa. As a friend, he insisted, not as a fuck buddy. Just as well, it would have been like doing one of my brothers.

One Friday evening, toward the end of the month, Laurel asked me to finish off a document she needed for the annual report. Adrian had been away for a few days, apparently visiting relatives in Northern California. I didn't mind being by myself. I got much more done when the place was quiet.

When I finished, I placed the file on Laurel's desk and went to return the music the boss had lent me: mostly blues artists I'd never heard of. Of course, I had ripped them all straight onto my iPod. There was something about the rasping voices that appealed to me.

After stacking the CDs on Adrian's desk, I took the opportunity to check the place out. The last few times I'd been in there, I'd been so worried about being fired that I hadn't taken much notice of my surroundings. Large photos on the wall stared down at me: Adrian's father and his late grandfather and great-grandfather, the founder of the company. No doubt when he finally inherited the business, a formal portrait of Adrian would join them. The empty feeling I had inside at the reminder he would probably be based in the New York office was only relieved by the thought that he'd take Laurel with him. Hopefully by then I would be a fully qualified associate or have even attained fellowship status. Maybe he'd leave me in charge. I grinned. *What would it be like to have that sort of power?* I sat in his chair and pushed it back, so I could rest my ankles on his desk. Mr. Ben Dutoit, Company President, Western Division. That had a nice ring to it.

Through the open doorway I gained a totally different perspective of the office layout. *Damn.* He could see right into my cubicle. I'd have to remember not to goof off too much.

What to do now? I glanced at my cell. Jason would already be out, cruising. Perhaps I could see if Mick had any plans for the evening. We could check out the pizza place on Noriega Street that Mrs. Christie recommended. Mick kept boasting that his father's restaurant in Little Italy had the best ones in San Francisco, but he would, wouldn't he!

As I locked up, I noticed a light shining out of the washroom doorway. Great. Maybe Tyrone was around. I needed to talk to him about his pool selections. Now we were into the play-offs, and the Golden State Warriors were out of the comp, he didn't have to keep screwing his chances by backing his favorite team.

I glanced in the open door and blinked in surprise. Definitely not Tyrone. This guy was white, or should I say a nice shade of golden brown. He had his back turned and was pulling his T-shirt over his head. All I could see was a broad expanse of muscles rippling under tanned skin and a great jeans-covered ass. *Wow. Nice. Who the heck was that?* My cock certainly wanted to know.

Muffled noises came from the area of the shirt. The guy had become tangled up inside and was having difficulty getting it off.

"Need some help?"

"Fuck!"

The muffled expletive was precisely what I was thinking, but the word wasn't meant to be an invitation. *Pity.* I moved to face him and eased my hands up under his shirt, trying to discover the problem by feel alone.

"Careful, glasses."

I breathed in and all the blood rushed from my head. I knew that after-shave. Adrian Sutherland. *Damn.* I was committed now. I swallowed and tried to tell the bottom half of me to behave as I fumbled inside. "Take your hands away and let me do it," I suggested, trying in vain to keep my voice from betraying how I felt.

He sighed, but did what he was told. As I worked to resolve the problem, the backs of my fingers brushed against his smooth, warm skin. More blood rushed from my head, making it even harder for me to think, let alone see. I tried to ease his shirt back down, but a loose thread had wound itself around one of the screws of his glasses. Eventually I managed to free him. As soon as I did, he pulled the shirt off and threw it down in disgust. "That's what you get for buying cheap crap."

At least the cheap crap would effectively disguise the raging boner I now sported. I picked the offending garment up off the floor, and draped it casually in front of me to hide the evidence. "What are you doing here? I thought you'd gone away." Hopefully once my brain slipped back into gear, I'd settle down. Currently, my heart was beating like I'd just run a marathon on the treadmill.

"My grandfather needed some help with the weeding."

Huh? Grandfather? Weeds? I'd just been looking at a photo of his grandfather, his very dead grandfather. Some blood made its way back to where it belonged and I gave myself a virtual clip upside of the head. *He's talking about his other grandfather, dummy. Everyone has two.* I stood there staring at him as he leaned over, displaying that tight ass I'd been admiring earlier, and extracted a new shirt from a parcel adorned with an Alfio's logo. If one of his grandfathers was still alive, Adrian couldn't be as old as I assumed he was. Dressed in faded jeans with his chest bare, he looked completely different. Much younger. Apart from the gray in his hair, now that he'd lost some weight, he certainly didn't look middle-aged anymore. He looked quite hot. I really envied the way he tanned so easily. I wouldn't have been surprised if he'd said he'd been to the Bahamas or somewhere equally trendy. But outside, weeding? I was dying to ask him for more details, but even though we had been spending a lot of time together, working out, we never really exchanged personal information.

"Are you going to use the gym?" Most Fridays he met up with Laurel, but she'd gone away somewhere for the weekend.

"No, I just came in to change. How come you're still here?"

"I had a document to fix for the end of year report, but I'm finished now." A thought struck me. *What if he'd come into his office and caught me sitting in his chair as if I owned the joint!* "I put the CDs you lent me on your desk."

"Thanks. Did you like them?"

"Yeah." The smile he gave me sent more tingles up my spine.

A mad idea sprang into my head. What would he say if, instead of calling Mick, I invited *him* out for a pizza? Pretend I owed him one for lending me the CDs. My imagination kicked into overdrive. We could sit in one of those intimate booths and discuss the music.

After a quizzical look, as if he wondered why I had become this inarticulate dummy, he slowly fastened the buttons on his shirt, locking away all the bare skin that had turned me on earlier. Nah. The man was obviously going somewhere classy; he wouldn't want to hang out with me. I bundled up the other shirt and placed it on the bench. I needed to leave before the temptation got the better of me.

"See you," I spluttered, my brain/mouth link finally kicking back into gear. By the time I made it out the door, my body was nearly back under control. How weird was that? Getting turned on by my boss, of all people.

CHAPTER
+++
SIX

Red

May '09

Q165: *Beginning with the first full moon in October, deer are hit by cars at a Poisson rate of 20 per day. The time between when a deer is hit and when it is discovered by highway maintenance has an exponential distribution with a mean of 7 days. The number hit and the times until they are discovered are independent.*

Calculate the expected number of deer that will be discovered in the first 10 days following the first full moon in October.

(A) 78 (B) 82 (C) 86 (D) 90 (E) 94

I hadn't seen any deer for months, let alone hit one with my Ranger. The ASM manual made a satisfying thunk as it hit the wall. Equations, variables, 3-premiums, premium-ratios.... I gazed out the window. The apartment's garden had initially been one of the attractions, but now every manicured inch reminded me of what it wasn't. Back home, the woods around the lakes would be bursting with life again. Who cared if the skeeters were buzzing; at least, there was action there, not just problem after problem to solve. *Damn.* One week to the MLC exam, and I still had a crap-load of sample problems to go through.

Thanks to the banshee, I was often too tired to do much study on week nights. If I didn't go to the gym, I could cram in an extra hour, but apart from the fact I sort of felt compelled to, the exercise stopped me crawling up the walls. Otherwise, I just stared at rows and rows of numbers with none of them making any sense. That left me with the weekend, but after a few hours of mind-numbing problems, I usually felt mentally drained.

The familiar ringtone pealed out. "Jason."

"Hiya, Red. Wanna come over to my place?"

I checked my watch. Three o'clock in the afternoon! "What? Now?"

"Yeah. I'm horny, big guy. Need someone to give me a good fuck."

"But what about the guy you live with?"

"He's out."

Oh, what the heck.

Jason greeted me with open arms, as if we'd been together every day since Christmas.

At last I had a chance to see inside. His house was every bit as grand as it looked from the street. Modern décor, white walls. "When's he due back?" I asked as I stroked the sides of his hips. Jason felt real good.

"Not for ages." He ran his hand under my shirt, opened my belt, and reached inside. My knees buckled at his touch, and a shudder ran up my spine. The glance he gave me was pure Jason: one hundred percent mischief. "Let's do it here," he said, and squeezed my cock hard.

"Here?" I managed to squeak out while surveying the entranceway. As he stroked, my brain vaguely took in polished timber floors glowing under the light of a chandelier. Pure class.

"Yeah, here," Jason repeated, his hand slick with my pre-come, sliding along the shaft, getting me hard. It didn't take long. Like I said, I hadn't been getting much action lately.

"But, what if someone can see?" I whispered, leaning into his touch. I could hear pedestrians walking up the street.

"The door's solid, no windows." Jason gave my erection an affectionate pat and eased my jeans over my hips. The buckle made a loud thud as it hit the floor.

Now he wasn't touching me, I could think again. Sort of. "Isn't your bedroom up there?" I gestured to the staircase leading to the upper floor.

He repeated, "Here," more firmly this time. "You know I like to watch, and these mirrors are perfect." He had to stand on tiptoe to pull the T-shirt over my head. He was being unusually helpful. Usually we took off our own clothes and got down to it.

As soon as he had me naked, Jason stood back as if admiring the view. I could see my body reflected in the gilt mirrors that stood on both sides of the entranceway. In fact, there were multiple bodies as each reflection was in turn reflected back. I struck a few poses, admiring the effect while Jason shed his clothes.

A little plant sat on a narrow, marble side table beneath one of the mirrors. As soon as Jason stripped, I carefully moved the pot onto the floor and perched him in its place. At this height, he could check out the floorshow while I got busy.

His cock was as hard as mine. I bent to take it into my mouth, but stopped when I heard a movement outside. I tried to check the front door, but Jason trapped my head between his hands and guided it back down. "Stop worrying, Ben. There's no one there."

The voices moved away. I blocked out the noise and concentrated on what I was doing. Jason tasted so good. I soon had him squirming and moaning my name over and over again. "Yeah, Red, more." I bared my teeth and gave him a nip on the inside of his leg at the sound of my nickname, but that only made him cry out louder. Hopefully the building had good soundproofing.

As soon as he was good and hard, I pulled him forward so I could get at his ass as well. First one finger, then two. The staircase had given me an idea. "Wrap your legs around me." I had always wanted to fuck someone while standing up, but it's not as easy as it sounds.

A wicked grin crossed his face as he clung to my front like a monkey. "Ooh, Ben, I do like it when you give me orders."

Yeah, as long as they were ones he wanted to follow. I carried him over and rested his butt on the side of the steps. "Now grab onto the railing above your head." For once, he did what he was told.

He sure looked sexy, arched back like that; his smooth, tanned skin glowed under the bright lights. His eyes were closed, every inch of him looked primed and ready for sex. I stared over at my pile of clothes on the floor. “Fuck. I should have got the condom first.” It had taken me ages to get Jason at the right height, and I didn’t want to start all over again.

He groaned and opened his eyes to glare at me. “Oh, come on, Ben. Don’t stop now. Forget about the latex. I want to feel your big prick inside me.”

“No.” I tried to pull away, but he clasped his legs tighter, trapping me.

“It’s not like we’ve never done it before.” The wicked glint was back in his eyes.

I stopped trying to break away and stared at him. “When?” I was normally very careful about things like that.

“The night of your birthday.”

I blinked and racked my brain. “I don’t remember going bareback.” From memory, I was pretty drunk at the time.

“You liked it… a lot.” Jason smiled at me from under his eyelashes. “You kept going on about how much better it felt.”

Just the thought of fucking Jason like that made more pre-come ooze out. I smeared it over my cock and stared at him. His eyelids drooped shut again, and he arched back farther.

Oh, fuck it, why not. After applying as much spit as I could and adjusting my stance, I worked my cock into his hole. Damn, he was tight, but Jason never minded a bit of pain. “Fuck, yeah.” He gave a loud cry as I finally sank all the way in.

I clamped my hand over his mouth. “Shush. You sound like I’m trying to rape you.”

He giggled and squirmed away from my hand.

Shit. My legs trembled as I savored the bare contact against warm flesh. No wonder guys raved about the difference. I waited for Jason to relax around me, then I pulled back and thrust in again. *Sweet.*

After a few goes, I finally got the angle right. Jason moaned as I massaged his prostate with my cockhead. “Yeah, that’s the spot. Do it again!”

I drew back and snapped my hips forward, faster this time.

"Yeah, yeah!" Jason, threw his head back and called out, "That's it, Red. Harder, harder!"

If only I had another hand to gag him with, but both mine were now hanging on to his hips to make sure he didn't fall. I shut my eyes and grunted as I started pounding away. Each thrust was better than the last. A tingling started in the base of my spine. Above the roaring in my ears, I heard a startled gasp. Opening my eyes, I glanced at the front door. *Shit.* Adrian Sutherland was poised inside the entrance. He looked as if he had been out running. His face and arms were slick with sweat, and a sleeveless red T stuck to dark patches on his chest. Hastily, he closed the door and turned around.

What the fucking hell was he *doing here?* Needless to say my cock wilted faster than a burst balloon as I pulled out and eased Jason down onto solid ground. I tried to turn my back, but no matter where I faced, the mirrors reflected every detail of my embarrassment.

Crap, crap, crap. I grabbed my clothes, shoved one leg in my jeans and frantically worked on the other one, jumping around the hallway.

"Keep it quieter, please Jason, I could hear you half-way down the street." Adrian made his request as calmly as if he needed one of the office girls to do some photocopying, but when he straightened from picking up the pot and replacing it on the table, I noticed that his face was red. So was mine.

"Sorry, sir." My voice sounded croaky as a noose tightened around my throat.

We stared at each other for a few seconds, then Adrian's face changed from red to ashen white. He turned away after a brief nod of acknowledgement at my apology and bounded up the stairs. A door banged, followed shortly by what sounded like a glass shattering.

Shit. I took a deep breath and finally managed to get my jeans zipped. Jason had pulled on his pants. The bastard was chuckling quietly, not the slightest bit perturbed that we'd been caught fucking like rabbits, and by our boss of all people.

"Why didn't you tell me you lived with Adrian!*?"* My hands shook so much I had trouble fastening my belt.

"Oh, didn't you know?" Jason flipped the hair out of his eyes. His face had that fuck-the-world expression I knew so well. "He owns this house. When my last lease ran out, he suggested I stay here with him."

"You could have warned me."

A sly smile twisted Jason's lips.

I grabbed the rest of my clothes, staggered out the door, and collapsed in a heap on the top step. Jason didn't give a hoot. He was out of the office most of the day, looking after his clients. I'd be stuck at my desk, knowing every time the boss saw me, he'd remember. *Damn.* The expression on his face as he headed upstairs wasn't going to be easy to forget. For once, the polite mask had slipped, revealing something raw underneath. Embarrassment? Definitely not amusement. Grief or some other emotion I couldn't identify. A pang of guilt stirred in my gut. Why did I have this weird feeling I'd been caught cheating? Talk about crazy.

Then the thought hit me. In March, Adrian warned me that I had one more chance. I sighed and buried my head in my hands. What a mess. My job was probably on the line again, and given my limited preparation, I'd be lucky to pass the upcoming exam.

The door behind me opened. I cringed, but it was only Jason. He grinned sheepishly. "Come on, Ben. We can use my bedroom."

I shook my head. "Fuck off. No way am I ever going back in there."

THAT night, my restless sleep was disturbed by the recurring vision of being sent back to Minnesota in disgrace, but this time instead of Adrian whipping me on my way, for some reason, the person I was fucking against the balustrade turned out to be him instead of Jason. I woke in a sticky mess, the dream turning into a sick fantasy. The only way I could get back to sleep was imagining Adrian making love to Laurel. That one turned into a real nightmare.

All week at work, I waited for the axe to fall, but the feared request for a meeting never materialized. There are only so many times you can accidentally drop something on the floor when the person you're dreading to make eye contact with walks out of his office.

Laurel had gone to a lunchtime appointment. The coast was clear. I took a deep breath and knocked on the boss's door.

A quiet "Enter" came in response.

Inside, I stopped in surprise. I'd never seen the place so messy. Files lay scattered about instead of in their normal neat piles. His suit jacket was draped over the back of his chair. Even Adrian didn't look the same. His blue tie was half pulled down, his sleeves rolled up, displaying his golden tan. He might not look so immaculate, but hot damn, he looked good enough to eat. I made sure the door was properly closed, then stood in front of his desk. *Here goes.* I took a deep breath. "I'm sorry about the other day, sir."

A faint smile twisted his lips. "Ben, you don't have to call me *sir.*"

My hands felt huge, heavy, as if they could actually recall what it felt like to grip his hips while I slammed into him instead of Jason, like in my dream. I fidgeted with my watch and tried to block the alternate image from my brain.

He sighed and waved a hand in my general direction. "Sit down, please. You're so tall, I'll get a crick in my neck if you keep standing."

I sat, relieved to take the weight off legs that had never felt so shaky. I took another deep breath and lifted my head, even though I would have much preferred to study the carpet. The dreamed vision still toyed with the edge of my consciousness. New words failed me, so I just repeated my apology. "I'm sorry about the other day, Mr. Sutherland."

He sat and stared at me in silence. Lately, I noticed that he smiled less often. The business was definitely going through a rough patch. This was the man who had virtually guaranteed me a job, as long as I wanted to work here. Was that why he hadn't fired me? Should I offer to resign? My skin went clammy at the thought of leaving. I couldn't meet those steel gray eyes any longer. I stared at the carpet instead, debating what to do.

The softness of his voice made me glance up. "Ben, you and Jason are adults. What you get up to out of work hours is no business of mine... although I've always found bedrooms beat entrance halls for comfort." He smiled slightly after delivering the punch line.

I swallowed, but my tongue felt much too large for my mouth. "If I had known it was your place, I wouldn't have done it... where we could be disturbed by you... by anyone." *I certainly wouldn't have been fucking in the middle of your hallway.* It would have been bad enough in Jason's bedroom.

Adrian sighed and picked up his pen. "You're young, Ben, and life may seem simple, but even small actions you do now can have consequences in the future. People with more experience can hurt you before you realize it's happening."

"People with more experience"? *Was he referring to Jason?* And what did he mean by alluding to my youth? "I'm twenty-four," I spluttered. "Not some wet-behind-the-ears kid!"

He snorted. "I'm well aware how old you are."

The firm's literature disclosed how old he was. Thirty-five. Only eleven years older than me. The gray hair had me fooled completely. I shifted uncomfortably in my chair. "Anyway, I just wanted to apologize."

"Apology accepted." Adrian straightened some papers on his desk.

"Thank you, sir, um, Mr. Sutherland," I answered quietly and stared at the carpet again. There were actually tiny flecks of white in the blue, creating the smoky gray-blue color that exactly matched his eyes. He kept silent, so I assumed I was dismissed.

I had my hand on the doorknob, ready to open it, when he spoke again, his voice pitched low, uncertain. "You haven't been coming to the gym."

I turned to stare at him, my pulse suddenly beating faster. "I've been too embarrassed."

The return of his slow, sexy smile sent my heart to a shuddering halt. "I still need someone to spot for me."

Words of thanks stuck in my throat. I bit my lips together and gave a quick nod of assent before closing the door quietly behind me. *Need someone.* Such a simple phrase for a strong emotion. One I could relate to.

CHAPTER
+++
SEVEN

Red

June '09

I PASSED my exam. The shock of being caught fucking by the boss worked as a wake-up call. Ever since arriving in San Francisco, I hadn't done much to earn his respect, so from then on, I spent every spare minute working through as many sample questions as I could. In the end, it must have been enough.

Another one down, my next one on Financial Economics wasn't until November. Apparently, there was a lot of algebra involved, so that part would be fine. The rest was based more on understanding and the ability to think on your feet. Hopefully mine were big enough.

I would have gone out to celebrate, but I was still pissed off at Jason, and Mick had started going out with a guy named Steve. I toyed with the idea of cruising and seeing who or what I could pick up, but the image of Adrian's gray eyes staring at me kept tugging at my brain.

My cell rang. The caller ID read: Mick.

"Ben, sorry to wake you."

I rolled my legs out of bed and glanced at the clock on the nightstand. After midnight. "Is this a Gayday?" Mick had called me a couple of times when his dates went sour.

"Sort of. I'll explain when you get here. The battery in my cell is running out."

"Where are you?"

I blinked when I heard the familiar name. Mick usually didn't visit places like that. I pulled on a pair of jeans and a black shirt. Usually my size was enough to intimidate anyone who tried to give Mick a hard time.

The thumping bass of disco music greeted me again when I arrived at the converted warehouse. The dance floor was heaving, but Mick was nowhere in sight. I headed upstairs. Still no sign of him or any crazy boyfriend.

I grabbed a bottled water from the bar and guzzled it down while I scanned the upstairs dance floor. I choked as water gushed down my throat. Mick and Jason were dancing together. Or rather Jason's arms were draped around Mick's neck while he shuffled around. I chuckled at the incongruous couple. Jason had on his usual skintight pants, an open leather vest above black boots. Mick was his usual geeky self. He looked as if he didn't know where to put his hands. As soon as he saw me, the look of relief on his face made me laugh.

"Thank God, you're here."

Jason disengaged himself from Mick and transferred his arms to my neck. "Ben, I didn't know you were coming." He gave a weak smile and swayed on his feet.

I grabbed his hips to steady him.

Jason took a while to focus as he leaned in for a kiss. *Damn.* He was as high as a kite.

I leaned back and took in the vision in my arms. Jason had gel in his hair, making him look more like a *GQ* model than ever, and, was that kohl around his eyes? They certainly looked darker than usual.

Between the two of us, we managed to maneuver Jason off the dance floor and found a secluded corner. Jason collapsed against me while I propped up the wall.

Mick put his hands in his pocket and shrugged. "I wasn't sure whether I should call you or not. I know you guys broke up…."

"Broke up? We were never going steady."

Jason gave a start, and I realized he had actually passed out for a second. He twisted his head to look up at me. There was a bleakness in his gaze I hadn't seen before. "Are you okay?" I asked.

"Yeah, just tired."

"Sure you should be out partying?"

"Shit, Ben, you're as bad as Adrian." A scowl crossed Jason's face. At first, hanging out with him had been fun, especially when I didn't know anyone in the city, but lately there'd been more arguments than laughs. Arguments about barebacking, going out on weeknights, where we went. I didn't need all that crap in my life. The final straw had been the incident at Adrian's house.

"I'm worried about him," Mick said quietly. "He doesn't look too good." He tried to feel Jason's forehead, but Jason swatted his hand away. Mick gave me a sad smile. "I've been keeping an eye on him all night. Guys keep trying to drag him into the back rooms. I wouldn't have interfered, but sometimes when he came out afterward, you could tell he'd been crying. Dancing with him was the only way I could keep him occupied."

"Yeah, and you're a shit dancer," Jason muttered.

I knew Jason liked it rough, but that didn't sound normal. "I'm happy to punch someone out if they haven't been nice to you. Point me at them."

Jason gave a low chuckle. "Nah. I just feel like crap."

I straightened away from the wall and held onto Jason's arm when he staggered. "Looks like I better take you home."

"Don't you love it when Ben does the Sir Galahad act?" Jason smirked at Mick.

Mick raised his eyebrows. He thought Jason was a rich prick who only worked because he was bored. I hadn't told him about the episode at Adrian's place. If I had, he wouldn't have intervened. "Do you want me to come with you?" he offered quietly. "He looks very pale."

Jason pushed him away, muttering, "I don't need two fuckin' nursemaids."

I shook my head and gave a dry laugh. "Looks like I'll have to manage on my own. Sorry to ruin your evening, Mick. Thanks for keeping an eye on him." We gripped hands, then I thought, *What the fuck,"* so I hugged him. Good friends are hard to find.

When we arrived outside Adrian's house, I waited for Jason to leave the car. No way was I going inside. Too many embarrassing memories. I reached across and opened the passenger door. "Good *night*, Jason."

He didn't move. His eyes were closed, and he seemed half asleep again. *Fuck.* I went around and helped him out. He walked shakily up to the door. I leaned back against the car, watching him.

He paused when he finally managed to get his key in the lock. Glancing back at me, he mouthed, "Come on." He still looked as if he was going to fall down any minute. Much as I didn't want to go inside, I had to. Jason was so out of it, he would have been lucky to get up the stairs. I put my arm around his shoulders and helped him into the house.

"Where's your room?"

He pointed wordlessly to the upper floor.

I took a deep breath and tried to block out images of my previous visit. At the top, two closed doors were situated on opposite sides of a short corridor. A light underneath one suggested Adrian was awake. Hopefully, I could get Jason into bed and leave before the boss even knew I was there.

I opened the door Jason indicated and turned on the light. The room was pretty austere. Conservative, even. More polished floorboards, a red Persian rug, and a double bed in the center covered by a simple, pale-blue spread. What had I expected? Mirrors on the ceiling? Leopard-skin rugs. Red satin sheets? Yep, to all of the above.

I bullied Jason into drinking a glass of water and helped him undress. I wasn't sure whether his shakiness was from drugs or alcohol, but a drink wouldn't hurt either way.

I felt like his freakin' mother when I tucked him in. He started muttering something and tossed his head around. I touched his forehead and wiped away beads of sweat. I couldn't leave him like that. In the adjoining bathroom, I found a rag, wet it with cool water, and wiped his brow a few times. He settled slightly, but his temperature was still way too high. Then it hit me. It wasn't drink or drugs; he had a fever.

Crap. Any chance of a speedy exit vanished. I crossed the corridor and knocked on the other door. A couple of seconds later, it opened, and the boss stood there. I felt like someone had punched me in the gut. All he had on were low-slung, slinky lounge pajamas. The soft blue material clung to the outline of cock. *Geez, he was hung.* I tore my gaze upward before he caught me looking. The combination of muted light and high cheekbones threw shadows across his face, their darkness increased by the salt-and-pepper stubble on the edge of his jaw. Gone was the clean-cut businessman. Now he was rough, untamed, wicked. I gulped.

He'd obviously been reading; a book was clasped in one hand, his glasses in the other. Thank Christ he didn't have his girlfriend over. Seeing Laurel with him would have been too embarrassing for words.

"Good evening, Ben—is something the matter?" The warmth of his smiling enquiry startled me. Whoops. The sight of my boss had completely driven thoughts of Jason from my mind. "Sorry to disturb you, s… It's Jason." I shifted uncomfortably from one foot to the other, my mouth bone-dry. We'd settled back into our gym sessions, so I didn't feel awkward with him at work. Here was different; I couldn't help remembering our previous embarrassing encounter downstairs.

"What's wrong?" His voice switched from tired to alert immediately.

"Jason's got a fever. He keeps muttering something about flames. At first, I thought he was drunk. Now I think he's sick."

I followed Adrian back into Jason's room. He was still unsettled. The boss touched his forehead and drew his hand back immediately. "Wow, he *is* hot."

"I tried cooling him down." I remoistened the rag and smoothed it over Jason's forehead and under his neck again.

"Don't. It burns," Jason moaned a couple of times.

Adrian grimaced, left the room, and reappeared moments later with a medical kit. He removed a probe, put on a small plastic cover, and placed it in Jason's ear. He glanced at me and smiled. "Don't look so surprised. Sometimes, when there's a board meeting, my cousin Bill and his family stay here. Natalie's only four, so I make sure I'm prepared in case she gets sick." After checking the reading, he sighed. "A hundred and two. Could be why he's delirious." He replaced the probe and shut the kit. "I've got some liquid child-strength ibuprofen. I'll give him a double dose. Maybe he'll be able to keep that down."

I kept up my sponging until he returned.

"Jason, drink this." The command was firm, as was the shake the boss gave him.

Jason's eyes flew open. He stared around as if unsure where he was or who he was with. Adrian tried to dose him, but Jason spluttered, and the medicine ran out the side of his mouth. I clambered behind him and sat with my back against the headboard, legs on each side, pulling Jason up, so he was supported by my chest and my arms. "Try it now."

That worked; Jason managed to swallow the medicine and the glass of water that followed. As soon as he finished drinking, he collapsed back against me with his eyes closed.

I glanced up at Adrian. His lips were a thin white line. "What do you think is wrong with him?" I asked.

The boss shut his eyes and did the—by now familiar—neck rub. When he opened them again, his eyes flickered away from mine, avoiding contact. "It could be a number of things, but until I get him to the doctor tomorrow, all we can do is treat the symptoms."

Adrian placed the empty containers on the nightstand and turned off most of the lights, leaving only a couple above the bed. He moved a small, hard-backed chair closer, sat, and opened his book.

I gazed at the top of Jason's head. *What should I do now?* I half expected Adrian to tell me to go home, but I didn't want to leave. I wanted to stay and check out this sexy version of my boss. Mind you, it was hard to think of him in that capacity when he was shirtless and just wearing his PJs. He'd donned his glasses again, and in a weird way they made him look younger. With his trendy stubble, he reminded me of one of those models in optometrist ads who never seem to need glasses but look so good in them, they're more like a fashion statement.

My eyes drifted lower, and I studied his bare chest. He'd obviously been topless out in the sun again lately. His skin was now the color of golden chestnuts. There wasn't a hair to be seen above the waistband, not even a happy trail. *How far down did he wax?* I wondered. Reluctantly, I dragged my gaze up again, hoping there wasn't any drool running down my chin. The weight sessions in the gym were definitely paying off. Stark shadows cast by the bedside lamp delineated his abs. My tongue itched to trace the indents on his chest, lick the dark-brown nipples, make them hard. *Talking about hard.* I squirmed slightly, trying to get my cock into a more comfortable position without touching it. *What sort of a relationship did these two have, anyway?* Jason was cagey anytime I fished for more information, but they must be pretty close. The concern Adrian showed tonight definitely wasn't faked.

I laughed to myself. *Isn't life strange?* I'd decided to stop hanging out with Jason and vowed never to step inside this house again, yet here he was, in my arms while I sat on his bed. He'd actually fallen asleep snuggled up against my shoulder. If I shifted too much, he'd wake up. Careful not to disturb him, I reached for a pillow and slid it behind my back. Jason stirred for a second but settled again immediately. *Ah, that was better.*

Adrian glanced up when I moved and smiled. Christ. Those come-to-bed eyes and a bed in close proximity were a bad mix. I needed something to take my mind off sex. Anything.

I couldn't see the front of the book. "What are you reading?" I whispered.

"*The Billionaire's Vinegar* by Benjamin Wallace." Adrian angled the cover so I could see the title. "It's about the most expensive bottle of wine ever sold. A 1787 Château Lafite Bordeaux that allegedly belonged to Thomas Jefferson."

"Is it a novel?"

"No. Narrative nonfiction written like a whodunit. The author traces its origins after doubts arose about its authenticity when Christie's auctioned it for $156,000."

"You're kidding me."

He laughed. "No. I'll lend it to you when I've finished, if you like. Do you know much about wine?"

"No, but I know what I like. Isn't that the standard answer?" I grinned when he rolled his eyes. My ploy worked; soon Adrian was busy talking about wine, and I stopped thinking about sex and my boss in the same sentence. Mostly, anyway.

A hand touched my shoulder; I looked up into his pale gray eyes. Whoops, his "midnight-to-dawn" voice must have lulled me to sleep.

"Do you want to go lie down on one of the beds?" he asked quietly.

I rubbed my eyes and tried to wake up. The clock on the nightstand said 2 a.m. Pity he woke me; I was in the middle of a great dream where I was having hot sex among the wild flowers in a vineyard. It seemed so real.

Adrian's expression was polite, concerned. The good host checking on the welfare of his guest. I recalled what the guy I'd been pounding into the ground looked like. My face grew warm; I was blushing again. The heat of his hand on my shoulder sent a tingle clear down to my groin. I shifted to break contact and struggled to catch my breath. He waited for my answer.

"No, I better go home now." I eased myself off the bed, settled Jason down, and adjusted the sheet. He didn't even stir. I stood there and stared at him for a while. Asleep, he lost all the prickles that poisoned his personality when he was awake. He really was a beautiful bastard. "Will he be all right?" I glanced up to see Adrian watching me intently.

He shrugged and checked Jason's temperature again. "It's come down a bit." He still looked worried. "I'm going to take him to the doctor even if he's better in the morning. You go get some sleep."

Before I left, I leaned over and kissed Jason's forehead. His long lashes looked like black moths resting on his cheeks. Shame he was so unsettled. Deep down, I knew I wasn't the person he needed. Pity. We'd had some good times together.

Adrian accompanied me down the stairs and let me out the front door. All the way I was conscious of his clean smell and bare chest. I often saw him like that in the washroom after a gym session, but tonight was different somehow. Maybe it was the proximity of the beds or memories of him walking in when I was fucking Jason downstairs; or maybe it was just the dream. *Fuck*. Luckily there's no law against gay guys lusting after straight ones.

When I said good night, he gripped my hand tightly. "Thanks for your help. I'll let you know how Jason is tomorrow." He glanced at his watch. "I mean today." He smiled one of those devastating smiles again. I could get addicted to those. *Damn, why were all the good ones straight?*

PART TWO

BLUE

INTRODUCING BLUE

I HAVEN'T always been blue.

During my five happy, rebellious, stolen years of freedom, I was the life of the party, guaranteed to get people laughing the minute I walked in. But all that changed when my father had a heart attack and said it was time to stop fooling around and learn the business before I inherited it.

You see, from the day I was born, my destiny has been the lead role in the long-running saga of Sydney Sutherland Family Insurance: A Family Looking after Families. After my mother died, I prayed that there would be other candidates for the part, hoped that my father would re-marry and have other kids. Over the years, he'd had a number of girlfriends—mostly blondes, the complete opposite of my mother—but he stayed resolutely single, and I remained an only child, with my life carved out in stone.

The trouble is that the firm is, literally, a family affair, carried on generation after generation. Even my cousin Bill is Senior Vice President in Charge of Administration. In fact, strangers often get confused as to who's who, because Bill is the spitting image of our mutual grandfather and looks more like my father than I do.

I take after my mother's side of the family, long time owners of a vineyard in the Dry Creek Valley region of North Cal. Even though Pop and Nonna had migrated to the States soon after they got married, wine was in their blood, and they carried on a tradition started years ago by their forebears in the Tre Venezie region located in the northeast of Italy.

That's where I was when the call from "casting" came through: working on the vineyard that belonged to my maternal grandfather's brother, enjoying life, finding love and living openly in Europe as a gay man, something I would never dare to do under my father's watchful, homophobic eye. Leaving Italy wasn't easy, especially as it meant leaving everything I loved. But having to deny my sexuality made it even worse.

Now, I live my life in the closet. I'm a closeted blues music fan, a closeted drunk, a closeted Democrat, a closeted New York Jets fan… the list goes on.

No, I'm wrong. I don't *live* in my closet. I can't. There isn't enough room, because it's chock full of Bill Blass, Armani, Ralph Lauren, and other designers. The days are long gone when I could fit all my possessions in a backpack. Back in the States, I decided that if I had to act the starring role of Adrian Sydney Sutherland IV, I might as well win the Oscar for costume design.

Things were fine at first. I threw myself into my work, building the division into something I could be proud of, something worth the sacrifices I'd made. Like many others, though, I got caught by the credit crunch.

On the surface, I acted as if I didn't have a care in the world, and until my good friend, beard, and ex-colleague, Evelyn Archer, decided to come out herself and settle down, the suits and fancy clothes received regular airings. Now, most nights I sit on the sofa in my heavily mortgaged Pacific Heights house and listen to music with my closest companion, Jack Daniels.

Perhaps listening to the blues isn't the best way to cope with the demands of my life, but hearing Muddy Waters and Tom Waits sing about their problems makes me feel as if I'm not alone.

Although I'm not really alone, as I share the house with Jason Parr, the son of one of my father's oldest buddies. But he's out partying most nights. I've known Jason for years, as we grew up near each other on Long Island. I'm supposed to be making sure he doesn't get into too much trouble, but keeping a gay guy like Jason on the straight and narrow in San Francisco is nigh on impossible.

The trouble is that ever since he realized I'm gay, he's taunted me about what I'm missing. Every time he goes out, I hear all about it when he gets home. I don't mind, so long as it's innocuous reports about what bars he's been to, but I cracked when he tried to tell me what his latest boyfriend was like in bed. Especially when it turned out to be Ben Dutoit, the firm's new actuarial recruit.

My gaydar is notoriously inadequate, so I'd been surprised when Jason told me he'd seen Ben in a Castro bar. Not that that meant anything, because to Jason, every good-looking stud he sees there is gay or at least fair game. It's only when he fails to get them into bed that they suddenly become heteros.

When I realized he was telling the truth, I was pleasantly surprised. Maybe now he'd settle down and stop playing the field, but I did ask him to spare me the details. It's bad enough hearing tales behind his lovers' backs; impossible if they're an employee.

Jason sulked for days.

CHAPTER
+++
ONE

Blue
December '08

LIFE continued without incident until early December, at the end-of-year industry luncheon. Carl Hausfeldt and I had been discussing whether to have the fish or the chicken when he'd gone into a massive cardiac arrest. Only some frantic CPR and first-class medical care saved his life.

He was asleep when my father and I visited him in the hospital a couple of days later. The harsh lighting made his pale skin not much darker than the sheet covering him. The monitor beside his bed showed a regular beat, which was encouraging. The number of tubes inserted into his body wasn't.

Ever since September, the stress had been horrendous. At least, thanks to Carl, none of our reserves had been too badly affected, because he'd insisted on adequate hedging programs back when the rest of the board were all for ignoring the risky nature of the finance sectors' love affair with flashy speculative derivatives and credit default swaps.

Our financial future still remained uncertain. Nose-diving house prices and a free-falling stock market affected everyone. Life insurance was often one of the first expenses people cut, but if it hadn't been for Carl, we would have been in a much worse position.

Having been assured his long-time friend was on the mend, and with the data he needed, my father took the next flight home. Carl's temporary replacement, Laurel Marchison, arrived a few days later. Dad had planned to accompany her; however, another attack of gout intervened. Instead, he called and told me to make sure she settled in okay.

"I'm thrilled at the opportunity to relocate to the western division, Adrian." Laurel's manicured fingers pulled the tight skirt down over her silk stockings, drawing my attention to her legs. They were shapely, and she knew it.

I gave a vague smile of acknowledgement and concentrated on steering through the typical pre-Christmas traffic snarl. When I picked her up from the airport, she exemplified the epitome of NY corporate chic: long, blonde hair tied into a chignon, Donna Karan suit, and sensible pumps. "How was New York?"

"Cold and snowy. Your father promised me lots of Californian sunshine."

"LA, maybe. Let's see how you feel after a few weeks of fog and rain."

She laughed and turned to gaze out the window. Bright sunlight glinted off water as we drove along Bayshore Freeway, making me into a liar.

"Won't you miss the nightlife?" I asked. "My father said you'd accompanied him to the Met a few times."

She turned and smiled. "He assured me there'd be plenty of cultural opportunities here. He said you often go to the ballet and SFS concerts."

I had, with Evelyn. I flicked another glance at Laurel; she seemed very comfortable in my company, super-confident, sophisticated. "San Francisco is a village in comparison."

"Anyone would think you're trying to put me off relocating." She smiled again.

I would have described her as beautiful if her smiles actually reached her eyes. Instead, there was a calculating wariness; as if she was monitoring my reaction, checking to see if I was buying the product she was selling. "It's not going to be easy," I warned.

"I'm looking forward to the challenge. When he offered me the position, I told your father it would be a privilege to work in a division that has garnered so much attention for its innovative approach to life insurance."

I snorted inside. All the innovative policies Carl and I had introduced were won inch by inch in the face of my father's reluctance.

After she checked in, I carried her bags to the room and told her I'd pick her up later.

I DON'T care what anybody wants to call it. For me, it will always be the staff Christmas party. I can still remember when Mom used to dress a pine tree and ask Dave Simmons to don a Santa costume to entertain our employees' children.

Jason must have been watching out for me, because I saw him move away from the window when I helped Laurel out of the car. As soon as we walked in, he started kissing Ben. As he did, the little brat caught my eye and actually smirked. Obviously, if he couldn't *tell* me about their relationship, he was going to *show* me. Moments later, Ben took refuge in the kitchen, blushing so badly his face was nearly as red as his hair. I didn't blame him; I'd have been just as embarrassed at his age. Luckily, everyone was more interested in the sight of me arriving with a new female.

Laurel hadn't been too impressed when she saw them kissing. As soon as we moved away, she pursed her lips and said quietly, "I hardly think behavior like that is appropriate for a family-focused firm." Her disapproval deepened later when Jason put his arm around Ben.

What was I going to do about the boy? Carl had asked me to look after him, but if Laurel relocated, there really wasn't a position. It would be a pity to have to let him go. He was competent, and you could tell by the way all his fellow employees talked to him that he was definitely well-liked.

I didn't find out until I took her home at Christmas time that Laurel had blabbed to my father that Ben was gay.

"THANK you for making the effort to join us."

I ignored the underlying sarcasm in my father's tone and stared out the large mullioned window in his study. The bare trees in the snow-covered woodland reminded me once again why my presence was such a rarity at this time of year. I never minded visiting in fall, but winter chilled me to the bone.

Usually, I managed to avoid coming by pleading Nonna and Pop wanted me to spend Christmas with them. It was always a battle about who had priority. This year, my father insisted I attend the family dinner and bring Laurel along. The wind had risen steadily since we arrived. Whitecaps now adorned the waves in Long Island Sound.

"What's this I hear about that new actuarial trainee I met? Laurel says he's gay."

The leather sofa squished underneath me as I sat on its overstuffed cushions. Sometimes I wondered if the phrases anti-discrimination and equal opportunity even existed in my father's vocabulary. "Jason's gay, and you've never mentioned his sexuality before."

Not only was my father's gout acting up, judging by the flush that crossed his face, his blood pressure wasn't too good either. "Jason's father, Vernon, is a good friend. I wouldn't want to upset him."

"Would it help to know Ben and Jason are an item, and he's keeping Jason in line?"

"It's...." My father's gaze roamed the room, landing anywhere but on me.

My jaw tightened uncomfortably. "What's your problem?"

"We're a family firm...."

I held my breath and waited for him to continue.

"Some of the salesmen report customers are saying our policy on providing life insurance for people with AIDS is anti-family."

I ignored the *family* word for the moment, as over the years it had become a touchy subject. "HIV isn't exclusive to homosexuals, Dad. The incidence in the heterosexual community is rising. Even children have been diagnosed positive. Anyway, it's a treatable, chronic illness, not an immediate death sentence." I'd explained it many times before, until I was blue in the face, but he was a hard man to convince.

My father turned to me, his eyes narrowed in determination. I knew that expression all too well. "There's still no cure."

"There's no cure for cancer or diabetes either, and we insure people with those. I thought you were proud of our position as one of the country's foremost high-risk insurers."

"It's not the same. Anyway, in this downturn, we have to be extra careful."

"Carl adjusted the premiums to account for the higher risk."

"I'm talking perception, not money."

Perception. I knew from bitter experience I was never going to win this debate. "I don't see how it relates to Ben. He isn't out on the road, selling policies."

"Like I said, we're a family company looking after families." My father wasn't used to his dutiful son arguing with him. Irritation brightened his cheeks even more.

"And gays aren't welcome in families?" I rose to my feet; I couldn't stay seated any longer. "Do you realize how hard it is for me to have you continually harp on the subject?"

"Well, you have to settle down and get married some day."

If I hadn't known how important the concept of passing the firm down, father to son, was to him, I'd have thought he was joking. "Is that why you told me to invite Laurel?"

"She's very attractive."

A scrunch of tires on raked gravel almost drowned his comment. I checked out the window. Bill and Lindy had arrived for our Christmas dinner. No doubt they'd be up here soon, and we might not get a chance to talk one-on-one again.

"Look, Dad, when you asked me to come back to the States, I did, even though that decision cost me dearly." I'd never told my father exactly what happened; he wouldn't have understood, much less had any sympathy for either of us. "You promised me I could run the West Coast division the way I wanted as long as I *suppressed my gay tendencies.* I think that was the phrase you used, wasn't it?"

He gave an impatient snort.

"Well I've done that." I sighed. "Isn't that enough?"

"But you're my only child."

"I'm hardly to blame for that!"

66

"Keep your voice down." His face flushed again as he glanced quickly at the door. Footsteps, along with Chester's excited barking, could be heard outside. "I just ask that you consider the prospect," he added quietly. "You wouldn't be the first gay man to lead a normal life and keep that part of yourself hidden."

My stomach churned, but the door opened before I could tell him what I thought of his revolting suggestion. A small, fair-haired child and a yapping Jack Russell terrier erupted inside.

"Uncle Adrian!"

Suppressing my anger, I gathered Natalie in my arms and welcomed my cousin Bill and his wife.

CHAPTER
TWO

Blue

January '09

EVEN though it was more than three months since the September stock market crash, I knew that many members of staff had serious concerns about the economy in general and their own jobs in particular. The start of a new year seemed the perfect occasion to get them into a more positive frame of mind. The meeting opened in its usual way, with the welcome speech. Ben and Millie arrived late. When they reached their seats, Jason caught my eye and adjusted his cuffs—his "check out the threads" signal. The difference between the two men couldn't have been more marked. Jason was wearing the new Kiton suit he had picked up when we visited Saks for its post-Christmas sale. Ben's white shirt didn't even look as if it had been pressed.

A ray of sunlight caressed his hair as a cloud passed from in front of the sun. The fiery highlights reflected the glint in his eyes as they both laughed. The tension in my grip slipped away. Who cared what Ben's clothes looked like? It was good to see him again.

Everything proceeded according to plan until Laurel spoke. We'd had a long discussion on the flight back about who would say what, and I had specifically pointed out that, until the board met, neither of us should foreshadow moves that, at that stage, were only my father's suggestions. They certainly didn't have my support. When her speech hinted at policy changes in the high-risk area, I realized I had obviously wasted my breath. First day back, and I missed Carl already.

She also did her best to monopolize the meeting in my office. I could sense Ben's nervousness from the other side of the desk as he stared at me. I debated what to say while she cross-examined him about the progress of his qualification. If she hadn't been there, I would have had a heart-to-heart talk to him about his future. Now she was replacing Carl permanently, there really wasn't room for him.

When she subtly suggested that he resign because the firm was too small, even though I'd been thinking the same thing, I nearly hit the roof. She should have consulted me first.

Ben's answer could have come straight from Carl's mouth—he obviously took on board the man's wisdom while they worked together—pointing out that being a family-owned company, we didn't need to cater to shareholders' demands for ever-increasing returns. We could be a niche operator and look after people the big firms ignore.

If only Carl hadn't had that heart attack. Given a few years, when he finished his course, Ben would have made a great replacement.

IT WASN'T until the end of January that I finally managed to get away to visit my grandparents.

"Adrian, *caro mio*." I had barely alighted from the car when my grandmother came hurrying toward me, wiping her hands on her apron.

I hugged her more gently than I used to; she was getting really frail. "*Ci dispiace, non arrivo in tempo per Natale, Nonna*." I continued speaking to her in Italian, the language as comforting to me as an old pair of slippers.

She pushed a wisp of gray hair back from her face. "Come inside. Pop's inspecting the vines."

"Of course he is. Where else would he be?" I grabbed my overnight bag and followed her into the cool interior. The thick, stone walls kept the heat in or out, depending on the weather. The house itself hadn't changed much ever since I remembered first visiting with my mother.

"Have some iced tea before you start." She fingered my hair as I sat at the kitchen table. "Soon you will be as gray as I am."

"At least I'm not losing it." I grinned at her. "I could be bald, like Pop."

She clucked at me and told me to make sure we cleaned up in time for lunch.

When I met him shortly after, my grandfather had a spare pair of the new French power shears ready and a pair of gloves tucked into his belt. "You made good time." He flexed his fingers after handing me the gear. His arthritic joints were as bumpy as the grape vines.

I laughed. "It helps if you get to bed at a decent hour the night before."

He studied my face for a moment. "You look better. Your eyes are clearer."

"That's a first. Everyone's been commenting on how old I look lately."

He poked my stomach. "Still carrying a bit of weight, I see." He snorted at my expression. "City life doesn't agree with you. You never looked better than after you'd spent those years working in my brother's vineyard in Friuli."

A lifetime ago. So much had happened since then. Time that could never be recaptured, no matter how much I wished for it. "People change."

He stared at me. "You know there's always a future for you here, if you want it." He leaned down and started pruning.

I worked on the next trellis. For some people, pruning is boring, but I enjoyed it. Every cut had a purpose, a result. *Want it?* What good was wanting something you could never have? Anyway, much as I enjoyed coming up to help my grandfather, it brought back too many memories. Memories I kept locked away. The past was dead and buried… literally.

When the call for lunch came and we walked back along the rows, I noticed my grandfather was limping. "How's the hip?"

"It needs replacing, and that costs money." A flash of anger crossed his face. "What's the use of getting a new one at my age? I'm too old, and who would look after the place while I recovered? You can't supervise workers from a chair."

He often hired people to help him. They pulled out the canes after he cut them, but pruning was one thing he hated delegating. He trusted me. As a child, I'd followed him around, watching where he made the cuts, the angle, which shoots he chose to retain for the following year's crop. He used to boast to my mother how I'd make a fine *vigneron* one day. She just smiled and nodded, biting her lip. Those were the times she cried when he wasn't looking.

My father never came with us when we visited her parents. After she died, it wasn't until I was at Cornell that I visited them again. They welcomed me with open arms and encouraged me to travel when I finished studying. "See the world," they said, and I did.

That's where I met and fell in love with Antonio, my great-uncle's grandson. The years we spent together in Italy, picking up jobs where we could, then travelling around Europe whenever work was sparse, were still the best years of my life. Heck. They *were* my life. The rest was all a performance by someone named Adrian Sydney Sutherland IV.

CHAPTER
╬
THREE

Blue
February '09

AT THE start of February, my cousin's wife Lindy had another miscarriage. The second since Natalie was born.

My father was devastated when he heard it had been a boy. He asked me to come and look after the East Coast office, so Bill and Lindy could go on a cruise. While they were away Natalie would stay with us, under the care of his housekeeper. I suspect my father could have handled the office as well, but I think he wanted to expose me to a normal family life. Make me see what I was missing.

Lindy and Bill were waiting at JFK when I arrived. Lindy's wan smile showed her grief, and Bill's frequent glances at her betrayed his concern.

"Uncle Adrian." The familiar shriek as Natalie's chubby arms clung to my legs.

"Hey, honey, have you been eating growing pills?"

"No, just my vegibubbles."

I lifted her onto my back. Her legs wrapped around my waist as she clung on tightly, giggling nonstop. Every now and then she placed her hands over my eyes and squealed as I staggered from side to side. Lindy guided us, making sure we didn't bang into anything as we walked to the car.

Natalie had Bill's peaches-and-cream complexion, topped by a cloud of ash-blond curls. Little wisps escaped the clips that Lindy inserted to keep it tidy. Her hair still had the baby softness that surprised me so much when she was younger.

Before Natalie was born, I had once argued that Bill could take my place in the firm. My father shook his head. He got on well with his late sister's son, but I think he held that misguided idea that I could get over being gay, settle down, and start a family. Having a child wouldn't be too bad, but I certainly didn't want to lock them into the same straightjacket I was trapped in.

Bill and Lindy knew I was gay, and they respected my determination to renounce that way of life even if they didn't agree with my decision. As I explained to them, it wasn't as if I was living as a heterosexual or even in the closet. I was doing what other famous people had done before me and still do, living my life as a celibate.

Bill had been amazed. "What's the matter, Adrian. Lost your mojo?"

I just shrugged. My time with Antonio proved that my sex drive was stuck in high gear. Alcohol helped kill the urge, and there was always gay porn on the Internet.

Having lost both his parents in a light plane crash when Bill was twelve, we had grown up as close as brothers. I think he suspected the truth around the same time I became aware I was "different". What Bill knew, Lindy knew, because they had one of those relationships. That was one of things I envied them for—that, and their daughter.

I swung Natalie onto her feet as we approached their car. She held my hand tightly and jerked it to gain my attention. "Uncle Adrian."

I squatted down to her eye level. "Yes, cherub, what is it?"

The dimples in each cheek showed when she giggled. "Will you take me fishing while I stay with you?"

We'd done that last time I visited. At her age, I was amazed she remembered. I wasn't going to make it easy for her. I plastered a serious expression onto my face. "Wouldn't you rather play with your dolls?"

She shook her head so wildly, one of the clips fell out.

"What about dressing up?" I teased as I carefully replaced it.

Again the head shake. She put her thumb in her mouth.

"Tea parties?" Same response.

"But what about the worms? They're wriggly, slimy things—surely you don't want to touch those. Then there's the fish, if you catch them." I mimicked a fish gulping out of water.

"Fishing," she yelled and ran around in circles with her arms out, opening and shutting her mouth like I had.

Lindy smiled as we buckled her daughter up in her car seat. "It's fine by me. I'm just grateful you'll be here while we're away."

Natalie fell asleep soon after we started driving. Bill glanced at me in the mirror and said, "You're looking tired, Adrian."

"Don't you start."

"I'm worried about you... we're worried about you."

"Want to change places?"

Lindy repressed a startled protest.

I continued speaking as if she hadn't said anything. "The last thing you need at the moment is this kind of pressure, this expectation." I indicated Natalie, who was sleeping peacefully in the car seat beside me. "While Bill would make a great head of the company, you know what my father's like. He'd keep badgering you to get pregnant again, and if you didn't, he'd start treating Natalie as the heir-in-waiting. It's been bad enough for me, and I was groomed for this job from day one. It wouldn't be fair to her. Not at her age. Maybe later, when she's had a normal childhood, we can talk about it again."

While on paper the business was worth a lot, it didn't make a fortune. Bill's wage was very generous. In comparison, because I'd be the major shareholder one day, my salary was much lower.

The two week break passed quickly. My father did go into the office a few times, suggesting I spend some time with Natalie. It was often too cold to fish, so Natalie, Chester, and I would wander through the woods on my father's estate, exploring every nook and cranny. When she grew too tired, I carried her on my back, while Chester chased squirrels and generally made a nuisance of himself.

Before I left, my father asked how I was getting on with Laurel.

I managed to give him the impression we were getting on fine. I had discovered which buttons to push as far as she was concerned. Any time she suggested making changes, I made sure the topic quickly shifted to the latest freebie ticket we'd been sent. She loved going to venues where she could parade me on her arm like another handbag: the opera, concerts, art gallery openings. She made a perfect beard without knowing it.

My father definitely wanted the match. He kept hinting as much all the time I was there. To him, I was only gay because I hadn't found the "right woman" yet. Stalling was the only option. If I said I wasn't interested in Laurel, he'd find someone else. The daughter of one of his friends had recently relocated to San Francisco, and he was already hinting she'd be suitable. At times I felt like he was lining up a breeding pair, but no matter how much I enjoyed the time with Natalie, I was determined not to give in to his demands.

Everyone seemed pleased to see me when I got back. Once I sorted out the problem with Ben and the office pool, I had to admit he was right. The atmosphere was much happier with something to distract from their money worries.

CHAPTER
+++
FOUR

Blue
March '09

FORTUNATELY, Laurel fell in with my scheme and put her name down on the NBA pool sheet. She also finally recognized Ben's usefulness and stopped suggesting he be fired.

But the day after his birthday, I nearly fired him on the spot, or at least stressed that it would be in his best interest to find another job. Seeing him turn up to work half-drunk and disheveled shocked me. When he applied for the job, I thought we were getting a nice mid-Western boy with his feet planted firmly on the ground. And once they hooked up, I had hoped that Ben would be a steadying influence for Jason, but instead the opposite was happening. Lucky for Ben, before I had a chance to act, Jason admitted it was his fault Ben had got so drunk.

That conversation hadn't gone well. I'd been sitting on the sofa, downing a couple of glasses of Jack, dreading having to ask Ben to leave. At the time, I hadn't thought anything of Jason's plea to take the day off because of a migraine. When he came downstairs and asked why I was sitting in the dark, I told him what had happened. He laughed and said that, because it was Ben's birthday, he'd wanted to give him a good time.

"Jason, when are you going to start acting responsibly?" As soon as the words were out of my mouth, I grimaced, knowing that I sounded like my father. Jason said as much. When I reminded him that *his* father had begged me to let him move in so he wouldn't get into any more trouble, Jason snarled at me.

"What? I get caught once for DUI and possession, and now I need a keeper? Fuck off, Adrian." It had been lucky for him that the magistrate was a friend of his father.

At least the house felt alive when he was around. I'd been appalled when he discovered I was gay, fearing he would either out me or use it as a form of blackmail, but he never did. Like Ben, he also needed an outlet for his energy, but when I suggested as much, he told me I sounded just like his fucking parental unit.

Considering the incident and lecture that precipitated it, the solution I reached with Ben to spot for me in the gym worked well. Some days, when I saw Laurel being particularly bitchy to the staff, the sound of Ben whacking the punching bag expressed every frustration I felt.

His next visit to my office wasn't nearly as stressful.

"Are you coming, boss?"

I removed my glasses and gave them a quick polish while my brain flew through all the possible rejoinders. *Not yet, but if you hang around looking like that, I may,* was the first that sprang to mind. Then I sternly chastised myself. *Behave, Adrian. That's not in the script.* I'd been so engrossed in an article on insurancenews.net that I hadn't heard the office door open. The double meaning of his words must have struck Ben also, because he flushed and beat a hasty retreat to the shelter of the doorway. "Sorry, I didn't mean to disturb you, boss, but you did say you wanted to work out tonight."

"I do. Wait." I replaced my glasses and glanced at my watch. "Just trying to keep up to date with my reading."

"Why don't you do that on the exercise bike?"

I chuckled. "Bit hard with the laptop."

He grinned, but the grin faded quickly. "I wasn't sure what was happening."

"No, it's fine, I can read the article later." I quickly packed everything away while Ben waited at the door. He must have started without me; his old gray T-shirt already showed signs of sweat. I stood and winced as I bent over to pick up my gear.

"Are you all right?" His voice showed concern.

"Just a few aches and pains. I haven't done this much exercise for ages."

"Yeah, I know what you mean." Ben put his fists into the small of his back, arching his chest out in the process. He couldn't have showcased his pecs and nipples better if he tried. Maybe he did it deliberately, but I don't believe he was even aware of the effect he was creating. I swallowed and took the bag in one hand. "My quads are a bit tight."

"Any actual injuries?"

"No, coach. Nothing that a hot tub won't fix."

"Why don't you install one here?"

The cheeky grin had returned. Joining him in one of those would be a temptation I'd find hard to refuse. As I followed him down the stairs, I checked out his butt. His sweat molded the soft, gray material to the tight curves. Very nice. And his shoulders were even broader than I'd realized; the cheap shirts he usually wore disguised them effectively. Ever since that first day, when I'd watched him trying to bash the living daylights out of the punching bag, I'd seen a new side of Ben, a more physical side. His technique might be lacking, but raw power and aggression made up for it. No wonder Jason was attracted to him. He liked strong men too.

They really were an odd couple. I tried to picture Jason in the work gym, but couldn't. No one worth impressing—not that he spent much time actually working out at his usual place, from what I could gather. He kept his figure by eating like a bird. Ben looked like he would enjoy eating. The type to embrace everything with gusto. Food, life, exercise… sex. Perhaps that was the point. Opposites attract.

Ben handed me a bottle as soon as I finished changing. "Here, rub this in."

As I sat on the weight bench and rubbed the heat liniment into my legs, I watched him on the rowing machine. He reminded me of one of the guys in my nightly jerk-off DVD collection who had a habit of biting his lip when he fucked, then grinning as he changed positions. Ben was the same. In the office, he'd be concentrating on his work, one of the girls might ask him something, and then it was as if someone switched on an overhead halogen—the whole room would light up.

I closed my eyes and continued rubbing my legs. How sick was that? Comparing my employee to a porn star.

"Careful, you don't want to overdo it."

Ben had removed his T-shirt to wipe off the sweat, and the sight of his uncovered, pumped-up muscles made me drop the bottle cap. His milk-white flesh now glowed a healthy shade of Indian red. Scrabbling around to find the lid allowed my heartbeat to return to normal. "Just thinking about the report I was reading, about an HIV discrimination case." Hopefully my voice sounded steady.

"Too much doom and gloom can make a guy depressed."

When I looked up after replacing the cap, I discovered that Ben was standing right in front of me, wiping himself down. My head was now at crotch level. A very impressive crotch level. I closed my eyes again.

"You're kinda pale, boss. Maybe you should have an early night?"

The reminder of our employer/employee relationship doused the urge to jump him as effectively as a bucket of cold water. "No, I'll be fine." *You can look but don't touch,* I chanted to myself as I rode the exercise bike.

After that, my main problem was hiding the way my body responded to him: sweaty, clean, and all stages in between. I took to wearing a tight jock strap and kept reminding myself he was Jason's boyfriend.

Each night, when I reached the safety of my room, I put on my favorite jerk-off DVDs before going to bed. It didn't hurt that Ben was better-looking than half the studs in my porn collection, plus he could carry on a conversation on topics of interest to me. It was good to have someone to vent to; Jason didn't give a shit. As long as he got his commission and bonus at the end of the year, he was happy.

I enjoyed the gym sessions even when we weren't talking. The silence as we worked on the different machines made a pleasant contrast to the stresses of the day. Sometimes I brought my iPod along. We swapped them once just for the heck of it, but apart from blues music in general, we didn't have that much in common. I didn't like Ben's techno and dance mixes, and he didn't like my classical music. We were only a generation apart, but so much had happened to me in those eleven years that I felt old in comparison. At least I was getting back into shape.

CHAPTER
┼┼┼
FIVE

Blue

April '09

THE excess weight started to fall off me. By mid-April, when I took a couple of days off work to help Pop clear the weeds from the vineyard, my grandfather even noticed the improvement. It didn't come easy, though.

"Forty-seven, forty-eight, forty-nine, fifty." As soon as I gasped out the last number, I lay back on the mat, hands clasped against heaving chest, ankles trapped by Ben's. *Fuck it. Whose brilliant idea was it to get fit?*

"Had enough crunches for tonight, boss?"

Ben reached forward to help me up. I grimaced as I took hold of his hand. His lower legs, clad in his familiar soft, gray sweatpants, were clamped firmly on the outside of mine. "That's two hundred. How many more sets of these damn things did you say I had to do?"

"*We* have to do. I'm doing them too, remember."

"Yeah," I grunted. Ben's T-shirt clung to him like a second skin. Sweat stains ran down his abs. Earlier, he'd been doing Navy seal burpees while I rode the exercise bike. He suggested I join in, but hey, I'm not a complete masochist. "Don't forget you're younger than I am."

"Nah, you're doing great. Soon I'll have you doing one-handed push-ups." He grinned at me, those sky-blue eyes sparkling with unquenchable vitality.

I groaned. "Can't wait. I haven't done them since rowing training."

"We need to add variety, or it gets boring, plus there's less chance of injury that way."

"Yes, coach."

Boring was the last word I'd use to describe our workout sessions. Ben took my remark about being my personal trainer to heart, researching different exercises we could do in the restricted area between all the shoved-back pieces of equipment. "One more set and we'll call it quits. I have to go somewhere after this."

"Me, too, boss. Friday night. Whoopee. Look out, Castro, here I come."

I groaned as we went back to our next set of fifty. This time, my reaction wasn't my muscles objecting to the strain; I was imagining checking out the bars with Ben. The music would probably drive me crazy, but being surrounded by people out to have a good time would be fun. I wasn't jealous. Much.

After I finished in the shower, I slung the towel around my waist and checked my reflection in the washroom mirror. Definitely better definition. I was making progress.

"Worth all the pain, boss?"

I grinned. Actually, the pain hadn't been bad so far. Different muscles might be tender the next day, but never enough to bother me. Ben disappeared into the shower while I dressed.

When he finished, he leaned back against the washroom wall and watched me shave. His quickly dried red hair stuck up as if he'd just shoved his finger in a light socket. Scattered droplets of water still clung to his skin above the towel wrapped around his waist. He used to avoid being in that state around me, always dressing immediately after his shower, but gradually he had relaxed. I tried to keep my eyes above waist level, but I was always aware of his size and strength and his almost overwhelming virility. Tonight, even more so. I concentrated on not gouging a chunk out of my face with the razor and ignored the way my cock thickened inside my jockstrap.

"Where are you off to?" he asked.

"The charity 'do' that caused all the problem with Millie."

"What's this one in aid of?"

"Breast cancer research."

"Do you like going to those things?"

I lifted my chin to get at the stubble. "It's not really a question of liking, it's more of needing. It's a PR thing. My father supports a lot of arts organizations and medical charities with substantial donations. They send tickets in appreciation. As he can't go, he likes me to make use of them. If the press take a photo, and it gets published, it helps promote the charity, and because of my name, it promotes SSFI at the same time."

"So, you're still working." A wry grin curled his lips.

I shrugged, pretending a nonchalance I didn't feel as he continued watching me getting dressed. Splashing cold water on my face doused some of my desire and the sting of the after-shave helped.

Ben sniffed. "You always use the same one. What is it?"

Reality returned with a thud. I replaced the bottle in my wet pack. "Calvin Klein, Eternity." My response came out clipped and cold. The scent wasn't the latest or the most expensive, but it brought back memories. Why I could cope with that reminder of Antonio while avoiding so many others puzzled me. A therapist would have a field day. I sighed and put my shirt on. He was still watching me, a slight frown between his eyes. "What's wrong?" I asked.

"Nothing. Just admiring the shirt."

"Thank you. I bought it last week."

"Do you only wear designer clothing, stuff that's expensive?"

I grinned, remembering the frayed pair of cutoffs I always wore when helping Pop. "Depends where I am." I tried to picture Ben in a tux. Surprisingly, it wasn't difficult. "Have fun tonight," I said, and meant it.

"Likewise."

The event was a disaster from the get-go. I'd have done better going to the Castro with Ben instead. As usual, Laurel's outfit was stunning; she knew how to make the most of her attributes. I complimented her, and she purred sweetly all the way to the venue.

For a while, I thought the evening would be fine. Unfortunately, the organizers couldn't have devised a worse combination of people to put at our table if they'd tried. One was a staunch Republican who didn't stop complaining about how Obama was going to socialize the nation. Next to him was the widow of a man who'd committed suicide when his business failed in the recent downturn. Judging by the amount of jewelry she wore and the fact that the tickets were pricy, she wasn't destitute, but she still had plenty to complain about. As far as she was concerned, the government hadn't done enough to contain the crisis.

Charity dinners weren't usually hotbeds of political discussion, but somehow the mix of people didn't work. No matter what topic I tried to raise, someone was upset. Laurel chatted to the person sitting next to her, a Hollywood producer who was more than happy to share tales about the private lives of the actors he worked with, flattering her that she should relocate to Los Angeles where the weather was warmer and her talents would be appreciated. I felt like saying, "Take her, please." Then, when the main course arrived, the widow—who was slightly deaf and had obviously missed the introductions—wanted to know whether we were married. My head was already threatening to split open, and I took too long to answer. Laurel batted her fake eyelashes at me, and said, "Not yet."

I couldn't say, "Over my dead body," so I remained silent and smiled. From then on, Laurel's whole demeanor changed. I had to hand it to her; she really knew how to work the table. Whenever the discussion threatened to get out of hand, she switched it back to safer topics like books or movies, proving to me what an asset she would be: the perfect corporate wife. Her concern continued on the way back to her apartment where she suggested I come up for some coffee and a neck rub. I regretfully declined the latter, although there was nothing that I needed more.

Later, as I sat on the sofa at home, staring mindlessly at late-night TV and drinking a few too many slugs of Jack Daniels, I thought about the evening. If all my father wanted was someone to carry on the family name, maybe *he* should marry Laurel? I had overheard her speaking to him on the phone one day, enquiring about his gout, joking about how he needed someone to watch what he ate. Strike that: I could handle a lot of things, but the thought of Laurel ending up as my stepmother made me want to puke.

My thoughts kept drifting back to Ben, wondering where he and Jason were now, what they were doing. Before I went to bed, I downloaded some new porn. The drug of choice for a lonely sex-junkie.

The usual fake setup scene began. A quick meet and greet, obviously rehearsed. The young twink star blushed beautifully as he was asked by someone off camera when he had last partnered the top who was already stroking the promising bulge in his jeans. After a few meaningless comments, they started kissing. I grabbed the lube from the bedside table, smeared some on my cock, and tried to figure a way out of my predicament. Maybe I should give in to my father's demands. Find someone decent to marry and have a couple of kids. Immediately my stomach rebelled at the thought. No, I'd made my decision. Everything I'd given up or fought for would be wasted if I gave in now. I had to wait until I controlled the company. Then I could make my own rules. I didn't want my father to die, but while he was alive, there was no possibility of clambering out of the closet.

But even if I did, what were my chances of ever finding someone like Antonio again? Watching Ben and Jason kiss at the Christmas party had unlocked a memory deep inside of the first kiss I'd ever had. The first one that ever meant anything. We'd been working in the winery, cleaning up after bottling. I had a streak of dirt on my face, and Antonio leaned in to lick it off; then his tongue moved to lick my lips. I still remembered the jolt that had spiked right through me.

Muffled moans filled the air as the guys on screen sucked each other's dicks. I spat on my hand, resumed pounding my cock, and groaned with them. What would it feel like to have real lips drawing my hard length into moist heat again? What if they were Ben's lips? What if, earlier, he'd given me a blow job? What if I'd given him one? I pictured the scene again. Ben naked underneath the white towel draped around his powerful groin, his muscles pumped from exertion, beads of moisture still glistening on his body. I shuddered as spurts of come filled my cupped hand.

CHAPTER
+++
SIX

Blue

May '09

IN MAY, I stepped my fitness training up another level, gradually working my way up to a five-and-a-half-mile run around the Presidio. One Sunday, when I returned, I realized that Jason had a visitor.

"That's it, Red, harder, harder." Jason's unmistakable voice. I stopped with my key in the lock. *Who was Red? Another boyfriend?*

What should I do now? From the sounds of things, they were downstairs. *Should I do another circuit?* No, it was time someone called Jason out on the noise he was making. Whoever he was with might not like being caught in the act, but at least it wasn't Ben.

I opened the door and froze.

Fuck. It *was* Ben. The nickname should have been a dead giveaway. *How stupid could I get?*

His nakedness only emphasized his strength. Muscles developed from pushing against machines as we worked in the gym were thrusting hard against Jason. If it had been some random stranger, I might have coped better, but the sight of the familiar, strong body tore away something deep inside.

Images of Antonio making love to me cascaded down in a torrent. Another man, another time, another place. His Mediterranean complexion, the complete opposite of Ben's pale skin. *Why did someone so different bring out memories and feelings I had buried so efficiently?*

I managed to keep my wits together while I rescued my bonsai from the floor, Jason's glee a sure indication he had planned the whole thing. It wouldn't have been difficult. He knew that if I left for my run at three o'clock, I'd be back an hour later. He probably thought it would be a lark. Show Adrian what he was missing. I didn't need reminding; it took me years to learn to wake up without longing for the comforting presence of my lover by my side.

I'm not even sure what I said in the end. My brain refused to register anything except the image of Ben fucking Jason.

Did the bastard even realize how lucky he was to have a boyfriend like that? Someone who would look after him? Protect him? Even while they were struggling to get their clothes on, Ben was the one trying to fix the situation, make it right. Jason couldn't give a shit.

I managed to hold my emotions at bay until Ben apologized when I walked past, calling me "Sir". *Sir.* A word with so many connotations. He used it as a mark of respect.

Fucking hell. I made it up the stairs and into my room just in time. I didn't cry. Not on the outside, anyway. Instead, I picked up a glass from the nightstand and threw it against the wall. The crash made me feel a bit better before I collapsed on the bed.

By the time I moved again, the house was quiet. The light of a street lamp shone across the room, breaking the darkness into two halves. I clambered to my feet and headed for the shower. As I rotated under the warm spray, my brain continued to berate me, the monster of self-pity unleashed in full destructive force. *What was the point of getting fit? Looking good? Why? Who for?*

The following morning, I resolved to take the initiative for once. My pity party was over, but anger at his actions still burned in my gut. "Jason, can you come in here please?"

He looked up at me from under his lashes and smirked as he sauntered into the living room. "Yes, Adrian."

"Why the hell did you do that?"

"I wanted to shake you up a bit," he muttered.

"Shake me up? It takes a lot more than that to shock me, if that's what you mean."

"No, not *shock* you. *Shake* you." He walked over to the window and stared out for a few seconds before turning back. "When are you going to stand up to your father? Tell him to fuck off and just be as gay as you want to be."

"Do you know how many people would be out of a job if I did?"

"They'll find other work."

"No, they won't. Not in this economic climate. Not everyone is rolling in money like your parents, Jason."

"So, goody two-shoes is going to keep on sucking Daddy's ass. Hope you enjoy it."

I bit back the expletives I wanted to throw at him. "Show a little more respect. You may not care about who you hurt and how you do it, but you shouldn't involve other people."

"Which other people?" He actually looked confused.

"Ben, of course. You might get off on having as many people watch you having sex as possible, but you shouldn't involve your boyfriend."

"What, jealous are we, Adrian?" He stood toe-to-toe with me, his dark brown eyes flashing a personal challenge. "You should try him someday. He's a great fucker, you know. Hot as hell. A real piston pumper when he gets going. Big, too. Ooh right, you saw that."

I drew my clenched fist back. He laughed and ran from the room. *Damn.* My East Coast WASP upbringing usually managed to keep a tight lid on my Italian temper.

Moments later he came down the stairs with an overnight bag, poked his head into the living room, and said, "I hope you enjoy talking to the walls for a few days. I've got some out-of-town clients to visit." He slammed the front door on his way out, making the glass in the chandelier tinkle.

Well, that went well.

Ben was avoiding me also. Each night as I cycled or rowed by myself, I kept hoping the door to the gym would open, and in he'd walk with that broad grin across his face. When I went home to an empty house, Jack Daniels became my best friend again. Of course I became maudlin and started thinking about Antonio. How could I give advice to Ben, anyway? For starters, I'd have to confess to being gay, and I couldn't do that. Not yet. How could I trust him not to reveal my secret? So far Jason hadn't said anything, but after the last blow-up, who knew what he would do?

Then, I'd have to explain to Ben why I had caved in to my father's demands. Even before Jason's tirade, I had started to ask that question of myself more often lately. If I hadn't, Antonio would still be alive. Before I left, I told Antonio that I loved him, and even apart I would always love him, but in the end it hadn't been enough. He screamed at me, "You don't love me. How can you leave me if you do? It's being together that matters." I'd hoped that, in time, he would find someone else, but he hadn't.

I didn't so much as look at men in that way after my father said it was time to learn the business before I inherited it. How could I? I still loved Antonio. It would have felt like I was cheating on him.

After Antonio died, even if I had met another guy, guilt still would have prevented me from doing anything. If it was okay to be with someone here, I should have brought Antonio to the States rather than walk out on him. Instead, I did as my father requested, buried my gay *tendencies* and transformed Adrian Sydney Sutherland IV into a fine, upstanding, all-American male, a proud member of a distinguished family: nothing queer about him.

But, now that they were over, I realized how much I had enjoyed those sessions in the gym with Ben. I could no longer kid myself that it was just appreciation of a magnificent specimen of the male form; every fiber of my being responded to him. Apart from the sheer joy of watching him work out, he cheered me up when I was down, kept me on my toes with new challenges, made me completely forget about the world outside the four walls of the gym when he was around. Oh, well. Another experience to file away in the "good while it lasted" box. My fault for forgetting he was Jason's lover.

Now, whenever he caught sight of me, the telltale blush would appear, signaling his discomfort. Perhaps he *would* be happier working somewhere else. No one was hiring lately, so I couldn't leave the task of finding him another job to the HR people. This would need the personal touch. I had just dragged out Evelyn's contact details at United Policy when Ben knocked on the door. He closed it behind him, gently, then cleared his throat. "I'm sorry about the other day, sir."

I conducted the rest of the interview on autopilot. All I registered was an overwhelming relief that he didn't want to leave and was even prepared to resume our gym sessions again. Life could now slip back into its comfortable pattern.

CHAPTER
┼┼┼
SEVEN

Blue

June '09

UNFORTUNATELY, my life didn't revert back into its normal comfortable pattern. By the time June rolled around, I was forced to admit that Jason was right. His actions had shaken me up. I spent some time questioning why I fell apart like that. It took me ages to admit that I was jealous. Immediately, I felt disgusted with myself. I should be happy for the two of them.

I gathered from Jason's remarks that now Ben had passed his exam, they were meeting up on a regular basis. *Why shouldn't they? I* had to remind myself. Better a regular boyfriend like Ben than have Jason out every night, cruising the bars and getting up to his old mischief. He'd been staying out later and later, though. Presumably over at Ben's place. Ben was probably too embarrassed to come here. One night, because Jason looked tired, I suggested he stay home for a change. He yelled at me before storming out of the house, "Fuck off, Adrian, I'm going out with Ben." *How could I keep them apart?*

Later that night, I lay in bed reading, but I couldn't concentrate. I kept picturing the two of them together, wondering where they were, what they were doing. Noises downstairs brought me to full alertness. Jason's distinctive giggle and Ben's unmistakable drawl, asking him where his room was. Sounds of footsteps on the stairs followed, then the soft click of his door closing. My mouth went dry as I waited for the inevitable evidence of lovemaking. Would Jason start screaming out "Red" again? I grabbed my book and tried to lose myself in the story.

The silence was shattered by an unexpected knock at my door. A fully clothed Ben stood there, looking embarrassed when I opened it. His black T-shirt was stretched tight over his chest. The dark color made his skin appear even whiter. Faded jeans clung to his long, strong legs. If he kept working out, he would need a whole new wardrobe soon. He really did look good.

"Sorry to disturb you, s.... It's Jason." I caught his slipup and nearly smiled before I realized there must be something wrong.

I should have insisted Jason see a doctor earlier; the fever was raging. I did what I could, and then we waited, Jason cradled in Ben's arms. They looked so good on the bed together. The jealousy I had successfully controlled threatened to erupt again. I tried reading my book, but the clear type blurred as memories resurfaced.

Shortly after I'd returned to the States, Antonio had started using heroin and mixing with the wrong crowd of people. If he was trying to punish me, it worked. Unprotected encounters and shared needles led to an HIV infection. When full-blown AIDS developed, he refused to allow me to visit. He said he didn't want me to see him like that, so someone else took on the role of caregiver.

Would he have survived if I'd been there? Would I have survived?

Movement caught my attention. Ben had snagged a pillow for his back. He was here for the long haul. He wasn't going to desert his lover, like I had. I know Antonio would have cared for me if our positions had been reversed. He would have defied family, public opinion, anything. What had I done? Given in. I sat staring at my book, turning a page every now and then. The words weren't even registering.

When Ben started asking questions about what I was reading, I was thankful for the distraction. He seemed genuinely interested in learning more, or at least to be distracted from worrying about Jason, so I tried to draw pictures of the vineyards as I remembered them from those magical years with Antonio. I explained the way organic farming principles use cover crops of radishes and turnips to keep the weeds down instead of spraying. I described how the vineyards became a riot of white and yellow blossoms on a pale-green carpet when they flowered. Poor Ben, I must have bored him silly. It didn't take long before his eyes closed, and his head lolled to rest on his lover's.

I stared at the tableau they made on the bed. An artist couldn't have posed them better. They were such a contrast. Jason had definitely lost weight and that, coupled with the shadows under his eyes, gave him a fragile beauty he hadn't had before. Angelic almost, a clever cover for the devil that lurked inside. In contrast, Ben was the picture of young strength and youthful innocence.

Suddenly, burning pain tore at my gut. Could Jason be infected with HIV? I'd never seen him look so ill. When young, he'd been in hospital a fair bit, but nothing recently. Usually his tanned skin would have been in stark contrast to Ben's paleness, but tonight there was definitely an unhealthy sheen present—or were recollections of ancient history making me paranoid? I chewed some Gaviscon to ease my heartburn. *Heartburn*: what an appropriate name.

Then I woke Ben. He couldn't sleep properly sitting up, and Jason appeared to be more settled. The tender kiss he gave Jason sent another stab of pain right through me. Damn. *Why were all the good ones taken?*

As we walked down the stairs, the heat from his body seemed to seep into mine, warming me. When he left, I stood there for a while and watched the pickup disappear.

I returned to the house, but didn't sleep. Instead, I sat with Jason until he woke.

PART
THREE

RED + BLUE

CHAPTER
+++
ONE

THREE days later, Adrian let himself into the office. A light still shone in the gym. *Ben.* In one respect, he couldn't wait to see the young man again, but in another he dreaded the meeting. He dumped his overnight bag and walked down the corridor. The clank of the quad machine met him as he approached. Taking a deep breath, he opened the door.

Crash. The weight fell back into place as Ben rolled off onto his feet.

"Shit, boss. You look a mess. Are you alright?"

Am I alright? Adrian raked a trembling hand through his hair. He'd had no sleep on the flight east and not much more on the way back. He sat on the weight bench and buried his head in his hands.

Ben crouched on the floor, concern in his eyes. "What's wrong? Is it Jason?"

The question sent a shiver up Adrian's spine. "Hasn't he been in touch?"

Ben shook his head. "I've tried a couple of times, but he's not answering his calls."

Fuck, fuck, fuck. "He was supposed to contact you, so you could go and get tested."

"Tested?" Ben drew back, suspicion dawning in his eyes.

Adrian swallowed to wet a mouth suddenly too dry to form words. "I took Jason to the hospital as soon as he woke up. They took some blood and urine samples." The moment would be forever etched in Adrian's memory. Jason waiting in stony silence, arms crossed, scowling at the floor. "He tested positive."

Ben sprang up, his hands in clenched fists at his side.

"I'm sorry, Ben. Jason should have told you himself, or at least the clinic should have." *You shouldn't have to hear it from me.* "We're waiting for official confirmation via the Western blot analysis test, but that result won't be back for a couple of weeks. In the meantime, he's on antiretrovirals." *Drugs that weren't around in Antonio's time. Would they have helped him survive for longer? Slowed the disease down?*

Ben shook his head slowly as if he didn't believe the news. "Where is he?"

"I took him back to his parents' place on Long Island."

"Why?"

A simple question, but it tore at Adrian's heart. *Another two lovers forced apart.* "When Jason gets sick, he really gets sick. As a kid, he spent a fair bit of time in the hospital because of various illnesses. So far, they think he's just in the acute stage that some people get during the first couple of months after exposure. But at the moment, he needs lots of rest and a good diet, plus the treatment has to be strictly adhered to, or it won't be effective. You know what Jason's like."

Ben moved to sit at his feet, resting his chin on his knees, staring into space. *Listening, but thinking what?* Given the amount of time they spent together, there was a real chance he was infected too. That possibility had been gnawing at Adrian's gut ever since he'd heard the news. It was bad enough about Jason. But Ben? Adrian shuddered and added into the quiet, "Jason won't be a good patient."

Ben glanced up at him but didn't comment, so Adrian continued speaking, hoping to explain his reasons for taking Jason back to Long Island. "Apart from the illness, the strong antiretrovirals they're giving him may produce all sorts of side effects. He needs full-time care." Still the young man didn't respond. His knuckles were white as he gripped his knees. "His parents are very wealthy." Adrian reassured him. "They're employing a full-time caregiver."

That got a reaction, the disbelief in Ben's voice unmistakable. "Jason says his parents hate him and have never forgiven him for being gay."

The meeting with Jason's parents, Vernon and Consuela, hadn't been easy because, to a certain degree, Adrian *had* felt responsible. "He's their only child, Ben." *Like me*, he felt like adding. Though in Jason's case, it wasn't seventy years of tradition and control of a family business that constrained him; instead, the burden of eventually inheriting a huge mansion complete with guesthouse, pool, tennis courts—one that had been in the family for generations and which they had hoped still would be for generations to come.

Ben rubbed his fingers through his hair, making it even spikier than usual. Adrian was having trouble dealing with the fact that Jason hadn't told him. The bleakness in Ben's eyes made Adrian ache inside.

"Did he tell you how and when he became infected?" Ben's question was barely above a whisper.

Did Ben know Jason had been unfaithful? "No." Adrian gripped his hands together to stop himself from reaching out to offer comfort. Ben sprang to his feet and walked across to the punching bag, hitting it with a wild swing. *Ouch, that must have hurt.* Ben caught the bag and turned back, rubbing his bare knuckles, a rueful smile on his face. He still hadn't made the connection to his own vulnerability. Adrian had to know; Jason had refused to tell him. "Did you often have unprotected sex with Jason?" He knew Ben hadn't been wearing a condom when he'd interrupted them in the hallway.

Ben's face, normally white, went even paler. Adrian feared for a moment that he'd faint. He seemed to collapse at the knees, then swung around and ran into the nearby washroom. Retching sounds followed.

Adrian allowed him time to clean up before entering himself. Ben was sitting on the floor next to the sinks, chin on his knees, but this time, the borders of his eyes glistened with unshed tears. *What kind of support did he have?* "Would you like me to go to the clinic with you?"

Ben shook his head, wordlessly. "I'll be fine." Blue eyes flickered upward. He shook off Adrian's proffered arm, scrambled to his feet, and ran off without a word.

THE receptionist nodded at the clinic door. "Mr. Dutoit, you may go in now."

The doctor ushered out the previous patient. He was about Ben's age, and judging by his red eyes and slumped shoulders, he'd been crying. An older guy was with him, grief etched into his face.

The counselor, a middle-aged woman, looked like the last interview affected her as much as it had her patient. *What a shit job.* She handed across an envelope and gestured to the chair. Ben's fingers shook as he sat and opened it.

"Your urine test came up clear, and the blood test showed an absence of HIV antibodies."

Figures and letters swam before his eyes, so Ben latched onto her words instead.

"That doesn't mean you haven't been infected. The seroconversion isn't always immediate. Sometimes the antibodies can take two to six weeks to show up. In any case, you'll need to come back for another round of tests in three months."

Ben gulped. So an "all clear" but not an "all clear".

She tapped her notes with a pen. "The good news is your CD4 count is over 820 per cubic millimeter, and your immune system doesn't seem compromised. If your T count was lower than 500, I'd suggest you immediately go on a course of antiviral drugs."

Ben stared at his hands. Jason had been put on a whole cocktail of pills and things, some of them still in the experimental stage and not covered by insurance; according to the e-mail Ben finally received, they cost his parents a small fortune. From its typical flippant tone, he gathered Jason was getting over his body's initial reaction to the virus. No apology. No wishes of good luck, just the bald statement that he didn't know who the fucking hell he'd contracted the virus from, let alone *when.* "Do I have to?"

"No, as I said, so far your immune system is fine. It all depends on how much exposure you had to the person who tested positive."

Not much ever since I started concentrating on my studies. Ben shuddered inside in relief, yet the possibility was still there. That incident at Adrian's place might end up being disastrous in more ways than one. "What do I do now? Wait?" He hated waiting ten minutes for a MUNI, let alone three months.

"I'm afraid that's exactly what you have to do." She tapped the results. "Think about your options and get back to us. It's a slow-onset disease, so there's no frantic rush, but if you have been infected, the sooner we start the triple therapy the better."

For the next two hours, Ben wandered the streets, giving himself virtual thumps on the head. He dealt with stats all day long and still behaved like an idiot who didn't understand the risk of not using a condom. Should he tell anyone? Mom, Mick? He'd only be sharing a worry that might not be justified. Knowing his brothers, if they found out, all four would turn up on the doorstep and forcibly drag him back to Minnesota. *No way.*

He groaned. No fucking for three months! That was going to feel like forever. Maybe it was going to extremes, but until he got the all clear, he wouldn't risk getting anyone else infected. What if the condom broke? *Damn.* He shouldn't have been so goddamned irresponsible and given in to Jason's demands; of course he must be fucking other guys, probably bareback.

CHAPTER
TWO

WORD spread quickly about Jason's illness; morale was at an all-time low, so Adrian asked all the available staff to assemble in the training room. After telling them what he could about Jason without breaching privacy guidelines, he finished up by giving a pep talk about how the company was faring. "I don't ascribe to the theory that in times of trouble we should shed staff and reduce programs." Relieved expressions suggested that's exactly what they *had* been expecting. "Instead, we need to work harder, sell more policies, and look after our clients. Every customer who is annoyed by that extra ten minutes on the phone waiting for someone to respond, or every time we hassle them about a claim, we increase the chance they'll find an excuse to cancel their life insurance. Our job is to go that little bit farther and give them customer satisfaction. Prevention is better than cure. Word of mouth is an extremely powerful influence. It doesn't matter how much money we spend on advertising; one disgruntled customer who complains to his sister, her neighbor, their workmate has a snowballing effect."

The applause at the end came as a surprise.

Laurel followed him into the office. "Adrian, those feel-good platitudes are all very well, but sometimes I wonder if you appreciate how much at risk the whole viability of this company is."

Lately, all their meetings had degenerated into slanging matches. At times, Adrian wondered whether she was getting more impossible, or if his level of control was slipping. The weird thing was that, ever since the charity dinner, people treated them as a couple. Even Evelyn joshed him about it, asking for the date of the wedding. Outside work, Laurel was all sweetness and light; the ever-present cameras saw to that. But once behind closed doors, her personality reversed. Now she was tapping her foot, waiting for his response.

Adrian sighed. "I'm under no illusions. I can assure you. Every night I go through scenarios and try to devise ways we can address this threat without changing who we are and what we do."

A sudden burst of laughter penetrated the door. Ben's cackle. Once, it had been a common occurrence, but now rarely heard since he went for the test. Ben hadn't divulged the results, and Adrian was too afraid to ask.

"Well, we can't afford pay raises." She'd recognized who was out there.

"If you're referring to Ben, he completed another exam, and the increase was in his starting contract. You would have received them as you progressed through *your* training."

She sniffed and straightened her skirt. "Installing gyms—a waste of money. And that stupid office pool for the NBA." She'd been a convert for a few weeks, especially while she was winning; then Tyrone and June Christie had surged ahead in the final rounds.

Adrian shook his head. "Employee morale is important. We can't afford to give them bonuses, so anything we can do to raise their spirits in other ways will compensate to some degree until the crisis is over."

"You pander to them too much." As usual, irritated or not, her appearance didn't change. Her suit was as immaculate as ever.

It was like arguing with a brick wall. "A happy work team will go that extra mile. Give-and-take works much more effectively than a punch-clock mentality."

"Well, if that's the case, your precious protégé can handle this seminar presentation." She threw a bundle of papers on the desk.

Adrian recognized what they were without picking them up. "Would he have the required knowledge?"

She waved her manicured hand dismissively. "If he doesn't, he can research it. He needs to cover the material for his course anyway. Unfortunately, seeing as he has so much to do in normal office hours, I'm afraid he'll have to do it after." She smiled as she stood to leave. "Let's see if your comment about employees being happy to go the extra mile holds true."

The bitch set me up. Adrian followed her to the door. Ben and Millie were standing near the water cooler. As soon as she caught sight of Laurel, Millie's smile vanished, and she scampered off for the front desk. Ben turned and slowly finished drinking his water before throwing the empty cup in the bin. He didn't take his eyes off Laurel, and the smile had been replaced by a cool look of challenge.

"Ben, could you come here for a minute?"

WHAT have I done wrong now? Ben followed Adrian inside. The look Laurel threw on her way past telegraphed: "Let's see how you get out of this one, buddy."

The boss pulled down his tie and rubbed the back of his neck. His normally well-groomed hair stood up in one section as if he'd been running his hand through it, making the silver-gray even more noticeable. With his glasses on, he looked the perfect model of a harassed businessman. *No, definitely not good news.* All sorts of scenarios ran through Ben's brain. Despite what he'd heard at the staff meeting, was his job on the line again? He took a deep breath.

Adrian handed over a folder from a pile on his desk. "I need your help."

Help? Phew, that was a relief.

"There's an industry seminar in Napa in August. Laurel accepted an invitation for the company to present a talk on predictive analytics for small to medium-sized insurance companies…. You do know what predictive analytics are, don't you?"

Ben nodded. "Yes, they allow us to look at patterns in current and historical data to make predictions about future events, but Carl always used to say our smaller data volume made the concept irrelevant or at least statistically inconclusive." There were ways they could be used, but Ben had felt too junior to contradict his superior.

"Did he?" Adrian removed his glasses and polished them: an unconscious habit he had whenever he was thinking what to say next.

Geez, I'm starting to read the man like a book. Ben grinned inwardly.

Adrian replaced his glasses and continued. "Anyway, Laurel did a presentation on the subject in Vegas last year and was going to reuse that material." He gestured to the packet.

Ben drew out the sheets of paper and flipped through pages of slides. Familiar terms jumped out: multivariate adaptive regression splines, generalized additive models, equations, tables, columns of data, graphs on slide after slide. Typical actuarial stuff. "What's the problem?" Ben caught a flicker of frustration before his boss's face cleared to its usual polite professionalism.

"The seminar isn't only for actuaries. There'll be CEOs and other management people present. Many of the delegates won't be able to make head nor tail of all these charts, let alone acronyms like GAMS, MARS and the other jargon. Laurel says she won't have time to prepare a new paper because of the board meeting a couple of days beforehand."

"What do you want me to do?"

"Can you adapt her material into something that won't have them snoring within the first five minutes?"

A guilty grin flashed across Adrian's face, as they probably shared similar visions of bored delegates nodding off in their chairs. *Fuck it.* The assignment appealed and would fit in with Ben's course work, but the banshee had handed over a stack of "top-priority" jobs that morning. "I'd like to, but I'm not sure I'll have enough time."

"Yes, Laurel told me you were busy, but I don't feel this is what the organizers are looking for." Adrian sighed and rubbed the back of his neck again.

Next birthday, seeing as he couldn't do it himself, Ben was definitely giving the man a voucher for a massage clinic. "What the heck," he said and shrugged. "I can stay late if needed."

"Are you sure? I'm worried it might be too much for you." Adrian paused. "Have you received your test results?"

Oops, maybe I should have let him know? Briefly, Ben told Adrian the good news. Well, good for now at least. The initial clinic visit had been over a week ago, but he'd been avoiding the boss ever since he knew there might be a chance, no matter how slight, that he'd been exposed to HIV by Jason. Everyone had the concept drilled into them, when they started working at SSF Insurance, that people infected with HIV weren't "dirty" in any way, therefore the use of the word "clean" to suggest the opposite was totally inappropriate. The fact that they were one of the few firms that agreed to provide impaired-risk life insurance to people who *were* infected was one of the many reasons Ben accepted their offer of an internship in the first place. They understood. His brain may have told him that, but he still didn't feel as easy in Adrian's presence.

That didn't stop him thinking about the man though. Now, whenever he jerked off, a picture of Adrian drifted into his mind: bare-chested, reading quietly while Ben wedged his slinky pants under his balls and gave him a blow job he wouldn't forget in a hurry. He had to keep reminding himself that Adrian was his boss, and not just a very fuckable man.

Ben shifted on the seat, glad that the folder covered his lap, and immediately felt ashamed. Heck, given the recent pep talk, if improving this presentation removed one of Adrian's worries, Ben owed him that much at least. Anyway, spending time here would be better than going home and tossing and turning in bed, trying to get to sleep.

"Is there a problem?" Adrian's quiet voice penetrated his thoughts.

Yes, there was a big problem, but he couldn't very well tell him that. "Predictive analytics haven't been used much with life insurance. It's more for automotive and health claims."

Adrian shrugged. "The conference topic is changes that will affect the industry. Don't ask me why Laurel volunteered. If you don't feel capable of handling it, I suppose she can give the original speech."

Not if you don't want her to. An idea started to gel, based on something Ben had done during his course. "I've got a couple of ideas. If I stay late for an hour or so each night, I should get it finished in time. The only problem is that then I don't get to work out." He felt like adding *with you.*

"Hm." Adrian tapped his fingers on the desk. "If we can avoid cancelling that, we should. But I don't want to put too much stress on you. When's your next exam?"

"November… lots of time."

Adrian didn't reply immediately; he removed his glasses and started polishing them again. "I don't know about you, but I can't work out on a full stomach. How about we exercise for an hour, then you can do your research. I'll order some food, and you can eat while you work on the project. There's always some reading I need to catch up with. Let me know if there's anything I can do to help."

"Sounds fine to me."

Adrian's relieved smile made Ben feel all warm and fuzzy inside.

IF, THROUGH some weird sense of jealousy, Laurel thought that the added workload would ensure they spent less time together, her plan backfired big time. After a couple of nights working out, showering, and then sharing a couple of pizzas together, Adrian found he was rediscovering a part of himself he thought he'd lost forever.

Perched on the edge of Ben's desk, dressed in jeans and a casual shirt, he felt he was back in college, discussing an upcoming assignment with his friends. It was hard to maintain the boss-employee relationship when you were fighting over who had the last piece of pizza or which one to order.

HOWEVER, when he made the offer, Adrian realized he should have defined exactly what he meant by "help." On the third evening, they'd barely finished eating when Ben gave him that look he was getting to know so well. The one where he was challenging him to do something he'd never done before: those extra reps on the equipment or to finish a set of exercises when the young man knew he was at his limit. It hadn't taken long for Ben to discover his competitive side, the one that had served him so well all his life. In some ways, Adrian was more like his father than he cared to admit, but in his case it wasn't business that brought out that willful streak, but the need to prove something to himself.

"You said you'd help me with the project." Ben's wicked grin lit up his face.

Mrs. C had commented that the girls would do anything for Ben when he looked at them like that. Adrian understood why. "I did," he said and realized there was a hint of nervousness under that bravado. "What do you need me to do?"

"Come shopping with me."

"Shopping?"

"You'll see."

Ben refused to explain further, just adding that he needed some props for the presentation.

Adrian paused before getting into Ben's Ranger. After working out and having a quick shower, he'd changed into casual gear. "I hope it's nowhere fancy."

Ben grinned and said, "Nah, you'll be fine."

"We don't have a huge budget for this project, you know."

"Don't worry, I'm paying."

Adrian was intrigued, but Ben refused to elaborate.

"Have you ever been in one of these before?" Ben asked him quietly as they entered the local Goodwill.

"Actually, I have." Adrian glanced around, wondering why they were there. "Not buying, just dropping off clothes and things," he hastened to add.

"Come on, then." Ben led the way to a rack of clothing that might have suited Nonna. He held up dress after dress, checking the price each time. "This one is the best," he finally announced and tucked the garment under his arm.

The dark-blue summer outfit would have fitted his grandmother's stout figure. "Who's the dress for?" Adrian asked as he followed Ben over to the next aisle.

The grin he got in return was pure devil. "You."

"Me?"

"Yup." Ben kept walking, so Adrian had to keep going, otherwise he'd lose him between all the racks. "We just need to pad you out with something, so it fits." Ben threw the comment back over his shoulder without interrupting his steady progress. Now he was in a section best suited to Pop.

"Wait up, Ben."

The young man stopped and turned around. The determined expression was back, but now Adrian realized that he wasn't the only one being challenged here, Ben had made a decision that he knew his boss wouldn't be happy with, and he was trying to pass it off as being simple, so that Adrian wouldn't freak out. Like when he proposed a new set of exercises that he had dreamed up. "Did you say *I* was going to wear the dress?"

The smile changed to one of pure innocence, but the sparkle in Ben's eyes was anything but. Adrian took a deep breath. No one had looked at him like that in years. Not since Antonio. He flinched when the back of Ben's hand brushed him as he held a sweater against his chest, muttering something about it matching his eyes. To Adrian, it looked like a perfectly plain gray-blue sweater. Ben fingered the wool at the elbows. "I think I can make a few holes to make this look old."

Adrian shut his mouth with a clang.

"Problem?" Ben asked calmly, but Adrian noticed that his fingers were shaking slightly as if he wasn't as confident as he was trying to appear.

"What are we doing?"

"Getting costumes for the DVD."

Over the last couple of evenings, they had tossed ideas around while eating their pizzas. Ben had suggested livening up the presentation by transferring Laurel's data to a more visual format with someone pointing to graphs and explaining them as if they were the character the data related to. Producing one wouldn't be a problem. They often made training videos for new staff. "And who exactly is going to be in this video?" Adrian had a nasty suspicion he didn't want to hear the answer.

"Why, you're the star, of course!" Ben smiled and turned to pick up a pair of horrible, brown men's slacks. Adrian would need a belt to hold them up; they were way too big.

"But, you don't expect me to wear a dress, do you?" Adrian asked, reluctantly accepting all the different articles of clothing Ben shoved into his arms.

"You said you'd worn one before. When you were at Cornell!"

They'd been discussing their different experiences at University, and Adrian had mentioned that he'd once played the part of Lady Bracknell in *The Importance of Being Earnest*. Ben had been intrigued by the fact that Adrian hadn't minded dressing like a female and had nodded his head thoughtfully when he learnt that his boss had some acting experience. Now it seemed like he'd set himself up for this. *That's what you get for letting your guard down.* Adrian sighed. "Point taken."

Next, Ben placed a lilac dress on the pile, something a drag queen might wear. *Whoa.* Adrian stopped dead in his tracks again. In the end, Ben had to come back, because Adrian's feet were firmly rooted to the spot.

"Hey, there are limits." Adrian stared pointedly at the offending garment. Part of him was intrigued to wonder what he would look like when it was on. Until now, he'd never been tempted to wear drag, not in public anyway.

"Don't worry, once we put a wig on and loads of makeup, no one will recognize you."

Ben seemed oblivious to the difference between dressing as an old, cantankerous woman and a seductive female. "But why me? Why not you?"

"Bit hard to find dresses when you're six-foot-two."

Not in a Goodwill store, Adrian acknowledged to himself, dryly. But there were definitely dressmakers around who excelled in making drag costumes for tall men. Adrian tried to visualize Ben in a dress, but failed miserably. The image wouldn't stick. "What about someone else at work?"

Ben shook his head as he added a tattered pair of jeans to the pile. "We don't have enough time, and I can't really ask them to stay late without pay. You *did* offer to help." He batted his eyelashes and smiled.

Adrian smirked. Ben had been hanging around Jason too long. Jason could tempt a vegetarian to eat steak. On Ben, the flirty expression looked funny, but it still worked for Adrian.

"Okay." He was finding it hard to get his head around the fact that Ben hadn't thought twice about dragging him into a Goodwill store. The fact that he was his boss didn't seem to faze Ben in the slightest. Adrian sighed and piled all the clothes except the trousers back into Ben's arms. "You tell me what characters you want, and I'll choose the clothes, okay? Your taste in pants sucks."

Ben grinned and started moving even faster around the store.

"What about accessories?" Adrian asked when Ben finally worked out that he had enough characters to show the different types of people he wanted to portray.

"Accessories?"

"What's wrong with you, Ben?" Adrian flicked his wrist and did his best Carson Kressley impersonation. "Haven't you heard that the only thing separating gay men from heteros is their ability to accessorize?"

Ben looked stunned.

Adrian gave a quick laugh, hoping he hadn't given the game away. He'd forgotten for a second that Ben wasn't one of his college friends who knew he was gay. "I told you I could act." He felt like adding that after playing the part of a straight man for years, he'd been getting practice 24/7.

Adrian managed to prevent Ben from buying a few items, saying he could borrow them from his girlfriend. He was sure that, if he asked her nicely, Evelyn would lend some of her makeup and accessories. The bill came to more than Ben anticipated, so Adrian insisted on paying.

IT TOOK them a couple of weeks, but in the end, the making of the DVD was just as much fun for Ben as the shopping. Adrian's theatrical expertise complemented his own technical know-how perfectly. While they worked out in the gym each night, they discussed the different scenarios and decided how to best illustrate them. The characters were way over the top, of course, but that would keep the audience amused while the accompanying graph or data set gave the specifics. The last one was the best, although Adrian didn't seem to think so at the time.

"… can't help it, I'm… sorry." Ben wiped his eyes with the back of his hand and sniffed. No good—he burst out laughing again.

Adrian twisted around and glared at him. "Do you want me to do this or not?"

"Yes, *Mr. Sutherland*." Ben deliberately used the full name, even though he'd been calling him Adrian to his face for so long, it felt natural. The thought that the apparition staring at him was his boss set off another round of giggles.

"If Tyrone comes in to investigate and catches me like this, you're fired."

"Yes, Mr. Sutherland."

"So, be quiet and hold still."

"*Yes*, Mr. Sutherland."

Adrian turned back and applied another couple of strokes. After a while, Ben couldn't help himself; he had to say something. "Um, you've got the angle all wrong, sir. It needs to be straighter."

Adrian sighed and shook his head. "Ben, have you ever done this before?"

"No... *sir*...." Another snigger.

"Well, I have, so look and learn."

Adrian lifted his hand again, and this time, he got it right. Ben checked the photo in his hand. Perfect. Adrian put down the kohl pencil and swiveled around on the stool. "What do you think? Will I do?"

Do? Ben swallowed. He could do the man in front of him, no problem. Now that he was standing inside Adrian's parted legs, all he had to do was move forward a few inches, and they'd be crotch to crotch. *What was I supposed to be doing?* Oh, right. For once, Ben had a good excuse to gaze into those unblinking, come-to-bed eyes, but that wasn't much better than letting his gaze fall to where their bodies nearly touched. He risked taking another step closer. "Hang on, some mascara has smudged on the makeup." He pretended to wipe it off Adrian's cheek, but his fingers trembled so much, he had to disguise the reaction with another giggle. "You look great." Ben swallowed and stepped back, feeling another blush starting. At least the blood was better up there than down where it seemed to have taken up permanent residence lately. *Thank God for tight Jockeys.*

He tipped the bag of clothes up and found the black, fingerless gloves. "Put these on." Adrian slid his hands into them, taking care not to smudge the nail polish he'd applied earlier.

"Perfect, just one more thing. You might want to sit down for this bit."

"What now?" The words sounded impatient, but the twinkle in his boss's eye showed he didn't hate it as much as he tried to make out. The first few days had been awkward, but gradually Adrian got into the groove of acting again—although he never admitted he was actually enjoying the experience. In fact, he didn't stop bitching the whole time: the shoes pinched, the woolen sweater itched. After a while, Ben tuned out his complaints. He'd reached the stage where he instinctively knew how his boss was feeling despite his facial expression or lack thereof. There was something about the way his shoulders imperceptibly stiffened or he held his head that told Ben whether he was happy or sad. Lately, there hadn't been as much of the latter, which suited Ben just fine.

"This will sting a bit, but they really set off the outfit. Shut your eyes for a sec."

Adrian stared at him warily as Ben approached, then he obeyed his command.

"Ow!"

Ben's fingers brushed against bare skin as he adjusted the fake nose ring, sending tingles zinging through his body. Adrian opened his eyes, and a completely different atmosphere descended. Those gray irises grew dark and smoky as the two men stared at each other in silence. No giggles now. Ben's heart skipped a couple of beats. Eventually, he managed to regain his sanity and stop gazing at his boss like a besotted idiot.

As soon as everything else was ready, he helped him shrug on the black leather jacket. Lucky for their budget, Adrian owned one already, though they did have to buy the wig on eBay. Ben helped by tucking in some loose strands of hair. Adrian could have done it himself, but they'd got into the habit of Ben playing valet. He didn't mind. It gave him lots of excuses to touch his boss. Ben swallowed and stepped back. "Is something wrong?" Adrian asked and frowned. "Don't tell me the mascara is smudged again."

Wrong? No. I just had an overwhelming urge to kiss you. Ben shook his head and bit his lip as he admired the finished result. No one would have ever recognized the person in front of him as Adrian Sutherland. Hiding the gray in his hair made the boss look years younger, and with makeup and an all-black outfit—skinny jeans, leather jacket, and platform boots—he looked nothing like his usual conservative self. Before his boss could move, Ben stepped forward and adjusted the wig again, fluffing up the strands they'd sprayed bright blue so they showed up better. He didn't really need to, but the chance of being this close wasn't likely to happen again, and he had discovered that he liked it. He really, really liked it.

"Well, what do you think?"

Ben drew in a deep breath, letting the familiar cologne tease his nostrils. No way could he tell Adrian what he really thought. He spun his boss around so he faced the mirror.

Adrian gave a start, as if he'd seen a ghost. "Fucking hell! I look like Adam Lambert!"

Ben's mouth dropped open when he heard his boss swear. First time for everything. "No, you're a Goth, just like in the picture." He held the photo up to show him.

Adrian tugged at the wig a little and combed his fingers through his fake bangs, settling them over one eye so he looked even more like the original. "Couldn't you have downloaded some images from the Internet for the DVD?" He stood back, angling his body, to get a better view.

Ben giggled, and adjusted the collar of Adrian's jacket. "But you look so cute in all your different getups, pointing to the different things on the chart."

What a contrast they made: the pissed-off Goth and the all-American farm boy standing behind him. Ben found it difficult to think when Adrian glared at him like that. All he wanted to do was wrap him in his arms and make everything better.

"Just as well I have my back to the camera most of the time." Adrian took a step toward the mirror, putting some distance between them and shook his head. "Explain to me again how a Goth fits into your predictive analytics scenario."

Ben resisted the temptation to close the gap and pull Adrian against his body, so the man would feel *exactly* how a Goth fitted into him, or rather how he would fit into this particular Goth. Instead, he started packing everything away, dragging his mind out of the gutter and back into work mode. "It isn't so much *who* each character is, more a recognition of the specific features that go into identifying them. In

112

this instance, it's the black eye makeup, the hair, the clothes, the boots—all the things that set them apart. Wait until you watch the finished product. It'll be great!"

"Don't forget I get final approval. If I don't like it, you'll be putting in extra hours of your own time, fixing it up."

"Yes, Mr. Lambert. Of course, Mr. Lambert." Ben snickered at the resulting glare. The twinkling eyes gave the game away.

A knock sounded on the washroom door. The look of horror on Adrian's face was priceless.

"Relax. It's only Tyrone, with tonight's order." They'd gradually been sampling all the local pizza places, but Ben was beginning to think Mick might be right. They had tried his father's pizza one night, and it was way better than any of the others. The security guard placed the boxes on the bench. Adrian had his back half-turned, and was trying to avoid being recognized. So far they'd been able to escape detection, though Tyrone must have suspected something, given the amount of laughing and giggling they'd done.

"Will there be enough here for three when Mr. Sutherland gets back?"

Ben chuckled. "Sure. Adam doesn't eat much, do you?"

Adrian shook his head and put his gloved hand up to his face to hide his smile. If Tyrone didn't recognize Adrian, then no one would.

The actual filming of the segment took less time than it did for Adrian to remove his black nail polish and makeup. When he removed the wig and his familiar gray was uncovered, Ben couldn't resist saying, "Maybe you should dye your hair. Black suits you. Makes you look years younger."

Adrian smiled and shook his head. "Not going to happen."

The casual, swearing equal was gone. Ben sighed inwardly, missing him already. Now Adrian was back in his normal clothes, his behavior reverted, as did his speech. The man was not only a great character actor, he was a chameleon. The film proved it.

The day after they finished working on the video, Laurel called Ben into her office and tartly informed him that *she* would be going with Adrian. She thanked him for his contribution, but said it would be more appropriate if she went, so she could answer any questions that might arise.

A sudden flare of jealousy raged for a second, but then Ben remembered the banshee was Adrian's girlfriend. Of course they would be going together. Pity. He would have liked to see the conference delegates' faces when they saw the presentation.

DESPITE staying back and working on the presentation so Laurel could concentrate on the next board meeting, by the time it came around, she still wasn't ready, and demanded Ben leave what he was doing and print and bind the report for her: "Pronto!" Luckily Millie offered to help, so the meeting had only been going for fifteen minutes when Ben knocked, made his excuses for interrupting them, and walked in.

Working his way around the boardroom table, he placed a copy in front of each of the people present. Some, like Adrian's father and his cousin Bill, the manager of the East Coast office, he recognized immediately, but there were a few people he hadn't seen before. Adrian had been speaking and making notes on the whiteboard. Most of them acknowledged Ben's presence with a smile or nod of the head; Laurel didn't even thank him.

"Wait, please, Ben." Adrian's voice stopped him as he turned to leave. His boss cleared his throat and continued. "For those of you who haven't met him, Ben Dutoit is our extremely talented and very competent trainee actuary. He'll be accompanying me to the industry conference in Sonoma County next weekend when we do our presentation on predictive analytics."

Adrian had checked that Ben was available that weekend, but after Laurel's comment, Ben assumed his boss had changed his mind. What could Ben say? Everyone nodded their heads and smiled. Laurel pretended she was fine with the announcement, but her talons were making little indents in the table. The prospect of spending two days with the person who'd become his night-time fantasy lover made Ben's throat dry, but knowing he'd piss off the man's girlfriend in the process made it even better. Ben stammered his thanks, and left.

CHAPTER
+++
THREE

JASON'S familiar ringtone woke Ben. He rubbed his eyes. Why did falling asleep at 3 a.m. after tossing and turning all night, feel worse than crashing after a party at the same time? "Hi, Jason."

"Hi, Ben."

"How ya' doin'?" Ben's jaw nearly dislocated with his deep yawn.

"Are you okay? You sound weird." For once Jason sounded honestly concerned about another person.

"Nah, I'm fine. Just didn't get much sleep last night." At work, everything had been so full-on frantic, first putting the finishing touches to the presentation and then the board meeting, that there'd been no time to think about anything else. But when he finally turned out the light, reality set in—he was about to spend a weekend away with Adrian.

Ben checked his watch. 8.45 a.m. *Shit.* Tucking the cell under his chin, he scrambled out of bed. Thank God he packed last night. "Look, can you call me back later? I'm meeting Adrian soon, and I slept through the alarm."

"Sorry."

Ben paused, one foot in his Jockeys, his brain clearing instantly. Jason never apologized. For anything. "Did you say 'sorry'? What for?"

"For waking you so early and…." Jason's voice died away, but Ben could still hear quiet breathing.

"Nah, lucky you rang or I'd be even later." Ben finished pulling up his briefs and reached for his jeans, his cell phone still tucked under his chin. "Are you okay? You don't sound too good. How's the treatment going?"

Jason's quick snort of disgust told Ben everything he needed to know on that front.

"Like that, eh?"

"Yeah."

"How bad is it?"

"I feel like shit, but according to Vincent, I'll live for years if I do what I'm told."

Ben had learned from their time together that Jason hated being fussed over. "I gather this isn't some kind of deathbed reconciliation scene, then."

"Nope." Jason chuckled. "That's what I like about you, Ben, no bullshit."

Ben struggled into his jeans. "Anyway, who's Vincent?"

"My nurse…."

"Your nurse?"

"Yeah, my parents employed him to look after me. Long story."

"Tell me some other time, eh? I've got to get ready."

"Okay. But, Ben, guess what?"

"What, Jason?"

"He's into leather!" The note of awe in Jason's voice didn't surprise Ben. Jason had flirted with the scene when he'd been here. From the sound of things, he'd hit pay dirt.

Ben breathed in so he could fasten his button, the cell clamped tight under his chin again. Whoops, he must have bulked up with all the gym work. "A whip-wielding nurse, eh? Sounds interesting."

"He's not your average nurse, either, more a psychologist."

"Why do you need one of those?"

"He says the mind plays a big part in getting over illnesses. He reckons the main reason I'm so depressed is that I have all this guilt inside. Until I deal with a number of outstanding issues, I won't get better."

"What outstanding issues?" Ben pulled on his best T-shirt and looked at his watch again; Adrian would be arriving any minute. One-handed, he checked through his bag to make sure he had everything.

"An apology to you, for starters." Ben could hear Jason take a big breath. "I shouldn't have kept bugging you to bareback me, especially after having unprotected sex with other guys." Jason's voice sounded quieter than normal. Gone was his usual brashness.

Ben blinked in surprise. The Jason on the other end of the line was totally different from the reckless party boy he'd been only weeks before. "Apology accepted."

"And I should have contacted you straight away, not let you find out from Adrian."

"True." The three days might not matter in the long run, but it was the principle.

"How are *you*?" Jason asked.

Another first—Jason thinking of someone other than himself. Obviously this Vincent character *did* have his measure. "So far, so good," Ben replied. "Now I'm waiting for the follow-up test to confirm I'm in the clear." Jason made a small sound, but Ben cut in over the top. "Look, Jason, I was as much to blame; I shouldn't have been so shit-faced I gave in the first time." He paused, memories of their different encounters flashing through his head. "… and I could have always said no afterward."

Jason sighed. "Fair enough." He was silent again.

Ben glanced at his watch. "Is that all?"

"No." It was almost a minute before Jason spoke again. Ben slipped on his boots, giving him time to elaborate. "I have to apologize about something else."

"*Have* to? That doesn't sound very sincere, Jason."

A spark of the old spirit filtered over the connection. "Do you think this is easy? Give me a break, will you? I'm trying."

"Sorry." Ben waited again.

"You remember that day I invited you over to my place?"

You mean Adrian's place. How could he ever forget? "Yes." Ben drew the word out, wondering what was coming next.

"I intended for us to get caught. I set you up."

"What in the fuckin' hell are you going on about?"

"I wanted him to think we were serious."

"Serious. You and me? Why would Adrian think that? I only went out with you, what… three times in the previous three months?"

"Er, I may have given him the impression we were still going out together on a regular basis."

"Why, Jason?" Ben rubbed his forehead; his hand came away sweaty. "I don't understand."

The belligerence was back. "Adrian kept harping on me to settle down and stop being a total slut, but whenever I said I was going out with you, he backed off."

So *that* was the reason for all the lectures in the gym about making sure he didn't spend all his nights out on the town, neglecting his studies. "Couldn't you have found someone else to be your imaginary boyfriend?"

"I wanted to shake him up a bit, too," Jason muttered.

"Shake him up?" A horn sounded from outside. Ben checked to see who it was and saw Adrian get out of a blue Prius. His boss walked to the front door without even glancing at some rough-looking locals leaning against the railings of a house three doors down. Ben opened the window and called out, "Won't be long."

Adrian smiled and nodded before walking back to the car.

Ben took a deep breath, trying to calm himself. Just the sight of Adrian set his heart pounding. For some reason, even though they had been spending a lot of time together lately, he was feeling on edge about this trip. Excitement? Nerves? He wasn't sure which. "Look, Jason, call me when I get back, eh? Adrian's here. We're going to a conference up at Napa this weekend."

"But…."

"Later, okay?" Ben cut the connection, grabbed what he needed, scrambled out the door and jumped down the steps two at a time.

"Got everything?" Adrian asked when he opened the car door.

Ben smiled and hoped his nervousness didn't show as he threw the small overnighter into the backseat and hung his suit next to Adrian's. "You betcha." Shoving the whole weird conversation with Jason out of his mind, he concentrated on his boss. The smoky-blue shirt fitted snug across his chest, giving a hint of bumps where his nipples were. The top few buttons lay tantalizingly open. Thinking about sucking those nipples made Ben's throat dry; he swallowed to wet it. "Nice car," he managed to blurt out, hoping Adrian would take the hint and start up a conversation.

"You can move the seat back if you're a bit squashed."

Ben needed more room but not for his legs. "Nah, it's cool."

Adrian studied his face before he started the engine and moved off. "What's wrong, Ben? Are you worried about the presentation?"

No, I'm not sure how I'll go being alone with you all weekend, dummy! "Yeah, a bit."

"We'll be fine. Our session isn't on until tomorrow afternoon. Plenty of time to go through things again."

The soothing sound of his boss's voice gradually calmed Ben down, and his mind drifted as Adrian maneuvered through the city traffic. If the rumors going around the office were correct, the announcement of Adrian's engagement to Laurel was due any day now. While they were at the conference, Ben resolved to keep his eye open for someone who'd make a better wife for him than that bitch. Heck, any female would be better. Even Millie. But if he didn't find a replacement, he might have to resort to dirty tactics. He nodded every now and then, not really paying attention to what Adrian was saying. Instead he was imagining his boss walking down the aisle with Laurel, his face rough and unshaven like it had been on that unforgettable night, but this time Adrian wore a gunmetal-gray suit, no shirt, just a tie in the same smoky blue he had on now. When the part came about anyone objecting, Ben pictured himself dashing forward, throwing him over his shoulder, and rescuing him from the clutches of that harpy. Back at his place, using his tie, he'd wrap Adrian's hands together and bind them to the railings of his brass bed, so he couldn't escape. Then he'd fuck him until he screamed louder than Jason.

AS HE drove, a strange thought crossed Adrian's mind. What if things were different? No parental expectations weighing him down, and no sick boyfriend waiting for Ben back East. He felt like turning on the childproof lock and spiriting Ben away. There were so many places they could visit. Alaska, maybe. Could they drive as far as Rio? Patagonia even? Lucky the kid didn't have his passport with him. The idea was awfully tempting.

After exchanging a few words of meaningless chitchat, he noticed Ben was blushing for some reason. *Did his skin change color all over when making love?* Adrian wondered. If Ben were his, Adrian would tease him until he became as hot and bothered as he'd been when he'd caught him fucking Jason. That would be fun.

An SUV suddenly cut in from the right. For the next few minutes, Adrian concentrated on avoiding all the suburban shoppers and soccer moms. Even when the traffic thinned to a more ordered stream, he could sense that Ben was still on edge. To put him at ease, he ran through all the points they were due to cover.

On the surface, the DVD was pure entertainment, but underneath was some solid research. Ben had done a great job. He had a gift for presenting the material in a way everyone would understand. He hadn't been listening though; at one stage, he jumped as if he'd been bitten on the ass, and blushed again. Adrian sighed. He'd bored Ben to tears, and they weren't even over the bridge.

"ARE you okay with that?" Adrian's voice cut into his thoughts. "Ben?"

"Sorry, what did you say? I missed it."

"I'll introduce the film we made, and you can present the conclusions. You know the material better than I do, so if there are any questions, you'll know the answers."

Ben's daydreams popped like tiny balloons, and he landed back in the present with a thud. *Me, actually get up and speak?* "You're joking."

Adrian took his eye off the road and smiled.

God, I wish he'd stop doing that!

"No. I'm not joking. I meant what I said at the board meeting. You're extremely talented and very competent. The material you've put together for the presentation is first-rate, so you should get the credit. Think of it as part of your training."

Talented, competent. He doesn't think I'm a complete idiot. Ben shut his eyes to make sure the moment stayed in his memory bank. "Okay, if you think I'm capable."

"I'm sure you're capable of more things than you're aware of, Ben."

Ben knew what he was capable of then and there, and while Adrian might enjoy it, they'd probably have an accident. He rummaged around in his backpack, hoping his boss wouldn't notice his bright-red face. "Mind if I put on a CD?" At least his voice sounded normal.

"What have you got?"

Ben took a deep breath. "Nine Inch Nails, Usher, Lady Gaga… a bit of everything."

Adrian's face didn't change, but Ben noticed that his chest shook with silent chuckles. Oh well. Ben already knew *his* idea of everything was totally different. Adrian reached into the glove compartment and drew out a small parcel. "I bought you something, as thanks for your assistance. Put this on."

Ben tore open the package and found a couple of CDs. *So that's why Adrian asked me all those questions about which ones I owned.* "Thanks, but I was glad to help."

"Wait until you hear it. You might not like it."

Ben opened the case, extracted the CD and inserted it into the player. Who was Adrian kidding? He'd given him *Music by Ry Cooder* a compilation of backing tracks written for different films. They listened in silence for a while, the instrumentals and songs providing a perfect accompaniment for the landscape passing by.

At least his initial nervousness at being alone with the man he spent so much time fantasizing about was settling down. He still wasn't sure what triggered the reaction in the first place. All he could come up with was that this wasn't the same as being in the office together or in the gym. The enclosed space of Adrian's car made it seem more intimate, somehow.

Adrian's voice cut into a quiet section as Ben gazed out the window. "Ben, would you mind if I asked you a personal question?"

Personal? Ben's brain instantly set off in all sorts of directions at once. His mouth went dry. Mutely, he shook his head. *No.*

"Are you ever afraid of anything?"

Ben turned the volume down while he gathered his scattered thoughts back together. Talk about a question coming from left field. *Afraid? You betcha. I'm scared stiff of making myself look like a total idiot in your eyes.* "Afraid of what? Bears? Girls?"

Adrian grinned. "No. I was just surprised before when you said that you were nervous about speaking at the presentation. Most times you appear to be super-confident."

Super-confident? Me? Ben stared out the window, looking for inspiration, wondering how Adrian had got that impression. "Maybe it's bravado." He turned back in time to see Adrian's lips twitch a bit.

"No, it's more than that. When I was your age, I could never have dragged my employer into a Goodwill store, for example."

Woops. Heat rushed into Ben's face. He had never thought about his actions from that angle. He couldn't have afforded the clothes any other way, and at the time it felt perfectly natural. He stared at Adrian's profile as he thought about the question. His boss wasn't rushing him for an answer; he really wanted to know. Ben settled back into the car seat and tried to figure out where the courage had come from. Eventually, he came up with the only conclusion that made any sense. "I think it's because we work out together, and I see you in your casual clothes. If you'd been in your suit, I probably wouldn't have dared."

"So, it was just because I wore casual clothes," Adrian prompted.

"No, it is actually more than that." Because they were sitting side by side and not facing each other, Ben's thoughts flowed more freely.

He often found that happening on the long car trips to his grandma's house in Minneapolis when his mom dropped him off or picked him up at the start and end of each term. Chris usually accompanied them, so she'd have company on the way home, but his brother sprawled out in the backseat with his headphones on while Ben sat in the front. During the journey, Ben would tell his mom things that he could never discuss with her at home. Now it was the same. Though thinking about Adrian and his mother in the same sentence was a bit off somehow.

"You can't be in awe of someone if you've watched them groan and sweat on the machines beside you. Someone who gets sore, just like you. Who complains as much as you do when their abs hurt from too many crunches. I guess there's something about doing physical things with another person that breaks down barriers. Don't forget, we've been working out at least three nights a week for the last five months. That's a fair bit of time together."

Adrian turned and grinned, pulling in his abs and sitting a bit straighter. "One formerly overweight unfit executive is very grateful."

Ben returned the grin, but moments later all his so-called confidence dried up. "Did you mind me treating you like that? Making you come to the store with me, and getting you so involved with the presentation?"

Adrian reached across and placed his hand on Ben's thigh. "I enjoyed it. Haven't had that much fun in years." After a couple of seconds, Adrian's hand returned to the steering wheel. Ben stared at the spot where he had been touched. The area burned at a few degrees higher than the surroundings, and the image of Adrian rubbing his leg seemed so natural, so right, Ben felt confused by the fact that his hand no longer rested there. He stared out the window, hoping Adrian hadn't noticed his reaction. When his body was back under control, he extracted the CD from the slot and inserted the second disc. "Thanks for the present, by the way. It's great."

Adrian gave him another of those mouthwatering smiles; this time he didn't say anything.

In the end, they reached the conference hotel in Napa far too soon for Ben's liking.

After the easy camaraderie in the car, it felt weird walking beside Adrian in public. This was the real world, where their age and status difference became apparent and a sober reminder that the man was his boss. A number of people turned to watch as they passed by. Adrian was like that, someone you noticed.

As luck would have it, they arrived at the same time as a busload of wine lovers from Oklahoma and had to wait in line at the reception desk. The scent of Adrian's shampoo teased Ben's nostrils, sending more signals around his body. He felt like putting his arms around Adrian's waist and hugging him closer. Luckily the virtual slaps upside his head, telling him to settle down, were only imaginary ones, or he would have been black and blue.

After a quick, appreciative scan of Adrian, the girl at the desk studied her computer screen when he gave his name. She frowned and glanced up, biting her lip. "The booking for the room was done by an L. Marchison. She insisted on a room with a queen-size bed."

Ack. Now we have to share a bed? Part of Ben salivated at the prospect, the rest was downright petrified. He must have made some sort of noise. Adrian turned and glanced back before speaking to the girl; even *his* face was flushed. "Is there another room that we could have, or can you split the bed into two?"

She searched through the computer for a few minutes, every now and then tapping her pen on the screen. Finally, she pursed her lips. "I'm afraid, what with the insurance convention and the wine tour, there's nothing else available."

Adrian turned and gave a wry smile. "Don't panic, Ben; I'll see if I can find somewhere else to stay. Wait over there." He gestured to a seat away from the desk. "I'm going to make a call." He went outside. Ben did as instructed, placing his bag on his lap. Telling his cock to behave might have worked if he could just stop imagining them entwined in bed.

A few minutes later Adrian returned, a broad smile spreading across his face. "I've found some alternative accommodations. Let's register now, and we can return for our presentation tomorrow. Most of the other sessions aren't relevant."

Relief and disappointment waged a quick war. Relief won. Adrian took his agreement for granted and completed all the necessary paperwork.

Within minutes, they were back in the car, heading north. This time, Adrian hooked his iPod up to the radio and pressed "random," giving Ben a first-hand taste of *his* idea of "everything." Rows of vines now stretched each side of the highway.

"Um, boss, where are we going?" Ben assumed they were heading for another hotel, but they'd left the built-up area of Napa behind.

Adrian gave a quick grin. "To stay with my Nonna and Pop."

"Oh." These must be his mother's parents. The ones Adrian had said he helped with their weeding. Ben remembered the conversation vividly. That was the day he narrowly escaped being caught doing Goldilocks impressions in Adrian's office, trying out his chair for size. That was also the day he helped Adrian remove his shirt when it got caught in his glasses. The day he first noticed what a nice butt Adrian had. Mostly though, that was the day he stopped thinking of Adrian as a middle-aged man and started thinking about him far too much for his health and sanity.

Ben's cell played "Don't Call Me Red."

"Hi, Jason," he whispered, turning away, keeping his voice as low as possible. "I can't talk now. I'm in the car with Adrian."

"So you said. Where are you going?"

Ben explained about the conference and that they would be spending the night with Adrian's grandparents. He wanted to ask Jason what the comment about shaking Adrian up was all about, but he couldn't do it with the man in question sitting right beside him. "I'll call you when I get back, eh?" He could mention Laurel's role in the saga then.

"Okay, but it's important."

Ben tried to work out what Jason might consider to be important.

HIS young companion hadn't spoken for five minutes. For once the expression on his face was serious. "Cat got your tongue?" Adrian asked.

Ben's features relaxed into their usual grin. "Do I talk *that* much?"

"Well, you're not usually this quiet."

"What shall we talk about then, boss?"

"What about football?" Adrian prompted. "You said you're a Vikings fan."

"You betcha."

"Did you hear the rumor that Brett Favre will be signing up to play next season?" Ben looked stunned, and stared at him with his mouth half-open. "What's the matter? Surprised about Brett, or the fact I'm a football fan?"

"Both."

Adrian shook his head and laughed. "You're speaking to a lifelong Jets fan."

Ben snickered. "Being a Jets supporter must really test your loyalty."

Too true. "Yeah, but we keep hoping, don't we?"

When they finally ran out of stats to exchange, Adrian fiddled with his iPod, unleashing the raspy sounds of Tom Waits. He chuckled to himself. His love of football and the blues had already escaped from the closet; if he wasn't careful, everything would.

He glanced across at Ben. The young man's eyes were now closed, his head resting against the window, sunlight glinting off his hair, turning it to a ball of flame. Awake, the force of his personality filled every space or room he was in, so it was unusual seeing him so quiet and vulnerable.

After leaving the conference venue, everything had been perfect. Adrian could pretend once again they were just two guys going away for a weekend together. No big deal. Then Jason called, reminding Adrian that Ben wasn't *his* boyfriend. He was Jason's. At first, Adrian felt like throwing the cell out the window, but by the time the call finished, the hollow feeling inside had vanished. Ben hadn't sounded overjoyed while talking to his lover. No murmured endearments. No "wishing you were here". Maybe the fact that Jason had been fucking around had caused a rift between them?

Immediately, Adrian kicked himself for being so bitchy, hoping that they were breaking up. Maybe Ben didn't go in for public displays of affection. He and Antonio had, but everyone was different. Memories of different occasions ran through his mind as he drove. Instead of being disappointed that Ben slept during the last part of the journey, Adrian discovered that he enjoyed that part of the trip as well. There was something about Ben that allowed him to relax and let his thoughts roam freely without feeling overwhelmed.

BEN woke when the vibrations under the wheels changed as they left the paved highway in favor of a narrow secondary road. "Sorry." He glanced across, but Adrian didn't seem to mind the way his travelling companion had conked out on him.

"We're here," was all he said.

"Here" was an old stone cottage surrounded by a vineyard loaded with grapes. At the sound of the engine, an elderly couple emerged and enfolded Adrian in hugs as soon as he stepped out of the car.

Ben climbed out and stretched his legs. *Why are all cars made for midgets?* Even though the Prius was roomy, he still had pins and needles.

Adrian waited for him to approach, his arms draped lightly across his grandparent's shoulders—they were even shorter than he was. "Nonna and Pop, I'd like you to meet one of my best employees, Ben Dutoit."

Ben shook their hands and returned their warm smiles as they welcomed him to their home. The dark coolness inside came as a welcome relief from the hot sun. Adrian's grandpa disappeared out the back, returning with a bottle under one arm as he started to unscrew another. "Here's the latest Zinfandel. Tell me what you think."

Adrian and his grandma started chatting in Italian as they sat and drank the wine. The old man had a fair smattering of English, but his wife's wasn't the best. Adrian tried to include Ben, but he held up his hand. "Stop worrying. I'm okay."

His grandfather looked across and would have tried to engage him in conversation in English, but Ben shook his head and settled back in the chair. After a few minutes, he closed his eyes, letting their voices wash over him.

Maybe it was the wine, possibly the heat, or simply the fact he hadn't eaten for a few hours. Perhaps even the sound of Adrian's sexy voice, speaking in Italian, relaxed him completely. Whatever the reason, he soon drifted back off to sleep again.

BECAUSE the mix-up at the conference hotel was such a complicated story, it was much easier to converse in Italian. Nonna hadn't heard about Laurel, so Adrian left that part out. He just told her there'd been a problem with the hotel booking and described how Ben had made a video for the conference. She laughed when he told her about having to pretend to be an old woman and clucked when he offered to pass on the dress.

Her attention kept wandering across to Ben as he slept. She wanted to know if he was sick. Adrian couldn't divulge the threat to Ben's health, so he told her that he'd been studying a lot. After a while, their conversation drifted to the economy, as it always did, and then updates on their relatives back in Italy. Pop's brother still grieved for the death of Antonio, his favorite grandson. On Adrian's first visit to the vineyard after returning to the States, he had discovered his grandparents already knew about their relationship. They were understandably disappointed that they wouldn't have great-grandchildren, but they never rejected him. Something Adrian would be forever grateful for. Sometimes he wondered if his mother had warned them he was gay before she died. She may have suspected the truth even back then. Although his grandparents loved their faith, they didn't love everything the Church decreed, so when it became a matter of which was more important, religion or family, family won out every time.

They never said exactly why they had come to terms with his homosexuality, but they had. In fact, in his Pop's eyes, hiding his *true nature*, as he called it, was as much a sin as exposing it was for Adrian's father.

WHEN Ben woke again, Adrian's grandma was moving around quietly, trying to set the table without disturbing him. He clambered to his feet and found himself blushing again. *Shit. I'm traveling with my boss, and I've already zonked out twice in his company.*

"It's all the fresh air after being in the city for so long." Adrian's grandpa handed across his overnight bag and gestured for him to follow.

"Sorry, that was very rude of me. Didn't sleep much last night."

"Well, at least you didn't snore." When Adrian's grandpa laughed, his eyes crinkled at the corners like his grandson's did. *I bet he was just as handsome in his youth.*

The old man led him out to a small stone cottage a few yards away from the main building. The walls looked as if they were a foot thick. Double doors led out onto a vine-covered deck, and three small windows were covered with yellow daisy-patterned curtains. In the middle of the room was a huge bed. Mesmerized, Ben's gaze latched onto the two sets of towels arranged neatly on top of the pillows. *Two?*

A quickly smothered expletive behind him broke the spell.

Adrian swooped in, gathered up one set and had an animated discussion in Italian with his grandpa. It eventually became clear that he would be sleeping in his old room in the main part of the house. As Adrian left, Ben tried to banish the alternate image from his mind.

His grandpa looked puzzled for a second, then shrugged and went on to explain that the building was originally used to store wine and apologized for the lack of hot water, pointing to a basic bathroom with an old showerhead.

Ben murmured his thanks.

The old man said, "Dinner will be ready soon," and left.

After removing as much dirt as possible and changing his shirt, Ben returned to the kitchen with empty-belly rumbles that threatened to become audible. After a diet of nonstop pizzas for the last couple of weeks, he was ready for something different. He patted his stomach after the first plate of lasagna and had to restrain a belch. Adrian looked at him and obviously found it difficult to restrain the twitch at the side of his mouth.

Adrian's grandma piled more food on their plates as soon as they were empty. "You boys are too skinny. Which one of you does the cooking?"

Neither of them spoke for a moment, then Adrian said, "Ben doesn't live with me, Nonna. He *works* with me."

She frowned, obviously confused, and was about to speak again when he said something in rapid Italian; Jason's name was mentioned. Ben lifted his eyebrows at her grunt of recognition. When Adrian finished speaking, she turned toward Ben with narrowed eyes, as if she was assessing him. "*I* like you," she said in heavily accented English.

Ben stammered his thanks. *Well, that was weird.* To disguise his confusion, he helped clear the table, then wandered around the room, checking out the photos on the wall. There was a wedding portrait of the couple, taken back in Italy from the look of it. He was right. Adrian did resemble his grandpa at the same age. There were also photos of an attractive young woman—Adrian's mother, he assumed. Standing next to her was a dark-haired boy with a cheeky grin spreading from ear to ear. Adrian didn't smile like that now. Pity.

"Do you have any siblings?" Adrian's grandpa came to stand beside him.

"Four older brothers, no sisters, sir."

"Where are you from?"

Ben carefully replaced a small photo of one of the older generation back onto the piano. "My mother lives in a small town outside Duluth, in Minnesota. My father died some years ago." He had a feeling Adrian's grandpa wanted to know his ethnic origins, and his next words confirmed it.

"But the name Dutoit sounds French."

As Ben turned to answer, he noticed Adrian standing in the kitchen doorway with a plate and dishtowel in his hand, eavesdropping. "We've never researched our family tree, but I gather at least one of my ancestors was a French *voyageur*, a trapper who travelled deep into the north woods collecting and transporting large bundles of furs in the late nineteenth century. My mother thinks he must have decided to settle in the area one day, and the family's been there ever since."

"What are you doing in San Francisco?"

Good question. Ben missed his family, the lakes and the woods, but he didn't miss the bigotry, the skeeters, and the long, freezing winters. "Work, the need to make a living."

Following that statement, a hush fell on the room.

Adrian's grandma's fractured English broke the silence. "The city is not a good place." She wiped away a tear and folded her hands in her apron.

"Nonna." Adrian gave her a hug.

Adrian's grandpa smiled sadly as he explained, "Adrian's mother, Rosalita, was our only child. Maria feels Adrian should stay here and work the vineyard instead of wasting his talents in San Francisco."

The stiff set of the old man's shoulders showed he agreed with her. Ben glanced out the window. The setting sun shone through the vine leaves, creating an idyllic scene, but he wondered if a place like this was viable. Wouldn't Adrian make more money in the insurance business?

NONNA'S suggestion about taking over the vineyard came up as it usually did each visit. The offer sure was tempting. Adrian wouldn't be the first businessman to own a winery as a weekend hobby, but he knew he'd want to be more hands-on than that. Driving or even flying up every now and then wouldn't be his style. He was too much like his Pop.

Nonna had confused Ben with Jason, who often answered the phone when she called and, as usual, turned on the charm. She never could believe Adrian didn't have a lover stashed away somewhere. To her, anyone related to Pop would. She had joshed with her husband when she said that, and he went red. Obviously that part of their marriage was still active. As far as she was concerned, if he and Jason lived together, they must be involved. In the end, Adrian had simply said Jason wasn't his type. Apparently, she thought Ben was.

After dinner, Nonna and Pop insisted he and Ben sit out on the back deck while they went to bed.

Out there, nothing disturbed the silence except for the soft whisper of a breeze blowing through the vines. Most of the house lights were off, and the moon was just a sliver, leaving them in almost total darkness except for a star-studded sky.

Whenever Adrian visited, he didn't mind sitting by himself after they went to bed, thinking and dreaming, but it was good to have someone to share the magic with. Ben seemed perfectly at ease as he sat cross-legged on the step near his chair, facing him and close enough so their voices wouldn't disturb the oldies.

"Tell me about your family. You said you have four brothers."

Ben didn't look at him as he replied. "Yep, Andrew, the eldest, is thirty-five. He owns a canoe-outfitting shop, supplying all the gear and boats for people who want to take trips into the Boundary Waters Canoe Area or the adjacent Canadian Quetico Provincial Park. Then comes, Rob. He's a year younger and works at the ranger station near Moose Lake."

Adrian had detected a wistful note in his voice. Ben was obviously close to his brothers. "And the others?" he prompted when Ben was silent for a few moments.

"Sure I'm not boring you?" The grin Ben flashed up was all bravado, but underneath Adrian detected a degree of uncertainty.

"I wouldn't have asked if I didn't want to know," he assured him gently.

Ben gave one of his shyest smiles, then glanced down again. "Dave, the next brother, is a drug-crime investigator for the Duluth Police Department. I mentioned Chris before. As well as being in a band, he's a plumber. Mom stays at home and gives pottery classes."

132

"And what about your father?"

"Dad had a heart attack while fighting a brush fire back in '99."

"He was a firefighter then?"

Ben was quiet for a while. "No, a volunteer." His serious expression vanished, to be replaced by his familiar grin. "But he was insured with SSFI under its high-risk policy. Otherwise Mom would have found it really difficult to cope. It was hard enough as it was."

Policies that Adrian was fighting hard to maintain. His determination to keep going grew stronger, especially with Ben looking at him with hero-worshipping eyes. Eyes that seemed to see something inside him—or someone. Adrian just wished he knew the person Ben was seeing. It certainly wasn't him.

It was late, they probably should go to bed, but Adrian didn't want to. Ben's head was bent forward again as he stared at the ground, placing it well within reach of his hand. His fingers itched to stroke through the soft red hair. It had grown longer than usual and wasn't so spiky on top. "Do you miss your family?" he asked quietly.

"Sure, and I miss the lakes too."

"They must be beautiful."

"Yep, they are." The familiar vitality returned in an instant. Ben was like that. Mercurial. His face a mirror of his emotions. Adrian wasn't sure whether that was a good thing or not. "Have you ever been there?" As he glanced up, Ben's head was cocked slightly to one side, almost like a dog anxiously waiting to find out whether a walk was in the cards.

"No, but they sound great." Adrian reassured him. "Dad has a cabin down at the Finger Lakes, so I did a bit of canoeing as a kid. Then I was in the Scouts. After that, I rowed in the eights at Cornell. I like being on the water. I always find a sense of serenity and peace I can't find anywhere else."

Ben nodded, his eyes now brimming with enthusiasm. Obviously the place was dear to his heart. "You should go there, you know." He was silent for a moment, then he laughed. "Let me know if you do. I'll act as your guide. I've got connections." He waggled his eyebrows.

How could Adrian resist *that* look? "Careful, I might take you up on that offer."

Ben stared at him for a second, all amusement gone from his face. "I wouldn't mind."

The thought of escaping with Ben into the lakes of Minnesota and Ontario set Adrian's heart racing. Just the two of them, out in the wild. To break the spell he was rapidly falling under, Adrian fetched some more Zinfandel. They finished off the bottle while they chatted about growing grapes and making wine. It was after midnight when Adrian finally said, "I should let you get some sleep. We have a big day tomorrow."

Resisting the temptation to join Ben in the big bed in the guest house, Adrian headed off to the small room he had used whenever he visited before his mom died.

The bed hadn't grown any since then, but he had.

After falling asleep fairly quickly, he woke while it was still dark. Apart from the cramped confines of the small bed, the incessant call of a bird prevented him from getting back to sleep. The same thing had happened once when he was a kid. In the morning, he'd armed himself with a slingshot and gone searching for the culprit. Pop had laughed and told him he had just heard something very rare in these parts: a male Northern Mockingbird calling for its mate. Adrian knew exactly how the bird felt. In some ways, he missed Antonio more than ever lately, or was it missing having someone of his own? A lifelong companion?

As if deliberately making a point, the bird's song grew louder.

Adrian sat on the edge of the mattress and buried his head in his hands, trying to shut out the irritating warbling. He didn't need reminding he was alone. As soon as the bird gave up and flew away to try somewhere else, he filled his lungs with the cool morning air. *God, I can almost taste the place, feel it.* His gaze caught on yellow dust motes dancing in the single ray of light shining through the open window. The sun had finally poked its head above the horizon. *Was Ben awake? Maybe he'd like to walk through the vineyard.* Adrian pulled on his cutoffs and donned some shoes. Long shadows covered the ground between the rows, and small drops of moisture clung to the hairs on the green leaves.

A lace curtain billowed out through the open door of the nearby guesthouse. Adrian walked over and looked inside. Ben lay facedown, spread-eagled across the bed. Naked. It had been hot last night. Another reason Adrian couldn't sleep. Only Ben's long legs and part of his ass were covered. Against the dark blue of the sheet, his flawless, pale skin looked like Carrara marble.

Adrian approached as quietly as he could, his fingers itching to peel back the top sheet so he could see everything. That same ray of sunlight that had pierced the blackness of his room set Ben's hair aflame again. Even in his sleep the light must have worried him, as he had cradled his face in the crook of his arm to shut out the glare. *Was he awake?* Adrian couldn't see his eyes, but Ben didn't stir as Adrian drew closer and crouched down to check. The broad, muscular back rose and fell rhythmically.

The breath caught in Adrian's throat at the sight of that glorious body. The possibility that Ben might be HIV positive often haunted him at night. Logically, he knew that nowadays it wasn't an immediate death sentence, but memories of Antonio kept intruding on his thoughts. Jason had looked terrible, but thankfully, according to his parents' latest report, the antivirals seemed to be working. His body had just reacted strongly during seroconversion. Hopefully, once he recovered from that, the virus would lie dormant in his system for years. At least Ben didn't look sick. His next test wasn't due for weeks yet, and even though the young man was pale, he looked so healthy, so alive.

Adrian took a long breath, drawing the air deep into his nostrils. This close, he could detect Ben's musky scent, overlaid by a blueberry tang that seemed to seep out of the stone floor and walls of the old wine store. If only he had a glass of Zinfandel with him. What a contrast the color would make against that white skin. He could pour it slowly over Ben's back, then lap up the purple liquid as it slid down into his crack.

The smell, the proximity, the sight of that naked perfection made Adrian's penis thicken until it was rock-hard against the denim of his shorts. He palmed the bulge at his crotch a few times to ease the pressure, but that only made it worse. *You can look, but not touch.* The mantra he chanted to himself more and more lately. In this case, even looking felt wrong, but he couldn't resist watching Ben sleep for a few more minutes.

The urge to touch him became overwhelming. Starting at the shoulders, keeping his open palm only an inch away, he slowly traced the curve of Ben's back down to the round globes of his fine, firm ass. Across the gap, he could just detect the warmth of Ben's skin.

SOMETHING stirred Ben awake. He'd been lying on his front, but even without opening his eyes, he could sense a presence in the room. A familiar cologne.

He could hear Adrian's quiet breathing, but he couldn't see him. *What was he doing here?* A war broke out in Ben's mind. Should he turn over and ask him? If he did, Adrian would see his hard-on. His normal morning wood had grown even fuller as soon as he realized who was there.

He needed some sort of signal to tell him what this was all about. *Please, just touch me.* The silent plea ran on a continuous loop inside his brain. That's all he needed. One touch. Then he'd spin around and tumble Adrian onto the bed beneath him. He'd wrestled with his brothers often enough to know how to get someone flat on their back in five seconds. Adrian was only Chris's size. No contest. Once Ben had him there, he'd kiss that gorgeous mouth with its perfect curve and grind into him until the man screamed and begged for mercy.

Ben could sense Adrian watching him. Should he wriggle his butt, or was that too clichéd a move? Even though he rarely bottomed, Ben would make an exception if Adrian wanted his ass. *Was that the reason? Was Adrian bi-curious?* If he wanted to be initiated into the pleasures of gay sex, Ben would be more than happy to oblige. Hopefully, Adrian wouldn't be a good student, then the lessons would have to be repeated over and over again until he got them right. *Oh, fuck, who was he kidding?* He didn't care if Adrian was straight, gay, bi, tri, or whatever.

Ben forced himself to stay as still as possible. If he moved suddenly, Adrian would flee. He knew that as surely as he knew his own name. Whatever motivated him to come into the room, didn't matter. The only thing that was important was that he was there.

Ben tried to visualize the scene. Was Adrian naked, too? He stifled the groan that threatened to break through at the thought. He wanted to move, needed to move. His cock was doing its best to drill a hole in the mattress.

A wave of heat slowly travelled from his shoulders down to his butt. Every tiny hair follicle on his back felt like it was standing on end, trying to reach the source of that warmth. Ben bit his lip and almost whimpered. *Touch me. That's all you have to do! I'll look after the rest.*

A low groan sounded, and Ben felt the air stir as Adrian moved.

No, don't go!

Next thing he heard was stones crunching underfoot as Adrian left the building. *Damn. Double damn.* Ben lifted himself up onto his elbow and pummeled the bed. Some bird outside started chirping. It sounded happy. He wasn't. Turning over, he released the moans that had been piling up inside. After a couple of quick strokes, he came, managing to catch most of the semen in his hand; an inspired load if ever there was one. As he lay idly massaging his softening cock, he tried to make sense of the whole incident.

Jerking off didn't solve much. By the time Ben dragged himself out of the bed, he was hard again. The cold shower Adrian's Pop had apologized for provided the perfect solution.

THE call of the bird greeted Adrian when he left the guesthouse. He searched around for a stone, then caught sight of his grandfather approaching. Pop glanced up at the culprit and grinned. He hadn't forgotten either.

"Come check the vines with me."

They walked silently, side by side, Adrian's thoughts still filled with the image of Ben asleep on the bed. In some ways, he regretted walking away; in others, he didn't. The setting was right. If he was casting the character, someone like Ben would be perfect. But the timing was wrong. He needed to sort out his life first. Work out what he wanted. Make it possible.

Pop didn't seem perturbed by his lack of conversation, making a snip here and a cut there, trimming back errant vines that escaped the confines of the canopy. Even they were meant to conform. After a while, Adrian's body and heart settled back into their normal, restricted state. "How have you been?" he asked his grandfather. "Is your hip troubling you?"

"No, it's only bad when it rains." Pop stopped and turned to face him. "Can you come up again at picking time?"

"I'll see if I can get away."

"You can't keep tearing yourself in two."

"Yet, you keep trying to pull me up here." Adrian shook his head at the irony of it all.

"Here is good for you," his grandfather said simply.

Adrian scuffed his loafer against the ground. The fine dust clung to the brown surface.

Pop picked up some dirt and let it run through his fingers. "You are like this soil: dry. The vines can't live without water, and you can't live without love. Some people need more than others, like some varieties of grape need more water than others. You are trying to be someone you are not."

Another way of saying what Nonna had said. "I've been doing alright until now."

"Nonsense. You arrive exhausted. Your eyes are dull, and there is no spring in your step. By the time you leave, you are a different man."

"Everyone benefits from time away."

Pop snorted. "It's not like you sit for a weekend and do nothing. You don't stop working when you are here. Helping me spray the weeds, pruning... but you are like a vine that grows without nourishment. You give of yourself all the time, but get nothing back in return. Your soil is becoming depleted. Each year you will produce a crop, but each year they will be smaller and drier."

The frustration Adrian had started the day with threatened to spill out as anger. "How many times do I have to tell you? I can't just pull up my roots and live here."

Pop ran more soil through his fingers. "After we run our petiole analysis, we add back to the earth the things it is missing. What you lack is love. I was overjoyed when you said you were bringing someone with you. I thought, at last he has laid Antonio to rest."

"I loved him." Adrian crossed his arms over his chest, battling to keep the tears away.

"I know you did, but you can't grieve for him forever. Grieving is a normal process that has an end. Once it does, it's healthy and good for life to reassert itself. You must find extra nourishment from somewhere, or you will wither away." He brushed the remaining dust off his hands.

Adrian remained silent, gritting his teeth.

Pop took one glance at his locked jaw and sighed. "I could not have survived without my Maria. You must find someone else. What about the lad you brought with you? That's the sort of person you need. Someone to remind you that you are still young."

Adrian unclenched his fists and rubbed the back of his neck. A lecture about love was the last thing he needed, as was the reminder of who and what had caused the buildup of emotions that threatened to spill over. "Ben?" He laughed bitterly. "He's Jason's boyfriend."

AFTER his cold shower, Ben dressed and walked onto the deck to breathe in the clean country air. Voices drifted up the hill, too far away to distinguish the words. He saw Adrian walking with his grandfather, studying the rows of vines that stretched across the slope. Adrian's bare chest glistened under the heat of the morning sun. He was wearing cutoffs, and the pale blue denim barely hid his butt. Nice.

Even though Ben wouldn't have minded a closer view, he didn't want to intrude, so he wandered into the cool of the kitchen to watch Adrian's grandma prepare breakfast. He offered to help, but she shooed him away, saying he was a guest.

When Adrian finally joined them, he acted as if nothing had happened. Well, in a way nothing had. Not a blink or furtive glance betrayed any curiosity on Adrian's part. Ben watched for all the usual clues to show he was interested in him as something more than an employee. But nothing. Either the man should win an Oscar, or this morning's episode was a dream brought on by all the fantasies Adrian starred in.

Anyway, Ben had more important things to think about. He had a presentation to make in front of a whole bunch of people.

On the drive south, he didn't fall asleep or think about sex once. Pretty good going, eh? Instead, he revised his notes until he knew them by heart. Adrian helped with the speech, and by the time they arrived, Ben was good to go.

The presentation worked like a dream. Adrian's intro was as professional and smooth as Ben had anticipated, and the DVD had the audience in stitches. Afterward, everyone congratulated them, and Ben walked around on a high for the rest of the day.

There were lots of attractive women among the delegates, so he circulated as much as possible, chatting to them, and using every bit of charm he possessed, hoping to find one to replace Laurel. He even managed to maneuver a couple of candidates across to meet Adrian, but after a while, someone would come along and claim them, or they'd drift off. Only one stayed around. According to the card she handed him, her name was Evelyn. She and Adrian laughed and chatted for ages. Her face was warm and friendly. She'd make a much better match than Laurel, but when he checked her hand, he saw she was married. Typical.

ADRIAN watched Ben do his usual party trick, chatting to everyone, even though he didn't know a soul there. He laughed to himself when Ben walked up with yet another female in tow. This would be the third he'd brought over; all with some flimsy excuse about something he thought they might have in common.

"Adrian, I was talking to...." Ben surreptitiously checked the name on his card. "Evelyn, and she said that she wanted to talk to you about the presentation."

Before Adrian could tell Ben who she was, he was off again.

"Where did you find him?" Evelyn's husky voice warmed him as much as her arm did as it wound around his waist. Adrian hadn't seen much of her lately, and found he really missed her. She was the sister he'd never had.

"He wandered in from the wilds of Minnesota a year ago."

"Hm, nice."

"Yes, he is." *Very nice.*

"He did a good job with the presentation."

One thing Adrian could always count on was that if Evelyn said something, she meant it. A refreshing change. "He's a natural behind the camera."

"You're a natural in front." She glanced slyly at Adrian. "But I always knew you were a good actor. The purple dress suited you, and the yellow boa I contributed was a nice touch."

"It was only a rear shot—do you think anyone recognized me?"

"How much is it worth to keep me quiet?" She laughed as Adrian stiffened. "Relax, you should know me better than that by now. Though there is something I might ask you for one day." She smiled and jabbed him lightly on the arm. "Oh, lighten up, Adrian. Anyway, I was surprised that my shoes fit you." She scanned his feet critically. "Have you got small feet, or are mine humungous?" She lifted up first one, then the other. "Rather a sobering thought that I could share my shoes with a man."

She wasn't exactly small. Definitely the butch one of the pair. Her partner, Liz, was dainty and feminine. "Nah, I've got small feet. Not that I have any ambition to borrow yours again. That was definitely a once-in-a-lifetime thing." Adrian shuddered.

"Well, it really brought the house down."

Adrian's laugh sounded a bit forced. Hopefully, the audience hadn't realized the same person was in each segment. From a drag queen whose high heels led to the risk of ankle injury, then an old man with an inflamed prostate, followed by a bag lady in a blue dress suffering from untreated thyroid problems, the assorted characters illustrated stereotypes with different insurance risks, finishing with the Adam Lambert look-alike who brought the house down. In hindsight, Adrian marveled at the way Ben had managed to persuade him to play them all. Even Evelyn hadn't realized the last one was him.

Now Ben was chatting to a group of people his own age. *Fellow students?* Jason had never mentioned anything about Ben having any other friends. They looked more the typical actuary type—studious, serious. Ben's more rugged earthiness made a stark contrast. As if he was aware he was under scrutiny, Ben glanced in their direction and then returned to his discussion, his face even more animated than before.

Evelyn snagged another glass of wine from a passing waiter as Adrian took a sip of his orange juice. They still had the drive back to San Francisco, so he'd been watching his intake.

"I noticed you weren't here for the morning sessions," she said.

Adrian sighed, glad for something to divert him from the hollow feeling that sprang into his gut when he saw Ben so obviously enjoying the company of younger people. "I wasn't in the mood to hear more bitching about Obama's proposed changes to the industry. It's not the end of the world."

Evelyn laughed. "Ever the optimist."

Adrian stiffened and tore his eyes away from Ben. "It's nothing to do with optimism. The country desperately needs change, too many people don't have access to basic health care."

"Hard to accomplish in the current economic climate."

"We need major reforms, not tinkering at the edges."

"People are scared of radical change." She wasn't checking out Ben any more, she was smiling at him. "Even though some people need it."

"What do you mean?"

Her smile softened. "The world didn't fall apart when Liz and I got together, Adrian."

"You know I can't."

"It's not the closet you're afraid of coming out of, it's making yourself vulnerable again."

She was another person who knew about Antonio. They'd spent many an evening drinking coffee at her place after attending a function together. Adrian swallowed. First Pop and now Evelyn. But was his reluctance really fear? He'd never thought about it that way. "How's Liz?" he said to change the subject.

"Getting broody." Evelyn laughed. "By the way, there was a reporter here earlier, looking for you."

A journalist was the last person Adrian wanted to speak to at this point in time. The longer he could keep work and the reality of his life at bay, the better. Ben's face lit up when he suggested they go somewhere to eat.

IN LESS than an hour, the maître d' was welcoming them inside the popular restaurant located not far from the conference venue. "How are you this evening, Mr. Sutherland?"

"Fine, Nicolas. Thanks for finding us a table at such short notice."

"It's good to see you again. How's your father?"

"Fighting fit." They both shared a laugh. Adrian took his seat and accepted the wine list. "Good to see that business is still brisk."

"It's not as busy as we'd like, but not bad considering the circumstances." Nicolas made sure Ben had everything he wanted, then, with a friendly nod, he left them alone.

Adrian knew he'd made a huge mistake as soon as Ben sat down, his unease in the formal atmosphere plainly apparent. What was he trying to do, impress the young man? Show him how clever he was, getting them into a world-famous restaurant at such short notice? It was his father's name that opened doors like this, not his. Ben hadn't even heard of the place.

A couple of people nodded at him when they walked past, cronies of his father's, no doubt, assessing Ben, trying to work out if he was related to anyone they knew. But Ben himself was drawing some admiring glances. Adrian felt like saying, *He looks even better with no clothes on.*

Ben was totally oblivious to all this, of course, and Adrian didn't want to spoil his evening by telling him. To say the young man was uncomfortable with his surroundings was an understatement. He was a fish out of water.

BEN glanced around. When Adrian made the suggestion to eat somewhere else, he hadn't expected anything like this: starched white tablecloths, red velvet-covered chairs. Real classy. Even though they'd been alone before, this was different somehow. They were surrounded by people and dining together, almost like a date.

An uncomfortable silence descended as Ben watched Adrian swirl some white wine around in his glass and take a sniff. He didn't feel like talking about football again, and Adrian had heard all about his family last night. He sighed and turned his attention back to the menu. *What the hell are Ficoide Glaciale or Lentils du Puys?* They should have picked up some takeout and shared it in the car somewhere, preferably in a secluded lane. A nice, dark secluded lane. Then they could feed each other bites of pizza and let the stringy bits of cheese link them together.

The waiter approached and took their order. Ben happily let Adrian choose. His boss was quiet again afterward. As soon as the waiter left them alone, Ben said, "Hey, thanks for taking me to meet your grandparents."

Adrian looked up and gave one of his slow, sexy smiles. "My pleasure, Ben."

"Do you get to see them very often?"

Adrian shook his head, and the smile disappeared. He dropped his gaze to his glass, and when he answered his voice was soft, reflective. "Not as often as I'd like to, or should."

As Adrian was their sole surviving relative, Ben could understand that comment. Before they left, his grandma had hugged Adrian tightly, as if she feared she'd never see him again. When you got to their age,

144

the chance of that was real. They would want him to have children, carry on the family tradition. Ben amused himself for a while, picturing Laurel tripping around the vines in her stiletto heels, complaining that picking the grapes chipped her fingernails.

"Your grandma said you should take over the vineyard. Would you like to?"

Adrian took a sip of wine before speaking. "When I was younger, I did. Before my mother died, she nearly convinced my father to let me study to be a *vigneron*."

"How *did* she die?" Ben asked.

"Breast cancer at thirty-six."

Ben couldn't stop himself. He reached out and covered Adrian's hand. As soon he did, Adrian pulled his hand away and placed it on his lap.

IT HAD taken every bit of Adrian's resolve to drag his hand away. Ben's sign of comfort, of compassion, felt like a touch of intimacy to him.

Look but don't touch. He drilled the mantra into his brain again. Being together at the conference had reminded him that the whole employer/employee relationship was a minefield he didn't wish to cross. Even if he admitted he was gay, while Ben worked for SSFI, Adrian couldn't do anything. It should have been easy because of the vow to his father and the fact Ben was Jason's lover, but it wasn't. Seeing Ben naked again had only etched the image deeper into his brain.

A couple nearby caught his attention. One man would have been fifty and the younger was in his twenties—much the same age as Ben. The older man glanced up and caught Adrian's gaze. As he did, his hand slid under the table and, judging by the youngster's blush, they were more than friends. A slow smile crossed the man's face as he held Adrian's gaze, and the young man's blush deepened. Adrian quickly swallowed more wine. The thought of teasing his dinner companion like that wasn't difficult. Ben looked downright miserable. He'd been on such a high at the conference and now this. Adrian was about to say, let's chuck it and go somewhere else, when the food arrived.

Mario's cooking was as superb as usual. Ben seemed to be enjoying his scampi, but Adrian had the impression more of his Nonna's lasagna would have suited Ben just as well. After they'd both had enough bites to dampen their hunger, Ben broke the silence. "Getting back to what we were talking about before."

Adrian's fork was poised halfway to his mouth as he waited for Ben to continue.

"Life can change, so why don't you at least learn what you can about the industry?"

Adrian snorted and replaced his fork on his plate. "I *have* been keeping up to date, as much as I can. I discuss things with Pop when I go up to visit." He stopped and gave a quick chuckle. "Argue might be a better word. But I can't exactly resign from SSF Insurance. From the time I was born, it's been my destiny."

"But if things were different, would it be possible?" Ben's eyes, only inches away from his on the other side of the table, seemed to burn into him, scraping the surface layer away, seeking out the truth.

"Possible…." Adrian took a deep breath. "But not easy. It would require a hefty infusion of capital. Like most people, the majority of my money is tied up in property or shares, and it's not a good time to sell either. But so much work needs to be done to bring the vineyard up to scratch: new electricity, modern plumbing." He smiled at Ben, surprised to see a faint flush steal over his face. "For starters, the guesthouse would need hot water before I could live there. I hate cold showers."

The color in Ben's face deepened further as the young man shifted in his seat, bringing their knees into contact. Immediately, an image of the dark sheet molding to those long legs flooded Adrian's mind. He felt a swelling at his groin and had to fiddle with the bread to stop himself from reaching down and running his palm over his crotch, or better still reaching under the table to touch Ben's thigh, just like the older man had at the other table. He didn't move his leg though. It had been too long since he'd been able to have that sort of intimate touch.

Ben's conversation about the vineyard helped to distract him. Adrian had gone over the subject with himself so many times, he managed to keep up his end without too much effort. He broke the piece of bread he'd been fingering and took a bite before continuing. "You're a numbers man, Ben. You've seen how small the vineyard is. In these days of multinational wine companies, how could I compete? The vines are old—they need to be replaced with a different variety, one that appeals to the boutique wine market. Or, if we don't do that, we have to introduce other things to create that difference: stop using pesticides for example and gain organic certification. Believe it or not, it's expensive going green." Adrian took a breath and sighed. "Anyway, it's probably too late now." Even to his own ears, his voice sounded tired and jaded.

"Bullshit." The fire in Ben's immediate reply made him look up, the bread falling from nerveless fingers. You're only in your thirties." Ben's eyes flashed as he spoke. "How old are your grandparents? Seventy, eighty? You've got the majority of your life ahead of you. It's never too late."

Oh, the impulsive certainty of youth. Adrian stared at the passion in Ben's eyes for a second before dragging his gaze back to his dinner.

Normally, he would have had some witty response to make to Ben's last comment, but everything he tried to say felt forced, unnatural. He kept looking at Ben's suit, wishing he could peel it off and touch the raw strength underneath. At twenty-four, the young man was still growing into his body. Even his facial features hadn't fully matured, but there were glimpses of the man he would become when they did.

"Adrian Sutherland, just the man I wanted to see."

Adrian started at the interruption and automatically grabbed his table napkin when he stood, preventing it from falling to the floor. Fortunately, the folds disguised his erection as he accepted the handshake. This was probably the guy Evelyn had warned him about. The hair on the back of his neck rose. "Damien...." Adrian struggled to remember the man's last name. It wasn't the one he was blogging under. As soon as he could, he released his grip and rubbed his hand on the napkin.

147

"Stanton will do. That's the name I go by nowadays."

The reporter glanced at Ben, obviously waiting for an introduction.

Adrian grudgingly complied. "Ben Dutoit, one of the firm's actuaries."

Ben stood awkwardly, shook the proffered hand, and immediately sat down again. Adrian remained standing.

The reporter's attention flicked between the two of them, no doubt trying to assess their relationship. "Your boss and I go way back," he said to Ben before smiling at Adrian, but the expression in his eyes didn't change. "Amsterdam, wasn't it? Eight years ago?"

Adrian nodded warily; Antonio had been with him at the time.

The man turned back to address Ben. "I've been trying to pin your boss down for an interview for ages."

Adrian stiffened. From his words, you'd think everything was rosy, but Damien Stanton had the capacity to destroy everything if he decided to out him. Since his return to the States, Adrian had managed to avoid contact with most people he'd encountered in his travels; going prematurely gray actually helped with that. He hadn't flashed his surname about when he was overseas, and if acquaintances recognized the face, no one twigged that the man they'd seen in some of the seedier establishments in Europe was now a pillar of the establishment, and straight. They probably assumed he was an older relative of the man they had once met.

"This isn't the time, or the place, Damien." Adrian felt like telling the reporter to fuck off. He knew the tone of his voice said as much.

"I heard a rumor that SSFI is going to stop offering life insurance to people who are HIV positive." The issue was one of the reporter's favorites. He'd written an opinion piece in his blog, *Damien Dishes the Dirt,* back in January when a discrimination case had appeared before the courts in Olympia.

"Not while I'm with the company." Adrian's hands curled into fists. He wanted to grab the man by the neck and wring out the name of his source; his best guess was Laurel.

RED+BLUE

"So, you categorically deny that there are any changes in the wind."

"The answer to that is *No Comment*. Back off, Damien. I'm not going to discuss rumors or grant you an interview while I'm having a private meal."

The reporter handed over his card, leaning in as he did, speaking too softly for Ben to hear. "I was sorry to hear about Antonio." He glanced back at Ben, his gaze frankly appraising. The bastard probably assumed Ben was his closeted lover.

Anger at feeling scared replaced Adrian's instinctive fear of being outed. He was tempted to rip the card into shreds, but he didn't want to create a scene. He'd already attracted too much attention by remaining standing. "If there are any changes, you'll be the first to know."

The reporter inclined his head and smirked before walking away.

As Adrian resumed his seat, Ben asked, "Is everything okay?"

"Yes, fine," he answered.

BEN glared at the retreating back. He could tell Adrian hadn't wanted to speak to the man. For a moment, he'd been tempted to physically toss him out of the restaurant. He had no doubt that he could. If his boss wanted a bodyguard, he'd gladly volunteer.

After the reporter left, Adrian apologized for the interruption, and the conversation slipped back into the boring, impersonal claptrap people talk about over dinner: discussions about the food, the wine, and the restaurant.

Ben marveled at the contradiction his boss presented. At work, he couldn't imagine him anywhere else. Adrian seemed to live in the place, arriving early and leaving late, acting like a stuffy suit. But in the gym, in the car, and at the vineyard, he was relaxed, strong, casual, younger. Which was the real Adrian?

FIRST thing next morning, Ben returned Jason's call.

"How did the weekend go?" Jason's voice sounded a lot perkier when he answered, his breathing more normal.

"Fine. His grandparents thought I was you."

Jason laughed. "I used to talk to them on the phone when they called."

"They're nice."

"Yes, they are." Jason sounded amused.

After another restless night, Ben was still tired and frustrated. He'd spent the whole weekend with his boss, and if anything just got hornier than ever in his presence. Jason's comment before they left had been bugging him all weekend. "You know when you told me how you staged the scene in his hallway. Did you say you wanted to shake Adrian up?"

"Yeah." Jason drawled the word.

"I don't understand. Did you mean embarrass him?"

"No, shake him out of the closet."

Out of the closet? "No, not possible. The guy's straight!"

Jason started laughing. "Oh, Ben, you are so clueless sometimes. Turn on your gaydar—Adrian's not straight."

"No way!"

"I've been living with him, I should know." Jason sounded offended about being doubted.

"You aren't pulling my leg?"

"Well, straight guys don't usually watch gay porn, I caught him one night when I returned home early from a trip. He was drunk as a skunk."

Ben's immediate reaction was: *Which ones? Sean Cody or TitanMen?* "Drunk?"

"Yeah, before you arrived on the scene, he used to drink… a lot."

"But what about Laurel? Maybe he's bi?"

Jason snorted into the phone. "His beard. He's had a couple of them."

"Does *she* know he's gay?"

"Not sure. If she does, she must have him by the short and curlies."

A big brass gong sounded in Ben's head. *Duh. You* should *have wiggled your butt yesterday.* He rose to his feet and took a couple of turns around the room. What other clues had he missed? The weird glances Adrian's Nonna and Pop sent his way, for starters. None of the usual signals, though. No package checking. No significant looks. *He said he could act; that proves it!!*

"Jason, I've known you for over a year. Why didn't you ever let on?"

"He asked me not to tell anyone. Said if the truth came out, there'd be hell to pay."

"So why tell me now?"

"I've been trying to persuade the guy to come out of the closet for five years."

"To fuck him, you mean?"

"Yes. No. It's not as simple as that, Ben." Jason didn't say anything for a while. "I'm worried about him. In a way, Adrian was the big brother I never had. I wanted him to respect me as much as I respected him. The only respect I ever got was for bringing in new business."

"Weird way to show it, by having sex in front of him."

"As I said, I wanted to shake him up a bit, make him jealous of what he was missing. He thinks the sun shines out of your ass." The bitterness in Jason's voice was unmistakable.

"Are you sure he doesn't have a secret boyfriend on the side?"

"Not that I know of. The guy's a monk. He must have an awfully well-developed JO hand. There's some hidden secret in his past that he refuses to talk about. Whatever it is, it's eating him up."

Ben thought back over the weekend, so many wasted opportunities. "Jason, you only ever call me when you want something. What is it?"

Jason was quiet for a long time, then he sighed. "Nothing for me. I just want you to keep an eye on him. Vincent says Adrian has issues with his father that need to be resolved. He's trying to win his affection by burying himself so deep in the closet he's nearly in Narnia."

If Adrian had resisted Jason, Ben didn't stand much chance. Adrian had been in the room with him while he was naked, and he hadn't even poked a toe out.

ADRIAN'S house felt dark and empty when he walked inside. He switched on the living room light and immediately wished he hadn't. After coping with the glare of oncoming traffic, streetlights, and the clash and clamor of civilization, the last thing he needed was the twinkling light of a crystal chandelier. The subdued glow from the lamp on the side table was a much better alternative.

After dropping his bag, he peeled off the suit jacket, and threw it over the back of one of the antique chairs his father had urged him to buy. A good investment, he had said. Investment for what? You couldn't sell them, at least not in today's market. They were too uncomfortable to sit on for long, and Adrian was always worried they'd break.

Instead, he perched on the edge of another more practical chair and unlaced his shoes. Ferragamo. Armani. What had Ben once asked him? Something about whether he only wore things that were designer or expensive? Isn't that what you did? *The clothes maketh the man* was his father's motto. A message to everyone that you were successful; you had it made.

The bottle of Jack Daniels was nearly full. Good. Adrian grabbed a glass and settled onto the sofa. He swirled the first sip in his mouth, savoring the taste. What a weekend. It was late, but he knew from experience sleep would be a long time coming. Too many images and incidents swirled in his brain. Highs, lows, and everywhere in between.

He dragged off his tie. If only Laurel were here. He felt like putting it over her head and yanking the damn thing tight. How dare she pull a stunt like that with the room booking? What was she doing? Trying to force him into marriage? And then the hints about the policy changes she must have made somewhere. Adrian knew the way the spin doctors worked: throw out a rumor, test the water, gauge the strength of the opposition, twist the angle if needed so that when the announcement came, it was old news.

The next gulp of liquid burnt all the way down. Hopefully, he had enough food in his stomach, otherwise there would be hell to pay later. He undid a few shirt buttons and slid off his belt.

The only thing breaking the silence was the tick of the antique grandfather clock counting off the hours of his life. *Tick.* One less second to live. *Tock.* And another one gone. Was that all his life had become now? A series of wasted opportunities?

First, the problem at the hotel, then his grandfather pointing out what he lacked. *Love!* As if he didn't know that. Then the frustration of trying to keep his hands off Ben. Was that all the young man was? An opportunity?

Adrian took another long drink. Should he put on a DVD? Watch some more porn? He sat for a while, sipping on the Jack, wondering why he didn't feel like it. It wasn't just their phoniness; if he needed something more real, he could always rescue his laptop out of his bag and watch Xtube. But even that lacked appeal. No, what he wanted was a person. Someone to sit beside and touch him. Someone who could make *him* feel real.

Even though he hadn't been totally involved in the conversation with Ben in the restaurant, he had felt alive then. Ben wasn't talking for the sake of it. He really wanted to know why he couldn't take over the winery, calling him on the old excuse of being too old. *Never too late.* Adrian took another long draught and closed his eyes.

The loud jangle of a telephone jerked him into full consciousness. He fumbled for the handset.

"Good, you're up."

Adrian rubbed his forehead and peered at the clock. "Dad? What's wrong?"

Outside, the sun did its best to penetrate a typical morning mist. Adrian's brain wasn't having much better luck with the fog in his head.

"Nothing. I just wanted to speak to you before you went to work."

Adrian groaned and stared at the nearly empty bottle. No wonder he felt so lousy. Acidic bile heaved in his stomach. He bit his lips together to stop it escaping. Wrong move. It tasted vile going back down.

"Are you alright, son?"

Adrian snorted. "Yeah. Rough night."

The room was quiet for a while; each tick of the clock reverberated against his skull.

"I had a call from Laurel yesterday."

The words shone like a fog lamp through the murk in Adrian's brain. Bile threatened to erupt again. This time his throat burned.

"What did she want?"

"She said you didn't spend the evening at the conference hotel."

"How did she know that?" Adrian rubbed the back of his neck. He needed a glass of water, and he needed it bad. The kitchen was too far away though.

"She called the hotel, and they said you canceled the room booking."

Adrian's hand shook as he sloshed more liquor into the glass. *Let's see if hair of the dog works.* He took a swig. The liquor met the next wave of nausea coming up. Luckily, it won, giving him a few more seconds of reprieve. "Fuck Laurel," he rasped out.

"Language, son." The horror in his father's voice wasn't faked. His dutiful son had never sworn at him before. As a teenager, Adrian wouldn't have dared.

"I've had it up to here with that bitch." He tried to stop his words slurring, but he failed. Miserably.

"Are you drunk?"

Adrian grunted a laugh. "Put it this way, if I drove to work, I'd probably cop a DUI."

"Son, I'm worried about you. When I came out for the meeting last week, I noticed you are grayer than ever."

"Thanks a lot, Dad. You just made my day."

"No, I mean it. I *am* worried about you." There was sincerity in his father's voice, but underlying that was something else. Adrian was too tired to work it out though.

"I'm fine," he muttered. He could be a good liar too.

"You've been working too hard. You need to get away for a while."

"Yeah, Dad, and who will look after the office while I'm gone?"

"I can."

"But you just got home again."

"I'll be fine. There's life in the old boy yet." The ironic thing was that the main reason Adrian had agreed to his father's demand to return to the States was the great job he had done convincing Adrian he was at death's door after the heart attack. That must be where his acting skills came from. "When did you last have some time off?"

First he starts talking to me about where I slept, and now he wants me to go on a vacation? "I've been up at the vineyard a couple of times, helping out, and then I came over and spent time with you when Lindy and Bill went on their cruise."

"Why don't you go on one too? The others were all work, no play." A cruise, his father's cure-all for everything.

"Take Laurel," his father added.

"That's never going to happen, Dad."

"If you weren't at the hotel, where *did* you go?" The enthusiasm had vanished as quickly as it came, the old hard edge returning in his father's query.

Adrian exploded. "We stayed with Nonna and Pop." He swallowed the rest of the contents of his glass in one gulp. The burn on its way down added to the fire in his voice. "And for your information—not that it's any of your business—I didn't sleep with Ben, if that's what this is all about. I stayed in my old bedroom, and he slept in the guesthouse. Call Pop and check if you like."

His father didn't reply. Even after all these years, he was still scared of his father-in-law. "You really should take a break, son. I'll see you in a few days. A trip on a boat is what you need."

"Yeah, maybe you're right." Adrian hung up and just managed to reach the bathroom in time.

CHAPTER
+++
FOUR

THE next day, Adrian turned to Ben, who happened to be standing behind him in the elevator. "As soon as you're settled, could you come into my office, please?"

Without waiting for an answer, he strode ahead, threw his briefcase into the corner, yanked down his tie, and ran his fingers across his scalp. By the time he was seated, Ben was standing in front of his desk, his face a mixture of apprehension and concern.

"Are you okay, Adrian?… I mean, Mr. Sutherland?"

"Sit, sit." Adrian waved at the chair and waited until Ben was comfortable. "I need your help… again."

"What's the matter?"

Adrian took a deep breath. "I've decided to take some leave." He picked up a pen and started fiddling with it; a much easier option than gazing into the blue eyes of the young man opposite. "You mentioned that one of your brothers owns a company that runs guided tours into the Minnesota lakes area. Is that right?"

"Yes—Andrew." Ben's smile eased some of the tension in the room. "Why?"

"When I checked out a few sites on the Internet, no one had any trips available. Too late in the season, apparently."

"You wanna go canoeing?"

The shock in the young man's reply made Adrian laugh. "You're a better salesman than you realize; maybe your talents are being wasted in the actuarial department." Ben's open-mouthed surprise made him laugh again. "That was a joke, Ben. But seriously, yes, I've decided I need a week off so I can escape from the rat race. Unfortunately, it would have to be before the end of September. Any chance you could pull some strings?"

The chair nearly fell over as Ben surged to his feet. "Leave it to me."

Adrian flinched as the door banged on Ben's way out. Even after taking a rare sick day, his head hadn't recovered from his drinking binge, nor had his stomach. He should have checked himself into a health resort instead of this harebrained scheme. His father thought he was going on a cruise. "If you aren't going to settle down with Laurel," had been his comment, "maybe you will meet someone else there; the female to male ratio is always way out of proportion."

Adrian did check them out, even the gay ones, but mixing with a crowd of strangers held no appeal at all. A single guide he could cope with, perhaps one of the native Ojibwe who showed people around their tribal homeland.

He hadn't actually lied to his father and said he was going on a cruise; the mere mention of taking his advice regarding boats and water had been enough. The fact that his father would be looking after the business in his absence nearly made Adrian change his mind, but in the end, he decided it was worth the risk. He had to take a break some day, and if he didn't take it soon, he'd be the one to break.

He needed to get away and sort out what he was going to do for the rest of his life. He couldn't continue to hide his past forever. Sooner or later the truth would come out. That damn reporter had shown him how lucky he'd been until now.

He also needed to get away from the temptation posed by the young man who had just left his office. Every time he closed his eyes, Adrian saw Ben sprawled naked on the bed again.

Riding up in the elevator together had been pure torture. Vaguely, he'd been conscious of being surrounded by other people, but all his awareness had been centered on the young man standing behind him. The urge to lean back and rest against his strong body had nearly overwhelmed him.

Adrian fired up his computer and scanned his diary, checking to see what would need to be done over the next few days. After a quick rat-a-tat-tat, the door opened. Ben burst into the room and leaned over the desk in front of him.

"Hey, boss. We're on. Monday the seventh of September, or is that too soon?"

Adrian dragged his brain back into gear and tried to stop staring at the soft lips only inches away from his. One word registered like the clang of a guillotine falling. *We?*

"I contacted both Rob and Andrew. Rob has a cancellation, so there's a space in their permit schedule as long as we can fly in and start from Lac la Croix on Tuesday. Andrew will supply a boat and all the gear. It's only a four-day, three-night deal, with a night at Mom's before and after, but it's better than nothing. Hey, it's not what you know, it's who you know." Ben's smile lit up his face.

We again. "You're coming too?"

All the joy drained away as Ben straightened, his hands gripping the edge of the desk. "You said that if you ever went, you wanted me to be your guide."

It had actually been Ben's suggestion, but he did agree to it. Adrian swallowed. The hurt in Ben's eyes shot straight into him, twisting his gut into a tight knot. "I wasn't sure whether you were just saying that." The knot twisted even tighter at the affronted look he received in reply.

"I don't say things I don't mean."

Please, help me here. He wasn't sure who he was praying to. The God of Pity, perhaps, if there was such a thing. "Can you get the time off?" Perhaps Laurel would come to his aid. It was really her call when Ben could take his vacation.

Ben stood so stiff and tall that Adrian had to crane his neck to look up at him as he awaited the verdict. "I asked her. Told her I was owed two weeks, and that I wanted to take a week off to see my mother. I didn't mention where I was going or who with." A wary look crossed his eyes.

Adrian rubbed the back of his neck. He hadn't meant to hurt Ben's feelings, but his brain still reeled from the shock. This week was supposed to be time away, a chance to get the young man out of his system. "What did she say?"

"She said it would be fine."

Just when I needed her to be a bitch and refuse. Adrian nodded his head and said, "Good." His brain had been sliced in two by that falling blade.

Ben stood even straighter as he added quietly, "I'll give you a list of things to bring. The lighter the better, as we have to carry everything on our backs during the portages. I've checked the weather report. They're predicting a couple of weeks of Indian summer."

"Good," Adrian repeated, his head continuing to do a bobble-head doll impression.

THE "Fasten Seat Belt" sign clicked off. Ben glanced at Adrian out of the corner of his eye. Ever since he stepped into the cab for the ride to the airport, his boss had been quiet. Too quiet. Ben turned to stare out the plane window. Now they were airborne, he wondered again whether he had done the right thing. *Damn it, he had!* Despite taking a day off, the poor guy had looked exhausted when he arrived back at work after the conference. Ben should know—he'd been watching him like a hawk, trying to sort out whether Jason had been kidding about him being gay. All Ben saw was a man at the end of his tether. Adrian had even snapped at Millie once but then apologized profusely afterward.

As far as Ben could tell, he'd done nothing *but* work ever since they came back. In the week prior to their departure, Ben frequented the gym and used the rowing machine, getting his muscles ready, but Adrian shook his head whenever Ben suggested he join him, saying he had to ensure everything was under control.

A soft snuffle was the only warning he got as Adrian's head slumped against his shoulder. What should he do now? A faint snore sounded. Immediately, his own tiredness disappeared. He didn't move, couldn't move, even though part of him wanted to push up the armrest between them and hold Adrian tight. A flight attendant asked quietly if he needed a pillow. Ben waved her away. Adrian seemed comfortable enough.

All of a sudden, he became super conscious of Adrian the man, and not just Adrian his travelling companion or Adrian his boss: the proximity of their thighs, the hand lying on the armrest, his whole body. Ben eased back in his seat so they were more in line, every part touching that he could manage. He closed his eyes and breathed in deeply, absorbing the familiar smell that was Adrian into his lungs. Through the contact on his shoulder, he could tell they were now breathing in sync, perfectly in tune with each other.

What had he been thinking, though? When Adrian first mentioned the trip, Ben thought this would be a perfect opportunity to encourage him to come out of the closet. But what could he say? *"Excuse me, Adrian, Jason says you're gay. Wanna fuck?"* Ben snorted softly under his breath. He had tried variations on the theme, but they were all nearly as bad: *"There's no one around, and I don't scream as loud as Jason. Your secret's safe with me. Let's have sex."*

While packing, he stood beside the bag for twenty minutes, debating whether to bring the large packet of condoms and lube he bought especially. In the end, he didn't bring them. Reality had set in. There was no way he could make a move on his boss, no matter how much he wanted to. Anyway, he had made the vow not to fuck anyone until he received the all clear from his second round of test results, and they were still a month away.

At least in the future, no matter what happened over the next few days, he'd always have this moment to remember. His mind drifted back over all the other times they'd been alone together: the gym, their road trip, making the DVD.

In a way, he was getting to know the man better; but if he was gay, there was a whole side of him he had yet to discover. Why was he in the closet, for starters? And what about Jason's hint of some mystery in his past? Did he even want to know? Yes, he did. There was a connection between them. It wasn't merely a boss-employee relationship thing. There was more than that. Deep down, Ben knew there was more, wanted there to be more.

Adrian stirred and Ben tensed, thinking his companion was waking up, but his boss settled back again with a little snort as he drifted back into sleep.

Ben relaxed again. Hopefully when he got Adrian away from all the demands of work, he could get as close to him mentally as he now was physically.

When he felt Adrian stir in earnest, Ben pretended to be asleep too. Adrian muttered an almost inaudible apology and sat up straighter. Ben missed the contact. It felt so right.

As soon as Adrian was fully awake, Ben yawned and stretched, faking surprise that they'd gone so far and apologizing for falling asleep once again in his company.

Adrian blushed slightly, and said, "No problem."

The silence grew uncomfortable, with Adrian checking his wristwatch every five minutes.

To distract him, Ben told some local Minnesotan tech jokes. He started with: "What's a laptop?"

Adrian blinked and waited for the answer.

"Where the beer spills when you pass out."

Adrian chuckled and his face lost some of its tension. Ben dredged up some more. "What's a screen?"

A cocked eyebrow.

"The thing you shut during black fly season."

That went down better. "What's a screen saver?" Ben asked.

Adrian just shook his head and grinned.

"Duct tape for the torn window screen." Ben had lots more. One of his brothers would have had him in a headlock, by now, with a hand over his mouth, preventing him from telling any more, but Adrian was too polite for that.

By the time they changed planes in Minneapolis and switched to the Duluth flight, the ease they had in each other's company while making the DVD and during their trip to the vineyard had returned. Ben deliberately kept the conversation light, chatting about the NFL and another passion they had in common: ice hockey. At least talking about sports stopped Ben wondering about whether Adrian was cut or uncut. Whether the smooth skin he'd seen above waist level continued all the way down. What he tasted like. Most of the time, at any rate.

When they touched down, Ben piled all their things into Dave's Ranger. His third-oldest brother had left his pickup parked beside the police station with keys in the ignition and a note saying he'd pick it up from Mom's later. "Luckily, he's out on a case." Ben grinned at Adrian. "So that's one less brother to deal with."

Adrian's eyebrow raised when he got into the passenger seat. "Let me guess—you all drive one of these."

"Got it in one, mister."

Adrian snorted as Ben drove off.

"HOW you goin', little bro'?"

Andrew was a larger version of Ben. Adrian recognized him as soon as they walked into the outfitters. The same red hair, the same fair skin, and an even more pronounced drawl. He wasn't much taller, but definitely broader.

"Hi." Ben gave him a hug and then, leaving one arm around his shoulder, turned his eldest brother around to face Adrian. This was it, his first encounter with one of Ben's family. Something Adrian had been dreading ever since leaving San Francisco.

"This is Adrian."

Adrian detected a note of pride in Ben's voice when he made the introduction, but struggled to cover up a wince of pain when they shook hands. *Is he testing me?* A touch of hostility had replaced Ben's brother's initial welcoming smile, but disappeared almost immediately.

"Did you manage to get everything I requested?" Ben seemed oblivious to the underlying tension in the greeting.

"Request. Seemed more like a demand to me." Andrew casually cuffed his younger brother across the back of his head. Ben grinned and wandered over to one of the displays.

Judging by the fond look in Andrew's gaze, Ben could demand anything, and his brother would bend over backward to supply it.

"Are we taking the Grumman?" Ben was poking his fingers into the different life jackets he'd put aside, laying them flat and bouncing on them.

"Nah, it's too heavy. When you get to Lac la Croix, there'll be a brand new Kevlar canoe waiting. Make sure it comes back without too

162

many dings, eh. Carry it around the rapids. With this dry spell we've been having, there isn't much water in them."

Adrian smothered a grin at their interaction: typical brotherly offhand affection.

Ben checked through the gathered bundles of equipment and food, and set a few aside, muttering under his breath as he did so. Adrian watched his brother's face. The similar blue eyes narrowed more with each decision Ben made, but he kept silent. Sensing he was being watched, Andrew glanced up, caught Adrian's gaze, and blushed. *Another thing in common.*

"Why aren't you taking both tents?" Andrew eventually asked as Ben picked up one of the bags and stashed it back with the others in the storage bay.

"I said I only wanted one in the e-mail."

"You won't both fit into that one." Andrew gestured at the green bag left on the pile.

"I'm taking my own as well," Ben muttered and crouched back down over the gear.

"That old thing? These new ones are smaller and much lighter." Adrian could almost feel Andrew's gaze assessing him. He had deliberately packed his most basic clothes. Things he wore when helping his Pop, but he still felt the other man had pegged him as a weak city slicker.

"He'll be able to carry them both." Ben's defensive tone made Adrian stand that little bit taller and square his shoulders.

Andrew sniffed. "Are you sure?"

Adrian caught the glance of appeal Ben threw his way and said, "If Ben thinks I can handle the pack, I should be fine. He knows how much weight I lift in the gym." Adrian gave Ben a smile of encouragement and was rewarded by a quick grin in return. Ben's decision to separate some more equipment out of the pile prompted another query from his brother. "Aren't you going to do any fishing?"

"I don't need new stuff. There's enough gear at home."

"You always were a stubborn young brat."

Ben switched over the life jackets as well, selecting two older, bulkier versions from the bottom of the pile.

"Oh, come on, now you're being crazy." Andrew's impatience with his younger sibling was threatening to boil over.

Ben grinned as he spread them out. "These can double as seats; those new ones are fine for paddling, but that's all." He stood and faced his brother, toe-to-toe.

Adrian smirked at the sight of the young buck challenging the old stag. Andrew noticed his reaction, glancing at him briefly before turning his attention back to Ben.

"Seems you've made up your mind. I'd just be wasting my breath."

"Yup." Ben gave him a hug. "You know I love ya, Andy, and I do appreciate all you've done, but I have my reasons."

There hadn't been any hesitation in his choices, either. Ben knew what he wanted to do and did it. No doubts. Impressive. Adrian helped the young man carry the equipment out of the shop. Just before they drove away, Andrew called out, "Say hi to Mom for me."

It was nearly dark by the time they arrived. Ben's mother was cleaning down the wheel in her pottery studio. She was gorgeous. Slim, with salt-and-pepper hair cut short for convenience, not fashion. She possessed an inner beauty that didn't need makeup. The bones of her face were fine, delicate, nothing like Ben and his brother. Adrian wasn't sure what he'd expected—another clone maybe.

"Hey, Mom." Ben's voice broke slightly as he picked her up in a bear hug before setting her down.

She brushed her hair aside with the back of her hands. "Careful, you big lummox, what have you been eating? I'm sure you're twice as big as you were at Christmas time."

The twinkle in her blue eyes was a carbon copy of Ben and Andrew's. When Ben finally released her and introduced her to Adrian as his mother, she wiped a tear away with the back of her hand and extended it for him to shake. "Call me Cathie if you don't want to call me Mom." She flashed an exasperated sigh at her son and received an unrepentant grin back. "Thanks for bringing my boy home." The warm welcome of her smile to Adrian contradicted the cold wetness of her grip.

As soon as she realized what she had done, she blushed. "Sorry for the dirty hands," she added as she wiped them on her overalls.

Judging by the pale-cream stains on the material, she'd done that more than once today.

"It's fine. We should have let you clean up first."

"Anyway, he didn't bring me. I brought him." Ben's cheeky grin erupted.

While Ben asked nonstop questions about what his brothers were up to, Adrian wandered around her studio. Cathie Dutoit wasn't just a potter; she was an artist. Her completed pieces all had a deceptively simple grace and symmetry about them. He especially admired the variations of blue she had achieved in her glazes, ranging from the cool turquoise of a glacier lake to the deep indigo of unfathomable water.

Inside the house itself, each piece of furniture or decoration looked like it belonged: treasured and loved. Not discarded because it had gone out of fashion or didn't match the latest purchase. Unusually shaped pieces of bleached driftwood and arrangements of dried leaves made a stark contrast to the thousands of dollars spent on fresh hothouse flowers at his father's residence. Instead of the starkness of bare stainless steel, her refrigerator was covered with children's drawings. American Primitive art at its best.

Before they sat down to eat dinner, Ben sprawled on the sofa and told his mother about his visit to the vineyard. It was interesting to see the trip from the young man's perspective. Ben saw the potential: how good the guest house would be once it had decent plumbing, how much energy and life Adrian's grandparents exhibited despite their age. He also repeated the changes Adrian had told him he wanted to make to the vineyard, word for word.

Without drawing a breath, Ben went on to tell his mother about the DVD and the conference. Adrian relaxed back in the comfy sofa, crossed his ankle over his knee, and enjoyed the performance. Every now and then Ben's mother would glance at him with raised eyebrows, especially when Ben described how he'd been persuaded to portray the different characters.

When Ben started on a description of the restaurant, she put her hands over her ears and laughed. "You haven't changed. Give Adrian a turn. The poor man hasn't had a chance to get a word in edgewise."

Adrian laughed and shook his head. "His stories are much more interesting than mine." After a while, he tuned out and took delight in watching the younger man interact with his mother. He laughed inside as Ben skillfully deflected her questions about what he got up to after work finished, sparing her the details of the Castro club scene he'd heard from Jason.

Almost as if she was telepathic, Cathie asked, "And what about your friend, Jason? You used to mention him a lot in your letters. How is he?"

Adrian's ears pricked up. How was Ben going to answer this one? Would he mention the HIV and the risk to himself?

Ben stole a glance his way before facing his mother again. "Aaah… he's gone back to live with his parents on Long Island."

"Oh, that's a shame. I had the feeling the two of you had a thing going there for a while."

The blush on Ben's face grew even redder. Adrian was about to step in and rescue him when Ben said, "He's got a new boyfriend."

A weird fluttering began in the pit of Adrian's stomach, and he only vaguely heard Ben's story about how Jason was more interested in a guy called Vincent now.

"Oh, that's a shame. Never mind, no doubt you'll meet someone else."

Ben's quick, sidelong glance in his direction started Adrian's pulse beating twice as fast. All sorts of questions hammered in his brain. When, how, why? The most important thing, though, was that Ben didn't seem unhappy.

"Anyway, Mom, how are the pottery classes going?"

The conversation shifted, and tearing his speculation away from what Ben's news meant, Adrian added his sincere compliments. Her knowledge and enthusiasm filled the remaining hours of the evening.

Once dinner was cleared away, she started showing Adrian the family photos. The large number of brothers, cousins, and grandchildren soon became a blur.

"You sure you want to look at those?"

Adrian gave a quick nod. He wanted to discover what had made Ben the well-adjusted and confident man he was today.

Ben gave a big yawn and stretched. "Okay, while you're doing that, I'll dig out the fishing gear and my tent."

As soon as her son left the room, Cathie turned and placed her hand on Adrian's arm. "Is he alright?"

Adrian swallowed. *What could he say?* Before they left, Ben had made him promise that he wouldn't divulge anything about the threat to his health. Not that Adrian would have anyway, as that would have been way out of line, but she had, possibly, detected a degree of nervousness mixed with Ben's excitement at being back in his home territory.

Adrian trapped her hand with his and rubbed it, trying to hide his own fear that Jason had passed on his infection to Ben. "I'm keeping an eye on him. If there's ever a serious problem, I'll make sure he tells you."

She bit her bottom lip and tried to smile. "I worry too much." She studied his face for a minute. "His brothers didn't want him to leave, but he wasn't happy. It was as if he was searching for something, or someone, and knew he wouldn't find it or them here." She shook her head slightly as if her words didn't really reflect the whole story.

Adrian patted her hand again. "I'll look after him." *Good one, Adrian—now you're the one making it sound like Ben is a kid who needs to be taken care of.* He laughed. "As much as he'll let me, at any rate."

Her face cleared at his words, and a snort of laughter escaped. "You *do* know him well." Heavy footsteps sounded. She sniffed and grabbed another album from the pile. A wicked grin crossed her face as she opened it. "You should have seen how many freckles he had when he was younger."

"Wow, no time for that." Ben grabbed the book out of her hand and replaced them all on the shelf. "I found everything we need. We've got an early start tomorrow—time for bed."

Adrian picked up his bag and followed Ben down a short hallway. Caught unawares, he almost collided with the young man when he stopped to open one of the doors.

Ben turned to face him. Neither moved. They were standing so close, their chests nearly touched. Adrian's throat felt dry as he swallowed. Every brain cell screamed at him to step back, break the contact, but his feet refused to move. He raised his eyes slowly, expecting to see the lighthearted grin that usually covered the younger man's face. Instead, the blue eyes blazed with an intensity he hadn't seen there before. *Oh, fuck.* All the air escaped out of his lungs. *Desire.* He could have coped with anything but that. His body responded immediately, his cock trying to bridge the gap between them. Adrian closed his eyes and took a deep breath, willing his body to behave, but it wouldn't listen. Another swallow didn't make much difference. It was like they were waiting for outside direction. Someone to break the spell that froze them to the spot. One of them had to move.

BEN took a step back so he was hard against the open doorway. "This… is… ah… Chris's old room. You'll be sleeping here tonight." He cringed as his laugh betrayed his nervousness. "My bedroom is next door." He jerked his head back, not taking his eyes off Adrian's face.

They say you can always tell by the eyes. If that was the case, then Jason was right. There was no way he had interpreted that look wrongly. Adrian wanted him as much as he wanted Adrian. His simple exercise in lustful fantasies had taken another turn. One where those fantasies might come true.

Ben groaned inside and forced himself to smile. "I need to go through all your clothes." Oh, shit. His brain wasn't working properly; that came out all wrong. He turned and had to force himself not to run as he quickly crossed the short space to his room and found what he was looking for in one of the cupboards. By the time he returned, Adrian had put his bag on the bed and was slowly undoing his shirt buttons.

The whack Ben gave his erection before he walked back to the room hadn't made much difference. He tried to pretend he didn't have a raging hard-on as he held out the stuff sack he'd retrieved. "I meant, we should pack your clothes in this waterproof bag, ready for the morning. I need to make sure you're not taking too much." There. Two complete sentences. He could do this; he just had to concentrate and not mentally undress the man.

It didn't make sense. They worked out all the time, so he'd seen Adrian with only a towel around him. Why was he having this crazy reaction? He'd never seen Adrian look at him like that, though. Not while he knew he was gay. Those eyes weren't suggesting he come to bed, they were outright begging him to. Ben felt the heat rise in his face. Fuck it, he was blushing again.

Adrian's chuckle caused Ben to flush even more. "It's alright, Ben. I won't bite you."

But what if I want you to?

His boss turned and upended his case so all the contents spilled out onto the mattress.

Ben let out his breath and a shudder ran up his spine as he watched Adrian sort through them. Talk about going through his clothes. He wanted to pick up each article and check them out, especially the little blue slip of a swimsuit. Should he mention they often swam naked once they were away from the more public areas? The pair of denim cutoffs snagged his attention, and his breath caught. Adrian glanced up at him through eyelashes that were nearly as long as Jason's. Whenever Jason looked at him like that, it was an invitation to tumble him onto the bed and fuck his brains out.

Ben tugged at the neckline of his T-shirt. "That all looks… fine." He gave himself a mental clap on the head. Much as he wanted to do one of those dramatic moves where he swept all the clothes onto the floor with one hand and pulled Adrian onto the bed with the other, he did have a job to do here. He swallowed his lust and picked up Adrian's rain jacket. "You use this for sailing, eh?"

"Yes, it's great for keeping out the cold."

"You'll get hot, though, if you try to paddle in it." Ben bundled it up in his hand, testing its weight. "And it's heavy." He reached into Chris's cupboard and rummaged around in the bottom. "Good, he hasn't taken it with him." He dragged out an old, blue lightweight rain jacket. "This should fit. Leave the other one here. We can pick it up on the way back."

Adrian turned around automatically as Ben helped him slip Chris's jacket over his clothes. "Yeah, that's great." He took a step back and checked his boss up and down, catching Adrian's amused gaze when he reached eye level.

The cocked eyebrow said it all. "We seem to spend a lot of time playing dress-up."

Ben started bundling all the clothes into the waterproof stuff sack. *I'd much rather play take-'em-off,* he thought to himself and snickered.

After checking that Adrian wasn't carrying any glass bottles or cans and had his passport ready for checking into Canada, he glanced at the bed. "Make the most of the comfy mattress. It'll be the last you see for a few days." He watched Adrian's expression as his face lost all its teasing laughter. "No regrets, boss?"

"No. Not yet," came the quiet reply. "Good night, Ben."

"Yeah." Ben lingered at the door, wishing he had some other excuse to stay. "See ya in the morning."

AS SOON as the door closed, Adrian spun around and sank onto the mattress. He hadn't been this giddy since he was fourteen at summer camp. He was thirty-five, damn it, well past the age where his pulse sped up just from standing near another male. But every time Ben touched him lately, he ripped off one of the layers Adrian hid behind, just like a wax strip, causing exquisite pain and exposing skin denuded of all the crap of the past. The carefully constructed persona that had taken him years to craft: the responsible executive, the dutiful son, the sexless robot were all becoming harder and harder to maintain. Instead, glimpses of a young, carefree man were starting to break through. The person he had been with Antonio.

After rescuing his toiletries and getting ready for bed, Adrian sat and stared out the window. The moon cast long shadows across the grass.

The urge to escape had been overwhelming, but now he was here, his life seemed as unclear as the woods on the horizon: an impenetrable dark mass, hard to see a way in, let alone the way out. He couldn't decide whether that scared or excited him.

Goose bumps ran over his skin as he crawled under the covers. Sleep was a long time coming. In the morning he didn't get a chance to exchange any more words with Cathie Dutoit without Ben overhearing them.

She gripped Adrian's hand hard when they made their farewells. "You will take care of him, won't you?"

"Stop worrying, Mom. We've got a GPS and satellite radio."

But she wasn't looking at Ben when she spoke. Adrian nodded.

ROB came down the steps as they pulled up at the forestry station.

Ben tensed as his brother shook hands with Adrian and exchanged small talk. His greeting was about the same as Andrew's: big brother is watching you.

With a Jets cap now covering Adrian's salt-and-pepper hair, they didn't seem all that different in age. Adrian looked good. Nowhere near as tall or broad as Rob, yet still in perfect proportion. Neat.

After their paperwork was checked, Adrian wandered off to look at the posters and information on the wall, his hands resting in the pockets of his jeans.

Rob spread out the map. "Why are you using the Bottle Rapid Portage?"

"Because I want to show him Argo Lake." *Here it comes, the third degree.* Rob always thought of a better way. Ben felt himself tense again.

"You've set yourself a pretty challenging route to complete in four days."

Rob's dismissive glance at Adrian made Ben's blood boil. "Just because he works in an office doesn't mean he can't cope."

"I hope you're right. Once you get out there, you're on your own."

"I know."

"You'll have to work together as a team."

"Lay off it, Rob. Adrian and I will be fine."

By the time they settled into the light plane that would take them to the Canadian Custom's post on Sand Point Lake, Ben had almost simmered down.

Judging from the occasional glances Adrian threw back at him over his shoulder, Ben's foul mood hadn't gone unnoticed. He watched as his boss listened politely to the pilot's spiel as she shared her love of the lakes they were flying over. It wasn't until they had their passports stamped and were packing the canoe that Adrian asked quietly, "What's up?"

Ben shook his head and mouthed, "Brothers."

171

Adrian snorted before picking up the gear he was helping stow into the different waterproof containers. "It's interesting seeing you on your home turf."

"Innerestin', eh? Covers a lot of differnt bases, her-ya." Ben deliberately slipped into his best Minnesotan drawl.

Adrian grinned back, but his smile faded. "Well, Rob and Andrew obviously love you to death, but they act as if they'll never believe you're capable of looking after yourself."

"You noticed?" Ben snorted. "Why do you think I went to San Francisco in the first place?" He shook his head. "I was only ten when Dad died, so I was brought up by *four* fathers who still reckon I can't tie my shoelaces." Ben took the closed container from Adrian's hands. "What do you think? Can I?" As he bent down to place the plastic bottle into the canoe, his ears strained to hear the reply.

"You'll be fine. I have every confidence you'll look after my safety as well as your own." Adrian slapped Ben's butt while he was bent over. "But don't forget to tie a double knot in the laces while you're down there, okay?"

Ben straightened and grinned at Adrian's joshing. He wasn't sure what had made the most impact: his vote of confidence, or the jolt of electricity that arced through his body at Adrian's touch.

The sun shone on them as the towboat operator took them toward their entry point into the lakes system. On the way, they stopped to admire the pictographs on Painted Rock, but the wind was up, so they didn't stay long. They also paused at Warrior Hill, where Ben told Adrian the Indian legend associated with the large rock. When the towboat driver suggested they might like to climb it, Ben shook his head. The sooner they were alone, the better.

CHAPTER
✝✝✝
FIVE

"IS THAT too heavy?" Ben tightened the buckle around Adrian's waist.

Adrian flexed his shoulders, settling the larger pack more comfortably on his back. "I can see why you insisted on packing light."

"Just pretend you're lifting weights in the gym."

"Yes, coach." Adrian smiled when he caught the quick grin Ben gave him.

Adrian checked out his companion as Ben tucked the bent-handled paddles under the gunwales. Out of the office environment, he looked much more relaxed, more at home. Here, in his red-and-black-checked shirt with the sleeves rolled up, he looked like he belonged. He'd unzipped the bottom section of his cargo pants, converting them into shorts, so the fine, pale hairs on his long, muscular legs shone under the glare of the sun. He looked very fuckable. Adrian took a deep breath. "Where to now?"

Ben pointed to the hill behind them. "Over that ridge, then we can start paddling."

"How do we get the canoe there?" Adrian gave his pack another hitch.

"Like this." Ben bent his knees to form a support, lifted the canoe until it rested on his thighs, then stopped. With a quick crisscross movement of his arms, he had the canoe resting on his shoulders. "At least it's lighter than the seventy-five pound Grummans I learned on."

All his muscles had rippled under the soft fabric of his shirt when he swung the canoe over his head. No wonder his shoulders were so big. Adrian drank in a couple more moments, gazing at the young man. "I wondered why you were giving me the heavy pack."

"You can have a turn carrying this, if you like."

"Tomorrow, perhaps." Adrian could sense that Ben was anxious to get going before the sun went down. "Lead on, Macduff!"

Ben pointed to a narrow path leading away from the landing area. "No, you go first. The trail is pretty distinct in this section, so you won't get lost. That way I can keep an eye on you, and make sure you're handling everything okay."

"Okay." Adrian nearly added, *"You just want to ogle my butt,"* but stopped just in time. Damn, this keeping up a façade of being a boring, straight man was hard enough to maintain in the city, out here it promised to be nigh on impossible. There was something about being outside, where everything was stripped back to the basics, raw and real, that made hiding who he was a farce. Suppressing a grimace, Adrian set off up the steep hill.

The portage seemed to go on forever. Running on treadmills or even around the streets near home wasn't the same. A large boulder beside the trail offered a convenient resting place. Adrian balanced the pack on the rock so he could take a breather. Perspiration trickled down his face.

Ben grinned, then laughed at the glare he got in return. "Having second thoughts, boss?"

"Fuck off." Adrian laughed. "I thought we were going paddling, not lugging blocks of lead. What have you got in this thing?"

"All our camping gear, food, a few containers of wine. Fuel. A stove. After a few days you won't even notice it's on your back. Come on, we're nearly at the top. It's all downhill from there."

Once they relaunched the canoe and started paddling, Adrian finally felt he had reached his destination. It was fun being back on the water again; he hadn't realized how much he missed it. He manned the front of the boat while Ben sat in the back. The only downside of that position was that he had to turn around whenever he wanted to say something. After a while, he stopped trying to carry on a conversation and just uttered a quiet "stroke" whenever he wanted to change sides, content to listen to Ben as he pointed out the different things he might miss.

"Beaver."

Adrian turned and saw Ben point at something with his paddle. All he could see was a V-shaped ripple in the water.

"They're shy creatures. You won't see them much, but you'll see plenty evidence that they're around. We have to portage around their dams. Trouble is, sometimes they build new ones, so you end up carrying everything more often than you expected."

After an hour's paddling, Ben steered the canoe into the lee of a rock and opened his daypack. Moving cautiously forward, the young man straddled the large pack that sat in the middle of the boat between them. "I don't know about you, but I'm starving." He handed Adrian a big, flat, square cookie that looked like an over-sized muesli bar. "Granola bars. Mom made them for us."

"Thanks." Adrian flexed his fingers, glad for an excuse to stop paddling. He took a bite of the oats, honey, and nut mixture. "Hmm, these are great."

Ben stopped chewing and grinned at him. "Better than the bought stuff. That's one of the things I miss most in San Francisco: Mom's cooking."

"Well, it certainly beats the pizza we lived on while making the DVD."

"You betcha, but it was fun." Ben pulled a plastic bottle out of his pack and handed it to Adrian. "They're pretty dry, you'll need something to drink." He hesitated for a moment. "Apart from wine, I only brought water and some fruit juices. Sorry, we didn't really have time to go through a menu, I hope you like what I chose. I'm warning you that it won't be restaurant standard."

Adrian had deliberately left out the Jack Daniels. Since returning to the States, he had thought nothing of consuming half a bottle a night, but the latest drinking bout had unnerved him. Everything seemed to have happened at once. The financial meltdown, too many nights spent alone after Evelyn took up with Liz, Ben's arrival on the scene making him more aware of what he was missing. Alcohol had quickly become a convenient crutch. Time he stopped.

"I suspect by the end of the day, I'll be glad for anything."

After sharing a bottle of water, they continued paddling. Unloading the boat and preparing for the next portage went a lot faster. Although the path was just as steep, Adrian found he could manage a lot easier this time. Maybe the food he'd consumed was the reason, or the fact he knew what to expect. Ben even suggested he take a turn carrying the canoe, saying it was actually lighter. Adrian tried, and Ben was correct as far as the weight went, but the length made it awkward. In the end, he was quite happy, trudging up the hill with the huge pack on his back, lost in his thoughts.

The one thing that kept coming into his mind was Ben's conversation with his mother. *Jason has a new boyfriend.* And more importantly, Ben didn't seem to be unhappy about the fact. Jason was a fool for not holding on to someone like Ben. If Ben were *his*, he wouldn't let him go in a hurry. All the things Adrian would like to do to and with him ran through his mind. First off, he'd play Ben like an instrument until he was writhing and begging for his touch. Then he'd strip off all those clothes and tease him just so he could see how far the color extended when he blushed. Did his whole, magnificent body go pink when he made love, like some of the guys in the DVDs?

Adrian stopped and turned around. Ben had propped his canoe between two close-growing birches and stepped out from underneath, rolling his shoulders and flexing his muscles. Adrian groaned and felt his cock thicken. Did Ben realize what a big turn-on that action was?

Ben caught him looking, and a flush spread over his skin. Adrian's pulse quickened. *Maybe he did! Oh, what the fuck.* He'd been dreaming about having sex with the young man for weeks now. It was obvious Ben wanted him or was at least interested. He should just do it.

His grandfather was right. It was time to let Antonio go. He would always think of him as his first love, but he couldn't change the past. The only other thing that might have stopped him was the promise he'd made to his father to repress his gay tendencies when he returned to the States. Well, he wasn't even in the States now; he was in Canada. The significance hadn't really hit him until they stamped his passport.

His father's words ate at Adrian as he walked along. *Suppress his gay tendencies.* How he hated that phrase. He was *gay*, damn it. No tendency about it. He liked men. He liked having sex with men. He wasn't ashamed of being that way. In fact, he wanted to fuck the young man walking behind him so much, it actually hurt.

176

CHAPTER
+++
SIX

BEN could tell Adrian was finding the going difficult, but he hadn't complained once. Only the usual grumbles, like he did in the gym. *Coach*—he liked it when Adrian called him that. Matched up with the way he called him *boss*. They were just names, not titles out here.

By the time they reached the end of the portage, the midday sun had created enough heat to work up a decent sweat. The forecast of an Indian summer had been accurate, with temperatures in the high eighties. Ben pointed to a large rock overhanging the water's edge. "The paddle along Crooked Lake will take a while, so we'll have lunch first."

They took off their boots and dangled their feet in the cool water. As he slowly chewed his turkey sandwich, Ben glanced at Adrian. His gaze was darting everywhere, as if he was searching for something. "Lost something?"

Adrian grinned at him. "I give up. There aren't any signs or flashing lights on the portages. How do you know where they are?"

Ben shrugged. "Map and compass. It's basic navigation. You work out where your destination is and aim toward it."

"But all the edges of the lake look the same. How do you know how far we've gone?"

"Easy. I check off each headland or island that we pass and mentally mark it on the map." *That's as long as you don't get distracted by watching the man in front of you and wondering what he'd do if you kissed him*, Ben added under his breath.

"It's hard working out the correct way to go sometimes." Adrian turned to stare across the lake.

"Now it's fall, it's sometimes easier." Ben pointed to a hill at the other end of the lake. "See that patch of red." Adrian peered at the area he was indicating and nodded. "I took the compass bearing when we arrived. That's our next portage. The red birch along the edge of the path are changing color, so now I have something distinctive to steer toward. Dad always used to say that you shouldn't fear change, you should see how it can work in your favor."

Adrian continued chewing in silence; when he finished his sandwich he brushed the crumbs off his hand and leaned back on the rock, resting on his elbows.

Instead of suggesting they should push on, Ben enjoyed the opportunity to relax and steal glances at Adrian whenever he could. After a while, Adrian rolled over onto his side and propped himself up on one elbow, resting his chin in his hand. Ben tried to keep his gaze trained on Adrian's face, but his eyes had a mind of their own, drifting along that trim body, checking to see if there was a bulge in his faded blue jeans.

"Wouldn't you have preferred to come here with someone closer to your age?" The low sexy drawl jerked Ben's attention back to where it belonged. He shifted uncomfortably as those cool gray eyes rested on him without blinking.

Although the eleven year difference didn't bother him, Ben wondered if the gap might be an issue with Adrian. "Not really." He shrugged. "I used to love coming here with my brothers. They're around your age." Ben groaned inside as soon as he made the comment. Him and his big mouth. He might as well have said, *I think of you as one of my brothers*. Except he never thought about falling in love with one of his brothers. The day seemed to get gloomier, but maybe it was because a cloud passed in front of the sun.

Adrian gave a small laugh.

"What's so funny?" Ben asked, his sandwich poised halfway to his lips.

"I was trying to imagine you out here with Jason."

"Jason?" Ben waved his hand around, scattering some turkey into the water in the process. "No mirror, no gel, no hair dryer?"

"You don't appear to be upset that he has a new boyfriend." Adrian's gaze didn't waver as he waited for Ben's response.

Oh, that's right, Jason told him we were going steady. Should he tell Adrian the truth? Na, that would just make Ben sound desperate, as if he were angling for Adrian to become interested in him. "Vincent probably doesn't even realize that's what he is yet. Knowing Jason, he will be before long. He always gets what he wants." Ben sighed. "But from what I can gather, he's the sort of person Jason needs, especially now."

Adrian didn't say anything for a while; his concentration fixed on the area they were headed for. Ben didn't disturb him. Ever since they started out that morning, he noticed his boss was more relaxed. So far, he hadn't rubbed the back of his neck once. Ben smiled to himself. Adrian was definitely going to need more than a neck rub after paddling all day.

As soon as they finished eating, Ben stowed everything into the canoe ready to head off. Before they did, Adrian grabbed something from his pack and headed into the trees.

Call of nature probably. Ben was tempted to suggest they do what he and his brothers usually did: have pissing contests to see who could aim farther into the lake. That way at least his cut or uncut question would be answered. *Damn.* Too late.

"That sun sure packs a punch."

Ben glanced up and gulped. Adrian had stripped off his shirt and changed into his denim cut-offs. Ben bent back down, hoping the heat in his face had gone unnoticed. "Sure does. I probably should cover up more." He pulled his neck bandana out of his daypack. When he straightened, he noticed Adrian was watching him. Ben tried to ignore the intent look as he rolled down his sleeves and slathered sunscreen onto the bare areas. Not that there were many; he covered himself up pretty well. "Aren't you afraid of getting burnt?" he asked, finally plucking up enough courage to glance at the man again.

"Best present Nonna and Pop ever gave me. I just get darker and darker." Adrian sat on the rock and put his boots back on, planting his feet on the rock in front of him, displaying his crotch to perfection.

Ben dragged his gaze away. The temptation to check Adrian out almost too strong to resist. *How loose were the legs of the cut-offs? Could he see up them?* A wave of heat swept over his body, and it wasn't from the sun. *Stop acting like a total idiot, Ben. Concentrate on the conversation. What were they talking about? Oh, yeah, getting sunburned.* Ben swallowed and slathered some sunscreen onto his face. "Don't make me jealous. I have to use +30." Keeping his brain focused on what he was doing rather than the example of tanned perfection on the rock, he capped the tube, replaced it in his pack, and wiped his hands on a towel. Gripping the paddles was a pain in the ass otherwise. "I hate being so fair," he muttered as he straightened, finally risking a glance as Adrian left his position and walked toward him.

"Pale skin has its own kind of beauty," Adrian said quietly, taking his place at the front of the canoe. Ben pushed off and jumped in.

Damn. Now Adrian's muscles were even more obvious! Especially the way they rippled under his skin as he thrust his paddle through the water. After a while, the urge to touch what he hadn't been able to take his gaze off became too much to resist. "Are you sure you wouldn't like me to rub in some sunscreen?" *Shit, Ben. Why do you have to sound so pathetic?* He sounded like he was begging for permission to touch. Hopefully Adrian hadn't noticed.

Adrian turned and gave him one of those slow smiles that always got Ben's heart racing. Not that it could go much faster. "If you insist."

Ben reached for his sunscreen, but Adrian beat him to it, retrieving a plastic bottle from the big pack he'd been carrying and handing it over. "Use this."

Ben glanced at the label. Coconut oil SPF 6. "Hey. Not fair."

"That's the general idea, Ben." Adrian smirked and turned to the front.

The wind had abated, so they didn't need to pull into the shore. After shelving the paddle and perching on the big pack again, Ben kept up a constant mantra of *idiot, idiot* as he rubbed in the tanning oil. Just as well Adrian was facing the other way and didn't realize how turned on he was. When he started paddling again, he'd have to drape a towel over his lap to hide his erection. After slathering enough oil on Adrian's back, he worked his fingers into the muscles at the shoulder and neck. He may not have had any training, but he could feel where the knots were under the skin. Finally, he was able to give Adrian the massage he'd wanted to give him so many times before.

Adrian groaned as he rolled his muscles around under Ben's touch. "At least by covering yourself up, you don't have to worry about tan lines." His voice came out kind of spacey, as if he wasn't really aware what he was saying.

"There's another way to avoid them," Ben said, picturing Adrian lying in the sun without even a pair of Speedos on. He found a particularly lumpy spot on the top of Adrian's shoulder and kneaded it as hard as possible.

"You mean sun lamps?" Adrian turned his head to one side and grinned up at him. Ben had leaned forward to apply extra pressure, so their mouths ended up only inches apart. Eventually Ben managed to tear his gaze away from Adrian's lips, only to watch spellbound as pale eyes darkened into a smoldering gray.

"Look out," Adrian warned.

The canoe tipped alarmingly as it glanced against a branch sticking out of the water. Ben hurriedly returned to his seat. The wind was pushing them toward the open section of the lake. If they didn't start paddling soon, they'd end up back in the United States. He hurriedly wiped his hands on the towel and yelled, "Paddle."

The moment was broken. Adrian's muscles bunched as he put effort into his strokes. *Fuck it! So close and yet so far!*

From then on, all Ben could think about was the look in Adrian's eyes. To take his mind off his sexual frustration, he concentrated on paddling.

Adrian turned his head. "Are we in a race or something?"

"No, but I want to get to Argo Lake before it gets dark." Ben's recent frustration erupted again. "Hey, if we do, I'll give you a *proper* back massage."

Adrian raised his eyebrows and smirked. "Promise?"

"Cross my heart and hope to die."

The canoe's speed almost doubled.

Dusk was falling as Ben jumped out of the boat and pulled the craft up onto the sand. He'd been overly optimistic about how far they

181

could go the first day. Getting away was always the hardest part. They would have to hurry if they wanted to eat before the sun went down.

Judging by the way Adrian lifted the pack out of the boat and lugged it up to the flat area, you'd have thought they'd done this together heaps of times. Once there, Adrian quickly sorted out the things they would need for the night, taking out the tents and the sleeping gear.

Ben indicated the two spots he felt would provide the flattest surface. "If I do the cooking, can you set up the tents by yourself?"

"Sure thing, coach."

Adrian went to work while Ben gathered all the things for dinner and knelt on the ground to fill the gas stove. The foil on the packet of precooked chicken cordon bleu soon surrendered to his all-purpose scissors. He arranged the pieces carefully and placed the pan on top of the burner. A soft scrunch sounded as Adrian came over to stand beside him. "Do you think it will rain?" he asked softly.

Ben's gaze drifted slowly upward: across the short, brown work boots, over the carefully folded-over socks, then along the tanned legs. Even though Adrian was nowhere near as tall as he was, his legs seemed to go on forever until they reached his short cutoffs and a promising bulge that looked huge from this angle. Ben gulped hard. "You never can tell." *The bastard. He stood that close on purpose.*

Adrian smiled down at him without moving. "Do you want me to erect the small one as well as the big one?"

The two words *erect* and *big* hit Ben's brain, but not the context. "Ouch." He shook his hand. He'd been gripping the pan by the side as well as the handle.

"Are you alright?" Adrian crouched down in front of him.

Ben stuck his fingers into his mouth and sucked. Without taking them out, he managed to mumble, "Just a little bit... burnt." He removed his fingers and waved them around as he added. "Can you string up the fly between them? That way we can sleep outside, and just use our tent.... I mean, tents if it rains." He stuffed his fingers back into his mouth, wondering if maybe he should put his foot in there instead.

"You sure I can't do that for you?"

Ben gazed into the concerned eyes of the man in front of him. "What? Suck my fingers?" He felt the heat rise and knew he was blushing again.

With a perfectly straight face, Adrian pointedly stared at the pan where the chicken was sizzling nicely. "Cook dinner."

Ben jumped as if someone had stuck a pin in him, his sore fingers instantly forgotten. He shoved the pan handle around to face Adrian. "They won't take long." He stumbled off, and found he was trembling. Was Adrian teasing him deliberately, or was he so fixated on having sex with the man that he was reading all the signs wrong? Ben took a deep breath and counted to twenty, then he buried his confusion away and concentrated on his task, taking comfort from the familiar. Years of practice allowed him to have everything set up by the time Adrian called him over to eat. Delaying the venture back into unknown territory, Ben carefully arranged the self-inflating sleeping mattresses under the nylon fly that he'd strung between the two tents. Then he stood back, checking the arrangement.

At the start of the journey, his goal seemed so simple. Get to know his boss better and entice him out of the closet. The Adrian he knew from San Francisco—his reserved employer, or even his gym buddy and travel companion—was one thing; the confident, sexy man cooking the dinner was another thing altogether.

"I've poured some wine for you, I hope that's okay." The smile Adrian gave him was one of those special come-to-bed smiles. Exactly what Ben didn't need.

"Sure," Ben replied softly. "Thanks for taking over."

Adrian had arranged the life jackets on a nearby rock to act as cushions. Ben put a pot of lake water on to boil, then sat next to Adrian. There was just enough light to see by.

"Do I still get that massage, or are your fingers too sore?" The twinkle was back in Adrian's eye as he glanced sideways at Ben while they ate.

Ben choked on a mouthful of food. "They're okay, now. The pan wasn't that hot."

"That's good, I've been looking forward to feeling those fingers on me for the last couple of hours."

Ben gulped and his gaze darted down below Adrian's waist level. He couldn't help it. *Yep, definitely awake.* He started eating quicker. "Um. We have to clean up first." Ben waved his hand around wildly. "Bears."

"No problem." Adrian finished the last mouthful of his dinner and walked over to the eating pack. Without bending his knees, he delved inside and extracted all the cleaning gear.

Ben groaned as he was presented with a perfect ass: two round globes straining at the denim material. From the glimpse of bare butt through the frayed edges, Adrian had gone commando too. There was no way the man didn't know what he was doing, or the effect it was having on him. Ben shifted uncomfortably; the tents weren't the only thing erect for the last half hour. In fact, now he thought about it, he'd been semi-hard for most of the day. He swallowed the last piece of chicken. *What a waste of a perfectly good meal,* he thought to himself as he took the plate over for cleaning. His mouth was salivating so much, he hadn't been able to taste it properly. He grabbed a dishtowel and dried the cooking utensils as soon as Adrian washed them.

"Did you bring any oil?"

At Adrian's question, Ben's thoughts broke away from the images of sex flashing through his brain and immediately translated the last word into lube. "What?"

Adrian didn't let go of the plate he passed him, so they were both hanging onto it at the same time. "Fingers slide better with lubrication," he added dryly.

Was the man a mind reader? Ben closed his eyes, trying to break the spell the words had over him.

Adrian jerked the plate in his hands until Ben looked at him. A wicked grin turned up the edges of his mouth. "For the back massage, Ben." The grin turned smoldering as Adrian's gaze raked him from head to toe. "You are *so* cute when you blush." Adrian leaned in and brushed his lips against Ben's briefly before letting go of the plate. "Never mind, we can use my suntan oil again."

Ben found himself standing with a plate in one hand, dishtowel hanging limply from the other and a raging boner tenting his pants between the two. *Adrian kissed me!*

His heart beat double-time as he frantically stashed all the kitchen things in the food pack and suspended it from one of the overhanging branches of a nearby pine tree. By the time everything was packed away, his legs were shaking. A still form lay on the ground under the nylon fly; on the mat beside him was the suntan oil. Adrian had taken off his boots, so he was only wearing his shorts and socks. Ben approached quietly, and stood near his boss's head. Maybe, when he woke up, the original version would be back, the predictable one.

A hand shot out and gripped his ankle. Ben forgot to breathe until a thumb started to stroke the skin above where his boot finished. The featherlight touch sent tingles up his leg. Ben collapsed onto his knees. Adrian propped his head on one hand and half turned so he could look at Ben. "You sure you want to go through with this?"

Ben nodded enthusiastically and then found the cat hadn't got his tongue. "Yeah, I'm sure."

"That's good."

"What about you?" he asked, suddenly uncertain.

"I think I'm up for it in more ways than one." A small smile played across Adrian's lips as he lay back down.

Before he could lose his nerve, Ben shucked off his own shirt and threw it to one side. He picked up the bottle, poured a little liquid onto his hand, then tried to stop his hands shaking so he could replace the cap. He wanted an excuse to touch that tanned skin all over, every day they were here, as often as possible. No way could he afford to spill any.

Straddling Adrian's back, he sank to his knees and slowly and systematically massaged the tension out of the muscles again. As he worked, Ben found it difficult to stifle the moans that welled up inside. Heck, *he* wasn't the one who was supposed to be showing their appreciation; it was supposed to be the man underneath him. Was he asleep this time? Ben leaned cautiously in to check, and before he knew it, Adrian rolled over, grasped the back of his head, and pulled him into a kiss.

A huge jolt of electricity surged down Ben's spine, zapping all the strength from his body. Without breaking contact with Adrian's mouth, he collapsed onto his side, drawing Adrian into his embrace, and in the process swallowed a murmur from the man that could have been words of approval.

After a quick fumble, they started testing and teasing, neither taking full control. First one tongue then the other would dart inside, as if eager to explore new territory. The previous featherlight touch on his lips didn't count. This was different. The real deal. Ben had imagined himself kissing Adrian hundreds of times before, but he would never have imagined something like this. He'd always concentrated on how Adrian would feel. Would his lips be soft or firm? Ben had never taken into account how *he* would react. Now his body felt like it belonged to someone else, someone alien, a stranger. He'd certainly never felt like this before. The world outside ceased to exist, even the rest of his body was ignored as everything became centered on touch and taste. Touch like liquid velvet and taste as heady as wine.

Gradually, Ben relaxed into the moment, and soon there was a familiarity between them as if they'd been kissing each other for years.

Finally, Adrian stopped and rolled him over so Ben lay on his back. "Comfortable?" he asked in that honey-soaked voice that always sent chills up and down Ben's spine.

Ben didn't answer, too busy reliving the last five minutes of the best kiss ever. Kissing had never been a big part of his relationship with Jason; it had all been about the sex. Sure, there'd been the usual lip-locking, to get in the mood, but if it went on for too long, Jason would get impatient. Adrian poked him with his finger. Ben detected amusement in the beautiful eyes, only inches away from his. "What?" he asked, his brain finally functioning again.

"I asked whether you were comfortable or not. I don't plan on going anywhere soon, and I don't want stones or sticks digging into your back."

Ben wriggled around a bit to check. He'd been so wrapped up in what he was doing, there could have been a dozen boulders underneath the sleeping mat and he wouldn't have noticed. "Nope, the only thing digging into me is your cock." Ben felt his face flush as soon as he finished speaking.

"Good, that's how it should be."

Adrian dived lower on Ben's body, licking his chest, sucking his nipples, cooling his skin down before returning to his face. "You are so adorable when you blush. Did you know that?"

Ben stared up into those laughing eyes. Now they were like they'd been in the picture with his mother. Devilish. "Is that why you've been teasing me all day?"

"Uh-huh. I knew you were a clever boy."

Ben groaned at the description. "I... am... not... a... boy."

"Well, you certainly ain't a girl." Adrian wiggled so their cocks rubbed together.

Ben moaned. "Kiss me again. Please."

"Hm, like this?" Adrian planted a teasing kiss on his lips and pulled back.

"No... more... harder." Ben lifted his head to see that Adrian's eyes had darkened to that stormy gray he'd seen there so often lately.

This time Adrian kissed him like a man possessed, his lips bruising in their intensity. Then he started moving, grinding into him, pressing their trapped cocks together. Ben shuddered at the onslaught. Trying to get closer, he ran his hand down Adrian's slippery back and slid it under the waistband of his shorts. With one hand cradling Adrian's head and the other palming the delicious curve of Adrian's butt, Ben pressed into the kiss again.

"Aaagh, Ben, you'll be the death of me." The words were muffled by his mouth, but Ben heard them anyway.

CHAPTER
+++
SEVEN

ADRIAN closed his eyes and arched back, pushing his groin down. Between the friction of the denim and the pressure against Ben's body, he nearly lost control and came like a horny teenager. He levered his body away and forced the urge back. As if on cue, the nearly full moon came out from behind a cloud, illuminating the area strongly enough to cast shadows. In the soft light, Ben's skin took on the hue of a translucent pearl, so totally at odds with the ruggedness and strength of the body underneath. For so long, Adrian had resisted the urge to do more than look; now he wondered if he'd ever be able to stop touching him. Supported on his elbows and taking his time, Adrian studied Ben's face, noting the serenity and the smile curving his lips. The young man's eyes were shut, as if he was pouring all his other senses into what his hands were doing—one threaded through Adrian's hair, the other clasping his ass. Adrian leaned in and kissed Ben's eyelids; they fluttered open and all movement stopped as they gazed at each other.

"Hi," Adrian whispered softly. In a way this *did* feel like they had just met. The Ben underneath him was nothing like the young man who sat in his cubicle day after day, always on the edge of his awareness, no matter what he was doing. This Ben filled every sense he possessed. Adrian leaned in and ran his tongue over the edges of those beautiful pink lips, now rosy from the intensity of their first kisses. The contented sound he received in response went straight to his dick. Ben hadn't stopped kneading his butt, and judging by the hard cock pressing against his belly and the expression of pure bliss on his face, Adrian was sure he was doing something right. But Ben had too many clothes on. They both did. Adrian wanted skin touching skin. All the way.

His fingers fumbled at the buttons on Ben's fly. Finally Ben must have realized he was having a problem; he stopped his kneading and used both hands to feverishly open the fastenings and slide the pants down his legs. Adrian shimmied off his own shorts and threw himself back on that glorious body, generating a small "Oomph" as he drove all the air out of Ben's lungs.

"Hey, careful!"

Adrian eased back and grinned. "You make a real comfy mattress."

"And you make a nice warm quilt." Ben replied softly. Neither of them moved for a while as they resumed their silent contemplation. Eventually, Ben sighed and ran his fingers along the edge of Adrian's jaw. "Are you going to let your beard grow while we're out here?"

Adrian rubbed against the questing touch, marveling at how that simple caress sent shivers up and down his spine. He smiled and twisted his head, trapping a finger in his mouth, sucking it. He'd only been half-joking when he'd teased the young man earlier. The thought of sucking Ben's injured fingers to lubricate them before they entered him had made him rock-hard.

He let the finger slide from his mouth with a little pop. "Would you like me to?" His voice grew husky. Prolonging the act was pure torture, but he didn't want to rush.

Ben went back to running his fingers through his stubble as he whispered, "I like you like this. Suits you." He stopped stroking, reached up, cupped Adrian's head in both of his strong hands and brought Adrian's mouth back to his, moaning softly the instant before contact.

It was lucky Ben enjoyed kissing as much as he did. Adrian nibbled at the full bottom lip, drawing in the soft skin, playing with it for a while, then returning to the intensity of before. Ben seemed to instinctively latch onto the changes in Adrian's rhythms and matched him at every turn.

He'd dreamed of kissing Ben for so long that, in a way, this felt more like a dream, but dreams never captured the intensity of being held by strong arms, of feeling another person's heart beat, of the way their cocks were pressed between them. Just touching and holding Ben had as much impact as the actual kiss. Adrian balanced on one elbow and ran his hands over Ben's pale skin. In the moonlight, Ben's alabaster skin had taken on a delicate flush, not of embarrassment this time, but the deeper hue of sexual excitement. Just the sight of it made Adrian harder than ever.

"You... are... so... beautiful." The breath caught in his throat as he said the words. He had never meant them so much before. Everything about Ben *was* beautiful, from the swell of his muscles showing under his skin to the thick cock, jutting up in anticipation. Adrian stroked the hard length, smoothing in some of the pre-come that had leaked out. Ben flinched at his touch. Adrian dropped a light kiss on the tip. "I hope you packed the condoms."

Ben gave an anguished cry and threw Adrian off. He ran a few paces and stood facing the water, his arms wrapped around his body. Even from a distance, Adrian could tell he was shaking, and not from the cold.

Adrian walked up behind him and slid both arms around his waist, trying to stop the trembling. "What's wrong?"

"I didn't bring any. I took them out."

"You took them out? What on earth for?"

Ben turned and pushed him away. "I don't know. Lots of reasons. For a start, I didn't think you were interested in me that way."

Adrian shook his head and snorted at the irony of it all. That's what he got for being such a good actor. "Not interested?" He ran the tip of his finger all the way down Ben's cheek, under his chin, down his chest, circling his left nipple a few times. Then he brushed the back of his hand against Ben's erect cock as his finger traced the treasure trail right down to the soft, red curls at its base. He swallowed and felt himself grow even harder as he cupped the large, low-hanging balls in his hand before resuming the trace up the other side, around the hard nub of the right nipple, back up to stroke over Ben's soft lips. "Oh, I've been interested in you for a long, long time. I've dreamed about having you inside me."

Ben shuddered and rested his head on Adrian's shoulder, his body still quivering. "I can't." The words were whispered into his neck.

"What do you mean, you can't?" Adrian stroked his fingers through Ben's hair.

"I promised myself: no more fucking until I get the all clear. Even if I had condoms, what if they broke? I can't take the risk of infecting you. I won't." With a soft cry, Ben tore himself away and returned to sit on the mat, his arms clenched around his folded knees. Adrian knelt beside him and gathered him up in his embrace, letting his head rest against his chest, stroking the young man's back as the tears fell unimpeded.

"Shush, Ben, it's alright. I'm sure you're fine."

"No one can be sure! During the window period, I don't know whether I am or not, and until I am sure, I'm not going to do anything that endangers you." He glanced up at Adrian, the tracks of his tears glistening in the moonlight. "All I've thought about for so long is how I wanted to fuck you until you screamed with pleasure. Now, I can't." The last words came out with an anguished sob as he buried his head in his knees again.

Adrian stroked his back, torn between telling him he didn't care, but knowing that even if he didn't, Ben would never do anything that might hurt him. "There are other alternatives." He smiled at the hopeful look in Ben's upturned eyes. "Come on." He held out his hand and pulled the younger man to his feet. "Let's put these mats into that nice big tent you brought. It's getting late, and much as I like the idea of sleeping under the stars, I don't think we should take a risk with the weather tonight."

CHAPTER
+++
EIGHT

BEN hugged himself as Adrian briskly shifted the big pack of clothes to the borrowed tent, then spread the mats and sleeping bags inside his old tent. Just as well he hadn't brought the condoms. He wouldn't have been able to resist the temptation that Adrian offered, especially now he knew the attraction was reciprocated. He had made that vow, and he was not going to break it.

He swallowed and found that he already felt better. There was something about the way Adrian treated the matter so calmly, collecting their shed clothing, fixing everything for the night, comfortable in his nakedness.

Absently, Ben noted the tan line where Adrian's shorts ended. Ben wanted to bury his face against the smooth skin. Suck those balls into his mouth, see what they felt like. He glanced up to find Adrian watching him, that familiar twinkle back in his eyes. "Like what you see?"

Ben nodded wordlessly, his mouth once again too dry to talk. Seemed it only took a look from Adrian and an invitation from those come-to-bed eyes to get him hard again.

Adrian stretched out his hand. "Come here."

Ben's legs had never felt so shaky as he crouched down and followed him into the tent, their hands clasped tightly together.

Adrian directed him to lie on his back again. Without waiting to be asked, he wriggled around to test the surface. "I'm fine." He stretched out his hands, and Adrian slid into his embrace as naturally as if they'd been doing this forever.

"You're more than fine." Adrian reached over and pulled the bottle of oil out of a pile of things he'd stashed behind their heads. Soon oil-slicked fingers greased his shaft and, by the feel of it, Adrian's too. Ben groaned.

Stowing the oil away safely, Adrian shifted lower so their bodies aligned with their erect cocks touching. Then he placed one of Ben's hands on the ground near his head, and did the same with the other, entwining their fingers so Ben couldn't move. The darkness prevented him from seeing the expression in Adrian's eyes, but the lilt in his voice when he whispered, "Ready?" made Ben tense in expectation.

"Yes." His reply wasn't much louder.

Adrian gave him a featherlight kiss, then he started moving, making their cocks slide together, using the oil to lubricate their progress. First a dip, lining up their cocks, then the long, slow glide. Ben emitted a groan every time Adrian pressed down. All the while, Adrian kept muttering his name between kisses, planting them all over his face, then coming back to his lips.

"Need more." Ben managed to utter, trying to release his hand. "Not enough friction."

"Don't move." Adrian's boardroom voice was back, but lower this time, the soft whisky tones that always turned Ben on. All the while, Adrian didn't lose a beat, just dip and glide, dip and glide, dip and glide.

"I want to touch you." Ben squirmed again, arching his body up to increase the contact, meeting implacable resistance as he tried to free his hands. Every press of Adrian's cock added to the frustration. No matter how much he thrust his body up, the slick oil prevented him from capturing the burn he needed. All he wanted to do was enclose both cocks within his fist and rock into the tight grip.

"Stop it." Adrian nipped the edge of his chin sharply, then turned it into nibbles as he moved down the jawline.

"Please." Ben moved his head, searching for those elusive lips.

Adrian chuckled as he gave in to his insistent demands and kissed him again.

Ben's brain exploded. All his concentration centered on those lips and the feel of their hard cocks rubbing together. Still, the slow, languorous torture continued.

"I've *gotta* touch you." He tried to get Adrian to release his hand again.

"Mn-mn." Adrian shook his head without breaking off the contact with his lips. When he finally broke away to take a quick breath, he rasped out, "If you touch me, I'll come, and I want this to last forever."

No way. Ben had nearly come twice already, but each time he got close, Adrian levered his groin away, making him almost scream in frustration. Definitely a control freak. "Please," he whimpered as Adrian stopped him from coming the third time.

"If you insist." Adrian released his grip on one hand. Ben reached between their bodies and trapped their cocks in his hand. Adrian groaned out his name and gave an extra-hard couple of thrusts, forcing the two cocks through the encircling tunnel, shuddering through his eventual release. *Finally!* Ben let himself follow, and their warm, sticky jets of come mingled together.

BEN groaned. Despite the two mats beneath him, the ground was too damn hard. Maybe he should have brought along those sleeping hammocks, but then he wouldn't have been able to snuggle in close like this. Strange to think he had never woken with a man in his arms before. And not just any man. The man he'd been dreaming about for months. Adrian.

He couldn't think of him as his boss at a time like this. This was the man who worked out in the gym with him, the one who helped him make the DVD. The person who seemed to know what he was thinking all the time, sharing a quick grin with no need for words. Ben took a deep breath and nuzzled the top of Adrian's head. How many times had he wanted to do *that* before! Mind you, without the positive proof in his arms, he would never have believed this possible. Much as he might have wanted to, he hadn't expected to actually get this close to Adrian. Not so soon. He thought he would have been struggling to pry him out of the closet, with reasoned arguments about being true to his nature.

Judging by the soft rise and fall of the chest against his hand, Adrian was still asleep. Ben could give him a blow job to wake him up, but then he'd have to let him go. There'd be time for more later. For now, he savored the closeness of having Adrian's back pressed against his chest, spooned in his embrace. He probably needed the extra sleep. After that first long drawn-out session, even though they never actually fucked, the man had proved insatiable; Ben didn't think there was any part of him that Adrian hadn't caressed in some way.

Just the memory made him shiver. Each touch and kiss had been delivered like all of Adrian's actions, thoroughly and carefully. At one stage, he even worked his way from the tips of Ben's fingers, licking and kissing every section he could reach, then rolling him over to access the other side, discovering all his sensitive spots, tickling them, then sharing laughter. At other times, nothing was said, Ben's murmured sounds of appreciation speaking louder than words.

In Ben's limited experience with Jason and numerous one-night stands, he had never been with anyone so tactile, so caring. Every time he tried to reciprocate, Adrian would softly murmur, "No, let me, please." In the end, he just lay back, accepting the fact that Adrian needed this for some reason. By the time he finished, Ben's body thrummed like a tightly strung harp, each nerve, every thought, totally possessed by the man touching him.

During the night, Adrian had brought him to climax twice more, his hand proving as good as his own at knowing how hard and fast to stroke.

Outside, a loon gave a mournful cry, breaking the predawn silence. Ben snuggled in closer, trying to absorb some of Adrian's warmth. He could get used to this.

NEXT time he opened his eyes, the sun, shining through the tent, greeted him. Sometime after going back to sleep, Adrian must have woken and draped an open sleeping bag across him. Yuck. Crusty patches of come stuck to his skin. They had eventually both been so tired and blissed-out last night, they just grabbed whatever was handy to wipe themselves down. The sleeping bag, by the looks of it. Ben grimaced as he picked at dry flecks on his skin. *Where was a hot shower when you needed one?* He could heat up some water, but that would take time.

He crawled out of the tent. The sun might be up, but the early-morning chill hadn't disappeared; a mist formed in the cold air with every breath he took. He dragged out the sleeping bag and wrapped it around his bare shoulders. No sign of Adrian. A steady slapping sound on the water told him where he was: swimming. *Swimming?* Despite the hotter-than-usual weather, didn't the guy realize it was September? Ben walked down to the small beach and watched Adrian churn through the water. Like everything he did, Adrian swam properly, like a professional, his smooth, naked body gliding through the water like a fish.

Ben wanted to drag him out and suck the cold, wet cock that had ground against him last night until it was hot and hard again. See what it tasted like. Having him so close over the next few days and not being able to fuck him was going to be pure hell.

Eventually, Adrian must have sensed his presence. He stopped and stood in waist-deep water. "Good morning, Ben. Come on in, and I'll give you a wash. The water's lovely."

"That's what they all say." Ben stuck his toe in. "Jesus Christ! It's colder than a well-digger's butt!"

Adrian laughed. "Don't think about it." He splashed some water with his arm.

"You're crazy." Ben pulled the sleeping bag closer and shuddered.

Adrian turned and swam away from the shore, the huge splash of his kick obscuring him from view. Then he disappeared.

Ben waited for what seemed like hours, scanning the area, his stomach churning with anxiety. People who weren't used to swimming in water this cold sometimes underestimated the danger. Cramp, for one. Heart attack, for another. He dropped the bedding and dived in, biting back a scream. *Fuck.* The water *was* freezing. When he reached the point where he last saw Adrian, he stopped and searched around frantically.

Suddenly, he was grabbed from behind. In an instant, fear for Adrian's safety turned to fury. "Stupid idiot," he yelled. "I thought you'd drowned."

Ben tried to turn to face him, but Adrian's arms trapped him tight against his naked chest. Despite Adrian's smaller size, his grip felt like steel.

"Relax." The softly growled command was whispered into his ear, but the grip didn't loosen. Ben could feel his heart pounding strongly against Adrian's hand. Before he could protest again, Adrian started swimming on his back, pulling Ben along with him, his legs executing a long sidestroke kick. Ben tried to break free again, but all Adrian did was repeat quietly, "Stop struggling. I've got you."

Ben let himself float, his head resting against Adrian's shoulder.

"That's better," Adrian soothed softly. "I knew you were too chicken to brave the cold water. I didn't mean to scare you."

Bullshit, Ben thought, but his struggles were over. One of Adrian's arms was wrapped around his body in a classic life-saving hold. The other rubbed all the places within reach, cleaning away the traces of last night's activity. A war raged through Ben. Responding warmth from the caress versus the effect of the cold water. After a while the water temperature started to feel comfortable and they drifted, floating on their backs, Adrian's mouth nuzzling the side of his neck.

"Feeling clean now?"

Ben twisted out of his grip and pushed Adrian away. "I don't care if you *are* my boss; don't you ever scare me like that again. I'm responsible for your safety while we're out here." He started swimming for shore, but Adrian grabbed hold of his foot and pulled him closer, sending his head under water in the process. Ben kicked out and felt a jolt of satisfaction as his foot connected with something solid yet soft at the same time. Adrian's belly, most likely. *Oops.*

As his head broke through the surface, Ben was grabbed again, from the front this time. He tensed, ready to respond if Adrian retaliated to his clumsy kick, but he didn't. Ben glanced at his face and was instantly caught by the bedroom eyes that attracted him in the first place. *Damn.* He would never be able to resist those. Ben wrapped his

197

arms around Adrian, drawing him close for a kiss, feeling a shiver go through the body in his arms.

Their mouths stayed locked together while the steady scissor-kick beat of their legs kept them upright with only their shoulders above water. The warm wetness of Adrian's tongue licked the cold from his lips, then dove inside. Ben sighed and forgot to kick. Water covered his head as they sank below the surface.

Separated, they broke through the surface again, Adrian shaking his head, scattering water in all directions. "Definitely a dry-land activity," he said. "Last one back cooks breakfast."

Adrian might have the style, but Ben had the power. They hit the shallow water together. Adrian laughed as he ran up the bank and grabbed the towel he'd left hanging over the branch. Ben grabbed for it at the same time.

"It's mine!" Adrian yelled.

An all-out war erupted for possession, but Ben had a height, weight and reach advantage. No contest. He hadn't counted on low tactics, though. With a snorted battle cry, Adrian hooked a leg around his and yanked it out from under him. As Ben put out his hand to break his fall, Adrian whipped the towel out of his grasp and took off, laughing and waving it around in the air. Ben scrambled to his feet and followed.

Being lighter and just as fit, Adrian moved like one of the legendary lynxes that used to inhabit the lakes, ducking and weaving around the low-growing bushes, jumping over exposed roots. As soon as he was far enough in front, he turned around. Every time Ben approached, he flicked the twirled towel and jumped aside.

By this time, Ben was laughing so much, he had trouble doing more than putting out an arm to block the snapping material. In the end, he put up his hands in a "Peace" gesture. "You're crazy," he said, trying to regain his breath. He'd played those games often enough with his brothers, but he would never have imagined fooling around with Adrian like that. "What's got into you?"

Adrian shrugged and gave a little laugh. "I don't know. This morning, I woke and decided life was too short to be wasted." He frowned and walked closer. "What's wrong, Ben? Having trouble believing your boss is human?"

Ben shook his head. Nothing added up, ever since setting out. "No, I like you like this, but I didn't think you were into early-morning swims and things."

Adrian shrugged as he wiped off the last remaining drops. "When I rowed, I had to get out on the water while it was dark, and before that there were years of waking early for swim-training. Mind you, those pools were heated, but I've kind of missed it."

Ben shivered. "You're lucky the lake wasn't frozen over. It will be soon."

Adrian threw him the towel.

Ben clasped it to his chest and dabbed at the wet spots. "Come on, let's get warm."

CHAPTER
╬
NINE

ADRIAN walked a few paces behind Ben down to the water's edge, enjoying the way the muscles flexed in his firm butt, especially when he bent over to retrieve the sleeping bag he had dropped before diving in to rescue him. Adrian knew he'd been watching and deliberately kept swimming as he tried to work out what to do.

When he woke, he'd feared everything had been a dream, but the reassuring weight of the arm resting across his naked thigh soon told him different.

Guilt threatened to engulf him, but he pushed the negative thoughts aside and just reveled in the memory of how good Ben felt. How good *he* had felt. Ben certainly made him feel young again.

Now he could admire all the parts he'd only touched and tasted last night; the lack of light had prevented him from doing more. Ben's arms were open wide, with the sleeping bag draped around his shoulders, displaying his body; a shy smile twisted his lips. Adrian had seen him shirtless in the gym and even caught glimpses of him naked before, but never like this. The muscles of his broad chest and his slim hips were showcased to perfection. The cold had shriveled Ben's prick, and his balls were nowhere to be seen, but this wasn't about size or even sex, this was about sharing, giving. After one glance at the invitation in those sparkling eyes, Adrian moved into the warm embrace. To him, Ben *was* a gift and the sleeping bag the wrapping.

Ben widened his stance so their bodies lined up and, as soon as their chests touched, he closed the sleeping bag around Adrian's back, forming a warm cocoon. While Ben's arms were occupied keeping the bedding secure, Adrian's hands were free. He spat on his palms and wrapped them around their cocks. They were much the same size, although Ben's may have been longer and a tad wider. As Adrian pressed them together, a loud hiss sounded. He glanced at Ben. The cheeky grin had vanished completely. Adrian leaned in, pressing their lips together, letting his tongue explore the soft, full surface before deepening into a kiss that sent shivers up and down his spine.

"That's a much better way to say, 'Good Morning'," Ben said shakily as Adrian eventually let him come up for air. He rested his forehead against Adrian's and tightened his embrace.

Adrian continued to stroke slowly as the sun came up, wetting his hands whenever the friction started to burn, enjoying the slow, sensual kisses and watching the desire and need shine through that blue-eyed gaze. Soon they were both warm again, and Ben's breathing grew ragged.

"Please, Adrian, finish it."

Adrian increased the pressure, feeling the strength go out of Ben's knees as he leant on him more.

"Fuck it. I'm going to come."

Soon they both needed another swim.

Afterward, completely relaxed, they sat in sweats and jackets on the rock they'd used as a dinner table the previous evening. Ben had his arm draped around Adrian's shoulder while Adrian had his wrapped around Ben's waist. Before them, Argo Lake stretched in all its beauty: white sandy shoreline, rocky headlands with tall pines. Adrian rested his head against Ben's shoulder, much as he'd been when they'd both fallen asleep on the plane. This was much nicer though. He sighed. "Why is the lake so incredibly blue? It reminds me of one of the glazes your mom used on the pots in her studio."

"Dad once told me that it isn't fed by any streams, so the water has a really high mineral content with very little algae growth."

"It's cold."

Ben snuggled in closer.

Adrian laughed and squeezed his arm tighter. "No, I mean the water."

"You betcha. Times like this I wish I had Mick's wetsuit."

Adrian tried to stop a sharp pang of jealousy rising to the surface. "Who's Mick?"

"A guy I met soon after I arrived in San Francisco. He hired a tandem, so we could ride together in the Mikes on Bikes during Pride." Ben snorted. "You should have seen us. Mick wore a tux, and I donned a white dress and veil and went as his 'wife'."

"Sounds like fun." Once again Adrian blessed his acting skills as he managed to paste a smile on his face.

"Sure was." Ben gave small chuckle. "Lucky I had him along to defend my virtue at the party afterward though. A number of guys were hell-bent on deflowering the virgin bride. I hated having to tell them they were too late."

Adrian laughed along with him as he stared out over the lake. Logically, he knew that Ben must have had other lovers before Jason, but accepting that fact wasn't the same. "I gather you see a fair bit of Mick then."

Without breaking contact, Ben managed to turn his head so he could look at Adrian. "He's not my boyfriend, if that's what you're getting at. We just hang out together."

Their faces were as close as they had been in the canoe the previous day. This time, Adrian acted on the impulse. The resulting kiss was brief, not sensual, more a recognition that they were on the same page. He liked sitting beside the young man; liked being with him, hearing stories of the sort of things he would have once enjoyed doing. "So how come you were wearing his wetsuit?"

Ben proceeded to relate a long and convoluted tale about how, the weekend after the parade, he'd gone down to Malibu with Mick, who was a keen surfer. The way Ben told it, surfing was one thing he wasn't good at. Adrian admired the way he didn't mind admitting how he kept falling off, banging his nose so badly that he'd ended up with a black eye. Adrian vaguely recalled Ben turning up for work one day last year with a shiner, but he just assumed he must have been involved in a drunken bar brawl or something.

As Ben continued with his tale, Adrian stopped castigating himself for making such a crass snap judgment and paid attention. "To look at Mick, he's the last person you'd expect to be a good board-rider. But he's a whiz. It took me ages to even kneel, let alone stand up. I kept persevering, even though Mick told me to give it a rest.

Eventually I managed to stand up, for all of ten seconds. Can't imagine myself doing that again. Can *you* surf?"

Adrian shook his head. "No. I can sail, I can row, but that's one thing I've never tried." They chatted about the different activities they'd done as kids and later as college students, all the while, scanning the horizon, hoping to see a bald eagle, but without any luck. The morning was well advanced by the time Ben tapped Adrian on the shoulder. "Time to make like a tree and leave."

Adrian glanced at the worried expression on Ben's face as they changed into their paddling gear. "What's the rush?"

Ben fastened the last of his buttons and came to face him, wrapping his arms loosely around his waist. "Much as I hate to put an end to our fun, there'll be more paddlers through here soon. This is a pretty popular spot."

Adrian, smoothed back the frown lines that had appeared on Ben's brow. "That's okay. Don't know if I'm up for an all-day fuck-fest anyway. I'm not as young as you are."

Ben smiled, but the grin faded as quickly as it came.

"What's the matter?"

Ben rested his elbows on Adrian's shoulders and stared at him without answering.

"Are you still mad at me for giving you that scare?" Adrian added quietly. "It's strange being the irresponsible one for a change."

Ben sighed and kissed him, deeply this time.

Adrian dropped the shirt he was holding. His brain might have told him he wasn't ready for another round, but his body had other ideas. He leaned in and enjoyed the touch and taste that was becoming familiar. After a while, Ben pulled away. "The problem is that I want to stick to our original route. Rob and Andy both said I was overly ambitious, but I want you to see as much as possible in the time available."

"I've seen the best part already." Adrian palmed the bulge tenting the front of Ben's pants.

Ben just laughed.

Adrian gazed at the wistful expression on the young man's face. Being able to touch what he'd only been able to look at before was becoming an addiction for him, but he could sense Ben's need to prove his brothers wrong. "So, finding somewhere else that's private and seeing how many times I can make you come isn't going to work either?"

Ben shook his head, though by the way his cock responded, he wasn't averse to the idea. "No, we better have breakfast and get going." He broke away and walked slowly to the suspended food pack. "Anyway, judging by these paw prints, it's just as well we're moving on."

Adrian studied the marks in the soft ground. "Bears?" He scanned the area but couldn't see anything.

"Just one. Black, by the look of it."

"Can't get away from them!"

Ben looked at him quizzically.

Adrian shrugged. "Bears. Traders who love it when the stock market falls."

Ben caught on and gave a short laugh. "Hey, no thinking about work. That's banned while you're out here." He deftly retrieved the food pack, and before long they were fed and on their way.

BEN didn't talk much for the rest of that morning. Although he missed his friendly chatter, Adrian found the silence serene. All the doubts and fears of work and city living cleared from his mind as he limited his concentration to each stroke. Lean forward, place, pull. When the routine became automatic, his consciousness started to push out and explore his situation.

Out here, life was reduced to the basics. Travel from point A to point B, find somewhere to sleep and get something to eat. So simple, so easy. No responsibilities, no manipulations, no expectations. So tempting to throw it all in and just continue doing this. Each lake they paddled through had its own distinctive presence. Even the color of the water varied, and while pines predominated, other species of trees peeked through, their autumn foliage making them stand out against the blue-green background. No other living creature intruded into their solitude except for a few birds, flitting across the surface of the water.

As they traversed the next portage, Ben identified the different trees and plants, showing him how to distinguish the birches with their black and white papery bark from the smaller aspen. All the leaves were starting to turn yellow. The scenery would be spectacular in a couple of weeks. After that, though, it would be transformed by snow and ice. This freedom and escape from his cares and commitments couldn't last forever, no matter how much he wished it could.

Adrian watched Ben closely as he trudged up the hill in front of him. He hadn't missed the fear in his eyes when they'd been messing around. It wasn't only fear for his safety, it was a fear of failure on his part. Adrian had already noted how his brothers questioned every decision he made. Even his mother wasn't convinced Ben was a man yet.

Physically, there was no doubt he was. But Adrian had seen enough of him on other occasions to know that they were all misjudging him. Since the lecture he'd given Ben a few months ago, Adrian had noticed a distinct change in attitude. There was maturity there now, well beyond his years. He had demonstrated incredible focus and determination to get the DVD finished on time. Then, when it came to organizing the expedition, he hadn't hesitated to take charge, possessing enough self-assurance to carry it off.

The young man now took his responsibilities seriously. The problem was that his family never gave him the opportunity to shine in that regard. This trip was a chance for Ben to show them what he was capable of. Adrian vowed to do everything in his power to help him reach his goals.

"Damn dam." Once again, Ben rested the end of the canoe in the V formed by two close-growing trees. He eased himself out from underneath and used the bottom of his shirt to wipe the perspiration off his face.

Adrian was hot too, especially with the pack on. He hitched it higher and put his arm around Ben's waist, leaning in against his strength. "What's the problem?"

"Much as I love beavers, they are a nuisance sometimes."

"How so?" Adrian eased the pack off his shoulders and stared down the path. All he could see was leaf litter lying on the ground.

"There's usually a navigable stream here, leading into the next lake, but the little critters have dammed up a section, turning this into a swamp. Water can flow through the sticks they used to build the barrier, but everything behind it just becomes a squishy mess."

"Why don't the rangers remove the obstruction?"

Ben turned toward him, a horrified look on his face. "Are you kidding? The Canadian authorities are fanatical about keeping this place as nature intended it to be. We're not allowed to do anything to tamper with the environment."

"So what do we do?"

"We'll have to portage around it." Ben smiled ruefully at Adrian. "Sorry."

"Hey. It's not your fault." Adrian gave him a hug. Glad of the excuse to touch him again. "Nothing's insurmountable."

"It's going to make our journey longer and more difficult."

"That's life. We should only worry about the things we have control over. Come and help me with my pack." Adrian broke away reluctantly and flinched as the heavy weight settled on his shoulders.

"You okay?"

"Yeah," Adrian twitched his shoulders to get the straps into the right position. "Just got a little sunburned, yesterday."

"I...."

"Told you so." Adrian finished for him. "Come on, the quicker we get to the end, the sooner you can rub in some more oil."

"It's a deal."

For once they were able to walk side by side because they were no longer on a portage path. Adrian glanced across at Ben's profile as they trudged through the mud. He looked worried: chewing on his bottom lip, his face tense. Probably concerned they wouldn't reach their planned stopping place in time. Adrian searched for a topic to distract him. "How heavy were the packs the *voyageurs* carried?" Ben had mentioned something to Pop up at the vineyard, but Adrian hadn't had a chance to follow up.

"Often two ninety-pound bales at a time. One on the back, one on the front."

"You're kidding."

Ben shook his head and grinned. "Time was money as far as they were concerned. They even had contests to see how much they could carry."

For the rest of the portage, Ben chatted about the people who treated the glacier-formed lakes as a highway, stretching from Alaska to the eastern seaboard via the Great Lakes. Adrian absorbed the information and was pleased to see that his ploy had worked. Ben's face gradually lost its worried look, and his usual sunny nature returned.

Nothing much was visible when they reached the dam wall; only a few twigs and chewed-off branches poked above the surface. Behind it, leaves eddied in the small pond created by the barrier. "Where are the beavers?"

Ben lifted the front of the canoe and smiled. "We can hang around and wait if you like, but they're pretty shy creatures, so we might be here for a while."

Adrian's boots were sinking into the mud, and the day had been long enough as it was. According to Ben, they'd already paddled thirty miles. "Nah, let's keep going. I've seen enough on the Discovery channel."

Ben snorted as Adrian helped him flip the canoe back down, and they loaded it, ready for the last paddle to their stopping place.

THAT evening's campsite was on a low headland under an ancient red pine. After setting up the tents, Adrian sat shredding pine needles as Ben stacked some dry timber together. "I'm surprised fires are allowed," he commented.

"As long as we keep the area around the fire clear and don't let it get out of hand, we should be okay." Ben blew on the kindling, encouraging the spark before he continued. "Depends on the amount of rain we've had. I checked the fire restrictions before we set out." He poked some small sticks in as the blaze took hold.

All around them the lake and surrounds were still, peaceful except for the soft lapping of waves against the shoreline. As dusk settled, the birds had, one by one, sought shelter for the night, leaving them alone in the wilderness. It had taken Adrian a while to let go of the city; now he couldn't picture being back there. The noise and bustle seemed a world away. Another place. Another planet.

"I suppose wildfire is always a risk, though." Adrian brushed off his hands and stood, staring down the lake as the sun slowly set.

"Yeah." Ben replied softly.

As the silence continued, Adrian turned to see what was wrong. "Oh, gee, I'm sorry. I should have remembered; your father died fighting fires, didn't he?" The conversation up at the vineyard sprang into his memory.

"The fire didn't kill him. He had a heart attack while fighting one close to home." Ben's soft response could hardly be heard above the crack and sizzle of the flames as tiny beads of moisture in the wood swelled and popped. "Some idiot probably flipped a cigarette out the car window." Ben's chin rested on his arms as they cradled his knees. "You can't fight them once they take hold. You have to let them run their course. Usually they burn themselves out pretty quickly, but the last one…"—he pointed to a wide section on the opposite side of the lake, where it looked like someone had shaved the tops off all the trees—"went through a blow-down area from a huge windstorm that swept through here back in '99."

Adrian pictured the fire's ferocity. "How do they fight the big ones?"

Ben shrugged. "Apart from water-bombing, there's not much they can do. Mostly they try to steer them away from sensitive areas. Current theory is that the park needs to burn sometimes, or it becomes stagnant." Ben's voice grew softer, more reflective as he picked up one of the larger branches they'd collected and worked one end into the blaze. "Sometimes it's better to stand back when things get out of hand and concentrate on protecting yourself and the people you love."

AFTER dinner, Adrian sat on the log they had dragged near the fire to act as a seat. Ben sat on the ground, nestled between his knees. Draping his arms across Ben's shoulders, Adrian hugged the strong body against his chest, resting his chin on Ben's head, sharing body warmth. Every now and then one would make a comment, but mostly they were silent, enjoying the closeness, mesmerized by the flames and the soft crackling as the wood burned. Adrian tried to recall a time when he had felt this settled before, this happy and couldn't.

After the flames died down, Ben doused the fire with water and buried the wet embers in the sand to prevent any spark flaring up again while they were asleep.

Tiredness dragged at Adrian's eyelids, but they still hadn't cleaned up.

Ben removed the pot of water they'd been heating and poured some into their wash-up container. "Your turn to dry." He threw Adrian the dishtowel.

"Slave driver," Adrian grumbled. "I should have gone on that cruise after all."

"What cruise?" Ben's look of innocent enquiry sent a jolt of guilt through Adrian. There was so much he had hidden from the young man. Too much history to explain. Too many scars to reveal. He took the dripping plate from Ben's grasp and concentrated on wiping that for a couple of seconds. "My father thinks that's where I've gone."

Ben laughed. "Some cruise."

"I suppose it qualifies as a gay one at any rate," Adrian muttered.

"You betcha."

What would his father say when he found out? Adrian decided not to worry about the reception he'd get when he returned to San Francisco. No, he'd cross that hurdle when he came to it. This time away was what he needed. *Ben* was what he needed. There was something about the young man that made his heart skip, let his own younger, happier self run free. "The food's not quite up to cruise standard," he teased as he stashed away the dry utensils.

Ben snorted and handed him the last cooking pot. "Beef teriyaki in sherry soy sauce with snow peas and peppers ain't good enough for you, boss?"

"At least you didn't burn yourself this time." Adrian grinned and gave the pan a perfunctory wipe before placing it with other gear. *Why did the twinkle in Ben's eye banish all tiredness?* One part of him was ready to rumble. He wiped his hands on the sides of his jeans, adjusting the fit. "Well, you must admit that the facilities *are* a bit primitive. I'm not used to living this close to nature. You sure I'm safe out here?"

Ben finished hauling the food sack up into the tree and stalked toward him, lurching slowly as he walked. "Argh," he snarled, beating his hands against his chest, doing a passable impression of a bear. "Bears round here, don't eat honey, ya know, their favorite food is trespassers who expect indoor plumbing."

Adrian laughed at the fierce expression on Ben's face and took a few steps backward in mock terror. "You should have warned me all I was getting was a trench digger and a squashed roll of toilet paper."

Ben loomed over him.

Adrian took another step and discovered he'd been backed against the trunk of the red pine.

Ben placed his hands on either side of his head, trapping him. "You should be glad I didn't make you use lumberjack toilet paper." At Adrian's look of bewilderment, he added, "Leaves."

"Yuck."

Ben grinned and leaned in closer. "Complaints, complaints, that's all we get from you city slickers. I suppose you got problems with the staff too?"

Plenty, especially when they look at me like that! Adrian's tight jeans became even tighter as his cock stiffened again. "No, I'm happy with the staff, especially yours." He didn't manage to get the last word out, as Ben laughed and trapped his mouth in a determined kiss.

Adrian could taste the chocolate cheesecake they'd shared. They kissed for what seemed like hours; Adrian was in no hurry to stop. The discomfort from the rough surface at his back only added to the high he was getting from Ben's bruising onslaught.

CHAPTER
+++
TEN

EVENTUALLY Ben managed to break away. He grinned at Adrian. "Slave driver, eh?"

"Yep." Adrian smiled back, lowered lids half covering his cool gray eyes.

"And who was the one who wouldn't let me move my hands last night, eh?" Ben pressed his groin hard against Adrian's, pressing their shafts together, layers of clothing separating them this time.

"Aah. You've got a point there."

Ben grinned at the pun. Good. He liked this Adrian. Relaxed. Not so serious. Ben leaned in closer, wedging his knee between Adrian's legs. His face only inches away. "And who teased and tortured me for ages, not letting me come?"

"Um, that would be me." Adrian drawled out the last word, glancing up through his long black eyelashes, flirting with danger.

They stared at each other for a few long seconds before Ben finally succumbed and leaned in to kiss him again. Even with only a soft press of lips against lips, the kiss stole all the air from Ben's lungs. This was different from last night. More intimate somehow, because they were both fully clothed. Eventually, Ben broke away. The playful smile had disappeared from Adrian's face, to be replaced by an intent look that Ben couldn't quite fathom. He took a quick breath and tried to remember what they were talking about. That's right. Teasing. Torture. "And you call *me* a slave driver!" Ben swallowed a laugh as Adrian tried to reach down to adjust his cock. Catching his hand, he growled, "No, you don't. Tonight it's *my* turn to frustrate the hell out of you." This could go two ways: either Adrian would refuse to play along and things would get mighty embarrassing, or he could show his boss how to let go and have someone else take charge for a change.

Hooking his fingers through the loops at Adrian's waist, Ben drew him closer. With one deft move, he planted one arm across his chest and swiveled him around until he faced the tree, placing first one hand then the other on the bark at head height. "Stay," he growled.

"Who's gonna make me?" Adrian's challenging smirk over his shoulder earned him a quick tap on the butt.

The short, sharp hiss he got in response made Ben's voice deeper than usual when he replied, "Me, your very own personal guide and paddling partner." Wedging his knee back in between Adrian's legs, he pressed him forward against the trunk. "And where would you be without my J-stroke, eh?" He ground his leg in a circular motion against Adrian's butt. A soft moan was the only response he got. "Still going round in circles, eh?"

Too much material. He pulled Adrian away from the tree so he could open the button on his waistband. Eventually, Ben managed to slip the plastic disk through the hole and carefully ease the zipper down. Adrian's soft hiss of relief when his cock flopped out made Ben smile. He ran his fingers over the soft skin on the tip and waited for some sign that he needed to back off, but judging by the wetness of the surface and the stillness of the body within his arms, things were going to plan. After just being the passive receptor of Adrian's attention last night, maybe Adrian needed this, needed to know he was wanted in return. Using his free arm, Ben hugged Adrian against his chest, kissing and sucking the skin where neck and shoulder joined.

Adrian's strangled, "Yes," and the violent shudder made Ben suck harder.

His own cock throbbed as the blood pulsed with his heartbeat. Reluctantly, he planted a long, lingering kiss and tore his mouth away from Adrian's neck. Then, in one swift movement, he stripped Adrian's jeans down around his ankles, hobbling him. Ben scanned the quivering figure before him from tip to toe. "Pity I ain't got any handcuffs with me, eh?"

Adrian turned his head, and their gazes met. The gray eyes were now as dark as a summer storm. Looking good so far. Seemed his boss liked bondage too, though Ben didn't remember his heart hammering this hard whenever he tied Jason up.

"Ow!" Adrian eased his hands away from the tree-trunk. "Shame this isn't padded."

Red marks showed on his palms where they'd been pressed against the rough bark. "Sorry, I must have been leaning in too hard." Despite the pain Adrian must be feeling, Ben noticed that his cock still curved proudly upward. He stroked his thumb gently over the pink indentations on Adrian's palm. "Do you want me to stop?" Reluctantly, he checked Adrian's face for a sign. He didn't *want* to stop, but he would if it was all too much for Adrian.

Adrian pulled his hands away and shook his head without breaking eye contact. Turning back to face the tree, he stripped off his T-shirt, wrapped the bundled up material around his hands and replaced them exactly where they had been before.

Ben's breath caught at the demonstration of his boss's willingness to play. Wrapping his left arm loosely around Adrian's chest again, he splayed his hand at the waist, and sighed in satisfaction as Adrian let his bared body relax against his hold. Ben ran the palm of his other hand slowly down the tanned back, enjoying the smoothness of his skin, feeling the hard muscles underneath, kneading the soft globes of his ass. "More squats when you get back, eh boss?" The words might have been flippant, but the huskiness in his voice betrayed his own arousal.

"If you say so, coach." Adrian's voice sounded spaced-out, like he, too, was lost in the moment.

Ben continued working his hand, not massaging, just soothing away tension with gentle caresses rather than strength. Adrian shivered against the outstretched palm that cradled and supported him. Ben flicked up his thumb and tweaked his nipples. Rock-hard. "Cold?" he murmured into Adrian's ear.

Adrian groaned and turned his head, snatching a quick kiss before responding quietly. "No, but I'm going to scream if you don't do something soon." Ben was pleased to see that those beautiful eyes were now clouded with lust. Unfocused. Dreamy.

213

Ben rolled the hard nub around under his palm, loving the ability to actually touch the body *he'd* dreamed about, let alone having it on display before him, so open, so willing. His cock felt like it would burst if he didn't fuck Adrian. Soon.

"What are you waiting for, an invitation?" Adrian let out a strangled groan and head-butted his trapped hands.

Ben forced out a laugh, but even to his ears it sounded false. "I can't."

"Just fuck my thighs, then, anything. I'm dying here." Adrian's anguished glance and the desperation in his voice might have sounded funny if Ben hadn't been feeling the same way. He unfastened his shirt and opened his jeans, allowing his cock to spring free, anxious to join the party. Moving in close behind Adrian, he stood still for a moment, nestling the hard shaft between their bodies, enjoying the sensation of skin against skin. They fitted so perfectly together.

Adrian arched back, increasing the number of points of contact. This time their groans came in unison. A harmony of need.

"Damn, Ben, stop being a tease." Adrian leaned forward again, resting his head on his wrapped hands; his whole body trembling as Ben shifted his hand from his chest to palm his cock. The hard shaft twitched in his grip, eliciting another stifled moan from Adrian's throat.

Ben parted the firm, round butt cheeks with his free hand and guided his cock into the gap. A few drops of pre-come smoothed the way for the first glide along Adrian's crack. He groaned as the tip slid across the puckered hole. "Shit, Adrian, this is going to be pure torture. You have the most fuckable ass ever." Ben bit down on his bottom lip. *Strong. He could be strong. He had to be.*

Adrian moaned, his cock growing even harder from Ben's gentle but firm tugging. "Just fuck me, please."

Don't tempt me! "No, I promised myself. Squeeze your legs together, tight as possible."

Warm heat surrounded his cock as Ben thrust between Adrian's clenched muscles. Every quiver of Adrian's body transferred from Ben's dick to his brain, reminding him of who he was with. This wasn't some random fuck in the backroom of a bar; this was Adrian, the man he'd been dreaming about for so long.

Adrian responded to his strength, coiling like a taut spring, letting him use the tension in his body. "Ben... Need... you.... Want." Each word punctuated by a long drawn-out moan.

What had started out as playful sex suddenly flipped into hot urgency. Ben grabbed Adrian's hip and tightened the grip on his cock. At each pass through that hot, dry channel, he had to struggle against the temptation to change direction and plunge into the waiting hole. Murmurs of endearment bubbled to the surface. *Love this. Love you. Where had they come from? This was just sex, wasn't it?* Ben clamped his mouth tight against the skin at Adrian's neck, trying to keep the words at bay. Adrian bucked within the restriction of his embrace, the cock throbbing in his grasp as Ben milked the hard shaft in time with his thrusts.

"Fuck me!" The strangled cry split the air as Adrian became a rigid pillar of need, giving Ben more friction to work against.

"No!" By now, so much pre-come had leaked from his cock, that the tight passage was slick enough to allow full, snapping thrusts. The impact of the tip of his cock slapping against Adrian's balls finally undid Ben. All the strength fled from his legs. The urge to come travelled like a missile locked onto its target. With one final, hard suck, he drew in the skin against his lips, and clenched his grip on Adrian's cock.

Adrian howled like a timber wolf. His thighs spasmed and jerked, sending shot after shot of semen spraying against the tree trunk. The sound alone pushed Ben over the edge, come erupting from his body, his own mangled grunts of relief adding to their primeval symphony. As their heartbeats gradually returned to normal, he collapsed over Adrian's sweaty back, and hugged Adrian against his chest, resting his head on Adrian's shoulder, panting quietly from the exertion.

"Who needs porn DVDs?" Adrian muttered and twisted his head around to give Ben a quick kiss.

Who indeed? Ben couldn't think, let alone move. He shakily pulled away and licked Adrian's neck. The skin he'd been gnawing at to prevent himself uttering silly words was now red raw. Maybe he really *was* an animal, trying to claim something that wasn't his. "Oops. How long do hickeys take to fade?"

Adrian tried to see the mark, but couldn't twist his head far enough. "Good one, Ben. It's right where the strap of the pack goes." He gave a weak laugh and looped his hands around Ben's neck as they rested against each other, much like two boxers getting their breath back before the referee pried them apart. "A bear would be less dangerous than you."

Ben growled again and grinned, thankful that the danger had passed and they were back into safer territory. "Wanna go hibernate in my tent and find out?"

CHAPTER
✠
ELEVEN

THE sun's rays filtered through the dark nylon, warming the interior. Adrian stretched and yawned. He hadn't slept that well in ages. Hot sex with Ben beat a sleeping pill hands down any day. His companion didn't stir. Soft snuffles tickled the back of his neck as Adrian lay there, welcoming the warmth and closeness of Ben's body wrapped around his.

Memories of last night's encounter drifted through his mind, bringing a smile to his lips as he fingered the mark at his neck. At first, Ben's caveman antics had just been amusing. At one stage, Adrian even wrestled with the thought of resisting his efforts, but in retrospect he was glad he hadn't. That would have been as bad as Ben's brothers not allowing him to take control of his life, questioning every decision, forcing him to remain in the position of the immature younger sibling.

For them, it was a case of too many stags already competing for primacy. The young buck needed new territory to allow that part of his personality to shine through. Adrian had no problems in that regard. After what seemed a lifetime of being responsible for so many people at work, he didn't mind giving up control in bed.

Last night, what initially had been a conscious decision became instinctive as his mind and body responded to Ben's desire to take the upper hand. All thoughts of age and job difference vanished as soon as the heat of the moment took over. Though, heat was too weak a word. Inferno was closer to the truth. Jason had said that Ben was a good lover. Now Adrian could see why. His body still trembled from the memory of how owned he had felt. God, what would full-on sex be like? Ben could do rough, but he could also be gentle. As lovers, their age difference seemed unimportant, irrelevant. What would he give to be able to just let go and let Ben take charge.

After returning to the tent to "hibernate", as Ben called it, they'd explored each other's bodies. Still wanting that closeness, that contact. Without any illumination except the soft glow of moon and stars filtering through the walls of the tent, they'd had to rely on touch, but even so, Adrian had been able to memorize each muscle, trace every bone. The perfect and the not-so-perfect. They'd laughed as they recounted the stories behind each flaw. The slight dent in Ben's collarbone, which he'd broken falling out of a tree. The bump on his shin from a particularly vicious clash with a hockey stick. Their bodies were a living record of their childhood and early years.

Ben's dad featured a lot in his tales. Although he'd still been young when his father had died, the lessons he'd imparted to the impressionable young boy formed the backbone of the man he was today. Adrian had heard the phrase: "Dad used to say," a lot last night; apparently, his father thought lessons learned in the wilderness could be applied to every problem in life. Maybe he was right.

Adrian's stories were not so interesting. He hadn't grown up with brothers who thought nothing of having younger siblings tag along as they did activities well beyond their years. "Careful, Adrian," had been said so often, it was a wonder people didn't think he had a hyphenated first name.

After these reminiscences finished, they kissed again, and Ben fell asleep in his arms, the day's exertion finally taking its toll.

Adrian had lain there for a while, absorbing the sensation of having Ben's head nestled against his chest. Every time thoughts of next week or the future tried to force their way in, he ruthlessly thrust them aside, jealous of every moment they spent together.

He sighed. There was a lot to be said for having a younger lover, but they liked sleeping in too much. He rolled over and stroked the tips of his fingers along Ben's morning wood. If he was anything like Adrian, he was bursting to take a leak.

"Hey." Ben's response was half-protest, half-greeting.

"Wake up, sleepyhead. It's getting late." Adrian gave a casual flick of his finger, catching the cock-tip.

Ben laughed. "Stop it, that one's already awake." He pointed to his head. "It's the one up here with the brain that's not."

Adrian slid his naked body up over Ben's and gave him a long, lingering kiss. "Awake now?"

Ben nodded and smiled lazily at him.

"Did you have a good sleep?"

Ben ran his hand down the side of Adrian's jaw, stroking through the stubble. "Sure did," he whispered. "I had this great dream where I found a hot, sexy guy wandering in the woods and fucked him up against a big pine tree."

"Funny. I had the same dream." Adrian smiled at the quick blush that stole over Ben's face and twisted his head to plant a quick kiss on the questing fingers. "Come on, lazybones. We better get moving."

"Do we have to?"

"If we want to follow the route you picked out."

"Bummer. I want to stay here all day, making love to you."

The breath caught in Adrian's throat at the honest, unguarded need in the young man's eyes; the temptation to do just that threatened to overwhelm him. He groaned and shook his head. "My bladder is busting." Reluctantly, he crawled out of the tent and headed toward the pine tree that had featured so vividly in last night's encounter. Ben followed soon after.

"Why aren't we pissing in the water?" Ben asked as he grinned and aimed his cock at the ground.

Adrian stared at him while watering the big pine. "And pollute the lake?"

Ben's steady stream wavered up and down as his body shook with laughter. "Talk about a drop in the ocean!"

Adrian grinned. "So what! One of the things I love about this place is how pristine everything is." He shook off the last drops and leaned against the tree, staring into the distance. "No matter where you go nowadays, there are always people around, making noise. It's so rare to go someplace where the footprints of man are seldom seen. Even around Long Island there's always something disturbing the silence. Here you can be sure there'll be no jet skis screaming around in circles, no motor launches creating a huge wake. We're here, but really we're insignificant when you consider everything around us."

Ben put an arm around his shoulder as they gazed across at the wilderness in front of them, his half-hard cock cradled loosely in his other hand.

Adrian glanced sideways at his face and saw awareness grow in Ben's gaze. Adrian pulled away from Ben's embrace and leaned back against the trunk of the tree, enjoying the sight of the strong, naked body in front of him.

"Like what you see?" Ben asked with a shy grin.

Adrian laughed as his own words were repeated back to him. "Very much. Now I'm going to dream about having that gorgeous cock inside me."

The smile on Ben's face dimmed at the reminder of what couldn't be, at least for now. Adrian shoved away the quick addition that sprang into his brain. *Not ever.* He wasn't prepared to think about what would happen when he returned to San Francisco. He swallowed as his gaze dwelled on the thick length lying in Ben's hand. "That reminds me of a dream *I* once had." As he started speaking, his voice sounded as far away as his thoughts.

Ben's gaze immediately became more alert, and he didn't interrupt as Adrian continued. "You and I were working in Pop's vineyard at pruning time." Adrian smiled as he added, "I was wearing my denim cutoffs that you seem to approve of."

Ben's low growl and lick of his lips went straight to Adrian's own cock, rekindling its interest. He gave the shaft a long, slow stroke. "You were wearing your cargo shorts and a loose button-up shirt to protect your pale skin, but you hadn't fastened the buttons, so the sides drooped open, showing off your perfect pecs."

Ben drew in his stomach, making them stand out even more.

Adrian deliberately dropped his voice and spoke slower, letting the words linger in the air, allowing time for Ben to conjure up the image. "You were pulling the canes off the wires after I cut them. The work was hot and dusty, and you were bored shitless." Ben gave a snort of laughter, but judging by the quick spit on his hand before transferring it to his cock he wasn't bored now. He had closed his eyes, focusing on the picture Adrian was creating.

"The hot sun beat down mercilessly."

Ben opened his eyes briefly and grinned at the cliché. "Let me guess, you weren't wearing a shirt, and I had just finished rubbing suntan oil all over your bare skin."

"Something like that." Adrian gave a quick snort of laughter. "But, no more interruptions, this is *my* dream."

"Okay." Ben's hand on his cock had gone from absent-minded stroking to a steady rhythm. Adrian watched in fascination as it grew even bigger under his touch. Blood fled from his brain, and he found it hard to remember what bit came next. Oh, that's right. "We were working halfway down the hill, well out of sight of the house and, before seeking refuge from the heat, Nonna left us a tray with iced tea and chicken sandwiches on the picnic table in the shade of a large tree."

Ben licked his lips, making them all moist and pink. Adrian was tempted to kiss him again, but first he wanted to see how far he could take him, using only his voice. "As soon as Nonna was out of sight, I perched on the edge of the table. You stood between my legs, and we fed each other bites of our sandwiches." Adrian paused for dramatic effect. He could almost taste the chicken himself. "Our gazes didn't waver as we ate. The smell of sweat, dust, and your musk filled my nostrils."

Ben groaned and threw back his head, his hand now stroking his erection more urgently.

"Wait," Adrian warned. "I haven't got to the good bit yet."

Ben opened his eyes and stared at him, his blue eyes clouded with lust. "Have you any idea what your voice is doing to me, let alone the words, or the images you're creating?"

Adrian laughed quietly. Did Ben have any idea how hot he looked? Comfortable in his nakedness, long legs planted strongly, shoulder-width apart, purple-tipped cock arching out as he stroked its full length, pre-come now seeping enough to add to the slickness. Adrian was hard too, but he deliberately folded his arms tight against his chest, resisting the temptation to touch himself.

He swallowed and forced himself to continue speaking. "As soon as we finished eating. I reached around and picked up one of the long, tall glasses from the table. Nonna had added a thin slice of lime. Before handing you the iced tea, I took out the piece of fruit and sucked it between my teeth, then you bent down and kissed me. The tartness added a new flavor to our long, passionate kiss." Ben's tongue darted out as if he were savoring the taste already. Adrian's cock gave a quick twitch. "Then you threw back your head as you drank, and I watched your throat undulate as you swallowed." Adrian's voice dropped even lower without trying. "I could picture what you would look like if you had my cock in there, deep-throating me."

Ben groaned. "Adrian, I don't think I can stand any more of this." His blue eyes pleaded with him as he stopped stroking and tugged impatiently on his balls.

"Nearly finished," Adrian promised. He didn't know if he could string it out much longer himself. "I drank my tea, and as I turned to place my glass back on the table, you picked me up roughly and spun me around so my chest slammed onto the hard surface."

Ben groaned again and gripped the base of his cock, his breath now coming in short bursts. Adrian laughed at the proof of his impatience. "The next bit is always a bit unclear, as somehow both glasses miraculously disappear, my shorts get ripped off, and yours are undone and down around your ankles. That's what happens in dreams. Convenient, isn't it?"

Ben opened his eyes, and they shared a quick grin. The break in tension worked. Ben took a deep gulp of air and went back to stroking his cock. Adrian couldn't resist a quick, reassuring stroke of his own. He'd been getting complaints from there ever since he'd started.

"Next thing I knew, you'd slammed your cock into my hole, and seconds later you were balls-deep inside. I think they heard me cry out up at the house. We both froze as we waited for someone to come down, but neither Nonna or Pop appeared. While we waited, my body became accustomed to having you inside, although I'd never felt you so long and hard before."

Ben staggered slightly as if his knees were going to give way.

Adrian took a deep breath, his own imagination threatening to get the better of him. "Then you started moving, thrusting into me hard and fast, grunting with the effort. Again and again you pistoned into me, thrilling me with every stroke. By this time, I was moaning your name and my cock jerked in time, rigid and leaking pre-come even though I wasn't touching it. Both my hands were needed to support myself so that I wasn't cannoned into its hard surface by your brute strength. Neither of us wanted this to end, but eventually you reached around and grabbed my twitching cock. At your firm touch, long jets of come spurted out all over the table. My whole body spasmed, helping to draw out your orgasm. Moments later, you screamed my name out loud as you shot inside me." This time Ben's face did screw up in agony as rope after rope of come erupted, splattering on the ground beneath the tree.

"Oh, shit, Adrian."

Adrian caught Ben as he collapsed in his arms. He held him tight as the seemingly boneless body shook with after-shocks, stroking his back, enjoying the aftermath of the impressive orgasm he had caused.

Eventually Ben pulled away, unshed tears glistening on his fair eyelashes. His voice wavered as he muttered hoarsely. "You bastard, you didn't even come." He reached for Adrian's cock, but Adrian swatted his hand away.

"Later. We should eat something first. You look like you need to replace some of the energy you just lost." He smiled slightly as Ben found it difficult to walk straight, though when he tried moments later he found he had the same difficulty. Out of nowhere, Antonio's face flashed across his mind, sobering him instantly. They had never done anything like that, although some of their encounters were nearly as hot.

It was weird how the quick flashback to actual events with Antonio felt less real than the imaginary encounter he had just described. He could actually *feel* Ben there with him as easily as he could see him now, watching quietly as he donned his loose cargo pants.

Adrian's paddling clothes were still damp. He'd rinsed out his shorts and laid them on a rock in the sun. Hopefully, by the time they were ready to leave, the denim would be dry or at least warm enough to wear. He sighed and extracted an old pair of sweatpants from his backpack.

CHAPTER
TWELVE

ADRIAN'S scenario played through Ben's mind as he stirred the pre-cooked bacon he'd chopped into the pancake mix. If Adrian ever needed a fallback job he could always do phone sex. The guy's voice was made for it. All the pauses in the right places. He hadn't just been talking about sex though; he'd been drawing Ben a picture, using all the adjectives to set the scene. And what a scene.

The strange thing was that even though Adrian hadn't touched him as he jerked off, he felt as if he'd been cradled in his arms, safe and secure. He'd never felt this close, this comfortable with anyone before. Able to let go and know he could be himself. But now his frustration at not being able to go all the way became even more acute. It wasn't about fucking Adrian anymore; it was about being joined, becoming one: heart, body, soul—everything.

He watched his boss methodically take down the tents. He hadn't missed the abrupt change of mood. Something was definitely wrong. Even though Adrian hadn't come, his hard-on had disappeared pretty quickly. Now his shoulders were slumped as he packed away the gear. Any minute Ben expected to see him rub the back of his neck. Had he started thinking about work again? Ben knew a solution for that.

Making sure he kept his fingers out of the way, he poured the mix into the heated and greased pan. While their breakfast cooked, he opened the foil sachet containing the apples and syrup. At least Adrian's pack was lighter because they'd eaten most of the food. Their original route, though, was definitely impossible. Half the morning had already gone. Ben sighed. His brothers were right as usual. He *had* been too ambitious.

"Anything the matter?" Adrian had finished packing and stood quietly beside him. Ben was so wrapped in his thoughts, he hadn't heard him approach.

"I need to work out an alternate path to get us back to the pickup point in time."

"Will that be a problem?"

Now it was Ben's turn to rub the back of his neck. "I haven't been on some of them, so I'm not sure what they're like. Uncharted territory for me."

Adrian crouched down as Ben slid the finished pancakes onto the plates and spread on the topping. "I'm sure we'll be fine. Pick whatever route you think is best."

Ben gave him a weak grin as he handed him a plate. "What about you? Something bothering you?" He took his breakfast over to the log they'd been using as seat.

Adrian sat beside him and snorted. "Only the fact that I'm missing my clothes dryer, and I'd kill for a hot shower." He lifted his arm and sniffed.

"Hey, check the other one next time!" Ben laughed and turned his head pointedly away. As far as he was concerned, Adrian smelled divine.

Adrian grinned. "Lucky for you, my deodorant works in the woods."

Ben shifted uncomfortably, for once regretting the fact he didn't have a fat ass. "Padded chairs would definitely be an improvement, and I'd kill for a comfy bed."

"You got that right." Adrian took a large mouthful. "Hey, this is good."

"You betcha. Food always tastes better when you're starving."

Adrian waved his fork in the air, still chewing. "No, I mean it. This is *really* good." He finished eating that mouthful and swallowed, his face suddenly intent. "No matter what happens, I'll always look back on this trip as some of the happiest days of my life."

Ben felt the heat rising in his face at Adrian's compliment. For him, they *were* the best, no argument, but what did the phrase *No matter what happens* mean? And was Adrian referring to the outdoors experience or the sex? The problem was that, for Ben, it was no longer just having sex. Somewhere along the line it had become more than that. Clearly, the feeling wasn't reciprocated. He ate the rest of his pancakes in silence.

After breakfast, while Ben stowed the gear in the canoe, Adrian sat on the big pack, wearing his glasses and intently studying the large detailed map spread out over his parted knees. Ben was reminded of his favorite jerk-off fantasy. Adrian sitting in Jason's bedroom, reading his book on wine while Ben gave him the blow job from heaven.

Adrian's stiff shoulders betrayed his tension. Ben stood behind him and ran his fingers over the tight muscles. Adrian rolled his head around and smiled dreamily up at him. "You're very good at that, you know."

Ben leaned over and gave him a quick kiss. For a second, he thought it wasn't going to be reciprocated, but after only a brief pause, Adrian responded. Ben didn't try for erotic; he only wanted to show Adrian he cared. When he broke contact, Adrian sighed and licked his lips. "You're very good at that too." They gazed into each other's eyes for a long moment. Eventually, Adrian turned around and went back to studying the map. "What are our options?" he asked quietly.

Ben kept up his massage with one hand and reached over with the other, pointing things out as he spoke. "This is the way we *were* going to go but, if we do, we won't get back in time. Of course we could use the satellite phone and say we'll be back a day later."

Adrian shook his head. "And have your brothers think I'm a wuss who couldn't walk or paddle fast enough?"

Ben snorted. "And that their kid brother had shit for brains."

Adrian smiled regretfully. "Anyway, I do have to get back to work."

"Yeah."

The smile disappeared. Adrian bit his lip and studied the map again, pointing to an inlet half way up Lake Conmee. "What if we go this way?"

"That's the shortest route, but take a look at those portages. The first one is longer than any we've done so far, and there are three of them, one after the other. Even if we do make it across before dark, we've still got a long paddle across Lake Poobah before we hit the creek."

"Poobah? I wonder why it's named after a character out of *The Mikado*? Impressive maybe?" Adrian smiled as he made the comment, but the smile disappeared pretty quickly. "Do we have an alternative?"

"Not really, but I've never gone that route, so we'll be flying blind." Ben dug his fingers in a bit harder, taking out some of his frustration on Adrian's tight muscles. Neither spoke for a while as Ben continued to work. As usual, after a few moments of being close to Adrian and stroking his bare skin, Ben thoughts turned naturally to sex again. He leaned over and saw that Adrian's cock was also forming a tent in his sweatpants. He'd refolded the map, but now his eyes were closed, and his glasses were perched precariously on the end of his nose. Ben grinned and quickly moved around to face him, kneeling between his legs. With a deft swipe, he twitched the map out of his loose grasp and shoved it under his knees. No way could he afford to have that blow away while he was blowing Adrian away.

Adrian blearily opened his eyes and raised his eyebrows enquiringly.

"Talking about dreams...." Ben began as he deftly grabbed the waistband of Adrian's pants, pulled them over his erection, and wedged them under his scrotum so both bat and balls were held up and out in an inviting package. Without pausing, Ben engulfed the twitching cock in his mouth in one gulp. Over the last two days, they'd used hands, thighs, all sorts of body parts to make each other come, but this time Ben wanted to finish Adrian off in his mouth, milk his cock and drink his essence.

"Hey," Adrian complained, his hands moving to Ben's head pushing him back. "I thought we were in a hurry?"

Ben let Adrian's cock slip out of his mouth as he looked up and grinned. "Five minutes isn't going to make much difference."

"Five minutes? Is that all I'm going to get?" The comment may have been flippant, but Ben noticed that Adrian's eyes had gone all smoky again as his pupils dilated.

Ben licked the head reverently. "We can fit in half an hour if we take the shortcut."

227

Adrian nodded wordlessly as Ben ran his tongue around the tip. This was something he could do. He'd dreamed about it often enough. He might not have Adrian's skill with words, but according to Jason, he did have some decent cock-sucking skills.

All thoughts about returning to city life sank into the background as he focused his attention on the task at hand. Adrian had a beautiful, cut cock. Not too big, not too small. Fine ridges covered the blue veins running under the surface. Ben drew the hard length all the way in, not even gagging slightly as the tip hit the back of his throat. He smiled as he heard Adrian's reaction and swallowed, making the gasp turn into a groan. Adrian's hand returned to caressing his head, his fingers only pausing when Ben's sucking made him falter.

Ben was quickly able to tell exactly what Adrian liked. He didn't need to hear the soft murmurs of encouragement, so he tuned out the words until the honey-soaked voice became a background accompaniment. Every hitch or gasp registered though. Soon he had Adrian moaning, a long-drawn-out keening. Fingers tightened on his scalp. Reluctantly, he let the cock slip from his lips and smiled at Adrian as he wiped his mouth and took a deep breath.

"Don't you dare stop." Adrian gave him the evil eye.

Ben grinned. "Relax, boss." Adrian's eyebrows went up at the word, but he kept silent, continuing to stroke through Ben's hair, a strange expression in his eyes.

Ben bent closer, lifting Adrian's cock with one hand and angling his head so he could watch his reaction as he carefully drew one of his balls into his mouth.

"Oh, fuck." Adrian arched back suddenly.

Ben squeezed the base of Adrian's cock to prevent him from coming, then rolled his tongue around the ball in his mouth, sucking it gently before releasing it. Prickles were scattered on Adrian's sac. Ben hummed softly to himself as he repeated the process with the other testicle. Seemed like Adrian hadn't manscaped for a while. Maybe he should volunteer to do it for him.

When he felt he'd showered Adrian's balls with sufficient homage, Ben turned his attention back to Adrian's cock. Blood pounded in his head as he drew the hard shaft in again, letting his breath tickle the slick surface. He was rewarded by a particularly loud groan as Adrian wound his fingers through his hair, not gripping tightly, more as if he needed that contact, that connection. Reality was so much better than dreams. Ben's brain ceased to function, and he worked by instinct, sucking in as he bobbed up and down.

ADRIAN released a shuddering gasp of pleasure as his cock slipped deeper into Ben's throat. At his heartfelt sign of appreciation, the young man kneeling between his legs gazed up with a curiously content expression on his face. Sheer sexual excitement and condensation on his glasses made it difficult to focus. Colors swirled and danced. The blue of Ben's eyes merged with the indigo lake and clear azure sky in the background. Flashes of yellow and red darted into the monochromatic mix. Autumn leaves. Ben's hair. Sparking off a virtual wildfire in his brain.

The urge to tighten his grip and draw Ben in closer, to keep him there forever, was nearly driving him insane. After letting go, Adrian reached out blindly for something else to hang on to. The pack he was sitting on provided the only alternative.

Having Ben touch him, stroke his cock was one thing. Being encased in Ben's mouth overwhelmed him, triggering memories and feelings from the past. The first time he did this for Antonio. Expressing everything he felt inside. Tentatively at first and then with growing assurance as pleasing his lover supplanted his own selfish needs.

But despite his youth, Ben had this down to a fine art: the suction was perfect, the way he worked his throat around Adrian's cock as he swallowed. Never gagging. The slurps noisy but not distractingly so. More blood left Adrian's brain and surged into his cock. Adrian opened his eyes again and stared blindly at the vision at his feet.

Another strong suck set off another shivering shudder. Ben's abilities definitely surpassed any of Adrian's own early fumbling efforts. A surge of jealousy swept through him as an image of Ben giving Jason a blow job flashed into his brain. And if Jason was now out of the picture, what of the future? Men who might use Ben and abuse him without caring for him? Without taking precautions? Men like Antonio? With a strangled gasp as he came, Adrian tried to push Ben away, but the young man resisted his efforts, spluttering for a second, then regaining enough control to swallow. "Fuck no! Don't!" Adrian finally succeeded in freeing himself.

"What's wrong?" Ben's expression mirrored the way Adrian felt. Pain and confusion obliterating the pleasure.

Adrian didn't answer straightaway. Playing for time, he dragged his pants back up slowly, then wiped his glasses, trying to make sense of his violent reaction. How could he explain that when he ejaculated, he'd totally lost it, imagining it wasn't *his* semen pumping into Ben's mouth, but Antonio's? As if, somehow, his dead lover and all the nameless men Ben might meet in his future were infecting Ben through him. "Did you even think to check with me before you swallowed?"

Ben clambered to his feet. "Are you positive? Is that why you don't fuck guys anymore?"

No, but I can't tell you the real reason. "HIV isn't the only thing you can catch from consuming body fluids. Don't forget Hep C and other delightful diseases."

"Are you...."

"No, I don't have any infections. But you didn't even ask. Haven't you learned *anything* from your experience with Jason?"

Ben's stance: arms folded tight across his chest, broad shoulders shaking slightly betrayed his hurt. "I assumed from the way you were so keen for me to fuck you, that you would have said something by now if you were."

Adrian raked his hand through his hair. "I suppose so, but you should always check first."

Ben stiffened. "Are you implying that I'm a slut who gives blow jobs to anyone?"

"No!" *Not yet!* But he couldn't help remembering Antonio's reaction when they split up. Adrian gripped Ben's arms, but the young man refused to meet his gaze, staring fixedly at the ground instead. He looked like a kid who had just enjoyed a huge lollipop only to be told it was medicine. "I know you would never have played around, so how did you feel when you discovered that Jason must have been unfaithful?"

When he finally looked up, a brief blush of embarrassment suffused Ben's face. "There was never anything like that between us. Jason was leading you on."

Leading me on? Huh? Adrian found it difficult to concentrate as Ben related how Jason had recently confessed to using Ben as a cover so Adrian wouldn't realize that Jason had really been out on the prowl. Not that Adrian would have said anything, but if he'd known the truth, he would have found it difficult to reassure Vernon and Consuela that their son was behaving himself. Concerned for their only child and in their ignorance, they immediately equated being gay with getting AIDS. They had been relieved when Adrian told them Jason had a steady boyfriend, assuming monogamy would keep him safe. Fury at being manipulated made Adrian lash out at Ben as the full implications of the situation occurred to him. "If you weren't in a serious relationship, why the *fucking* hell did you bareback?"

Ben broke away from his grasp and walked to the water's edge. After watching his rigid back for a few seconds, Adrian approached from behind and spun him around. Anger had replaced Ben's earlier hurt and confusion.

"I wanted to see what it was like, alright?" Ben yelled at him. "Weren't you ever young and wanted to do something just for the heck of it?"

Adrian dropped his hand as if he'd been burnt. "Yes, but I wasn't stupid!" he snapped. "That's the trouble with your generation; you never think it will happen to you. Always to some other guy."

"But HIV is treatable nowadays."

"It's still not a walk in the park. Money won't be an issue for Jason, but each med has a different long-term effect on other parts of the body. No matter what happens, his entire life has been altered."

Ben was silent for a while. "You sound as if you have firsthand experience."

"I have. The man who was the love of my life died of AIDS."

As soon as the words left his mouth, Adrian realized they might imply he would never love anyone that way again. Ben stared at him, his face even paler than usual, obviously upset again. Adrian's stomach started churning. The sensation was nothing like the acidic burn he got from drinking too much Jack Daniels; this was lower, more visceral, an emptiness that threatened to well up and engulf him. Previously, he'd only ever gotten this gut-wrenching feeling when he and Antonio argued. Nothing could be a clearer indication that this young man meant much more to him than merely a chance to have sex again.

But even if things were different, when Adrian returned to the States, there was no room for Ben in his life. This relationship had to be nipped in the bud before they became too involved. Resisting the urge to embrace Ben and take that haunted look away, Adrian broke eye contact and muttered, "Come on. It's getting late. We better get moving." Without another word, he walked back up the hill and changed into his paddling gear.

BEN pushed the paddle away from the canoe at the end of the stroke and heaved a sigh of frustration. A stiff breeze had sprung up soon after they left shore. That didn't help matters. Nor did Adrian's paddling. He kept switching to the right side, his strongest side, but that was the direction the wind was blowing from. To make matters worse, they hadn't spoken ever since this morning's blowup.

Adrian's stark statement still ricocheted around in his head. *The love of my life died of AIDS.* Maybe he should have asked the obvious questions earlier, like: *Why are you in the closet? Why have you been pretending you're straight?* There was no way Adrian hadn't had sex with a man before. Ben might be young, but he wasn't a complete idiot. While shocking, it wasn't the last part of the sentence that affected him so much. He knew Jason would forever have that fear at the back of his mind. But it was the phrase *the love of my life* that really hurt. From the sound of things, Adrian didn't intend to ever fall in love again. He grunted as he dug the paddle in deeper to bring the canoe back on track. The fact that the wind was blowing hard today seemed fitting. Blowup, blow job, blow to all his hopes…. Given their difference in status, he should never have thought differently. Another gust of wind hit the side of the canoe, slewing it off course again. *Fuck it.* No matter how efficient his J-strokes were, they weren't enough. He rested his paddle on the edge of the canoe and called out, "Stop paddling, boss."

He had to yell the words again before Adrian turned and stared at him.

"If you keep pulling so hard on one side, I can't keep the canoe straight. All my power is being lost in stopping us from going around in circles. We have to work together."

Adrian lowered his eyes and stared at the bottom of the canoe before raising them again. When he did, the anguish in them caught Ben by surprise. "I'm sorry," was all he said, but raw pain flittered across his features.

Ben dropped his voice back to a more even level. "Just paddle on the left hand side as much as possible to counteract the wind." He pointed to the cove where the long portage began. "There's not much farther to go."

Adrian started paddling again, more evenly this time.

CHAPTER
+++
THIRTEEN

ADRIAN grimaced as the skin at the base of his thumbs protested. Blisters. That was the last fucking straw. From what Ben said, they were nearly there. For once he would welcome the portage. Now all he had to do was paddle like Ben wanted and help keep the canoe on track. Adrian bent back over the task and pulled, welcoming the pain.

The canoe scraped on a submerged rock as they approached the beach. *Damn.* He was supposed to keep an eye out for underwater obstacles and warn Ben. "Sorry." He glanced at his companion, but all he got was a quickly masked sigh of frustration. No doubt Andrew would chalk that scratch up against Ben's incompetence.

Adrian studied the overgrown landing area as he dragged the pack out and balanced it on the ground. At most of the other portages, the grass was short and the start of the path stood out clearly. Nothing indicated this was the correct spot. Ben lifted the canoe out of the water and placed it on the bank before checking the map again. "According to my calculations, we *are* in the right place."

The blue eyes skittered away from him with a wariness that Adrian hadn't seen for months. He realized with a pang that he missed the direct gaze, the gaze of equals. "What are we going to do? There's no path."

Ben straightened and beckoned to him. "Follow me." Adrian trudged behind as Ben led him to the end of the beach. Once there, Ben walked inland about fifty yards and waited until Adrian caught up with him. "Here's a trick my father taught me." Ben began following an arc parallel to the water's edge. About a third of the way along, they came to a narrow but worn track, leading up the slope. Ben's face carried no sign of its usual cockiness as he explained, "Sometimes the path you need to take gets overgrown, especially in the flat section, so you have to get away from the problem area to see it clearly."

After they traced the path downhill to collect the gear, Adrian looked back. The first section of the trail was obscured by the long grass and low-growing trees. Indistinguishable. If they had blundered on ahead, they might never have found the correct route. He shouldered his pack and set off up the short but steep climb. As they walked, Adrian thought about what Ben had done. He never seemed to have any doubts that he'd find a solution to whatever difficult situation cropped up. Even when he was younger, Adrian couldn't remember ever being that sure of himself.

At the top of the ridge he looked around in surprise. Most times, the portage between two lakes was a steep walk up one side of a wooded hill and a path down the other side. This was more like a grassy meadow stretching away in all directions.

"Fuck." Ben's expletive matched the quick glare of anger in his eyes.

Adrian slipped the heavy load off his back and reached inside for a bottle of water. Ben walked up beside him and did his usual twist to remove the canoe from his back and settle it on the ground. Adrian passed him the drink. "What's wrong?"

Ben took a long swig and wiped his hand across his mouth. "What the fuck do you think is wrong?"

The knot in Adrian's stomach loosened. This time Ben's anger wasn't directed at him; it was directed at their situation. *That* he could deal with. "I trust if you said this is the right place, it *is* the right place."

A start of surprise at the unexpected vote of confidence replaced the anger in Ben's gaze. He opened his mouth, but before he could speak, Adrian held up his hand. "No, wait. Until now, I've felt like a passenger, having you do all the thinking for me. Let me see if I can work it out for myself, please."

Ben raised his eyebrows in acknowledgement and waited, the tension in his body visibly reducing, but still not back to the ease that had been there previously.

Adrian studied the boggy ground. The path had disappeared again, and this time walking a bit farther wouldn't reveal its location.

When Ben said this track wasn't used much, he wasn't kidding. The area looked so rough and wild, they could have been in the heart of Alaska. Scanning the distance didn't help either. There were no brightly colored or even dead skeletons of trees to mark the way. No distinctive hills to head for, nothing. He often wondered how Ben could see anything with his head stuck inside the canoe as he carried it, inverted, on his shoulders. Adrian turned to see that Ben was now sitting on the pack with the map and compass on his lap, scanning the horizon with binoculars. *That was it, visibility!* "I'll carry the canoe while you navigate."

Ben blinked in astonishment. "Are you sure?"

Adrian nodded. "You said it's lighter than the pack…."

"It probably isn't, now we've polished off most of the drinks and eaten a heap of food."

"Doesn't matter. That way you can use your compass and check where we're going."

"Thanks." The simple word sent a shiver up Adrian's spine, but still no affectionate touch. No shy grin.

Ben flipped the canoe over and lifted one end high enough so Adrian could get underneath and settle the pads onto his shoulders. Once he was in the right position, Adrian wedged his hands under the gunwales as Ben had showed him and straightened his legs. Apart from the sting on his shoulders, the weight didn't seem as bad as the first time he'd tried. He turned to see what Ben was doing and the canoe turned with him. At least now they weren't on a wooded path—he wasn't banging into the trees front and back as he had when he tried carrying the boat before.

Ben shouldered the large pack and folded the map into a small rectangle. The compass hung around his neck on a cord. "Ready, boss?"

The front of the canoe bobbed up and down in time with Adrian's nods.

Ben started walking.

Adrian couldn't look around unless he tilted the front of the canoe, but that upset the balance, so he stopped bothering and kept his focus on the bottom part of Ben's long legs as he strode along in front.

Now that Ben was leading, Adrian had no doubts they were heading in the right direction. He tuned out and thought about the morning's disastrous events.

His rant after the blow job had been completely over the top. Ben wasn't Antonio. He was much more levelheaded. Even if they *had* been more involved, the young man walking in front of him wouldn't have gone to pieces when Jason left and endangered his life deliberately. Maybe the intensity of his orgasm had made him light-headed. Maybe *he* was the one who was stupid. He should have fallen to his knees, thanking the young man, instead of yelling at him. Even now, every part of his body screamed at him to just shut the fuck up and apologize. But apologize for what? For falling in love with him?

Adrian had crossed so many boundaries out here. Forbidden ones. Ben had been right to rebuke him for not being more aware of what he was doing when they started paddling. The word *Boss* had slammed into Adrian's head as hard as a cannon ball. The phrase *work together* hit the same target shortly afterward. Those boundaries needed to be recrossed before they went home. Adrian bit his lip. He couldn't pretend this was a casual romp in the woods any longer. The sooner they reverted to a more professional footing, the better. Maybe somewhere down the track they could be friends again, but at least this tension prevented anything else developing on Ben's part.

Okay, Adrian, he thought to himself, *let's see how good an actor you are. From now on you have to keep the relationship friendly and professional. Talk about the weather. Whether the Wild will ever be as good as the North Stars. Whether this will be the Vikings' year or the Jets'. Who is better: Ry Cooder or Tom Waits? Anything. Just keep your fucking hands off your employee.* He snorted to himself. Like that was going to work. One touch from Ben was all it would take. One touch.

BEN had been right about the difficulty of the portage. There was a huge difference between lugging everything for a few hundred yards and carrying it for two miles. At the end of the first mile, they stopped and relaunched the canoe. This lake was so small they barely got their paddles wet before they had to stop and carry the gear again. Going around wasn't an option, Ben tersely informed him; that would have added even more miles to their journey. They didn't have a choice. The next section was even longer and uphill. Neither of them bothered to make any comments as they trudged along.

The weather was cooler, but the overcast sky only added to his misery. Adrian's shoulders screamed in agony. Theoretically, he shouldn't even be able to feel the love bite Ben had given him, but at every step, every jolt, a short, sharp twinge reminded him of their session against the tree. The worst thing was that recalling those details only served to remind him they could never be repeated.

At the end of the second portage, they took a short break to wolf down some of the oat cookies. Adrian tried to stick to his resolve and start up conversations about ice hockey, the NFL, and music, but Ben only gave him monosyllabic replies, pointedly staring at the scenery.

The paddle to the last portage took a bit longer. Adrian checked his hands when he finished, the redness betraying the blisters that were definitely forming. He probably should ask Ben to dress them, but that would have entailed enduring the young man's touch. Adrian didn't think he could handle that.

When they were ready to resume their journey, Ben asked him if he wanted to carry the pack again, but Adrian refused. Carrying the boat all the way had become his special goal, almost a penance for his stupidity in letting his defenses down and breaking his vow of celibacy. A loud crash in the bushes startled him out of his daze. He tilted the front of the canoe so he could see ahead. "What was that?"

Ben stopped and turned to face him. He looked as tired as Adrian felt. "Moose."

A part of his brain said he should be excited, but with his energy thoroughly depleted and his mood at an all-time low, Adrian just shrugged, settled the canoe back onto his shoulders, and kept walking. This track was much steeper. He kept his gaze fixed on the ground in front. It wasn't until sometime later that he noticed he couldn't see Ben's legs anymore. The path was well defined, so he hadn't taken a wrong turn. His lack of concern for his predicament puzzled him at first, then his sluggish brain gave him the answer. The mere fact they were on a defined portage meant that, once more, Ben's navigational skills had proved up to the task. They were going the right way. Adrian needed a break, but tired as he was, he wasn't going to risk using some of the trees to support the boat while he took a rest. If the canoe slipped and fell, he wouldn't be able to lift it back onto his shoulders by himself.

A loud pounding on the ground sounded again. *Was the moose back?* Adrian tilted the canoe to check. In front of him was a red-faced Ben who had obviously been running.

"I've taken the pack to the end of the portage. Give me the canoe."

"No. I can handle it." Adrian lowered the tip and took another step.

Ben didn't move. His feet were planted shoulder-width apart, his hands on his hips. Despite the fact he was out of breath, Ben looked the picture of strength. The expression in his eyes could have belonged to either Rob or Andrew. Hard, steely determination. "I don't give a damn whether you can handle it or not. We're running out of time, and I'll be quicker than you."

Adrian balked at handing it over. Stopping now would feel like failure on his part. "I said I would take it to the end, and I will."

Ben bent down and joined him under the canoe, lifting the sides, taking some of the weight off Adrian's shoulders. Now their faces were only inches apart.

"Fuck it, Adrian. I know you're capable of getting there by yourself, but would it kill you to accept some help for once?"

"I promised myself." Even to his ears, Adrian's statement sounded weak.

"What's more important? The goal or some ass-wipe sense of self-justification?"

The harsh truth stunned Adrian for a second, then Ben's proximity hit him as well. All he had to do was move his head forward an inch or two, and he could feel those lips on his again. He closed his eyes and nodded, accepting reality. Even though they didn't touch, his flesh burned as if they had. It seemed like his body remembered without any conscious effort on his part. As Ben took his place, he supported the side of the canoe, ensuring that at least his face didn't betray how deeply affected he was by Ben's raw, earthy smell.

With the weight off his back, Adrian felt like he was floating in air. At the top of the hill he paused and drank in the sight of Poobah Lake spread out majestically below them. Even under a gray sky, the picture was postcard perfect. *They'd made it!* Adrian started running, but tripped over a rock and fell. *Fuck!* He scrambled to his knees as Ben drew close.

"Most of the rescues out here are from injuries sustained like that. Stupid ones." Ben's face was red again, but this time more from anger than embarrassment.

Adrian hastily rose to his feet and brushed himself off. He felt like a kid being chastised by his superior. "I'm alright." He was going to add *coach*, but even that word seemed inappropriate now.

THEY set off in the canoe for the final paddle of the day. By now their mood was as leaden as the sky. Even if things had been better between them, tiredness would have kept them quiet. Adrian's hands burned as he thrust the paddle through the water. His knee ached from the fall, but he didn't want to check to see if he had grazed the skin or not. He'd wait until Ben wasn't looking.

Dark shadows and the heavy stillness of nightfall drew around them as they pulled into the first cleared area they came across on the northern side of the lake. Ben dragged the canoe out of the water and muttered tiredly, "There's a couple of short portages around rapids along the creek before we hit the Maligne River. Hopefully there'll be enough flow to help us on our way once we get there tomorrow."

Maligne by name, hopefully not malign by nature, Adrian reflected to himself while doing his part of setting up the campsite. He didn't think he could stand another day like this one. But he only had himself to blame.

Ben's cold silence continued while they prepared the evening meal and cleaned up afterward. They had learned to function well as a team, completing each task as needed without discussion; but Adrian missed their usual friendly banter as much as the little touches and kisses that usually accompanied those things. The lingering hands when passing something or the quickly shared grin or the telltale blush, indicating Ben's thoughts were on sex and not on the more mundane tasks he was involved in. Now every impatient move reflected the young man's mood.

Adrian flinched when Ben shoved the next plate for drying into his hands. Before he could react, Ben grabbed his wrist and twisted his palm over so he could inspect the red patches where blisters were forming.

"When were you going to tell me about these?"

The coldness in Ben's voice was in complete contrast to the warmth of his touch. Adrian jerked his hand away, finished drying the plate and stashed it in the pack.

"Shit, Adrian." Ben's coldness flared into heated anger like embers fanned by a stiff breeze.

Adrian straightened and stepped away, eyeing Ben warily, his hands dangling uselessly at his sides as he stared at the transformation in his face. "They're nothing."

Ben raked his hand through his hair. "They may not have formed into full blisters yet, but we've got a day of nonstop paddling tomorrow. How were you going to cope with that?"

"You'd be surprised how much pain I can put up with." Starting with the ache in his stomach that had flared up again, along with Ben's temper.

"It's not a question of putting up with pain, it's about being able to operate more effectively when you're not hurting." Ben glared at Adrian. "I won't wrap them now, but I'll put some moleskin on them tomorrow and dig out some fingerless gloves I brought. Remind me in the morning."

"I'll be fine," Adrian muttered as he shoved his hands in his pockets.

Ben stalked up, standing toe-to-toe, looming over him, but there was none of the playful bear about him tonight. Anger turned his eyes into glacial ice chips. "You won't be fine. I've had enough blisters in my time to know better."

"I've had my share. I used to get them while rowing."

"So what? Do you get off on being the suffering martyr?" Ben turned away from him in disgust. "First you refuse my assistance during the portage, and now your hands. Geez, you call *me* stupid."

Adrian winced at the reminder. "I shouldn't have called you that earlier. I'm sorry, but you of all people should know the risks."

Ben turned back and glared at him. "Don't talk to me about risk. What about the fact you're risking the whole outcome of this trip by not looking after yourself properly?" He raked his fingers through his hair again, making it stand on end. "You can't keep bottling everything up inside, trying to cope in isolation."

As if on cue, a loud thunderclap sounded, and the rain started pelting down. Everything sped up as they hastily completed their chores. Ben dived into the smaller tent after a brief "Good night", leaving Adrian to crawl into the larger one alone.

CHAPTER
✠✠✠
FOURTEEN

BEN squirmed around in his sleeping bag, trying to get comfortable. He couldn't wait to get home and have a proper pillow instead of a bundle of clothes to rest his head on. He groaned as his thoughts returned to what had to be one of the worst days of his life. First, Adrian calling him stupid; then, to be flatly informed Adrian had lost the love of his life to AIDS. Obviously, no matter how much Ben might want more, the only thing Adrian wanted from him was sex.

For a while, he thought his feelings were reciprocated. Surely no one could kiss like that without it meaning something. Seemed Adrian could. The man had enough acting ability to fool everyone he was straight; apparently those skills extended to kissing as well.

Adrian did have a point though. Ben trusted people too much. Just because he was open and honest, he shouldn't assume everyone else was the same. By all rights, he should still be angry. But despite being pissed off at Adrian for not asking for help, he had to respect him for the way he plodded on all day without complaining. Several times Ben's heart had been in his mouth when Adrian slipped on the logs laid in the boggy ground to provide some semblance of footing. Then to make matters worse, mud caked above his boots, all the way up to his calves. Considering how clean Adrian liked to keep himself, the poor guy probably regretted not going on that cruise.

Eventually Ben drifted off, to be woken by what sounded like someone calling his name. He lay there quietly, listening to the soft patter of raindrops on the tent.

"Ben!" This time there was desperation in the cry. *Bears!* Ben scrambled out of his sleeping bag, fearing the worst. He hadn't slung up the food pack before going to bed. What with the rain, their

243

exhaustion, and the lack of convenient overhanging branches, he had decided to take the risk.

If they'd been sleeping together as usual, he would have erected the spare tent and left the pack in there, or even stowed it under the upturned canoe, but their argument and the rain prevented that option. Instead, he simply stashed the pack up the far end of the larger tent, figuring Adrian would still have enough room. Maybe the smell of food had lured some of the local wildlife inside.

Ben opened the zip of his old tent and wriggled in through the flap. Cautiously, he switched on his flashlight, directing the beam away from Adrian's eyes so it wouldn't blind him too much. His boss lay prone on his back, but no wild creature threatened him. Ben played the Maglite beam closer to his head so he could see better.

No reaction.

Adrian lay on top of his unzipped sleeping bag with the sleeping sheet tangled around his legs; he was tossing and turning his head from side to side, much like Jason had done when he was sick. Despite being in the larger tent, Ben still had to straddle Adrian's body to check his temperature. Sweat coated his boss's forehead, but he didn't seem to have a fever.

Ben untangled the lining sheet and gathered up a corner to wipe the moisture off his brow. Adrian's hand shot up and captured his wrist.

"Shh," Ben crooned softly. "It's only a dream. You're all right."

Adrian blinked and turned away from the glare. Ben switched off the Maglite and dropped it beside him. Adrian's breathing grew jagged, uneven. "Are you okay?" Ben whispered. "You called out my name. Is anything wrong?"

The warmth of the body between Ben's legs and the closeness caused the inevitable reaction; his cock filled as blood rushed to his groin. He tried to ease away, but that just gave it more room to poke down; it still touched Adrian. *Damn.* He never thought that having a big dick would be a disadvantage. In the dark, Ben couldn't see his face, but Adrian's breath washed over him. Despite the exertions of the day, he smelled clean. *Fuck it.* He wanted to nuzzle Adrian's neck, taste him, touch him, lick him all over.

Adrian's breathing grew stronger and steadier. "Ben?" He reached up and drew the back of his fingers up the side of Ben's face.

"Yes."

He leaned down, drawn to Adrian like a moth to a flame. At the same time, Adrian's hand snaked around the back of his neck, pulling him closer. One quick fumble brought their lips together, and a collective sigh escaped. After a couple of seconds, all his strength evaporated, and Ben's elbows gave way as he collapsed on top of the warm body. Adrian turned slightly, so he didn't crush him, but all the time they never stopped kissing. It felt as natural as night and day.

Adrian groaned, and shifted farther, rolling around so they were lying side by side. The sleeping sheet tangled between them. Ben swore and pulled it away. That brought bare skin into contact. No matter how much his attitude might suggest otherwise, Adrian's body wanted Ben. Their erections did their own mating dance.

"Love you," Adrian murmured. The words were muttered so quietly, Ben wondered at first whether he imagined them.

Eventually, plucking up the courage to admit what had been growing in his heart, he whispered back, "I love you too."

Once again, Adrian kissed him like he really meant it, his lips bruising in their intensity as those firm lips covered every inch of his face. Chills ran up and down Ben's spine as the rough stubble on Adrian's chin and cheeks rasped his skin like sandpaper. Gradually, the kisses died away and Adrian's breath became lighter and longer until finally, a little snore erupted.

Ben lay quietly beside him in the dark. The rain had stopped. Sleep would be impossible while his brain reeled from the shock of hearing those two words. Carefully, he twisted out of Adrian's embrace and searched for his flashlight. *Damn, Adrian must be sleeping on it.* After pulling up the sheet lining to cover the sleeping figure he scrambled backward out of the tent. When he reached his own smaller one, he opened his plastic bag of clothes and dressed himself in the warmest things he could find.

Ben figured it must be around two in the morning. The full moon made the surface of Poobah Lake look like a silver mirror, shedding enough light to read by. Every now and then, some bushes would rustle as a creature of the night came out to feed. A large rock jutting out over the water provided a convenient place to sit. The rain clouds had cleared away, leaving everything fresh and clean. Near the horizon, a curtain of green danced. The Northern Lights.

Should he wake Adrian so they could watch the awesome display together? No, the man had been exhausted. *His* man had been exhausted. A shiver ran up Ben's spine at the thought. He couldn't wait until morning so they could revert to being friends again, lovers, and erase the horrible, awkward silences of the previous day.

A fish jumped, sending ripples back toward the rock, reminding him that he hadn't even had a chance to go fishing. There was still time to rectify that; the equipment was stashed under the canoe, easily accessible. Ben dragged out the gear and sat back on his haunches. The tackle box hadn't been in its usual place in his mother's shed, and he spent ages searching for it. In the end, he found it shoved under the old Grumman. Hoping for the best, he had just grabbed it, without checking the contents. *Who used it last? Chris, by the looks of the mess inside.*

Ben sorted the sinkers and hooks into their correct partitions, then extracted all the things that didn't belong. A pack of dog-eared playing cards. Can opener. Insect repellant. Tube of toothpaste. Deodorant, and underneath, another tube. Ben stared at the label. Lube? His heart started beating faster as he searched through the rest of the box. Tucked away in a corner was a small foil packet. Since when had Chris needed condoms on a fishing trip? No way would his prissy new wife ever be keen on going canoeing.

Ben sat for a while, thinking. Obviously he didn't know his brother as well as he thought he did. *How old was the condom? Was it in date?* He smoothed out the foil packet. Damn, his Maglite was still in Adrian's tent.

ADRIAN stretched all the kinks out of his back and sighed. Hopefully, when he returned to San Francisco, he'd have Ben's company in dreams, if nothing else. Last night's version seemed so real, he almost expected Ben to be there when he woke.

Gingerly, he pressed the sore patches on his hands. Ben had been right, as usual. He needed to pad them with something today. Adrian donned his thermal undershirt and added some more clothes on top to ward off the chill. If, and when, the day warmed up, it would be easier to peel off a layer than change completely. Much like the layers he had learned to clothe himself in over the years. The ski gloves at the bottom of his pack proved a little more elusive, but eventually he found them. They were too thick to paddle in, but would protect his hands until then. He donned them before stepping outside.

A pot of water bubbled merrily on the fire. Ben couldn't be too far away.

He missed him at first. The figure perched on the overhang was so still that, in the early morning fog, Adrian mistook him for part of the rock formation. As he approached, he realized Ben was fishing. At least his line dangled in the water, but his gaze was fixed on the horizon. A slight crack of a twig alerted the young man to his presence. He turned to face Adrian, and the familiar welcoming grin on his face released a knot of tension inside. In the predawn light, the young man's skin appeared even paler than usual though. Adrian stumbled slightly as he went to join him. Ben reached out a hand to prevent him from falling headlong into the water, and Adrian flinched at the coldness of his touch. "Are you okay?" he asked. "Your lips are blue with cold."

Ben's teeth chattered as he replied, "Yeeesss, but I keep hoping that the sun will chase the mist away. Anyway, who went swimming the other morning?"

"I was moving. Huge difference." Adrian stripped off his gloves. "At least get your hands warm."

Ben shook his head. "Can't feel the line then."

"Well, put one on."

Ben reluctantly donned the left glove, his breath coming in shallow bursts as he muttered, "Mother hen."

"What?"

"You're like a mother hen sometimes, worrying about her chick."

"Cluck, cluck." Adrian shook his head and made his way back to the campfire. At least the sick feeling that had plagued him all yesterday had disappeared. Usually, with Antonio, he had felt like that until they kissed and made up. Yesterday, he must have been imagining things. He wasn't in love; he just had an upset stomach. The water, maybe. He and Ben were friends, nothing more.

Adrian doled out spoonfuls of coffee and added boiling water and sugar. One for him and three for Ben, the way he liked it. He carried the full mugs back to where Ben was now clucking like a chicken as he approached. "Here—even if you don't want a drink, holding the cup will keep you warm."

"Thanks, Mom."

Ben's shy smile was enough to warm Adrian. "You're welcome," he said as he sat on the rock: close enough to provide body heat, just like a regular buddy would, but not close enough to suggest anything else. He blew on the mug and watched the steam spill out over the top. Neither spoke for a while as they enjoyed their morning cup of joe. The wispy tendrils of cloud clung to the surface of the lake as if reluctant to leave. *Just like me.* This was their last day. Monday, he'd be caught up in the rat race once more. Banishing the thought from his head, he dragged himself back to the present. "Catch anything?"

Ben indicated the dishpan. "I took the canoe out while you were asleep and let it drift. Two bronzebacks jumped into the boat, ready for your breakfast, sir." Despite his joking words, Ben's voice sounded strained, tired.

Adrian checked out where he was pointing, avoiding contact with Ben as he leaned over to inspect the decent-sized fish. "Are you expecting me to scale, clean, and fillet them?"

Ben's look of wide-eyed innocence made Adrian splutter in his coffee as he took another sip. "It's called teamwork, boss. I catch 'em—you cook 'em."

Boss. This time, the word made a welcome relief. Not love or lover. Adrian clambered down and set to work, taking care to do a good job. They were definitely enough for a hearty breakfast. By the time he brought the cooked fillets back, the air still felt chilly, but Ben's face had lost its paleness.

As soon as they finished eating, Adrian cleaned up the dirty dishes and started packing the tent. Ben dragged out the map, saying he needed to check the route.

FUCK. The tiny writing swam before Ben's eyes. He'd been waiting for some resumption of last night's affection, but so far nothing to suggest anything had happened. What if Adrian had just been dreaming? Having a nightmare? In the tent, his voice had been lower than usual, but Ben just assumed that was his boss's sexy "in-bed" voice.

If he *had* been dreaming, at least Adrian didn't suspect the truth, treating him no differently from usual this morning. Disappointment was followed by relief that Adrian wouldn't remember Ben making a fool of himself by declaring a love that wasn't returned.

A shadow fell across the map. "This is yours, I believe."

A small Maglite fell onto the paper. Ben grabbed it before it rolled into the water and stashed it away in his pocket. As he carefully folded the map, a cold feeling of dread settled in his stomach. Adrian's next words sounded like a death knell. "We need to talk."

How Ben hated that word. He could chat until the lakes froze over. But talk—talk, he'd rather have his toenails pulled.

Ben quickly shoved the map into another pocket and tried to scramble to his feet.

In a smooth catlike move, Adrian landed on the rock beside him and grabbed his wrist. "I mean it, Ben. We need to talk."

Shit. No escape.

Adrian was quiet for a few moments as they both sat side-by-side, looking out across the water. The early morning sun had finally made its way above the ridge, and the cloud had thinned and lifted enough so that the ripples in the water glinted like diamonds. Far above the opposite side of the lake, Ben could see a bird. Trust him to pick this time to see a bald eagle. They'd been looking for one ever since starting the trip. Should he point it out to Adrian? The bird was circling. It had found its prey and was getting ready to swoop. Ben wasn't sure whose side he was on at that moment. In a way, he felt closer to the unseen animal that had attracted the raptor's notice.

"Last night, I went to bed feeling miserable, but I was happy when I woke." Adrian's voice startled him. Ben had been watching the eagle for so long, he'd forgotten what they were supposed to be doing. He hadn't forgotten Adrian's presence though, not for one minute. How could he? The rock wasn't large, so their bodies touched. Adrian had changed into his paddling gear, but Ben still wore a few layers of clothing.

"During the night, I dreamed I held you in my arms, and you said you loved me."

You said you loved me too. Ben glanced sideways, but didn't speak. A lump of ice formed in his stomach.

"Finding the evidence of two Maglites confirmed that it wasn't a dream. No wonder I felt so good this morning." Adrian's expression was the antithesis of his words. "In a way, I would have preferred if it had been a dream," he added quietly.

"Why?" Ben managed to squeeze one word through the constriction in his throat.

"Because this can't go on."

"Why can't it go on?" *At least Adrian hadn't said he didn't love him back.* "Did you think I was someone else? Was the other guy called Ben, too?"

"What other guy?" Adrian seemed genuinely puzzled, then light dawned in his eyes. "You mean Antonio?" A flush covered his cheek. "No, I haven't dreamed about him for a long time."

"Don't I measure up? Is that the problem? Aren't I good enough for you?" Ben struggled and tried to move away, but Adrian grabbed his thigh, trapping him before leaning back and scanning Ben from head to toe.

"Not measure up? Who are you kidding? You're one heck of a guy. You're smart, you're funny, you're strong, you've got a great body, you've got everything going for you. Your youth, your looks, your smile...."

"Well, if I'm so hot, why are you pushing me away?"

The appreciative smile faded. "Because I have to."

Adrian's words took a moment to register. When they finally did, Ben felt as if some freak of nature had whipped up all the water in the lake, creating a huge wave that crashed over the rock where they were sitting, drowning him. "Why?" *Damn it. Why did he have to sound so pathetic?*

"It's impossible, can't you see that?"

Adrian started patting his leg, just like someone might console a dog for not being able to take them for a walk. Ben's mind played back the things he'd been complimented on: his looks, his youth. "You think I'm too young for you, don't you? Too immature."

Adrian didn't face him; his attention was fixed intently on the water, slowly nodding his head as he replied. "The thought did cross my mind… on a number of occasions." Still Adrian wouldn't look him in the eye when he spoke. "You need to concentrate on your studies and find someone closer to your own age."

"Whatta loada crap! I like being with you. You're still as hot as hell, and much more interesting than anyone my age will ever be. I've learned so much. About music and wine and the talks we had while working out in the gym, solving the world's problems." Ben tried to convey the truth of the statement in his voice, because words alone couldn't convey everything he felt inside. When he was with Adrian, he felt different, stronger, more focused. The man treated him as an equal, made him feel he was worth something.

The boardroom mask had slipped firmly back into place when Adrian finally turned to face him. "But that's what I'm talking about. You see me as a mentor, not a lover."

Was he right? Adrian had certainly taught Ben a lot, but so had Carl, and the thought of fucking Carl never crossed his mind. But it wasn't only about the sex. He could imagine the two of them sitting like this for hours. His arm draped over Adrian's shoulder. Adrian's arm around his waist, sharing their thoughts and feelings, watching the lake and all that nature had to offer.

While Ben tried to find a way to explain all this, Adrian faced forward again and started talking, his hand now rubbing along the inside of Ben's leg, keeping a steady rhythm in time with his words. Ben started to speak, but without taking his gaze off the lake, Adrian held up his hand. "Please, let me explain."

As far as Ben was concerned, when Adrian's hand returned to his leg, he might as well have been speaking Swahili. Every one of his senses concentrating on that firm, warm touch, his body recalling what it felt like when that hand travelled over other parts, exploring him, caressing him. Vaguely, Ben heard Adrian explain how he wasn't a good match for Ben. How he used to drink a lot. Yadda, yadda, yadda. Ben had heard all that from Jason. It didn't fit the way Ben had seen him. Adrian was always sober when he was around. Who cared anyway? He'd been known to get drunk as a skunk on many occasions. What was so different? Ben's cock filled even more, taking all the blood from his head as Adrian's hand started moving back and forth, stirring up all the heat inside. Now the man was talking about his father and the policies the firm had in place, saying how important it was for him to remain in the closet and not be with Ben. *Did Adrian even realize the different message his hand was conveying?* Ben doubted it.

Mentoring and teaching. Ben snorted to himself. Let's see him get out of this one. Ben knocked the distracting hand away. Adrian stopped mid-sentence and glanced around in surprise.

Ben dredged up a fake smile to hide his nervousness. "So, as far as you're concerned, this has all just been fun, nothing more."

Adrian gave a lopsided grin in return. "Well, I've certainly enjoyed myself." Now Adrian's questing hand was rubbing his own stomach as the smile faded.

Ben pressed on before he completely lost his nerve. "And what happens on vacation, stays on vacation."

"Yes." The long-drawn-out syllable betrayed Adrian's wariness.

"You're forgetting something." Ben paused, noting the stiffness of Adrian's shoulders, the tilt of his head, all the markers he'd come to recognize that told him Adrian's true feelings, the unhappiness inside. "We're still here." Ben leaned over and fastened his lips against Adrian's. The startled protest was swallowed as Ben pressed against his mouth.

As soon as he felt him respond. Ben rolled Adrian onto his back. Adrian lay stiff for a few seconds, and then he seemed to melt as he relaxed and welcomed Ben's tongue inside.

I TRIED to be strong! With a low moan of defeat, Adrian circled his arms around Ben, pulling him closer. Finally, the young man stopped the onslaught on his mouth and levered himself away, staring down with a wistful expression on his face as he whispered. "I want you to fuck me."

Adrian's body liked the idea even if his brain didn't. "Ben, we can't."

"I've been thinking about it while you were asleep. I know the risks. Even if I am HIV positive, it's safer for the top."

The beat of Adrian's heart almost doubled at the thought of being inside Ben. He'd have been more than happy the other way around, but the thought of that strong body submitting to him made every nerve stand on end. "Maybe if we had a condom, but we don't."

"Yes, we do."

Ben's bald statement drove all the air out of Adrian's lungs. "What?"

"I found one in the tackle box." Ben delved into his pocket and extracted a crumpled foil square.

Without his glasses, Adrian couldn't check the date, but he trusted Ben. "Weren't you listening to a word I said before? We shouldn't."

"Why not? In a way, I figure you owe me for just using me as a fuck toy on vacation."

Adrian snorted. "It hasn't exactly been one-sided."

"Are you saying you're not interested?" Ben gave a sly grin. "Your cock is making you into a liar." He leaned back, uncovering Adrian's erection, proving the point.

Making love to Ben and then pretending afterward that nothing had happened between them was beyond even his acting skills. Adrian cast around for another good reason, anything. Then he had it. Ben so obviously wanted to dominate him physically. Adrian had been able to take control on a couple of occasions, but every vibe Ben gave off showed what he wanted. "You're a top."

Ben gritted his jaw stubbornly. "I did bottom once or twice when I first started. The other guy wasn't much older than me. I hated it. You seem to know what you're doing. Think of it as part of the mentoring process."

Adrian winced at the bitterness in Ben's voice. When they'd talked earlier, he had been clutching at straws, trying to come up with valid reasons why being together was such a bad idea. Seemed like that one was coming back to bite him in the butt. Or Ben's butt, at this rate. "We can't."

"Why not? Are you scared of being infected?" Ben started to stand up, anger firing instantly.

"No!" Adrian grabbed the young man's shoulder, preventing him from leaving. "I'm not scared of that!" He broke contact immediately and rubbed the back of his neck, disguising the fact that his hand was trembling as he desperately tried to think of another excuse. "I don't want to make it painful for you, but we can't use the suntan oil, it will weaken the latex."

Ben silently handed him the tube of lube. *Shit.* Now he really was screwed. "Oh, Ben. What am I going to do with you?"

"Fuck me."

The simple words were uttered without any sign of emotion, almost as if his request was no more significant than asking to be touched, but Adrian didn't have a hope of treating the act so clinically. Once he started, all the desires he had carefully squirreled away would be exposed again. His panic increased with each vanishing excuse while his body screamed at his brain to just shut the fuck up and get on with it. "We don't have time."

"If we're late, I'll use the satellite phone to delay the pickup."

No wonder his brothers accused him of being stubborn. "You're going to be sore afterward. You said yourself we have a long day's paddling in front of us."

"If you're usually on the receiving end, you should know how to make the experience as pleasant as possible." Ben settled onto his side, propped on his elbow. In a way, the more frantic Adrian got, the more relaxed Ben seemed to become. More certain that this was what he wanted. Now he was running the tip of his finger over Adrian's chest, making it hard for him to think straight.

Adrian swallowed. "Is that a challenge?"

Ben smirked. "Sort of."

Adrian groaned as those fingers tweaked his nipples through the fabric of his T-shirt. Every inch of his body wanted to give in; his cock positively strained at the seams of his shorts. There was only one card in the deck left to play. "It can get awfully messy if you haven't cleaned yourself properly."

Ben scrambled to his feet before Adrian had time to react. Within seconds, his clothes lay in a heap on the rock, and his naked body was scything through the water.

Adrian gave a deep sigh and gathered up the discarded garments, automatically turning them the right side out and folding them neatly. Before he put them down, he brought the bundle up to his face, stealing a quick breath, drinking in the scent, hoping the memory would stay with him long after.

Ben stopped in waist-high water and didn't take his eyes off Adrian as one hand disappeared behind his back. *Fuck.* The water must be freezing, but Ben's gaze didn't waver.

Adrian grabbed the toiletry bag from his pack and extracted the nail file. While Ben prepared himself, Adrian carefully smoothed the edges of his nails. Ben's actions faltered as he realized what he was doing. Adrian smirked as he placed the file back in its pouch. Maybe, in a way, this *would* give him closure. Be a fitting end to their time together.

Ben started swimming again.

Adrian went through the pack and found the towels, then he arranged the mats on top of each other, creating as comfortable a surface as possible. His father always said if a job was worth doing, it was worth doing well, and this one certainly qualified. If Ben preferred to top and wanted a demonstration of how to give a bottom the maximum amount of pleasure, he'd come to the right man. Adrian could always kid himself that it was his *duty* to teach Ben. The young man's future lovers might be grateful. Adrian sighed as he straightened and held out the towels to signal he was ready. All he had to do was convince the pain in his stomach to go away.

WHEN Ben finally plucked up enough courage to leave the water, Adrian draped one of the towels around his shoulders. The cold had stripped away his confidence as soon as he dived in. Too late to go back now. His teeth chattered as much with nerves as from the chill. Adrian rubbed him down vigorously with the other towel, not only removing every drop of moisture from his body, but making his skin tingle and turn red. When he finished, Ben clutched the towel around himself and stared into those come-to-bed eyes that he loved so much.

"Are you sure you want to go through with this?" Adrian asked quietly.

Even if he had been halfway to changing his mind, the sound of Adrian's low, sexy growl helped Ben answer. He nodded, lost for words. If there had been any sign of unwillingness on his boss's part, he might have wimped out, but Adrian had taken off all his clothes while Ben was swimming, and he'd never seen his cock so aroused, arching proudly up toward his navel. The thought of having all that inside him removed what little strength Ben had left. He stumbled over to the bedding and threw himself down on his front.

Resting his head on his folded arms, he gathered all his willpower together and cautiously moved up onto all fours, presenting his ass.

A soft chuckle sounded behind him, followed by a playful swat on his butt cheek. "I thought you said we had an hour. It'll all be over in five minutes, and you'll be screaming in agony if you're not careful."

Despite the flippant words, Adrian sounded as tense as he was. Ben settled back on to his knees and ankles, the breath hitching in his throat as Adrian moved into his field of vision, slowly stroking his erection. "Can I suck you off first?" Ben tore his gaze upward from the slick shaft and met cool, gray eyes that stared back at him with unblinking intensity. For a few seconds, he forgot how to breathe. Then Adrian gave him one of those slow, seductive smiles.

"Since you asked so nicely." He guided his cock into Ben's mouth, holding onto Ben's shoulder to support him. "This time, I give you permission to swallow."

Permission? The knot of tension in Ben's stomach eased a fraction. *Someone's been reading BDSM porn.* He grinned at the thought, but didn't stop what he was doing. He liked it when Adrian relaxed and let himself go. Sex should be fun. Ben sucked harder. Adrian groaned, and his next words came out sounding slurred. "Aren't you worried that I won't be able to get it up again?"

Ben shook his head, the cock in his mouth smothering his laugh. From what he'd seen so far, Adrian's recovery time was nearly as good as his. He sighed, sending a ripple of air into the slit. Adrian jerked and moaned his name. Ben smiled and swallowed him in. Now they were back into fucking, he felt on familiar territory. This he could do. All the thinking and talking just made his head spin. Shame they didn't have all day. He ran his tongue up and down the hard shaft, nearly letting the cock fall from his lips, drawing them together at the last minute, squeezing the tip, preventing its escape.

"Ben!" Adrian gripped his head and bucked into him, thrusting his hips forward, grunting as he came. This time, Ben relished the opportunity to finish the job properly, savoring the taste as he swallowed, licking all the remnants away. Judging by the hardness of his own cock, his body certainly enjoyed the experience. He reached down to ease the pressure.

"No."

Before he could react, Adrian tipped him onto his back. For a second, Ben thought his anger had returned, but Adrian gave him a reassuring smile as he lay on top, trapping Ben's hard erection between their bodies. "I don't want you to come yet. Believe me, you'll enjoy it much more if you're as horny as possible."

"I'm as horny as a mountain goat already." Ben tried to rub his cock against Adrian's body.

"No topping from the bottom, please. Lie there and learn." Ben groaned at the put-on, prissy voice as Adrian rose to his knees, removing the contact. "Now, let's see how flexible you are." He smiled at Ben and ran his hands up the underside of his legs, lifting them until they rested on his shoulders.

Ben shuddered at that simple contact, all the nerves in his skin still on fire from being rubbed so hard by the towel. "I'm flexible, I'm flexible," he promised and brought his legs over as far as he could, earning himself another laugh and playful swat on his butt. His cock jerked at the blow. Seemed as if he liked a bit of rough action too.

Adrian leaned over and kissed him, running his tongue inside his mouth, tasting his own semen. Ben groaned as the action went straight to his dick. If he got any hornier, he'd be giving a two-headed mountain goat a run for his money. "Please, just fuck me already."

"What a typical top you are—so impatient. Relax. I'm calling the shots now." Adrian rubbed his stubbly jaw against Ben's cheek, chafing him in the process. Even that sent a signal to Ben's dick, making it jerk in response. Those smoky gray eyes stared at Ben intently for a few minutes before Adrian moved lower, running his tongue over his chest, playing with his nipples, nipping them hard and then licking them to take away the sting.

Ben writhed beneath the magic touch. Somehow the sun seemed to have vanished and stars appeared behind his closed eyelids as he gave up control and let himself enjoy Adrian's attention. He couldn't stop himself trying to thrust up though as Adrian's tongue travelled south. "Don't move." Adrian's voice dropped about an octave lower as his shoulders disappeared. Ben clasped his hands behind his knees to keep them from collapsing now their support had been taken away. He locked his fingers together to stop them shaking.

Adrian completely bypassed his cock.

Ben couldn't help but be thankful. One touch of that hot mouth and he would have shot his load. Even now, every lick set off another wave of electricity.

Adrian bit at the back of Ben's scrotum, nipping and sucking all the way to his asshole. *How the fuck will that make me more receptive to his dick?* Ben groaned as he discovered his body knew better. Adrian spat on the entry point, then blew softly as if to say: *hello*. Ben opened his eyes. All his nerves tensed. "Are you going to…."

"No. You deserve a proper rimming, as the saying goes, but we don't have time."

"I'll take a rain check, then."

Adrian smiled and slowly inserted a finger. Ben squirmed at his touch.

"This isn't about penetration, Ben. It's about accepting. You need to let me in."

"Please, just do it already."

"Not yet." Adrian removed his finger and uncapped the tube. Moving with glacial slowness, ensuring Ben didn't miss a second of what he was doing, he rubbed the lube between his fingers for a second, then massaged all around the entrance. Ben found his grip relaxing. As far as he was concerned, he was ready, had been for ages, but obviously Adrian thought otherwise. Gradually, Ben found himself enjoying the sensation. The added jolts as Adrian's finger ventured inside and stroked his prostate made him writhe in pleasure.

Dimly, he became aware one hand had disappeared. Adrian swore. "Fuck, I should have opened this beforehand."

Ben smiled as he watched Adrian trying to juggle the condom wrapper one-handed with slippery fingers. "Been there, done that." He reached out and took the packet from Adrian's grasp, deftly removing the contents and returning the rubber to him. "Teamwork," he muttered, and smiled at Adrian's answering grin. The break in intensity allowed his body to come down from the plateau Adrian had managed to keep him on for the last fifteen minutes. Fifteen hours? Fifteen seconds? *Who knew?* Time meant nothing, anymore.

Adrian put his shoulders back under Ben's knees, allowing his hands to relax their grip. Ben locked them loosely around Adrian's neck, and drew him closer so their mouths touched.

Eventually, Adrian moaned and pulled away. Concentration screwed up his face as he lined up his prick and nudged Ben's hole. As if by magic, the tip worked its way in. Almost immediately, Adrian drew it out again. Ben protested. "Hush," Adrian said. "This is much better than the old two fingers, three fingers method. Trust me."

Beads of sweat gathered on Adrian's forehead as he repeated the process, only allowing the tip in, then withdrawing. Ben knew from experience how tempting it was to do more. A pang of guilt washed over him at how thoughtless he had been in the past, how rough. Never again. He sighed and relaxed a bit more as Adrian's patience continued. The temptation to do more must have been horrendous, but still he teased, until Ben found his body trying to drag Adrian in.

"SQUEEZE and release your butt around me." Adrian rasped the words out, the inclination to thrust mindlessly into that warm heat proving almost irresistible. Just looking at Ben's face as he lay there sent agonizing jolts zinging through him. If he had thought Ben beautiful before, he looked magnificent now. The sight of that strong body lying so passively, so receptive beneath him did strange things to his heart. Adrian trusted Ben implicitly when they were paddling; apparently the young man trusted him when it came to making love.

As expected, Ben grimaced at the first few thrusts, but his gaze never wavered from Adrian's face, his brow furrowing as he obeyed the new command. "You're thinking too much, just go with the flow." Adrian gave a smile of encouragement and stopped for a second, before thrusting in a bit deeper. This time a look of wonderment crossed Ben's face, of discovery, as Adrian's cock stroked across his prostate.

Adrian was vaguely aware of a whisper of wind blowing across the sweat on his back, cooling him down. He gritted his teeth. His first fuck in five years, and he had to control his every move when all he wanted to do was let go and rut like a stag.

"Fuck, Ben, you're tight."

"No… you're just… big."

"I'm not, you know. You're bigger than I am. Push down."

Ben grimaced again as he speared in farther, but did his best to accept the intrusion.

"Would you rather I stopped?"

"Don't you dare." Ben opened his eyes and glared at him in mock anger. Adrian smiled and didn't move, waiting for Ben to relax. As soon as he felt the pressure decrease, Adrian withdrew again and added more lube. Ah, that was better. This time he moved in quickly. Ben seemed surprised at how much easier it was.

Adrian bit his lip, stifling a groan as his cock was now fully enveloped in velvet heat. Even through the protective sheath, he rejoiced in the close contact. Thank God he had let Ben suck him off first, otherwise he would have come as soon as he was inside a man's body again. Years of hand jobs and even their earlier sexual encounters didn't come anywhere near this perfection. He turned his head and kissed Ben's legs, trying to express his thanks wordlessly.

Ben's soft moans greeted his actions as he lay there with his eyes closed, his body now fully accepting the unfamiliar intrusion. Balancing on one elbow, Adrian used some of Ben's pre-come to slick the young man's cock in time with his thrusts. The hardness alone showed how much he was enjoying himself. He wasn't the only one. Adrian eased away and slowed his action, marveling at the sight of his cock disappearing into the beautiful hole. His very own porn show. Ben opened his eyes and gazed at him dreamily, a small smile hovering on the edge of his lips as if he knew exactly what Adrian was thinking. Adrian leaned in and planted kisses on that sweet smile.

He let Ben's cock go and supported his weight better so he could play with him, swiveling his hips as he thrust back and forth. Soon he had Ben groaning as he stroked his gland, this time with his cock instead of his finger. Judging by the loudness of the response, Ben appreciated the action.

Now the young man's face was all concentration as he gripped Adrian's shoulders and worked with him. "Don't stop." The urgently uttered plea broke Adrian's resolve. Slow was no longer an option.

His movements accelerated to piston speed, grunting with the effort. Using Ben's body as a prop, Adrian tried to make up for lost pleasure. Thrust after thrust, for every chance he had denied himself during that long period of abstinence. He bit back a cry as he thought about all the future opportunities that would be denied to him. The chance of a repeat performance, or even better, to have Ben fuck him.

Adrian groaned as he finally lost all control and fucked harder than he meant to. He might have hurt a weaker man, but Ben absorbed all his punishment, soaking up his aggression. Again and again, Adrian thrust in mindlessly, his body taking over as he released the fetters that had restrained it for so long. The woods echoed with his cries as he almost sobbed in ecstasy with each stroke.

Despite the noise he was making, he heard Ben mutter hoarsely, "Fuck it, Adrian, I'm going to come."

"Do it."

Adrian leaned over and kissed Ben as the young man's hands tightened their grip on his shoulders; the only touch on his cock had been the occasional pressure as their bodies moved together. Ben's convulsions as he came tipped Adrian over, and he finally let himself go, howling like a wolf as he thundered his release, sending spurt after spurt into the condom. He hastily withdrew and ripped off the rubber, throwing it away as he collapsed onto Ben, helping him lower his legs and twine them around his body.

Just the sight of Ben's face as he came had nearly been enough to set Adrian off.

"Shit, Adrian. You make more noise than Jason." Ben still looked dazed from the encounter, his face a mix of contentment and bliss.

Adrian gave a shaky laugh and squirmed around on Ben's body, smearing Ben's sticky come between them. He felt rather than heard Ben's laugh as it rumbled through his chest. Desperately, he tried to remind himself that this wasn't about love; it was sex instruction, pure and simple. He eased back and rested on his elbows, gazing down at Ben. "Just remember, you can never have too much lube." Now those laughing blue eyes had the vividness of a midsummer sky rather than the winter's dawn they had been yesterday. Adrian faked a breezy, this-is-the-sort-of-thing-I-do-every-day-before-breakfast smile, his acting skills coming to the fore again as he hid how much the sex had meant to him. "Here endeth the lesson," he said playfully, even though he was crying inside. Not only had he broken his drought, but he had done so knowing this might be the last time he would ever make love to the gorgeous man beneath him. Anger and sadness welled up inside, making him want to howl again. He scrambled to his feet and put out a hand to help Ben up. The young man appeared to be as shaky as Adrian felt.

After an intense moment like that, they both needed to come down, to calm down, but time was slipping away from them. Without discussion, they both headed for the lake. The cold water quickly obliterated all traces of sex, both physically and emotionally. Adrian's concern grew as Ben stood in the shallows, clasping his arms around himself, his whole body shaking. "Are you all right?"

"Yeah... just cold."

"Did I hurt you? I tried to take it slow, but in the end I couldn't help myself." Adrian's voice trailed off as he noticed Ben's reaction. The broad shoulders straightened, and he stood tall.

"No, I'm fine."

"We better get going then."

"Sure." Ben looked away; when he turned back, his voice was as cold as the water they were standing in. "When you're dry, I'll fix your hands."

"Okay."

Adrian watched as the young man strode out of the water ahead of him. For once, he regretted not bringing a camera. It wasn't Venus rising from the waves, but a Norse god, cooling off after a long battle.

From that moment on, it felt like they had his father's dog, Chester, snapping at their heels, making them move faster as they prepared to leave. Adrian just managed to retrieve his discarded condom before Ben did, their heads almost colliding as they both reached down at the same time. Ben straightened with a blush and left Adrian to bury the evidence.

Just before they left, Adrian asked Ben to dress his blisters. Roughness he might have expected, but the gentle touch undid him.

Talk about elephants in the room; it felt more like a brontosaurus looming over their shoulders as they discussed everything except what would happen when they returned to civilization.

Soon they were paddling again, only stopping to finish off all the odd bits of food that didn't need preparation, drinking whenever they could. Having a shared objective helped. All Ben's comments revolved about how they could get to the rendezvous point in time, but Mother Nature seemed to conspire against them, sending a strong headwind to impede their progress. Adrian felt torn between wanting to help Ben achieve his aim and staying there as long as possible. The young man used every trick in his arsenal, paddling close to the bank to avoid the worst of the wind's power, taking the shortest line when out of its influence. Ultimately, they reached the pickup point with ten minutes to spare.

Andrew came to greet them and take care of their gear. By this stage, Ben was hardly talking. He appeared to be in pain, but just shook his head whenever Adrian checked to see what was wrong. Hopefully, his loss of control hadn't hurt Ben too much. The roughness at the end wouldn't have helped.

Naturally, Ben's brother wanted to know where they went and what they saw. As Ben remained silent, it was Adrian who ended up providing the details. Admittedly, he might not actually have *seen* the moose, beaver, bears, and eagles he listed, but they'd been around. When Ben realized that Adrian was building up the success of their expedition without exposing any of the problems or things not for general consumption, his face lost some of its tension, and he gave Adrian a wry smile.

Andrew was amazed when he heard how much territory they'd covered. The long trek from Conmee to Poobah especially impressed him. "You took a trip along the Memory Lane portage?" He laughed. "You won't forget that in a hurry."

Memory Lane? Adrian could see where the portage got its name from, but for him the whole trip would be Memory Lane. He wouldn't forget any of it in a hurry. The problem was that, although everything had changed, nothing had. He still had to return to San Francisco and resume his starring role as Adrian Sydney Sutherland IV.

CHAPTER
FIFTEEN

"BEN. Are you awake?"

Shit. Who dropped the ton of bricks on my head? Ben swung his feet onto the floor and managed to stand up without falling. By the time he opened the apartment door, he wondered whether someone had also extracted his bones when he wasn't looking.

"Hi, Mrs. Sanchez." He just managed to rasp the greeting out through a throat still too sore to talk properly.

His landlady took one look and elbowed him out of the way. "These were on the doorstep," she said, handing over an envelope and brandishing a bunch of red roses and a cellophane-wrapped basket. "You go back to bed, honey. I'll find a vase. I wondered why you didn't go to work today. Why didn't you tell me you were sick?"

Even through his snot-filled nose, Ben caught a whiff of a sweet, floral perfume as she carried the flowers into the kitchen. Soon bangs and clashes sounded as she rummaged around in the cupboards, fussing as if she had every right to be there. Eventually, she produced one of the large jars she always brought the cookies in and smiled as if she had won the lottery. "This will do." She shoved the flowers in and added water. When she finished, she put her hands on her hips and shook her head. "Just as well whoever sent you the flowers sent fruit also. You have no food in your cupboards."

Ben managed a weak smile. Luckily, the doorjamb kept him upright. His legs weren't really contributing.

"Well, open it." She nodded toward the envelope.

He hadn't dared to.

Sorry to hear you're not well. Thanks again for a memorable trip. Regards, Adrian.

Was that all the man had to say? Memorable? Regards? No love?

Ben's throat had begun to feel scratchy while they paddled down the final stretch toward the pickup point. Once it did, he hadn't felt much like talking, and his companion had grown progressively quieter on the journey back home. His mom took one look at him when they arrived back at her house and sent him straight to bed. Because his throat was so sore, he didn't sleep, tossing and turning in his bed, frustrated also by the knowledge that Adrian was near but unable to join him. That meant two sleepless nights in a row. The long trip back to San Francisco passed in a daze, dozing in the Minneapolis airport lounge between flights and falling asleep on the plane. After a brief wave of farewell when the cab reached his house, Adrian simply said he'd see him in the office. By then, Ben's throat felt like someone had scoured the inside out with a blowtorch. He slept the remainder of Saturday and all day Sunday, only just managing to muster up enough energy to call in sick as soon as he woke Monday morning. Laurel said she would pass on the message.

"I'll bring you some of my special homemade chicken soup." Mrs. Sanchez pointed him in the direction of the bed. "Make sure you call and thank whoever sent you the gifts."

As soon as she left and before he lost all courage, Ben grabbed his cell and dialed Adrian's private number. The low, sexy growl when he answered made Ben's knees so weak he had to sit down to take the call.

"Hi, Adrian." He could barely manage a whisper. "Thanks for the flowers and fruit."

"Ben, are you alright?"

Was that a note of panic? Oh, shit—given Adrian's experience with Jason, he probably feared the symptoms belonged to the retrovirus kicking in. Ben's confirmation test wasn't due for another three weeks. In the meantime, he had his fingers crossed that this was just a common cold. "Too much swimming in cold water."

"Are you sure that's all it is?"

"Cluck, cluck."

Adrian laughed softly, but his voice was dead serious when he spoke. "Perhaps you should see a doctor."

"Nah, I'll be okay. My landlady is bringing me some chicken soup. How are *you*?" The pause before Adrian replied had Ben sweating.

"I'm fine. Thanks for looking after me so well."

"I'm not sure which must have been worse: the blisters from paddling or the tough portages. If I warned you, though, you might not have come with me."

"I believe I did… a number of times."

Ben chuckled quietly. "Yeah, it was good."

Adrian's voice was equally quiet. "Yes, it was. Thank you, Ben."

Everything sounded so final, so formal. As soon as they took their seats in the seaplane, Adrian hadn't even touched him, let alone made any reference to what they'd done. In fact, those few words now were the only indication anything had happened at all.

Ben swallowed. "It wasn't long enough, though." He'd been tempted to get them lost so they could stay out there longer, but that wouldn't have worked. His brothers would have rescued them and then given him a ribbing he'd never live down.

"At least it took another week off your waiting period. When is your second test?"

"First Friday in October."

"Are you worried?" Ben could hear the concern in Adrian's voice.

"Yeah, a little, especially with this cold." Ben doubted he could have confessed the truth in a face-to-face conversation, but being separated gave him the freedom to express his fear. "The closer it gets, the more real it seems. I must have filed the possibility into the "too hard" basket, and now I have to deal with it." Ben waited for the response, hoping Adrian would offer to come over and see how he was for himself. A bit of clucking would be a small price to pay for Ben to be with Adrian again. They'd only been apart a couple of days and already he missed being able to wrap him up in his arms as they slept. It wasn't just the sex, more being with someone he felt so comfortable with.

"I'm sure you'll be fine." Adrian almost sounded sad when he finally added, "I better go. Make sure you see me first thing when you're well enough to return to work."

The seriousness in his voice brought Ben to earth with a thud. "Okay."

"COME in."

Ben's palms had been sweating ever since he left home. He was anxious to see Adrian again, but he also dreaded it.

This time, the office was immaculate: every file in its correct position, nothing out of place. Adrian stood staring out the window. Either he hadn't had time to take off his suit jacket, or he had deliberately kept it on.

"Shut the door, please."

Ben rubbed the sides of his pants and took a tentative step forward. Adrian's gaze raked him from head to toe. Ben felt his body responding. The situation had been awkward enough when he first learned his boss was gay; now that they had actually made love, it was almost impossible. Too many reminders of Adrian checking him out when he was naked. Too many memories of what they had done together.

"How are you feeling today?" Adrian asked quietly.

"Better," Ben lied. He would have much preferred to stay in bed for another couple of days, but he wanted to see Adrian again. Needed to. Being apart felt wrong. He didn't take the offered chair. Adrian remained on his feet also, the desk acting as a barrier between them. On the top lay two envelopes. A large manila one and a smaller white one. Nothing else. Ben felt his gaze being drawn to them, but forced his eyes to stay level.

Adrian took an audible breath and rubbed the back of his neck as he picked up the larger envelope and handed it over. "Here are the details of your new job and a reference. I spoke to Evelyn yesterday. She's more than happy to give you an internship. You made a big impression on her at the conference."

What the fuck? The boardroom mask was firmly in place, not even an eyelid flickered.

Ben had automatically extended his hand. Now they both gripped the envelope. "I don't understand." Well, that was the understatement of the century. A snapshot of them hanging onto the same plate that first night flashed through his mind. The situation couldn't have been more different.

"I warned you up at the lake. For all sorts of reasons, given what's happened, it's best if you leave SSF Insurance."

"Are you firing me?" Ben's hand dropped to his side.

Adrian still held out the large envelope, the paper trembling in his grasp. Ben searched the blank expression, trying to work out what was going on. He bit his lip. The man might as well have been a stranger; no trace of the carefree lover remained.

"Please, Ben." Adrian extended the hand again; for a second, Ben caught a glimpse of desperation, then the mask slipped firmly back into place.

Taking a deep breath, he plucked the envelope from Adrian's grasp. Inside was a reference, a letter of invitation for an interview from Evelyn Archer, CEO of United Policy, one of their main competitors, and some information about the firm.

Ben's legs finally gave way. He sat on the chair with a loud thump. "Let me get this clear. Because we had sex up at the lake, I can no longer work for you. Is that what you're saying?"

"No... Yes." Adrian sighed and turned back to the window before facing him again. He was obviously struggling to hold some emotion in check, but Ben wasn't quite sure what: embarrassment, fear, anger? "Laurel was right," Adrian continued in the same clipped, impersonal tones. "This firm *is* too small for you. We don't have enough variety to cover all the facets you need for the course."

Ben snorted. "Is it just a coincidence that you're coming to that conclusion now? Or is it more to do with you not having sex with one of your employees?" He'd been wondering about the nonfraternization angle; California didn't exactly make it illegal, but it was still frowned upon. He hadn't worried too much, figuring if Adrian thought it was okay to go out with Laurel then it would be okay to have him around, providing they were discreet, of course, and there was no abuse of their respective positions. The prospect of not seeing Adrian all day, every day had been something he hadn't even wanted to consider.

Adrian picked up the other envelope. "There's more. As it happens, while we were away, my father decided that changes needed to be made to the division. That's probably why he didn't mind filling in for me." The last words were accompanied by a wry grimace and a shrug. "He decided to eliminate your position, so there's a severance payout inside."

Ben stared at the proffered envelope, but didn't move. He'd rather touch poison ivy. "Is this your way of paying me for services rendered? What did you think I was offering? An escort service for the gay outdoors type?"

"No." Adrian almost roared the word, anger turning his eyes metallic gray. "Fuck it," he swore quietly and threw his head back, staring at the ceiling as he took a few deep breaths. Ben watched, fascinated, as Adrian brought his temper back under control. When his former lover finally met his gaze, unshed tears glistened at the corners of his eyes. "You know it wasn't like that."

Ben bit his lip to stop his own tears forming.

"Please take it." Adrian handed him the envelope again. "At least this way, you're better off financially."

"But if I'm not going to be employed here, when am I going to see you?" Given Adrian's stony expression, he didn't dare ask if they could date. "What about if I come over and work out in the gym with you after hours?" Ben hated the desperation that had crept into his voice, but the cold meds made it hard for him to think straight, let alone keep his emotions from trickling out.

"I think it would be best if you didn't. You'll soon find someone your age."

Surely the man wasn't trying to play the age card again? Ben gave a snort of disgust. "You don't seriously mean that, do you?"

Adrian had the grace to look uncomfortable at the accusation. Ben could accept other reasons, difference in status, difference in music tastes even, but age?

"Please don't make this any harder than it needs to be."

"Harder for you or harder for me?"

Adrian flushed, ran a finger under his collar, but he didn't answer.

Ben tried another tack. "Phone calls? You could do pretty good phone sex." Memories of the way Adrian made him come while describing his dream flashed through his brain.

Adrian shook his head.

"This is all crap." Ben stood again, anger replacing the hurt. "You're heading straight back into that stuffy old closet! Aren't you. Are you afraid I'm going to out you? Is that the problem? What's this? Hush money?"

"Please keep your voice down." Anger returned briefly to Adrian's eyes, then he sighed and rubbed his neck again. "Didn't you listen to me up at the lakes? I told you my reasons."

Ben flushed at the reminder of that final morning and frantically tried to remember what Adrian had said when he sat beside him on the rock. The warm hand on his leg hadn't helped then, and the crap in his head made it just as difficult to think now. All he could recall was that he'd been so desperately turned on by Adrian's touch that he hadn't listened properly. Obviously, he should have. "You better run through it again. From the top. I had something else on my mind at the time."

Adrian grimaced at the sarcastic undertone. "Do you remember once telling me how important it was to you that our firm carried all those high-risk policies? That if your dad hadn't been insured with SSF, your mom would have been left in financial difficulty?"

Ben nodded.

"For obvious reasons, we have higher premiums and restrict the maximum payout levels, but they're still only marginally profitable at the best of times. Now...." Adrian didn't need to elaborate further on that front, Ben knew the drill. "Also you must be aware that a large percentage of our policy holders live in the Midwest?" Adrian raised an eyebrow, checking Ben was listening this time.

Ben nodded again.

"While they might tolerate the odd musician or hairdresser being gay, many conservative states aren't too keen on their company owners and directors being homosexuals." A loud sigh erupted as Adrian gripped the back of his chair, his knuckles showing white through his deep tan. "I promised my father that I wouldn't jeopardize the firm in any way as long as he kept those high-risk policies intact."

"But couldn't we keep on meeting in private?" *Damn. Now I just sound like a whiny kid.*

Adrian sighed. "There isn't any such thing as privacy for people in my position. If the press found out I was gay, it would be all over the papers."

"That's what you get for being a media whore."

His words found their target. Adrian's face paled as he let go of the chair and stood straighter. In his immaculate suit, he was, once again, the perfect picture of a conservative business man. "It's expected."

"Bullshit." At Ben's half-shouted accusation, Adrian's lips narrowed into a firm, straight line, proving once again how stubborn the man could be. Inside, all hope withered and died. Ben shook his head, still unprepared to accept what he was hearing. "I can't believe you're willing to sacrifice your happiness and mine so easily. There must be some way you can fix things." He gripped the manila envelope tightly to prevent his hands from shaking.

"Do you think I haven't tried?" Adrian glanced at the door and lowered his voice, but the anger still sliced through. "Life seems so simple at your age, doesn't it? You have no problem in finding solutions for everything. Well, in this case, there isn't an easy way out. If there was, I would have taken it ages ago. Now, the current financial crisis has only made matters worse. You haven't been with the company all that long, so you may not realize that, over the years, the balance of work we do in the different offices has changed. When we expanded the high-risk side, rather than employ more staff, a lot of the ordinary policies were transferred to the other office. If I come out, my father will simply terminate *all* the high-risk ones, not only the HIV. Then, to reduce overheads, he'll consolidate the remaining, more profitable policies back to the east coast office. Every person here will be immediately out of a job, and they'll be lucky if they get severance pay. At least you got something." Adrian waved the white envelope again. "Take it."

Ben gripped the edge of the desk, leaning over so he was nearly close enough to kiss Adrian. But he didn't. Red, raw anger at having his love reduced to a monetary proposition roiled through him. "Okay, go back into the closet if that's what you want. I hope you suffocate among all the moth-eaten designer clothes." Tears threatened to overflow and his knees shook even more if that was possible. He had to leave before he broke down and cried.

Adrian opened the door and stepped back as he brushed past. In the mad rush to his desk, Ben even bumped into one of the underwriters. Blindly, he gathered all the personal things from his cubicle and shoved them into his briefcase. Millie said something before he entered the elevator, but he couldn't stop to speak to her, barely making it safely outside with his dignity more or less intact. The chill wind added another dampener to the day. At least it cooled off his temper some.

Back in his apartment again, he dosed himself up with more cold medication and tried to sleep his grief away. As he lay with the tears drying in his eyes, his thoughts roamed over the events of the past two weeks. For a while, up at the lakes, he'd thought he'd found the real thing. Found a person he wanted to spend the rest of his life with. The respect he'd felt for Adrian when he first joined the firm had morphed into friendship while they worked out together, and then into something deeper as he uncovered the man beneath the mask. Even though they had been limited in what they could do, the sexual attraction between them had been hot. Ben, for one, certainly hadn't been faking his reactions. But who was he to think he was worth risking the livelihoods of all his fellow employees, especially when his feelings weren't returned? The man had told him so himself. *The love of his life had died.* Ben sighed and buried his face in his arms. *Time to man up, dude.*

By the end of the week, he finally felt well enough to front up for the job interview. His new boss, Evelyn Archer, had requested a full rundown on what his role had been since joining SSFI as an intern, plus an update on where he was up to with his course. Somehow, he had to stir himself out of his apathy and prepare for his MFE exam in November. The likelihood of that happening was deteriorating by the day. While she flipped through his resume, Ben stared silently out the window. From where he sat, he could just see his old office building.

"I know you were happy at SSFI," she said when she finished perusing the papers. "But you'll have so many more opportunities working with us, because we're a much larger company."

Ben felt his hackles rise. That old excuse again! Why couldn't people accept that he might care more for ideals than ambition? At least he got the feeling she knew he wasn't happy about the change.

Ben sighed as he left his new place of employment. What would his life have been like if he left SSFI when Laurel first arrived on the scene? For starters, he would have been spared the embarrassment of hooking up with Adrian. The man had politely texted Ben to see if he was feeling better, but Ben didn't contact him back. The pain was still too raw.

He should have known not to get involved with the guy in the first place. He should have listened to his own advice. Even if he had known Adrian was gay, the man had been his boss. No getting over that fact. Since leaving Minnesota, his life had been one disaster after another. First Jason, then Adrian, and in two weeks' time, he had to front up for his HIV test. Didn't disaster always come in threes?

BY THE time the second of October finally arrived, Ben's brain had definitely gone AWOL. The cold had cleared away, although his cough lingered. The tension was killing him.

The appointment had been scheduled for 1 p.m., but they were running late, as usual. Ben flicked through the magazines and newspapers while he waited. There were two types there. Gay and straight. The mainstream ones were filled with photos and stories of movie stars getting drunk and behaving badly.

What right did the public or press have to judge them so harshly? The celebrities provided entertainment for the masses. The more the poor suckers whored around, the more money the media made from reporting their sins. They were only trying to drown their sorrows or enjoy their successes. Who knew what was really happening in their private lives? Shit, if his tests came back clear, no one could blame him if he went out and partied like there was no tomorrow.

273

The gay mags were much more serious. There were apparently moves afoot to target gay bars and sex clubs in an effort to stem the number of HIV infections in the gay community. Good luck.

The result from the rapid antibody tests didn't come through until 2 p.m.

Nil reaction.

Some of the other results wouldn't be back for a few days, but inside, Ben knew he was in the clear. He stared at the paper while his brain struggled to accept the fact that the torment was finally over.

Now what? Friday night. Go out and party, or study hard and behave? His MFE exam was only a few weeks away, but he'd already decided to give it a miss and wait until spring. It didn't take him long to make up his mind. He contacted Mick and arranged to meet him in the Castro.

A TEXT arrived at midnight. Ben had his cell set to vibrate, because he wouldn't have been able to hear it above the music. The place was packed and most of the dancers had worked up such a sweat that their T-shirts stuck to their bodies. Overhead, purple strobe lights pierced the darkness as he bopped to the DJ's house music along with a few hundred people. An older guy had been trying to cruise him for the past hour, dancing as close as possible and generally being a perfect pain in the ass. Ben was so over older men.

Trouble was, all the guys his age were either hooked up with their clones or didn't interest him. After knocking back a few drinks together, Mick had disappeared, chasing a slim-hipped surfer guy with long blond hair. His total opposite. Ben headed outside to check the text. Probably Jason. He had notified him of the result.

The cold night air hit him as he exited the club. Lucky he left the pickup at home; he was well over the limit. In the distance, lightning flashes split the dark clouds.

"What were the results?"

Shit. The SMS was from Adrian.

Ben rocked backward on his heels, staring at the screen. *Adrian, the ass wipe who fired me.* He rocked forward. *Adrian, the guy who*

274

remembered what day my test was on. He rocked backward again and took another swig of the Corona he managed to sneak past the doorman. *Adrian, the moron who was probably curled up in the bottom of his closet, hugging his boots to his chest.* Forward again, this swig barely touched the sides. *Adrian, the guy who owes me a rimming.* This time when he rocked back, his head started spinning. *Adrian, the prick who refuses to even talk to me....*

Ben threw the empty bottle in a nearby dumpster. "Yay, three pointer." He bowed for the nonexistent crowd. "Fuck it. I'm going to go tell him face to face." He burped and hitched up his leather pants.

After narrowly managing to avoid being flattened by a delivery truck, he made it to the other side of Market. By the time he reached the top of the hill, the fog in his brain had begun to clear, his drunken determination to confront Adrian lessening with every step. What the fuck was he doing here? A stream of people stopped his passage for a moment, and Ben stepped aside to let them by. Music rolled out onto the pavement from the door behind them. In the bright interior, people were laughing and calling out to each other. The nightspot was as welcome as a canoe rest. He made his way over to the bar.

"Whadda ya want?"

Ben didn't give a hoot. Anything, as long as it was alcoholic and wet. He pointed at one of the long glasses in the hands of the last customer. "Two of those." He only swayed slightly as he made the request. The bartender eyed him warily as she handed them over. Ben dredged up a bright smile as the cost emptied his pockets of all the cash he had left.

From a vantage point in the corner near a fireplace, he gloomily surveyed the crowd. Everyone was laughing and carrying on as if they didn't have a care in the world. The first drink took away the heavy weight that had settled on his shoulders, and the second gave him the courage to continue on his journey. He pocketed the little umbrellas and grabbed a flower from one of the tables on his way out.

Five minutes later he was on Adrian's doorstep with his finger on the buzzer.

"Ben, what are you doing here?" The guy didn't look too pleased. Funny 'bout that. It was only one in the morning. He wasn't even dressed for bed yet. No slinky blue pajamas. Ben hiccupped and handed over the flower and the little umbrellas. "Wanna thank ya for helpin' me."

Adrian hesitated, then put out a hand to accept the offering. As he did, Ben leaned in and kissed him. Those beautiful lips responded for a heartbreaking second. Ben shut his eyes and swayed.

Adrian took a step back. "You're drunk."

"No shit, Sherlock. Do you think I would have the guts to come here if I was sober?"

Adrian dragged him inside and quickly looked around before closing the door.

"Jus' me." Ben hiccupped again. "No paparazzi on my trail. Your secret's safe." Through the tears in his eyes, the cut glass of the chandelier looked like a waterfall of glistening diamonds.

Adrian grabbed his hand and led him into a formal living area. Ben didn't want to be down here. He wanted to go upstairs. "Bedroom," he protested, and tried to reverse their direction.

Adrian swore and shoved him onto a leather sofa.

Seated, he didn't have to worry whether his shaky legs would hold his weight. Ben picked up an empty glass that stood beside a bottle of Jack Daniels on the coffee table and took a sniff. Alcoholic fumes hung in its depths. "Looks like I'm not the only one who's been drinking." He raised his eyebrows.

"Not as much as you."

"Let's have a competition then, and see who can drink the most." Ben started to stand, but his knees gave away and he collapsed back on the sofa. Before Adrian could react, he grabbed the bottle and took a deep swig.

"Stop it!" Adrian removed the whiskey from his grasp.

"Why? It's what you do, isn't it? You told me so yourself."

Staring him straight in the eye, daring Adrian to stop him, Ben snatched the bottle back from Adrian's nerveless fingers and took another deep draught. The look of sadness on his former boss's face tore at Ben's gut. Shutting his eyes, he tipped the bottle up again. A dribble of whiskey ran down his chin, but liquid fire burned inside, taking away some of the chill. He was only vaguely aware of the bottle being removed from his grasp and a firm hand pushing at his chest.

All the tension in his body disappeared. He let his weight rest against the cushioned back, swallowing furiously in an effort to stop his misery from leaking out. Adrian's continued silence made him open his eyes.

The man's face had gone white as he crouched down beside him. "Was it positive?"

"What?" Ben's brain didn't want to function. "Positive? No." He shook his head violently. "Negative." He gave a loud snort. "I'm as clean and pure as the driven snow."

Adrian gave a huge sigh and sank back on his heels. "Shit, you scared me silly."

Ben stared into those come-to-bed eyes and swallowed. It had been weeks since he last saw them, but it seemed like only yesterday. He reached out and drew a shaky finger along the edge of Adrian's jaw. Soft bristles met his touch. Memories of the way his skin felt after Adrian had kissed him surged to the surface. *God, I want him.*

Adrian shut his eyes and didn't move, accepting his caress; then he turned his head away and brought Ben's hand to his lips. The simple kiss on his palm sent Ben's whole body into a convulsive shudder. There was no way Adrian could pretend this was all one-sided.

"Adrian, you're killing me."

Now that he wasn't hypnotized by those mesmerizing eyes, Ben finally found the courage to tell Adrian how he felt. The alcohol helped. Ever since his first day in the new job, everything had been building up inside. He thought he would be alright, then day after day without seeing Adrian only emphasized how much the man had come to mean to him. Words started tumbling out before he could control them. First slowly, then gathering pace as the emotions inside came free.

"Adrian. It hurts…." Adrian's head jerked slightly, but those soft lips didn't break contact with his palm as Ben continued speaking, his voice betraying his desperation. "I sit in the new office, and all I can do is think about you. I miss you so much. I miss your smile. I miss hearing your voice." Ben gave a weak laugh and tried to pull his hand away, but Adrian clung to it tighter. Ben brought his other hand up and stroked Adrian's hair briefly before allowing it to flop back onto his lap. "I used to get off just listening to you ask someone to do your photocopying. How sick is that?" He rested his head against the back of the sofa, blinking away the tears. Memories cascaded through his brain. "When we worked out, I used to watch you on the bike and on the rowing machine, always trying your hardest, determined to lose weight. I'd be hot and sweaty, and you looked so cool, everything about you so neat, so goddamned perfect." Adrian groaned and rubbed his face against Ben's hand, the dampness on his skin betraying the man's own tears. "Please." If that's what it took, Ben would beg, he'd grovel, he'd plead, he would promise anything. "No one need ever know. I can be discreet. I can come in via the garage. Make sure no one can see me. Come late at night." The words tumbled out like water over a rapid. "Isn't there room for me in the bottom of your closet?"

"No!" Adrian jerked away and started pacing back and forth, stopping at each turn, staring at him, his hands in tightly clenched fists at his sides.

"But I love you." There. This time Adrian couldn't doubt he heard him. The feeling should have gone away once he stopped seeing Adrian, but it hadn't. His stomach churned with hope, or was it fear? Adrian stopped in front of the sofa and shook his head. "Why? Why don't you love me? Is it because of the guy who died?"

"No." This time the word was whispered. "But it's like a nightmare happening all over again." Giving a sad laugh, Adrian rubbed his stomach. "I hurt Antonio too." He perched on the edge of the coffee table, out of Ben's reach.

"What happened?"

For a while, the ticking of a clock was the only sound in the room; then, in a voice tinged with bitter sadness, Adrian told him of his dead lover. Each revelation felt like a sword mercilessly stabbing at Ben's stomach, but despite his own pain, all he wanted to do was wrap Adrian in his arms and comfort him.

When he finished speaking, Ben struggled to his feet. A wave of nausea brought bile to his mouth; his stomach fought a losing battle as all the different drinks he'd consumed collided together. Swallowing the putrid result back down, he nearly gagged on the taste. He tried to stand again, but this time, the room spun and shifted. He couldn't help it. He threw up all over Adrian's beautiful blue rug.

Vaguely, he heard a muffled curse, then a warm cloth wiped his face as he sat frozen on the sofa. Next thing he knew Adrian was seated at one end, guiding him down so that he lay lengthwise on the leather cushions with his head resting on Adrian's lap. Soon, a steady stroking through his hair soothed his scalp and anchored him.

THE room was dark when he woke. Ben flipped off the light rug that covered him and sat up. The floor lurched for a few seconds, then settled. A streetlight outside gave enough illumination to let him know he was alone. The steady tick of the clock was the only sound in the room. His boots had been placed neatly beside the sofa.

Ben groaned and clutched his head. Vague memories surfaced of what had happened after he'd been ingloriously sick, but most was a blur. *Shit.* At one stage, Adrian had given him a pill and made him drink a glass of water. Ben snorted to himself. Mother hen. Adrian hadn't stayed, though. After a while, he tucked the blanket around Ben and whispered good night.

His most vivid recollection of the evening was of Adrian's face as he talked about his dead lover. Then the determined shake of the head followed by what sounded like a death knell: "Not again."

Carrying his boots to avoid making any noise, Ben quietly left the living room and entered the hallway, avoiding looking at his reflection in the gilt mirrors that would no doubt confirm how shattered he still felt. There was no sign of light or life upstairs. The front door wasn't deadlocked, so it opened easily. Ben closed it behind him, careful not to make a sound.

A hollow sense of déjà vu filled him as, once again, he sat on the top step and pulled on his boots. It was still dark when he started walking down the street, concentrating on his surroundings instead of dwelling on the memory of what a fool he'd made of himself. A faint light on the horizon told him dawn was breaking, and—judging by the way water gurgled merrily in the street gutters—while he was out cold, the storm that had threatened earlier must have broken, and only stopped recently. Ben tracked the water's path downstream, absently noting the way the piled-up debris formed mini-lakes beside the drains, just like the beaver dams did back home. The city slept. The only sound was his heels connecting with the rain-glistened pavement. In the distance, a siren started to howl, putting voice to the pain in his heart. Finally, he reached the end of the street-stream.

The wide expanse of San Francisco Bay loomed before him. In the distance, hidden behind the skeleton-like masts of the marina, the Golden Gate Bridge sent a glow into the night sky, making everything else blacker by comparison. Dark clouds obliterated whatever stars usually managed to overcome the city's light pollution. Ben walked away from the jumble of boats and buildings, and headed for a green park bench, facing an open stretch of water. Shoving his hands in his pockets, he sat and stretched out his legs. A full moon showed briefly below the cloud bank and then sank below the horizon, bringing back memories of the last time he'd seen it, while hunched on the rock in the wilderness.

Why the fuck had he ever left?

More memories of his time there with Adrian swirled around and around, then slipped from his brain like leaves being carried by the current. He tried to hang onto their happiness, but they sailed away, out to sea, reminding him once again of what he had lost. By the time he stood and walked as close as possible to the boundary of water and land, his head felt drained, empty. He stared down into the black depths and shivered.

A ferry's horn echoing the cry of the loon pierced the silence.

What time was it? Ben drew out his cell to check and saw a text must have arrived from Adrian while he slept. He opened it:

"Ben, much as I wish it were otherwise, you best forget me. Find someone else to give you the love you deserve. Good-bye. Adrian."

The cell phone barely made a splash as Ben threw it into the water. For a second, he wondered if he should wade in and retrieve it, but then he decided not to. Compared to losing Adrian, its loss seemed trivial.

Forget me. As if. Another shiver ran up his spine as he stared into the darkness. Why had he come here? Oh that's right. He had actually made a list of the three things he wanted to do when he reached the "promised land".

Gay bars. Check. Been in most of them and bopped the night away. Had fun. Met a few people like Mick who became friends. Even had a pleasurable fuck or three.

Pride Parade. Check. Been there, done that. Been out and proud.

Ahead, the first beams of sunlight shone under the bank of cloud. A few trees softened the horizon, but mostly it was only man-made constructs.

There'd been a third thing on his list. What was it again?

Oh, that's right. *Fall in love.*

Check. Why ever had he thought that would be a good idea? Ben sighed. What is love anyway? Just another bunch of letters on a Hallmark card.

A ripple from a passing boat surged toward the shore. Ben shivered again; it was freezing. He folded his arms tight against his chest and took a deep breath, trying to calm his mind. The salt in the air felt strange, alien.

What to do? Where to go? He decided to head east and use the shoreline as his guide. Luckily, he didn't need a compass or cunning navigational tricks here. Once, grass and dirt would have lined the edge of the bay just as they did back home, but over time, nearly all trace had been erased by man, reducing his options. He could only follow paths set down in concrete. In its own way, the city was as constricting as Minnesota had been.

Lights were on in some buildings on Fisherman's Wharf. Early-morning joggers and workers began to make their appearance on the city stage. A ferry ploughed past, the interior lights shining out onto the white wake of its stern and bow waves.

"Forget me?" Could he? Even if he wanted to?

The time with Adrian had been the happiest of his life. Every minute he spent in the man's company had been great. The trip to meet his grandparents, the fun they had making the DVD, the restaurant, making love up at the lakes. Did he want to forget all that? Forget the way Adrian felt when he touched him? The way *he* felt inside?

The skyscrapers of the Financial District loomed ahead.

One fact became crystal clear. He had to find a new internship. Working for Evelyn Archer would be too painful for words. Being Adrian's friend, she would probably feed him little tidbits about Ben over drinks and dinner. And, much as he loved his family, no way was he going home to Minnesota. Going back there would be admitting defeat. But if he didn't find another internship quickly, how could he keep paying his rent? *Shit.* He was so screwed. All the different problems swirled around in circles, going nowhere.

Then, as if he heard the words being spoken out loud, Ben remembered Mick asking him to come and rent the empty bedroom in his condo-loft. Ben stopped walking and stared at the pavement. That would be cheaper than staying with Mrs. Sanchez, and Mick needed the money to help pay off his mortgage. Previously, Ben had resisted his friend's urgings because, after sharing with brothers, he loved having a place of his own. Now he could no longer afford one. He should check to see if the offer was still open. Send him a text. Anyway, Mick was probably wondering where he disappeared to last night. Ben reached into his pocket for his cell and gave an ironic laugh. "Good one, Ben. You threw it in the Bay, remember!" No matter, he knew the address. If Mick was asleep, he wouldn't hear the buzzer, so Ben could come back later.

Avoiding the office, he turned onto Mission, heading toward SoMa. Mick's block came into view. Ben pressed the button on the panel near the entrance. Mick *was* awake. "Yo." The voice came immediately through the speaker.

"Hi, it's me, Ben."

"I'll let you in."

A click indicated the security lock had been released. Ben pushed the door open. The building was much classier than Mrs. Sanchez's place. Nice. He trudged up the stairs to Mick's apartment.

"What are you doing here?" Mick gestured for him to come inside.

"I need to talk to you about something."

The interior was neat, serviceable, a total contrast to Adrian's swank pad. "You look like shit," Mick said, ushering him into the kitchen.

"Thanks, I feel like shit."

"What's wrong?"

"Is that offer of a room still open?"

Mick raised his eyebrows. "Sure."

"Great." One problem solved.

"Why the change of heart?"

While Mick prepared the coffee, Ben sat on a stool, trying to work out how much to tell him. "I need to quit my new job."

Mick stopped in the middle of pouring and glanced sideways. "Why?" He knew of the recent switch to United Policy.

"Long story."

Mick finished pouring and placed the mug on the counter.

Ben sighed as the first sip hit his empty stomach. "Sorry, my brain isn't functioning properly. I haven't eaten since breakfast yesterday." Nerves had stopped him before he went to the clinic, and afterward he'd been too busy celebrating. That all seemed like a year ago, not seventeen hours.

"Okay. Eat first. Talk later. You look like you're going to pass out on my floor."

"Thanks a lot."

Mick grinned at the sarcasm and fed him some muesli and yogurt. The food helped settle his stomach at any rate. Ben's urge to punch a hole in the nearby cupboard erupted now and then, but there was something about Mick that calmed him down. He would be a good doctor one day simply because he was a great listener.

"Okay, tell me what's been going on."

In the end, Ben told him everything: Jason, his brush with HIV, the whole bit. Mick raised an eyebrow when he heard about Adrian being gay, but promised not to tell a soul. Ben didn't go into details about their time up at the Lakes, but Mick probably guessed they hadn't just been paddling. The decision to quit the new job didn't go down too well, but Ben assured him he'd find another one as soon as possible. In the end, Mick accepted his reasoning and promised he wouldn't hassle for rent until he could pay. Any income was better than nothing.

A look of pity crossed his friend's face. "What are you going to do?"

Good question. "I don't know."

"Move in whenever you want. It'll be fine." After clearing up the breakfast things, Mick gave his shoulder a sympathetic squeeze. "Come on. I'll show you the room."

Ben followed him up the stairs. The room wasn't anything special, a single bed large enough so his feet wouldn't hang over the end and a desk. It wouldn't be too hard to bury himself in the coursework. No distractions.

"Thanks Mick, I'll take it."

"Great. Do you want to go back and collect your things now?"

"May as well. Lucky I've got a pickup. Not that there's much parking around here."

"No sweat on that front. This apartment has a dedicated space, and I don't have a car."

Mick walked with him back to Haight-Ashbury. Along the way, they chatted about the future. Mick was his usual optimistic self. If nothing else cropped up, he was sure Ben could get a job at his parent's restaurant, waiting tables until he found another internship. In the meantime, there were heaps of things they could do together: games of soccer or basketball with his friends, noninterrupted study, leftover pizzas.

Mrs. Sanchez was cool, though she said she'd miss him. Apparently one of her nephews had recently arrived in the States and was staying with her while he attended Cal Berkley. He could take over the room, so she didn't mind Ben moving out immediately.

There wasn't much in the flat, so it didn't take them long to pack.

CHAPTER
+++
SIXTEEN

A GUST of wind rattled the windowpane, waking Adrian from a deep sleep. He stumbled out of bed, tripping over the pile of his discarded clothing, and staggered downstairs. The house was deathly quiet. *Damn.* Ben had gone. Adrian sank onto the cool surface of the sofa and buried his head in his hands.

Before he left, he'd meant to ask Ben for more time to sort out the mess he'd made of his life. Recounting the painful truth about his relationship with Antonio had felt like pulling slivers of glass from under his skin, leaving his nerve endings raw and tingling. Afterward, he'd sat there for ages, stroking his fingers through Ben's red hair, seeking solace from the touch as much as trying to give comfort after Ben's inglorious upchuck on the carpet. In the end, he'd resorted to the coward's way out, sending a text message to someone who was asleep on his lap and then walking away, needing the distance between them so he could think clearly. Touching Ben drove all thoughts from his brain. He hadn't meant to go to sleep, but he must have been more tired than he thought.

The trouble was that when he sent the text, telling Ben to forget him, he did so out of some crazy concept of being noble, but as he lay on the bed afterward, he realized he shouldn't have. You can't tell someone to forget the one you love.

Simply because he'd shared what Ben was going through, Adrian had no doubt that Ben *did* love him, even though he was drunk when he made that confession. Ben's departure from the firm had left a gaping hole in his life. Until then, he hadn't realized how much he'd come to depend on the happy grin of welcome each day, the sound of his cackling laugh, the shy glances every now and then when he thought

Adrian wasn't looking, the unqualified support that was always there if he needed it. The office hadn't been the same. Apart from Laurel, everyone missed him: Millie was awfully quiet, Mrs. C walked around with a frown on her face, hinting it was time to retire, and even Tyrone kept asking where he was.

As for the evenings, the less he thought about them the better. Who would have thought that three nights of being held as he slept could be missed so much when the comfort was gone? The sex had been great, but each recalled memory of whispered words and lingering kisses in the dark burnt like cigarette butts being stubbed out on his skin.

Trying to tire himself out in the gym hadn't worked either. All he did was wander around, remembering the way Ben looked when he used the different pieces of equipment. The encouraging smiles he sent whenever Adrian wanted to stop. The way he helped him with his crunches and devised their training regimes, changing them regularly to ensure no muscles got overworked, and that Adrian didn't get bored.

So far, he'd resisted the temptation to call Evelyn to see how Ben was getting on. If he did, she'd give him a piece of her mind. She already thought he was stupid for letting Ben go. "Guys like that don't grow on trees," she warned. "Someone will quickly pick him off."

Before he fell asleep, happy in the knowledge that Ben was close and safe downstairs, Adrian had listened to the rain pattering against the window, thinking about the sex, the fun times, but after a while his thoughts had turned more to the other aspects of the trip: Ben lifting the canoe and confronting him with his inability to accept help. The trouble was that ever since he left Italy, he felt like he'd been treading water, struggling to keep his head above the surface, knowing that if he stopped for a second, he'd sink to the bottom.

Another memory flashed up. Ben using the knowledge his father had taught him about how to find the right path when it wasn't clear. If only he had Ben's confidence to know which was the right path to take as far as his *life* went. It was like he'd gone through life, lately, with his head buried in an upturned canoe, restricting his vision. Somewhere along the way, he'd lost sight of the big picture: providing a means for people to insure themselves despite their existing medical conditions. Everyone deserved to know that their life was valuable, that they mattered, and that they should not give up. He'd lost sight of the goal itself and concentrated more on the fact that it was *his* responsibility to achieve it. Maybe the time had come to pass the burden on to someone else, just like he'd passed the canoe onto Ben. How had Ben put it? *"What's more important? The goal or some ass-wipe sense of self-justification."* In the long run, it didn't matter who provided the policies, as long as they were available.

In the end, it all came down to teamwork, because despite all their differences in age, status, and personality, they meshed well together. If he wanted Ben, and he now admitted that he did, he needed to confront his father about his ultimatum. Simple as that. He'd tried so many times before, but each time he'd taken the easy way, thinking that if he kept going, he'd eventually find his way out of the mess his life had become. However all he'd done was get lost in the labyrinth. At the lakes, Ben had showed him that sometimes you have to admit you have a problem and look for an alternate route, even if it is more difficult.

The whiskey bottle sat forlornly on the coffee table alongside the empty glass. Adrian picked them up with the tips of his fingers and carried them at arm's length into the kitchen. He didn't feel the slightest bit inclined to finish off the dregs. Seeing Ben so drunk had sobered him instantly. He needed to stop trying to find the solution to his problems there.

Adrian stared blindly at the golden liquid disappearing down the drain. Evelyn was right. Men like Ben didn't grow on trees. Adrian had to move fast. At least he had the whole weekend to get the ball rolling. He dropped the empty bottle into the sink and ran up the stairs, taking two at a time. The sooner he set off on this difficult journey to confront his father, the better. He could grab something to eat at the airport on his way to New York. First though, he needed to call Carl to see what his options were; whether the alternative they'd discussed before the financial crisis hit was still feasible. Adrian had dismissed the proposal out of hand, knowing that his father would never agree, but now his future was at stake, his life. If Carl thought there was a chance, then he had to next convince Evelyn. He definitely needed something to bargain with.

WHEN the cab dropped him off outside his father's home, the large Colonial-style house looked deserted except for a couple of lights in the living room. The sound of yapping and skidding feet greeted his arrival. "Hi, Chester." Adrian patted the dog's head and followed him up the winding staircase.

"Bill. Is that you?" His father sat sprawled on the sofa with a half-empty glass in his hand. Two small lamps on the liquor cabinet shone with a subdued glow. A half-full bottle of Jack Daniels sat nearby.

"No, it's me, Adrian."

The liquor in his father's glass sloshed as he set it down on the table beside him. "What the hell are you doing here?"

Adrian sat on one of the hard-backed leather chairs and tried to work out how best to approach the subject. Chester settled at his father's feet. "I need to talk to you about something—a few things actually."

Surprise clouded the patrician features, but all he did was shrug and wave a shaky hand at the liquor cabinet. "Get yourself a glass."

"No, thanks."

"Suit yourself." His father took another drink. The red flush on his face indicated his blood pressure was already elevated. When he heard Adrian's proposal, it would go sky-high. The bare branch of a tree brushing against the window drew Adrian's attention. Three red leaves clung determinedly, attempting to thwart the wind's effort to drive them into the darkness below.

No, he couldn't put this off to a better time. Every second had begun to feel crucial. Adrian took a deep breath. "Dad, you know how, for ages, you've been saying we can't afford the high-risk policies, and that you wanted to stop offering them to new customers."

The startled glance he received turned into suspicion as to why his son was, for once, raising the subject. "Go on." The glass was poised at his lips for a few seconds before he finished off the drink in one mouthful.

Adrian sighed. Winning this argument would not be easy. Most times, if he tried reason, his father would wear him out to the point where he gave in, simply because it was easier than beating his head against a brick wall. If he tried challenging him, the old man just kept raising the ante, becoming angrier by the minute. Usually, Adrian backed off pretty quickly, worried he would set off another heart attack. This time he had to change his tactics and meet every challenge. The trouble was he didn't have much to offer. *Now to see what my bluffing skills are like.* "What if I told you that I could *sell* all the high-risk policies?"

That got a reaction, the eyes softened and a satisfied smile curled his lips. "I'm glad to see you're finally coming around to my way of thinking. But who would be fool enough to take them on in this economic climate?"

"United Policy, the company my friend Evelyn Archer works for. I've only made a preliminary approach so far, but they're definitely interested."

His father's attention was hooked. He poured himself another drink and settled against the sofa cushions, resting one foot on his knee. Chester looked up, then went back to sleep. "Including the HIV policies?"

"Yes." *Now for the hard bit.* "But they need a sweetener."

The bristly eyebrows narrowed. "What sort of sweetener?"

Adrian swallowed and kept his voice level, trying to make it sound as if this were a normal business proposition, not one that was sure to get the old man's hackles up. "We need to package them with some basic life policies from the western division."

"Never." His father slammed the glass back down on the table, spilling his drink all over the polished mahogany surface. "Not while we can simply terminate the risk policies, close down the division, and consolidate everything into the East Coast office."

To his father, selling off a profitable part of the business was tantamount to a betrayal. He took great pride in the fact that the business had grown steadily ever since he took over from his own father. But that solution would mean an end to all Adrian's dreams and a bunch of people out of a job. The exact scenario he'd been trying to avoid ever since the financial crisis hit.

"If you do that, I will come out publicly, as flamboyantly as possible. I always did fancy creating a scandal. How about if I dress in drag and get my picture in the magazines? I could, you know. I have

289

enough contacts to make sure I get great exposure. I've even got the outfit. A nice lilac number with a yellow boa."

A loud harrumph erupted, the red complexion growing brighter by the second. "I would disown you."

Adrian strengthened his resolve, deriving courage from the fact that if he didn't win this fight, he was back to square one. "The damage would be done though. Even if the more conservative policyholders don't cancel, you'll lose a lot of people who sympathize with my plight. Wait until I tell them the whole story: how my father had a heart attack and claimed he was on his deathbed, how he pleaded for me to come back to the States to learn the business before he died, getting me to promise to stay in the closet and *suppress my gay tendencies*." Adrian couldn't help the sarcastic stress on the last phrase. His father flinched visibly.

"How dare you threaten me!"

Adrian had long ago realized that his father was a bully, but he maneuvered by stealth, getting Adrian to obey him by using loyalty and concern for his well-being as a weapon. Watching Ben stand up to his brothers made Adrian ashamed of the fact he'd never had the guts to do the same thing. "How can you accuse me of threatening you? What do you think you've been doing to me for the last five years? I'm fed up with your emotional blackmail."

"I'm warning you, Adrian, I'll cut you out of my will if you out yourself."

Now he had upped the ante, as Adrian expected he would. "You know what, Dad? I don't care if you do. I'm not interested in having vast wealth when you die. The only reason I went along with your demands was that I thought I could make a difference. That way, at least someone would benefit." That was why he hadn't returned to Europe when he'd realized his father's death wasn't imminent, even though Antonio's was. Deprived of the right to care for his lover, he took the next best option, staying in the States and turning what he always saw as a curse into something good.

His father's relaxed posture had disappeared some time ago. He stared at Adrian as if he'd never seen him before. In a way, he hadn't. "So, how come you suddenly found the balls to stand up to me?"

"I met someone I want to spend the rest of my life with." Adrian glanced back at the window. Two leaves still hung on grimly.

"Not that young punk you went paddling with?"

When they got back, Adrian's blisters had been a dead giveaway. His father didn't give a hoot what he got up to as long as no one knew, but if nothing else had, that had probably sealed Ben's fate. "Punk? I'd hardly call Ben a punk."

"Who cares what he is." His father stood and loomed over the chair, trying to crowd him, but Adrian didn't flinch. "You won't only be cut off from my will, you'll be out of a job. Have you worked out the implications of that? All your little company perks: the car, the phone, the laptop? How will you afford your house payments?"

The old man sure knew how to turn the screw. Adrian leaned back and deliberately placed his booted ankle on his knee, imitating his father's earlier casual pose, forcing him to retreat. He was far from feeling relaxed, but he needed to pretend he was confident; any backing down would be fatal. An image of Ben striding before him on the path gave Adrian another burst of courage. "I'm sure I could find some talk shows who would love all the gory details. Father makes gay son destitute. Human interest always sells."

Adrian swallowed a sigh of relief as his father turned and began to pace up and down the room. The conversation wasn't endangering the old man's health; if anything, he looked more alive than ever. Adrian shook his head at his past stupidity. He should have known that his father thrived on confrontation, whereas he avoided it wherever possible.

"You won't be able to sell your house, not in this economic climate." His father sounded as if he was taking delight in knowing how difficult it would be.

"I can always lease it and find somewhere else to live."

"What will you do for money?"

Unfortunately, the question was a good one. Adrian had been flat broke after he came back from Europe, then he had sent as much money to Antonio's family as he could to help them pay for his treatment. After his lover's death, what he hadn't spent keeping up a suitable image had been invested in shares that were now worth far less than he'd paid for them. "I'll get by. I have before."

"I'll make sure there's a clause in the final contract that stipulates you can't work for the company doing the buyout."

He would too; Adrian had seen him in action against other people. "Thanks, Dad."

This time, his sarcastic reply actually drew a startled pause before his father did another lap of the room. When he returned, the old man stood with his arms folded, a self-satisfied smirk on his face. "What's to stop me remarrying and having more children? Men older than I have done it."

As if that would be a worry! Adrian just pitied the poor kid. He was starting to wonder whether his father really cared about him as a person or whether he only saw him as his heir, another possession. "Maybe you should have done that long ago."

A deep flush erupted as he yelled, "I didn't because I loved your mother."

Adrian sniffed. "Funny way of showing it."

"You wouldn't understand."

Understand how much it hurt to let go and move on after losing the one you loved? Adrian didn't respond. He didn't want to acknowledge another example of how alike they were.

"Laurel would jump at the chance of marrying me."

The thought made Adrian want to puke, but if his father thought he could get at him that way, he might do it out of spite. "Go on. At least that means you won't have to pay her a proper wage."

When he realized his son wasn't going to rise to the bait, the flush on his father's face grew redder. The whole relaxed posture, fake as it was, added fuel to the fire. Adrian had never seen him so angry.

"I could kick you out tomorrow, and Laurel can close the place down."

He had raised the ante yet again, but Adrian still had one card left in the deck; the Goth he'd played in Ben's video came straight to mind. "If she does, I'll dye my hair blue and tattoo my ass with the words 'Screw SSF Insurance'. Then Ben and I can make a film of us fucking and put it up on Xtube." Adrian held his breath, waiting for the reaction.

At first, he thought the old man was having an epileptic fit; he shook with rage and almost foamed at the mouth. If it had been Chester, he would have been worried that he had rabies. Adrian forced himself to wait silently while his father brought himself back under control. The tension in the room escalated with each passing minute.

"What kind of a monster have I raised?"

"One exactly like you. A chip off the old block."

Maybe he shouldn't have painted him into a corner. But Adrian was desperate. His acting skills came in handy once again. He blanked every expression from his face. Eventually, his father took a deep breath and glanced away. When he turned back, he looked ten years older. "Okay, I'll give you a month. If I don't see some sort of proposal in writing, the deal is off." He waggled his finger. "And no outing yourself in the meantime."

The realization Adrian had reached his goal took a few seconds to set in. True, he had surrendered any prospect of inheriting the company and would soon be out of a job, but he felt as if a burden had been lifted off his shoulders, once again floating in the air like when Ben had taken the canoe from him toward the end of that long portage.

"What about the staff?" Adrian knew he was pushing his luck, but he couldn't go through all this again.

"What *about* the staff?" There was more impatience than anger in the voice now.

"Will you try to relocate as many as you can?" His father looked as if he was about to protest, so Adrian jumped in before he could. "A good news story about how important family is to SSFI would come in handy. About how you would bend over backward to look after your employees, like you do with your customers. Treating them like family."

The old man nodded. The wind's power hadn't decreased, but the only other sound that broke the silence was Chester's heavy panting. His father sighed. "Speaking of tattoos, you don't happen to know where Jason is by any chance, do you?"

293

"No." Adrian blinked in surprise at the sudden jump in conversation. "Why?"

"Vernon called a couple of hours ago. Apparently he's disappeared. The bikie nurse they had, that Vincent character, has gone off to see if he can find him. Consuela is beside herself with worry. He's their only child." He glared at Adrian as if that was his fault too.

One leaf still fluttered against the windowpane.

Adrian stood as his father returned to his seat on the sofa. The old man picked up Chester and gave him a reassuring pat. The dog's quivering showed he'd sensed the tension in the room. Before leaving, Adrian placed a pamphlet about PFLAG on the table beside the whiskey bottle. "Whatever happens, I'm coming out as soon as the month's over. You might as well learn to live with the fact that you have a gay son."

"I suppose you're going to waste your time up at the old winery. You won't make any money, you know." His father didn't even look up as he spoke.

"At least I'll be happy." Adrian pictured Ben greeting him with open arms. He was the only family he needed.

As he stared at the window, the final leaf fluttered out of sight.

Before leaving the room, Adrian turned back for a final glance. His father remained on the sofa, patting his Jack Russell, refusing to acknowledge his departure. He was probably never going to be acknowledged as his son again. The thought made Adrian sad rather than angry. He recognized his father for what he really was—a lonely old man. At least he had Chester for company. "Good-bye, Dad."

AS SOON as he returned to San Francisco, Adrian tried to call Ben. When he couldn't get through, he drove to Ben's apartment to give him the good news. A young Hispanic boy answered the door. Adrian checked the number to make sure he had the right address and then asked if Ben Dutoit was home. The boy shook his head. "Never heard of him."

The answer didn't want to sink in, or somehow his brain rejected it. When Adrian showed no signs of moving, the young man crossed to the neighboring apartment and rang the bell. A matronly woman appeared.

"Tia Tereza, this man is looking for a Ben Dutoit."

She pulled Adrian into her room and made him sit down while she made a cup of tea. As she was a bit deaf, it took a while to make her understand who he was and why he wanted to see Ben. Eventually, she shrugged. "He came with a friend, collected all his belongings, and paid a week's rent."

"When?"

"Yesterday morning, early."

"Was it the guy with the red Corvette?"

"No, I hadn't seen this one before. He was taller than Jason."

Maybe it was one of Ben's brothers? "Did he have red hair?"

"No. Dark hair. Like yours was once."

She was trying to be helpful.

ADRIAN didn't worry too much. He could wait until Ben went to work on Monday and see him there. The rest of Sunday afternoon, he spent visiting Carl Hausfeldt.

His former chief actuary was still recovering from his heart attack, but had managed to lose a fair amount of weight. He now looked after the children while his young wife went back to work. He had never been happier, he said. Fortunately, he knew enough about the business, and the policies they had put into place, to help formulate a serious proposal.

Adrian also visited a real estate office and told them to find a tenant for his house. The sooner he was out of there, the better. Perhaps he could move in with Ben, wherever he was. Thoughts of what they could do now filled every available moment.

First thing on Monday, Adrian paid a visit to the firm's doctor and had a thorough health check. He might as well make use of all the perks while he had access to the company's health coverage. He also made time for a full test for HIV and other infectious diseases.

Every time he tried to contact Ben, though, his phone still wasn't answering. In the end, he sent a long text, telling Ben that he loved him, and that in a few weeks he would be able to leave the closet for good, then they could be together.

He didn't get a reply.

As soon as he walked into the office after lunch, all his plans for contacting Ben at work came to a screeching halt. Obviously his father had let the cat out of the bag. Rumors were flying around like forest fires. No sooner did he smother one person's fears than another would knock on his office door and want to know if they were out of a job. Adrian tried to reassure them as best he could, but until he had something definite back from Evelyn's company, he couldn't be certain of anything.

One thing the day made him determined to do was to go public with his decision to come out. He contacted his father and told him how upset the staff was at the news being leaked. His father pleaded ignorance, but he did admit speaking to Laurel. He said Laurel couldn't have been the culprit, as she promised him she wouldn't say anything. He soon changed his tune when Adrian put Mrs. Christie on the line. She told his father in no uncertain terms what she thought of the bitch. He must have believed her, even if he didn't believe his son. Soon after, he contacted Laurel and said it would be best if she came back to New York.

Adrian wasn't sure whether to be pleased or scared. At least he wouldn't have to put up with her on a day-to-day basis. He would have enough to do, trying to find jobs for people he cared about. By the time he left the office at nine o'clock, he had a full-blown migraine. He would have given anything for Ben to give him a neck rub, but he still wasn't returning his calls.

AT MIDNIGHT, Adrian was working on the figures when the doorbell rang.

A vision in red waltzed in and prodded him in the chest, forcing him backwards. Before he could tell her what had happened with his father, she blurted out, "I told you he wouldn't wait forever."

Adrian hadn't had a drop of alcohol since seeing Ben, but the banging in his head made it difficult for her words to penetrate. "What the fuck's up, Evelyn?"

"Ben's disappeared." Adrian followed her into the kitchen, where Evelyn pulled a couple of coffee mugs out of the cupboard. She had visited often enough in the past to know exactly where everything was kept.

Adrian hung onto the doorframe. Her words still hadn't registered properly. "Did you say Ben's disappeared?" The parallel of this news with hearing about Jason hit him. Was the guy Mrs. Sanchez saw the mysterious Vincent? Perhaps they were both looking for Jason. He collapsed onto the nearest stool.

"Yes, disappeared—as in gone, vamoosed, and no one knows where he is." Making herself at home, as she had so many times when she'd acted as his beard, Evelyn dragged out all the ingredients and started up the machine, talking over her shoulder without even looking at him. "When he didn't turn up for work, I assumed he was sick again, but a letter of resignation arrived in this afternoon's mail. I would have called you earlier, but I had scheduled an emergency board meeting to discuss the proposal you couriered over."

Adrian didn't give a hoot about what the verdict was; no doubt she'd tell him later. All he wanted to hear was news of Ben. "What did the letter say?"

"Apparently he has decided he's not cut out to be an actuary, thank you very much. He was sorry to put me to all that trouble and deeply appreciated my help, blah blah blah. The only positive thing I could glean from the formal phrasing was that he was totally sober when he wrote it."

That removed one terrible possibility. "I've tried to call him, but keep getting a recorded message from the phone company, saying this number is unavailable."

Evelyn plonked the cup of black coffee down so hard, half the contents spilled out. The glare hadn't lessened one bit. "Well, he's gone."

Adrian stood and grabbed a glass of water and a couple of Excedrin. His stomach and liver might not thank him, but his head sure would. "Did he say where?"

"Nope." She poured another cup for herself and drew up the other stool.

"Does his mother know where he is?" Adrian pulled out his cell. "Damn, too late, I can't call her now."

"Don't bother. I did that this afternoon. She's away at the moment, but I spoke to someone called Chris. One of his brothers, I gather. He wasn't very polite either, just said Ben called to say he's gone to live with someone called Mick. Chris didn't know who he was—his boyfriend, he supposed. The young man sounded pretty sarcastic when he said that, as if he didn't approve. Have you heard of anyone called Mick?"

The friend he mentioned that he'd gone surfing with. The one Adrian had instantly been jealous of. All sorts of warning lights flashed in his head. How drunk had Ben been on Friday night? Had Adrian given up everything—his job, his money, his future—for someone who had immediately gone off with someone else? He couldn't help himself. He started to laugh.

Evelyn reached out and gripped his arm, shaking him roughly. "Don't you even care?"

Adrian flushed and pulled away. "Of course I care. It's fucking ironic. That's all."

He proceeded to tell her about the meeting with his father. She hadn't grasped the full implications of what would happen if he did come out.

Evelyn put a reassuring hand on his arm when he finished. "If it comes to having somewhere to stay, Liz and I have a spare room."

"Thanks. I may need to take you up on that."

"What will you do? Contact your father and say the deal is off?"

"No. What's done is done. I should have gone down this path ages ago. As soon as I realized my father wasn't really at death's door. I suppose I should be grateful to Ben for giving me the courage to act. My first priority is to get a deal put together as quickly as possible."

"You're not going to give up on Ben are you?"

Adrian stared at the empty cup, twisting it round and around in his hand. "No."

"If it's any consolation, I was nearly going to read him the riot act at work. All he's done since joining the firm was stare out the window all day."

Adrian was reminded of the time Ben had hurried on ahead during the trip down the Memory Lane portage. He was nowhere to be seen now either, but Adrian knew he was on the right track. Hopefully, he'd be there when Adrian got to the end. He had to believe that. He had to believe in Ben.

"Speaking of losing a job, if your board is keen to go ahead, I want to see how we can structure the deal so you take on some of our employees at the same time."

Evelyn patted his hand. "Definitely, and I'm happy to report that, so far, they're really happy with the initial proposal. It's a bummer you can't come and work for us, but anything you can do to promote the takeover will be a help. Contrary to what your father thinks, you *are* respected around town. At least, being a family-owned company, you can't be accused of insider trading, especially as it appears you're not going to benefit in any way."

ADRIAN sat on the sofa, gazing blindly at some college football on the television.

What if Ben's landlady wasn't telling the truth?

Adrian parked his Prius on the street near Ben's apartment and settled in to wait, squirming down in his seat to avoid detection. He'd been there every day for a week now. It was a wonder he didn't get arrested for being a stalker, but he justified the fact by saying he was making sure Ben was all right. A couple of bikes roared up. Adrian risked sitting up higher until he could see who it was. Two leather-clad guys dismounted. Adrian recognized Jason as soon as he took his helmet off. The jet-black hair had grown longer since he last saw him.

Ben came to the door when they knocked. Adrian couldn't hear what they said, but after a while Ben went back inside. Soon after he reappeared, carrying a small bag. Jason and the other guy looked warily from side to side. Adrian slouched down again so they couldn't see him. The roar of their hogs told him it was safe to sit up. When he did, all he saw was a rear view of Ben, riding behind one of the leatherclad figures. He didn't have a helmet on.

Adrian went home, utterly defeated.

He called Vernon and Consuela and got an earful. Turned out, Vincent had taken Jason on a road trip as a way of getting Jason's head out of his ass and to stop him feeling so sorry for himself. They were riding their Harleys cross-country, camping out. Jason had been horrified. No hot showers, no hair gel, and no morning macchiatos. Apparently Vincent was an alumnus of UC Berkeley and needed to attend a conference. While they were in San Francisco, Jason was going to wrap up his affairs on the West coast and see Ben. Afterward, they were headed for Baja. Adrian could imagine Ben filling Jason in on his intransigent stupidity. Seeing Ben was footloose and jobless, they invited him along for the ride. He didn't have his passport, so he told them to drop him off at Malibu. He wanted to go surfing again.

Three weeks passed. The longest three weeks of Adrian's life. He watched so much porn, his DVDs wore out. After another busy day at work, tying up loose ends, he downloaded a new surfer video. Settling onto the sofa, he yanked off his tie and poured some Jack with his remote poised to watch Beach Wood.

The first frame centered on the rear of a guy from his waist to his knees. He was holding a blue surfboard. He let it fall to the ground, revealing one of the finest asses Adrian had ever seen. The two perfectly formed globes were covered by a film of sand, as if the porn star had been covered in suntanning oil and rolled over and over until the grains coated his skin.

Adrian swallowed as the young man dusted off his butt, uncovering not the usual tan you expected in these beach porn flicks, but skin the color of alabaster. The hands moved away as the body turned slowly. In actual fact, the camera must have been on a track, as no muscles moved, just those hands that looked so familiar. Adrian groaned as his front came into view. The guy's cock stood proud and erect as he carefully flicked away the sand, grain by grain.

Then the camera tracked slowly upward, away from the soft, red curls at the base, up the happy trail, up, up farther until they reached those laughing blue eyes. Adrian's whole body shuddered as he came.

Adrian woke with a start and stared at the annoying infomercials that proliferated after midnight. He hadn't seen or heard from Ben since he'd left his house a week ago, but the young man still managed to haunt his dreams, though that one was more of a nightmare.

Egged on by his nightmare, Adrian rang Vernon to see if Jason was back, and to discover if Ben was with him. Turned out one part of his dream was true. Vincent had found Jason and brought him back to their house, but Ben definitely wasn't with them. When he finally got to talk to Jason, the young man didn't have a clue where Ben was, either. The fact that they had disappeared at the same time was nothing more than coincidence. Hearing that helped ease the pain a fraction. The thought that they were together again had made Adrian feel even worse.

Ben once said that he missed Adrian so much it hurt. Adrian knew exactly what he meant. He had stopped drinking, but his stomach still ached like it had up at the lakes when he'd first realized that he loved Ben. The only way he could deal with losing the job and all the company perks was comparing how little they mattered to the fact he had lost Ben.

As the days passed, the truth of that statement seemed more and more likely. Ben could be anywhere. Adrian didn't even know if Mick lived in San Francisco. They could be surfing together in Malibu, like in his dream, or travelling overseas.

Ben's mother was apparently away on a cruise somewhere, and whenever he called the house, the only person he managed to speak to was Chris, who told him in no uncertain terms to fuck off and not to try contacting Andrew or Rob either, as they both hated his guts and wouldn't tell him anything. Apparently he had broken Ben's heart. That's all he would say.

Adrian took to running around different parts of San Francisco, hoping he might stumble onto Ben or see his Ranger parked in the street, but the young man was like the elusive beaver. A glimpse of a figure in the distance would stir memories and give him hope. Once he even spotted a tall redhead playing soccer. As if.

In the end, it took just over a month to finalize everything and ensure the deal was irrevocably in place. In that period, Adrian managed to find a tenant for the house and moved in with Evelyn and Liz. They tried to cheer him up and even suggested he donate them some sperm. Apparently his name topped their list of potential fathers because he was good-looking, intelligent, and had finally grown some balls.

At least working on the takeover had kept him busy. The rumor mill had grabbed onto the story that SSFI was shedding its high-risk policies. Adrian had made a promise to the reporter who accosted him at the restaurant. Time to honor the deal, and step out of the closet.

CHAPTER
+++
SEVENTEEN

"Take a look at this, Ben."

Ben tucked his white shirt into his black dress pants and looked across to where Mick sat studying something on the computer. He checked his watch. "I have to be at the restaurant in ten minutes. I'm late as it is."

"I think you really need to read this, Ben."

Ben's attention was more fixed on his cuff. He glanced briefly at the page header: *Damien Dishes the Dirt*. "What's he going on about this time? Promiscuity in gay men giving them a bad rep?" He snorted. Mick was always trying to get him interested in gay rights and the politics behind it, but Ben didn't give a hoot.

Mick stood and gestured at the chair. "Life Insurance for people who are HIV positive. It's an interview with your old boss."

Ben slid into the vacant spot, his palms already too sweaty to guide the mouse. Quickly he skimmed over the intro, where the journo explained who Adrian was. A muffled whistle of surprise escaped when he read Adrian's account of how he gave up his birthright to ensure that at least one firm would continue to offer impaired-risk life insurance to people who had been infected with HIV. As his old boss explained, "They need to be reassured that their life still matters. That *they* matter. Society is too quick to shun them once they've been diagnosed, but the more encouragement we can give them to keep fit and healthy and keep their illness from progressing, the more likely they are to survive. With the new treatment regimes, many are living asymptomatic for years. Their life expectancy is almost an unknown. The longer they live, the more proof they're giving the bean counters that they are an acceptable risk."

Ben was pleased to read that Evelyn Archer would be at the head of a new division of United Policy. The reporter went on to note that the premiums were higher than SSFI had set them at. Ben could imagine the sigh that Adrian gave as he explained that the new entity, High Risk Solutions, wasn't a family firm, so they operated under a different structure. They even had plans to go global in the near future.

The reporter then congratulated Adrian's courage at coming out of the closet so publicly and regretted the fact that he was now estranged from his father. "Unfortunately, my case is not unusual." Adrian was quoted as saying. "Hopefully the day will come when gay people are not only tolerated but accepted with open arms by the community and their families."

As to his plans, Ben wasn't surprised to read that he was going to his grandfather's vineyard as soon as he had everything sorted out. "It's not going to be easy," Adrian admitted. "I won't have enough money to make some of the renovations and alterations the place really needs, but at least I'm accepted there."

The next paragraph made Ben's heart stop. "I lost my first lover because I was unwilling to put him first, and I vowed never to make the same mistake again, but it seems I have. Recently, I found someone who is the other half of me. Who complements me in every way, the yin to my yang. I just wish I knew where he was. I worry about him. Wherever you are, Ben. I want you to know that I love you."

Shit.

Ben stared at Mick. "How come he doesn't know where I am? He only has to call home to find out." A sudden suspicion crossed his mind. Chris had been staying at the house while his mom was in China. He had split up with his wife, and whenever Ben spoke to him, he was a perfect pain in the ass. Even the mention of the condom and lube in the tackle box earned him a "Fucking mind your own business" lecture.

He dialed his home number. His brother obviously had some explaining to do. If he had deliberately kept news of his whereabouts from Adrian, he'd wring Chris's neck.

"Hi, Pop."

"Where are you? I've been trying to contact you, but the phone company said you're no longer at the house."

"I'm sorry. I had so many things on my mind lately that I forgot that you didn't have my new number." Adrian ran his hand over the back of his neck.

"Oh." Pop's voice sounded guarded, gruff. "Are you coming up for Thanksgiving?"

"Yeah, if you'll have me. Sorry I missed the harvest, but work has been hectic."

In the two weeks since the article had appeared, he'd had all sorts of newspapers after him for the story. He managed to make sure SSFI didn't come out looking too bad, so now his father was at least speaking to him. Evelyn's company was ecstatic at the amount of positive coverage his plight had generated. He'd even been contacted by lots of "Bens," offering themselves as replacements. The thought that anyone could replace his Ben amused him for a while as he headed north.

In the end, his father had relented and given him the Prius as a severance payout. Adrian packed what he could fit and told Evelyn he'd return for the rest as soon as possible. She'd given him a hard time when he set off in his usual chinos and Polo shirt, kidding him that now he needed a complete new wardrobe of mesh tanks and ripped jeans. Yeah, not! At least his shirt was mauve. One Liz had given him as a "Coming Out" present. He'd managed to avoid having a rainbow flag sewn on the pocket. Just.

As he threaded his way through heavy traffic, Adrian felt like he was paddling into a headwind. Reminders of his previous trip up to the vineyard played on his mind as he drove. He kept glancing at the passenger seat as if, by will alone, he could conjure up Ben. After a while, the silence only reminded him of Ben's happy chatter. Adrian plugged in his iPod and pressed random. As soon as a Ry Cooder song came on, though, he ripped out the leads. Tears fell from his eyes, making it hard to see.

By the time he arrived, night had fallen, and for once, no one came out to greet him. His stomach lurched at the sight of the Ford

Ranger parked in the driveway, thinking it was Ben's, but this one was a different color. The main house was in darkness, though light streamed through the windows of the guesthouse. Adrian grabbed his overnight bag and headed for the old stone building, nearly colliding with someone coming out.

A dark-haired young man, about his size, recoiled and stared at him. Fuck, was he going to react this way whenever he saw eyes that looked like Ben's? These were more like the glacial ice chips they'd been that horrible day up at the lakes. The stranger snarled at him. "Out of my way, you bastard."

Adrian stared after the man in bemusement as he jumped into the green car and drove off. Heaving a loud sigh, he pushed open the door. Everything looked familiar, except for the fact that personal belongings scattered around showed someone was living there. Headlights shone in the window briefly as a vehicle came roaring up the driveway. The engine sounded the same as the car that had left a few minutes ago. Maybe the man had forgotten something in his haste. A light shone in the bathroom; Adrian walked inside, gazed around, and his heart stopped beating.

Two shower heads had been installed, one at each end of a recess large enough for two people. The killer, though, was the long metal hose. It reminded him of a snake. He turned on the tap and adjusted the temperature. Hot water. At least that was an improvement.

"Well, are you going to try it out?"

Adrian spun around at the sound of the familiar voice. "Ben!"

The young man stood in the entrance with his arms crossed. His smile sent Adrian's heart from zero to sixty in ten seconds. He couldn't move; he just stood there with his mouth open, wondering whether he'd stumbled into some kind of alternate universe when he opened the bathroom door.

"Chris said you were here."

"Chris?" Adrian finally managed to get a word out.

"My brother."

"Oh." *That's why he looked familiar.* "He takes after your mother."

"Sure does." Ben still stood there with that goofy smile on his face. "I've just brought Nonna and Pop back from visiting the doctor. Now that someone will be here full-time, your Pop has decided to have his hip replaced."

"I've been looking for you."

"I gathered that, but I figured you'd end up here eventually. In the meantime, I got Chris to come and fix the bathroom. He owed us both big time."

Adrian shook his head. "You could have called me."

"Given your unwillingness to accept help, I wasn't sure whether you'd knock back the offer, seeing it as charity." Ben's voice faltered for a second. "Anyway, I wanted it to be a surprise."

Surprise? My heart might never recover from the shock. Adrian walked out of the bathroom and into the bedroom. He hadn't known it was possible to love the young man standing on the opposite side of the bed any more than he did. Now he realized that, as he got to know Ben better, other facets would emerge that would make him more certain he wanted to spend the rest of his life with him.

"I love you, you know."

Ben smiled. "You've told me that three times now: once while you were asleep, and once in an interview. It's nice to be told face-to-face." As soon as he finished speaking, Ben turned around. For one heart-stopping moment, Adrian thought he was going to leave, but instead he carefully locked the door, then went over and systematically checked that all the windows were closed.

"What are you doing?"

Ben grinned at him. "I'm going to make you scream louder than Jason again."

"I'm not usually that noisy."

"You will be."

All the strength left Adrian's legs as Ben walked toward him. "I still can't believe you're here."

Ben's smile was a bit lopsided. "Let's just say I ran on ahead and fixed things up to make the campsite easier for you." He flicked a glance toward the bathroom and smiled. "As soon as I read that interview on the blog, I knew exactly what I wanted to do. Pop tried to call you."

"I gathered that." If he'd known Ben was here, Adrian would have broken every speed limit in his haste to join him.

Ben stood so close, the heat of his body swirled around Adrian. He clutched Ben's hips to keep himself upright. One by one, Ben carefully undid the buttons of his shirt, his blue-eyed gaze fixed on Adrian's face.

Adrian shut his eyes and breathed in. Rough hands caressed his skin; then, before he kissed him, Ben growled in his ear, "You owe me a rimming."

Adrian returned the kiss tenfold and pressed into his lover. Eventually he was able to break free so he could whisper in Ben's ear, before he nipped it. "You owe me a fuck."

Ben worked his lips down his neck, worrying at the spot he'd marked all those weeks before. "Planning on a few of those. Mind you, if we're playing tit for tat, you owe me a hickey." He clasped his arms tighter around Adrian and muttered, "Make that two."

Adrian arched back as Ben's hot mouth drew in skin, as he sucked up another mark. Oh fuck, this was even better than at the lake. Knowing that there was no reason they couldn't do this night after night made the act that much more special. He groaned and rubbed against Ben. "I haven't touched anyone since you."

"Likewise."

"What about Mick?"

Ben looked affronted that he'd even asked the question. "That's why I made Chris drive out with all his equipment and do the plumbing. He hasn't cottoned onto the notion that two gay guys can be friends without fucking each other." Ben stroked the side of his face. Adrian caught his hand again, the same way he had once before, and pressed it to his lips. Ben's voice cracked slightly when he whispered, "I packed condoms and lube this time."

Adrian pulled away and walked over to his bag. Rummaging around, he brought out a piece of paper and threw it on the bed. "You don't need the condom. I was tested to make sure."

Ben gave the report a cursory glance, then folded it carefully and placed it on the nightstand. By the time he'd dragged his T-shirt over his head, every trace of a smile had disappeared. Without taking his eyes off Adrian, he unbuckled his jeans and rolled them down over his hips.

Adrian quickly stripped off his clothes and lay down lengthwise on the bed.

Ben gave a chuckle and launched himself through the air, trapping Adrian underneath.

Adrian smiled up into Ben's laughing eyes as the young man eased back and straddled him. "You sure this bed isn't too soft for you?" He stroked his hand over Ben's chest, reminding himself of what his lover felt like.

"I'll cope."

The first kiss went on forever. By the time Ben eased back, Adrian's lips felt bruised from the onslaught. This time he'd been able to relax completely and get lost in the moment. No wondering whether rocks were sticking into anyone's back or wishing that the ground wasn't so hard. No worrying about diseases. No worrying about what he would do when he got back to San Francisco. He hadn't realized how those things had weighed on his mind. Now he could just enjoy the moment.

"Who's going first?" Ben asked.

"Shower or sex?"

"Good point." Ben checked under his arms and then blushed when he realized what Adrian meant. "Me, I suppose."

"Go for it. I'll wait here." Soon the sound of running water filled Adrian's ears. He was tempted to join Ben, then he decided against it. There would be plenty of time for shower sex in the future.

Ben walked out soon after with a towel around his waist, his face a rosy pink. Adrian didn't know or care whether it was a blush or the hot water. Either way he looked adorable. He picked up his overnight bag and gave Ben a quick kiss on the way past.

AS SOON as he heard the bathroom door shut, Ben dropped the towel, reached into the nightstand, and brought out the lube he purchased for the trip to the lakes.

He still found it hard to believe they were finally together.

Not far from the vineyard entrance, he had passed Chris's car coming in the opposite direction. Initially, he'd been alarmed by the anger on his brother's face, mistaking it for fear, thinking there'd been some sort of accident. Then he learned that Adrian had arrived. Chris had been urging Ben to return to Minnesota with him as soon as the bathroom was finished. "They're not your family," he said.

The strange thing was that for Ben, Nonna and Pop *did* feel like family. As soon as they arrived, and Ben made the offer to fix the bathroom, Adrian's grandpa had taken him aside and thanked him. "You are what he needs," he said. Ben had swallowed, wondering whether Adrian was what *he* needed. He was what he wanted, no doubt about that. He loved Adrian, but there were still so many things about him that he didn't know or understand.

Ben lay on the bed, thoughts swirling in his brain. How could Adrian give up his future as easily as that? How would he cope without the money? When Ben told Evelyn that he didn't want to be an actuary any more, it had been an excuse to avoid giving her the real reason, that he wanted to avoid seeing or hearing about Adrian. Now he had to contact her to see if she would give him another chance and allow him to finish his course. Maybe he would need to be the main breadwinner now. But then, how would their relationship survive if he spent his weeks in San Francisco and only saw Adrian on the weekends? So many things to sort through and discuss.

Ben's breath quickened as the water stopped running. He rolled over onto his front and cradled his head in his arms, suddenly uncertain about what to do next. Adrian's quiet footsteps stopped. Ben turned his head to see what he was doing, and discovered Adrian crouched down beside the bed, allowing Ben to stare directly into those beautiful eyes. Once again the pupils were flared so wide, he could get lost in their dark depths. The expression on his lover's face was intent, serious. Ben managed to give him a weak smile, but Adrian's expression didn't change. If he had any doubts about the way Adrian felt about him, he needed only one glimpse of those eyes for reassurance.

In one fluid motion, Adrian stood and moved until Ben could barely see him, then his hand came out and traversed all over his body.

At first Ben couldn't work out what he was doing, then he remembered the time Adrian came into the guesthouse on their previous trip when he thought Ben was asleep. Once again, heat seemed to travel between his hand and Ben's skin, even though they weren't in contact. But this time, that hand finally descended close enough to caress his skin, featherlight to start with, and then firmer.

Ben closed his eyes and sank deeper into the mattress. After a while, Adrian stopped. Then a smell he would always associate with Adrian wafted into his nostrils. The coconut suntanning oil. Ben couldn't believe that his dick could get any fuller, but somehow it did. This time when Adrian's hand came back, its slickness allowed him to press harder. Every muscle of Ben's body turned to mush. The smell alone sent his senses spiraling.

"You can't use it with a condom, but it makes a great lube." Adrian's low, sexy growl and the way his cock pressed against the sheets nearly tipped Ben over the edge. He groaned and shifted slightly to give his dick more room. Adrian slapped his butt, the sting reverberating right to his toes. "Up on all fours, Ben."

Oh, shit. Here it comes. Ben scrambled to his knees.

"You have the most perfect ass I've ever seen."

Ben twisted and tried to smile his appreciation for the compliment, but even his facial muscles didn't want to work. He shut his eyes and surrendered again as Adrian knelt behind him and caressed his butt. Every one of Ben's nerves tingled with anticipation as the circling thumbs worked their way closer and closer.

"Please, Adrian, just do it."

Ben rested his head on his forearms, all his muscles as useless as a baby's. Finally Adrian stopped torturing him and slid one thumb inside, working all the way along his crease. Ben bucked violently as each hand firmly palmed a butt cheek and pulled them apart.

"Think of this as part of your lesson," Adrian growled. Warm moisture hit his hole. A hot, wet tongue followed, licking all the way around the edge before working its way inside. Ben's whole body started shaking. The man sure knew what he was doing. No clumsy

311

fumbling here. Each lick, each thrust with his tongue had purpose to it, as if he knew exactly what Ben's body liked, needed, craved. Ben pulled himself up onto his elbows again and stared between his legs as his cock leaked drip after drip of pre-come.

By the time Adrian slipped one finger inside, Ben hardly noticed the intrusion, until the man stroked across his prostate, hitting it as surely as if he had a map. Oh, fuck. For a while Ben wondered if a skeeter had come along to spoil the party, then he realized he was making that whiny noise as he begged Adrian for more, again and again. All the time the man's fingers and tongue didn't stop working. Then a tingle started at the base of Ben's spine. He rested his head back on his forearms and let himself go. His whole body trembled as spurts of come splattered on the spread.

"Whoops." Adrian said as he grinned and laid the towel on the damp patch. "I didn't mean for you to come so quickly."

Ben collapsed on top and ran a shaky finger up the side of Adrian's jaw as he leaned over to kiss him. "You're awfully good at that."

Adrian just smiled. He didn't seem to be in any hurry to fuck him. Ben reached out and drew him closer into his arms. There was no rush. In a few minutes, he could return the favor, and then he could make love to the man he'd been dreaming about for so long.

Unlike many authors, A.B. GAYLE hasn't been writing stories all her life. Instead she's been living life.

Her travels have taken her from the fjords of Norway to the southern tip of New Zealand. In between, she's worked in so many different towns she's lost count. She's shoveled shit in cow yards, mustered sheep, been polite to customers, and traded insults with politicians.

Bored with traditional romances, she discovered M/M romance, where the story is about life and all its complexities, not just the ring, the wedding, and the babies. When pressed she'll admit she loves reading and writing about men, because they can do all the things she would love to do but can't, simply because she's female. And if reading about one man is good, reading about two must be better! Right?

Now living in Sydney, Australia, A.B. finally has enough time to allow her real-life experiences to morph with her fertile imagination to create fiction which she hope her readers will enjoy.

Visit her website at http://www.abgayle.com.

Also from A.B. GAYLE

CAUGHT

A.B. Gayle

http://www.dreamspinnerpress.com

Also from Dreamspinner Press

Irreversible eRROR

Wolf
Phoenix

http://www.dreamspinnerpress.com